"If I were not forsworn," Reynaud said, his voice deep, "I would wrap my hands in the wild silk of your hair and close you in my arms, until I could feel the heat of your heart. I would touch your lips with mine, taste the essence of your mouth and probe its source, inviting you with every wile at my command to do the same.

"I would kiss your forehead, your eyes, the softness of your cheeks, the small seductive hollow behind your ear. Gently I would slide your gown from your shoulders, following its fall with a trail of kisses."

"Please," Elise whispered, a heated flush rising to her face that was not entirely from embarrassment. She felt as if every word was a caress that she could feel against her skin.

"Your breasts I would take in my hands, stroking the nipples with my finger and tongue until they were tight buds of sweetness. I would press my face into the white flatness of your belly and breathe your scent. And when you were ready, when you yearned for me, only then, I would fill you, banishing thought of any other man. These things I would do, if I were not forsworn."

There rose inside Elise a terrible need to have him do precisely as he had said. . . .

FIERCE EDEN

Jennifer Blake

FAWCETT GOLD MEDAL • NEW YORK

I

T HE GATHERING WAS sparse. At the board of Commandant
Chepart, with its cloth of Flemish linen scattered with bread
crumbs and ringed with spilled wine, there were a number of
conspicuously empty chairs. It was not to be wondered at, of
course, not when every day brought fresh rumors of unrest
among the Indians. The village of the Natchez tribe was so close
and tempers so uncertain that few cared to risk being caught on
the road at dawn, should the evening be prolonged.

Elise Laffont had felt a qualm or two herself. She did not
usually attend such affairs as the commandant's *soirée*, nor
would she have this evening if it had not been most important.
She had kept to herself during the past three years since her
husband had died. Some considered it, she knew, a becoming
show of grief and modesty in such a young widow. The truth
was that she preferred her own company and had far too much
to do managing the estate left to her for frivolous amusement to
be an attraction.

From the head of the table came a roar of laughter. Chepart, chuckling at his own joke, signaled the servant behind
his chair to refill the glasses of his guests with the excellent
Madeira that was to accompany the dessert course. The light
of the candles in the crystal chandelier, hanging from the
rough rafters overhead, gleamed among the waves of Elise's
honey-brown hair, bright despite their dusting of white powder, as she turned her head to glance at her host. The warm
amber of her eyes turned cool with the disdain that rose to
her finely molded features.

1

Two places farther along the board, Madame Marie Doucet leaned across her husband to catch Elise's eye. Her plump face was alight with good-natured amusement and pleasure. "Commandant Chepart is quite the *bon vivant* tonight, is he not?"

"Certainly he thinks so," Elise said under her breath.

"What was that, *chère*? I didn't quite catch it."

The older woman had been quite pretty once, in a doll-like fashion. She had kept the quick coquettish mannerisms and light tone of voice despite the gray in her fading blond hair. She had been a good friend to Elise, however, in the past few years and a good neighbor who lived less than a third of a league away. Elise had learned to overlook much of the silliness for the sake of the kind heart underneath.

Elise shook her head in quick dismissal. "Nothing."

The commandant of Fort Rosalie, the representative of his Royal Majesty King Louis XV here in the wilderness known as Louisiana, was indeed given to good living. Elise, with a slight curl of her mouth, which was smooth and a trifle wide, thought that he was more of a debauchee than a *bon vivant*. Chepart had been a tankard friend of her husband. He and Vincent Laffont had spent many an evening drinking each other under the table and guffawing at crude stories. When her husband had had the consideration to drown himself while fishing on the Mississippi, the commandant had come to her. He had been all concern, most solicitous of her comfort and well-being; so solicitous in fact that he had pressed her down upon a settle and thrust his hand into her bodice to fondle her breasts. She had snatched a wooden knitting needle from the basket in the corner of the settle and done her best to skewer him with it, then had taken down Vincent's musket from over the fireplace and ordered the commandant from her property. When he had gone, she had cried for the first time since Vincent's death, tears of rage and disgust, and of gladness that she need never again submit to any man.

It was distressing, then, that she must now ask a favor of Commandant Chepart. She did not like to accept his hospitality, much less endure his company; still, she would do it until she had what she wanted from the fat fool.

She allowed her gaze to wander around the room, noting the jewel-colored Turkish rug underfoot, the silk hangings at the shuttered, glassless windows, the Watteau pastoral scene that hung above the enormous fireplace where red coals pulsed with fire and a back log smouldered. How out of place these things seemed in the simplicity of the house provided for the fort's commander. With the elaborate table setting and the ridiculous grandeur of the crystal chandelier that shed its light upon them, the furnishings were an indication of both the commandant's pretentious arrogance and his ambition. Chepart intended to use his office as a stepping-stone to greater things, perhaps an appointment at court, but in the meantime it pleased him to live in comfortable splendor, regardless of how his underhanded dealings with the commission merchants might affect supplies for the fort and the men who manned it.

What means could she use to persuade someone like Chepart to listen to her? She did not have the funds to offer him monetary inducement, and she refused to consider bartering that commodity she felt might interest him most: herself. But perhaps she was wrong in thinking that he would want something in return for what she would ask. It was not so great a request, not so unusual after all, however much it might mean to her. It would be no loss to the commandant to allow the prisoners now in the guardhouse at the fort to build a storage barn and poultry yard for her.

The men were not dangerous, being charged officially with nothing more serious than insubordination, for all of Chepart's railing about sedition and a blatant attempt to undermine his authority. The crime committed had been the spirited representation by these men, all of them officers of the fort, of the wisdom of preparing a defense against the coming Indian rising. That there was going to be one, they were positive. Their information had come straight from the Indian village of White Apple, from women who had heard it direct from Tattooed Arm, mother of the Great Sun who was the ruler of the Natchez.

Chepart had not been impressed by their source. He had declared that French soldiers should know better than to be swayed by their Indian whores and that his officers would learn better if he had to whip the skin from their backs to bring home the lesson. No puny Indian tribe would dare to challenge the might of France. Hadn't the diplomacy of the French governors of Louisiana always ensured amicable relations with their Indian allies? They were as children in the hands of men of intelligence and guile. Besides, no Indian chieftain would dare to order an attack knowing that the armed force of France would be turned against his people for such treachery.

In Elise's opinion, it was just such blatant disdain for the Natchez, just such lack of judgment in dealing with them, that was the reason for her pressing need for a barn and fenced yard. It was Chepart's bungling that had caused the recent unrest of the Indians, had turned them into marauders who took delight in carrying off her chickens and ducks, hogs and calves. Not that the Natchez had any great appreciation for property rights at the best of times, but everyone knew that their depredations in the last months were made from a sense of ill-usage and spite. And every day they became bolder.

Unconsciously Elise turned her amber gaze upon the corpulent figure of her host. Chepart, catching her eye, raised his glass to her. His expression held a hint of barely concealed lust as he surveyed her high-piled hair, the proud tilt of her chin and the determined self-possession of her features in the oval of her face. He lifted his hand to twist a curl of his long, full wig where it fell over his shoulder as he permitted his overwarm gaze to drop to the low bodice of her gold brocade gown that cupped the gentle swells of her breasts. His thick tongue came to lick his lips, leaving them wet.

Elise clenched her teeth, but could not prevent the shudder of repugnance that rippled through her. In sheer reaction, she covered herself as best she could by drawing up the edges of her shawl as if against a chill draft.

"Are you cold, my dear Madame Laffont?" Chepart called down the table, clapping his hands at the same time for a servant. "Now that we cannot allow!"

An African slave, little more than a boy, came running. The commandant gestured toward the fire and the boy went quickly to the hearth. At the same time, a serving woman emerged from the back of the house with a tray of cakes and custards. A small silence fell as the diners watched the mending of the fire and waited for their dessert to be placed before them. The only sound was the crash of logs being thrown on the hot coals and the crackling rush as they caught. The flames leaped up the chimney in a burst of yellow-orange light that chased the shadows from the corners of the room. The bright glow also penetrated, through a doorway that stood open, into the dimness of the connecting salon, a reception room with access to the outside.

A shrill scream shattered the quiet. "An Indian! Come to murder us!"

It was Madame Doucet, her eyes glassy with shock as she pointed with one trembling hand toward the salon. Men surged to their feet, looking around wildly. Women gasped and cried out, springing up to clutch at their husbands. The serving woman threw her tray into the air, then stood rooted as custard and cake dishes crashed to the floor, scattering their sticky contents over her feet. Chepart cursed, flinging down his glass so that wine streamed across the table and dripped like blood down the cloth to the floor. Elise clutched at her shawl with white-knuckled hands as she turned in the direction Madame Doucet indicated.

The Indian moved forward from the salon doorway into the dining room with silent animal vigor, tall as the Natchez were tall, magnificent in his sculptured barbarian grace, infinitely savage. The firelight was reflected in a copper shimmer from the muscled planes of his chest that were shadowed by intricate lines of tattooing unobscured by the faintest trace of body hair, lines that gave mute evidence of his ability to bear pain. The light also caught the beading that patterned the white doeskin of the moccasins on his feet and the breechclout that covered his loins, and shimmered in the soft white nap of the cape of woven swansdown that hung from his shoulders. More swan feathers had been used to form the circlet that he wore on the crown of his head in the fashion of the Natchez males of royal birth, those of the Sun class. Just behind that circlet was the knot of his hair where it had been drawn up, the thick, black knot that offered an easy hold for an enemy in deliberate scorn for any prowess other than his own, one that would become a scalp lock should that prowess fail. But his hairline had not been plucked for a higher brow in the Natchez fashion, and his eyes, watchful, dangerously opaque, were not black but gray.

"*Merde!*" the commandant exclaimed, the oath bursting from him in his relief. "It's Reynaud Chavalier!"

The fear that had gripped the men in the room dissolved into anger. Tight-lipped, they exchanged glances before turning back toward the intruder. The women sighed and whispered among themselves with nervous titters. Elise sat very still, staring in horrified fascination. She saw the man called Chavalier sweep the room with a glance that seemed to hold an edge of contempt, felt the glance touch her in stinging appraisal, pause, then move on as if there was nothing there to hold his interest.

Madame Doucet bent toward Elise over her husband's empty chair. "He's a half-breed," she said in a trilling undertone.

"I know," she replied.

She did know, as who did not? She had never met Reynaud Chavalier, but she had heard of him. He was the son of Robert Chavalier, Comte de Combourg, and the Natchez woman called Tattooed Arm, and the brother to the man now known as the Great Sun. He had been raised by the Indians until his thirteenth year. At that time he had been taken to France by his father, when the comte had returned to his native land after his service in Louisiana, to be educated. The old comte had died some years later, leaving Reynaud a sizable fortune and an immense tract of land on the west side of the Mississippi River. Reynaud had tarried in France to settle his father's affairs, which had included a French wife and a legitimate heir to the title and estates.

Then five years ago he had returned, melting into the wilderness of his holdings and dropping the mantle of civilization as easily as he had shed his satin smallclothes. He spent most of his time on his lands across the river where it was rumored that he had entertained the governor and his entourage in great state on occasion. No one believed it. When he visited the Grand Village of the Natchez in the jurisdiction of the commandant of Fort Rosalie, he always wore the trappings of his mother's people.

Reynaud Chavalier surveyed the startled faces before him with grim impatience. He was here on a fool's errand he was certain, but it must be carried out. At last he swung toward the commandant, sketching a bow totally without subservience. "I give you good evening."

"What is the meaning of this intrusion?" Chepart blustered, snatching at the remnants of his self-possession as he jerked his napkin from his neck and flung it down on the table.

"I sent a request to see you this afternoon and was told I must wait on your convenience. Not wanting to trouble you while you were occupied with the weighty affairs of your office, I thought to seek you out during your leisure." The words were smooth, but carried the whiplash flick of irony.

"You thought to see me at a time when I would be less likely to have you thrown in the guardhouse for your impudence! I've half a mind to call my men—"

"Certainly, if it pleases you. I trust you will not be too disturbed if they fail to come."

Chepart gripped the table edge as he leaned forward, demanding, "What have you done?"

"Merely disarmed them."

His speech carried the cultured tones of Paris, his voice was deep and vibrant. If she closed her eyes, Elise thought, it would be possible to suppose that she was listening, at the very least, to a courtier, if not a member of the French nobility. She stared at the silver armbands that compressed the muscles of his upper arms, aware of a feeling of disturbance inside her that she did not like.

"How dare you!" Chepart demanded.

Irritation gathered inside Reynaud, combining with a hard anger as he regarded the corpulent and self-important fool before him. "Because I felt it necessary. It is of the utmost urgency that you listen without doing something so stupid as ordering yet another arrest. The lives of your command, the people you are here to protect, even those assembled in this room, depend on it."

Chepart stared at Reynaud, then dropped heavily back into his seat. "I will disregard the insult," he drawled, "if you will tell me that you are not going to present to me yet again this rumor of imminent attack by the Natchez."

"It is no rumor, but fact."

"One I am to accept because you say it is so? What proof have you?"

"My mother was told of it by my brother, the Great Sun. Because of the love she had for my father, she does not wish those of his blood removed by violence from this land. She has charged others with this warning and you would not listen. Now she has charged me."

"That makes you a traitor to your mother's people, does it not?"

"I would be just as much at fault if I allowed the French, the people of my father, to be slaughtered. It is my hope that if the Natchez see you well-armed and prepared to defend yourselves, they will not attack."

"I don't doubt it, cowards that they are."

Reynaud Chavalier stared at the man before him until he had

conquered the strong urge to plant his fist in the greasy face of the commandant. "Not cowards, but realists who see no glory in dying without purpose."

"We won't quibble over the term," the other man said with expansive condescension.

"It's a distinction you would do well to remember, Chepart." Reynaud's voice was even, deadly earnest. "My mother's people are proud; yet you have, in the last weeks, had a warrior stripped and flogged for a misdemeanor that should have been brought to the attention of the Great Sun for punishment. They are just; and you have allowed a soldier of the fort to walk about free after shooting and killing an old man whose only crime was his failure to pay back a measure of corn on a given date, when his corn was not yet ripe in the fields. The Natchez have held this land for centuries, but you have demanded that they move from one of their oldest villages, that of White Apple, because you covet the richness of their cleared fields for your own use. These are only a few of the events that have tried their temper. They are sworn to move against you in concert with the Yazoos, Choctaws, Tioux, Tensas, and others. The date has been set and a bundle of reeds sent to every tribe; one reed must be removed daily until the day comes for the attack. My mother found the bundle in the Temple of the Sun, risking much to remove a handful of the reeds. Because of her action, the attack here will come early as a warning to the French in the Mississippi Valley. If you are ready, it will come to nothing. If not, then you must be ready to face the holy war of the Natchez called the Blood Vengeance."

"I fear I disappoint you, my dear Chavalier, with my lack of alarm. You must forgive me." The unctuous quality of the commandant's voice was maintained only with an effort. Perspiration stood out on his forehead.

"It is not my forgiveness you will need, but that of the seven hundred men, women, and children you are sworn to protect."

In the warmth of the room, there came to Elise, from the man on the other side of the table, the smell of well-tanned leather and woodsmoke, the bear oil scented with aromatic spikenard that had been used to seal his moccasins from water, and the sharp, wild freshness of the night air. The combination of scents was threatening as it clung to him, heightening the aura of virile masculinity and effortless power that he exuded. She turned her head in an attempt to escape it.

Chepart thumped the table. "I should have you run down, trussed up, and flogged just to teach you to respect this office!"

"Do so," came the instant, scathing reply. "If you think you can."

Impotent rage brought purple color into Chepart's face. "Get out. Get out of my house and don't come back! You half-breeds are all alike: lying, thieving, cunning bastards a thousand times worse than any blood Indian!"

"I understand your frustration, commandant, but it would be a mistake to let it blind you to your danger. I have delivered my warning and can do no more. I advise you to heed it."

Reynaud inclined his head once more in a curt gesture that did not begin to express the contempt he felt. He allowed his gaze to sweep over the company gathered at the table: the pale-faced women, including the beautiful creature in gold brocade with the cold features of one who feels no passion or else has learned to hide it well; the men still standing in stiff poses. Swinging around with his swansdown cape spreading wide around him, he stepped toward the door.

Madame Doucet drew a deep breath as if released from a spell. She flicked a glance at Elise, saying in hushed tones, "A noble savage."

"And a malodorous one," Elise murmured.

Reynaud Chavalier checked, turned, his hard gray glance striking her face as he caught the edge of spite in her words. He had never seen this woman before, that much he knew. What then had caused her enmity? He had little vanity; still, he had sampled enough of the perfumed embraces of the ladies at court, the gambolings of Indian maidens as unashamed of their hungers as kittens, and the practiced seductions of older widows to know that he was far from unattractive to women. His surprise and displeasure was so great that it was difficult to maintain the expression of implacable indifference suited to the occasion. That the attack was so unexpected must be his excuse. It was not every day that a Frenchwoman saw fit to fling the most deadly of insults at the head of a Natchez of the ruling Sun class.

Elise caught the flare of angry interest, quickly suppressed, in the half-breed's eyes. A wave of hot color sprang to her face as she realized what she had done. The lowest rank of Natchez, the common people who did the dirtiest work, were called Stink-ards and by inference she had applied just that name to Reynaud Chavalier. She had not meant it, had not intended that he should hear her, still she would not disavow her words. Holding his gaze, her heart beating with heavy, sickening thuds, she lifted her chin in defiance.

Reynaud studied the pure oval of her face, the sensitive mouth, the direct amber eyes with faint shadows of vulnerability in their rust-flecked depths. Something in his chest tightened and he felt the sudden warm rush of the blood along his veins. Still, neither a warrior nor a gentleman crossed swords with a woman. Swinging around once more, Reynaud strode from the room, but as he let himself out of the commandant's house he was frowning.

The evening had come to an abrupt end after that, of course. The commandant had stormed from the house to curse and kick at his trussed-up sentries. His guests, alarmed and yet at a loss as to what to think about the warning or what to do if Chepart would not act, had talked together in low voices while servants ran to bring them their wraps. Their host, profuse in his apologies and snide in his comments concerning Chavalier and the Natchez, had returned in time to see them off to their homes. He himself would go at once to the Natchez to look into this matter. He could promise them that he would be met with drink and feasting and all manner of merriment. They need not be concerned. The Great Sun was wily; there was no doubt that this talk of an attack was only an attempt to frighten the French, to prevent the takeover of their village. It would do them no good; this he, Chepart, would also promise.

Elise had left with the Doucets. There had been no opportunity to speak to Chepart concerning her barn, and so great was her distaste for the man after his display of choler and bad manners that she did not feel she could have taken advantage of it in any case.

She did not forget, however. She was up early the next morning. She put on her well-worn habit of hunter's green velvet and ate a quick breakfast in the kitchen while she instructed the African woman who saw to the house in her tasks for the day. Carrying her broad-brimmed cavalier's hat, she strode out to the small shed that served as a stable and barn. Her African man-of-all-work, Claude, was there. She talked with him about cleaning out the shed and making a dung heap for use on the fields in the spring, then went with him to show where she wanted him to start clearing the trees and brush from the site of the new barn. They looked at a cow that was due to drop her calf in late winter and discussed the possibility of trading milk and butter for some of the bantam chickens the Doucets were raising. As they turned toward the stable shed where Claude would saddle her mare, she paused to look around her, her chest swelling with pride at the sight of her well-kept arpents, four hundred in number, ten wide and forty deep. The land was solid, unchanging. It would never betray you, never hurt you. Here was something to love.

It was well after sunrise, nearly half-past eight by Elise's reckoning, when she mounted her mare. If she rode toward the fort, she should be able to see the commandant as he was leaving his house, before he barricaded himself in his office inside the stockade. It was possible, of course, that he would not work today since it was St. Andrew's Eve. Tomorrow would be a holy day, and it was the habit of many to indulge in feasting and relaxation from their labors before such religious observances. Not that there would be much made of the occasion here where they had only a small church that was without a priest except when one chose to visit on his way up or down the river.

The road that led from the fort to the Grand Village of the Natchez on St. Catherine Creek was little more than a muddy track rutted by the two-wheeled carts used by the French and flanked by a smooth path worn by the moccasin-clad feet of the Indians. It stretched the distance of a league and a half, winding uphill and down through woods that were thick with underbrush and hung with creepers, and was intersected here and there with trails that led to the lesser villages of the tribe. Now and then it passed a cleared area where the French held property. These open spaces contained neat houses, built of upright logs set in the ground, in the style of cabin derived from the Indians known as a *maison de poteaux en terre*, a house of posts set in the ground. The spaces between the log posts were packed with *bousillage* made of mud mixed with deer hair. These stout walls supported peaked roofs that spread out over surrounding galleries, protecting the windows closed only with *contrevents*, or shutters, from the wind and rain. In most cases, the floors were of earth packed and glazed by the tramp of feet. Spreading around the houses were fields with plowed rows lying fallow and cattle and sheep grazing in pastures still showing a little green among the brown grass of November.

The sun reached higher and was more brilliant as Elise trotted her chestnut mare out of her own front yard and along the track.

Her holdings were almost exactly halfway between the fort and the Indian village, so her ride would be no more than a pleasant jaunt. The air was crisp, but not overly cold; a brisk trot would keep her warm. There was a breeze drifting through the trees, bringing down showers of leaves in gold, scarlet, and brown. They carpeted the road, making a soft rustling sound as her mare trotted over them.

Elise had not gone two hundred yards when she heard a call. She glanced back to see three Indians standing in the road, one of them holding up his arm in a gesture of greeting. A sense of disquiet moved over her, then she dismissed it. It was not at all unusual to see Indians abroad. They traded regularly at the fort and often brought game or fish to the French farmers to exchange for chickens or geese. Indeed, quite a number had passed the house already that morning, moving along in groups of three or four.

Reining in her mount, she walked the mare back along the track to meet the Indians near her own outbuildings. She recognized one of them. He was the husband of Little Quail, an Indian woman who had been bought as a slave and used as a concubine by Elise's husband. They had been friends, she and Little Quail, rather than enemies; their common hatred for Vincent Laffont had made them so. On his death, Elise had freed the Indian woman, allowing her to return to her village.

Little Quail's husband was a dark, taciturn man. Elise had never liked him and was by no means sure that he was an improvement over Little Quail's last master. Now he stood back with a grim look on his face while another of the three men repeated his greeting.

Elise had learned quite a few words of the Natchez language from Little Quail and also of Chickasaw, the lingua franca of the other tribes in the region that encompassed land on both sides of the Mississippi River: the Chickasaws themselves, the Choctaws, Tensas, Tunicas, Yazoos, Natchitoches, Caddo, Ouachita, and a half-dozen others. She returned the salutation with proper ceremony and asked their destination.

They were on their way to visit her holdings, they replied. The Natchez planned a great hunt of many days' journey. They were sure to bring back much game, perhaps even buffalo, if they had weapons. They had been sent by the Great Sun to request the use of what firearms she might be able to spare for this noble purpose. In return, they would promise her ample meat to last her and the Africans who served her through the winter.

It was a tempting prospect, a gesture that certainly seemed peaceful and accommodating, instead of one of war. Being without a husband was most noticeable when it came to supplying game for the table. She could not afford to slaughter her cattle for food, not in quantity, and she did grow extremely tired of poultry. Sometimes she sent Claude out to hunt, but there was little to be had near the farm except for rabbits and an occasional squirrel. The big game had been driven farther into the forest.

She had only one musket, however. She did not like to let it out of her hands for any length of time, and it was entirely possible that the Indian who took it into his possession during the hunt might decide to keep it. She would receive recompense, doubtless, in furs and hides and meat, but that would not give her a weapon with which to protect herself. That last thought brought the night before, never very far from her mind, forcibly to the front of her thoughts.

She summoned a smile. "It is a fine prospect and I wish you the luck beyond your dreams. But I am in a hurry to see Commandant Chepart just now. Perhaps we could discuss it when I return."

"But, Madame Laffont, by then it may be too late. The men of the hunt may have gone, and those of us without weapons not among them."

"I shall not be gone long. In the meantime, you may ask M'sieu Doucet. If he does not give you firearms then you may still see me when I return."

She kept her voice firm with an effort despite the fact that the spokesman for the three had stepped forward within reach of her bridle.

"It would only take a moment to fetch out the weapon."

"But I do not have a moment," she answered, smiling stiffly. Tugging on her reins, she wheeled her mare and thrust her heel into the smooth chestnut side. "I'll see you when I return."

Little Quail's husband started forward, but the spokesman stopped him with a sharp gesture of one hand. Elise could feel them staring after her as she rode away and it was not a pleasant sensation. Her hands were trembling, she discovered, clutching tightly at the reins so that her mare jibbed at the bit. With a conscious effort she forced herself to relax.

The Indians had not approved of her refusal of the request of warriors. They thought that, a mere female, she should have a man to speak for her and to keep her in line. They were as bad, if not worse, in their way than the men of the French community at Fort Rosalie. Because she was a widow of property and not unattractive, there had been a number of bachelors, especially among the officers at the fort who had to subsist on their meager pay that was often slow in coming, who had thought she would do well to listen to their suits. She needed a husband to protect her, they had said, to do the heavy work, to warm her bed. She was foolish to think she could live alone. It was not a woman's way; it was not done. They had kissed her hands and brought her flowers and swaggered in and out of her house. Their friends had called and so had every matron they could interest in their cause. The suitors had given her no peace. The more distant and cooler she became, the more they persisted. She became a challenge to their manhood, one they swore to answer, wagering among themselves as to who would win her. When she had finally barred her door against them, refusing admittance to any unmarried man, they had called her a cold-hearted bitch, a widow of ice who froze men with a look. They had sworn that she would be sorry, that she would fail miserably to earn her own food and would dry up into a bitter hag eking out a living in a hovel with only a cat for company.

She had shown them. She had lived alone and prospered, and she would continue to do just that. She did not need a husband. She had no use for a man of any kind. If there was hoarfrost on her heart, then what did it matter? It hurt less, she had discovered, to care little.

Into the turmoil of her thoughts came a sudden vision of Reynaud Chavalier. He had not approved of her either, she was sure. She winced as she thought of her stupid gaffe, implying that he was a Stinkard. It bothered her; that error had robbed her of sleep during the night as she tossed and turned so that her straw-stuffed mattress set up a constant rustling. She did not usually make such mistakes. It would have been better if she had acknowledged it in some way, though the idea of apologizing to such a haughty barbarian set her teeth on edge.

What would he make of the Indian's offer of game in exchange for firearms? She would give much to know. The fact that she had no use for his kind of overbearing masculine self-assurance did not prevent her from recognizing that his opinion would be valuable. After the night before, however, it was doubtful that he would be inclined to give it, either to her or to any of the French around Fort Rosalie.

He had not been so much like the Natchez, after all, now that she had seen the Indian warriors once more. He had been as tall, towering nearly a head over Chepart, but his hair had been finer in texture, with a polished sheen, rather than the coarse black of his mother's people. His head had been well formed, without the flatness at the back caused by being bound to a cradle board in infancy, and his features had been more refined, with fewer harsh angles, doubtless the results of his French blood.

And yet for some reason he had appeared more dangerous. Was it the hard intelligence that shone from his gray eyes? Or was it perhaps his lack of any emotion about the message he had come to deliver except for disgust that it was not being heeded? Surely it would have been natural for him to express some concern for the lives of the women and children who would die if his warning was genuine, and yet there had been little more than anger that Chepart was not taking his responsibility toward them as seriously as Chavalier thought he should. Certainly he had not seemed to waste any time thinking of what the fate of women like herself might be if an attack came. Not that she needed his concern, not at all.

With a violent effort, she wrenched her thoughts away from Reynaud Chavalier. A pox on the man! That she was wasting her time thinking of him was a sign of how much the Indian warriors had disturbed her. She would do far better to turn her thoughts to how she was going to cajole Chepart into giving the order for his prisoners to build her barn. That would be much more to the purpose.

The dry leaves of a post oak rattled overhead as she passed beneath an overhanging limb. The thudding hoofbeats of her mare on the damp track seemed loud. Elise looked around at the bright morning, allowing her gaze to rise to where a turkey buzzard circled lazily against the intense blue of the sky. It was indeed a turkey buzzard and not a hawk, and yet she was aware abruptly of the singing quiet in which there was no sound of other birds. The breeze died away. The woods that lined the sides of the road seemed to crowd the track, closing in. She felt a prickle at the back of her neck.

The cracking boom of a shot rang out, echoing through the woods. Elise reined in, staring toward where the sound had come from just ahead of her while the mare danced and sidled with nervousness. It could be anything: a man out hunting, someone shooting at a fox or weasel sneaking around their chickens, a signal to bring a man in from the fields for some emergency. Ahead of her was the Doucet place. Monsieur Doucet, a woodcarver by trade who had been employed in France making woodcuts for the printing of books before he signed up as a colonist for Louisiana, had been known to let off a few shots of a morning to perfect his aim.

Abruptly there came the scattered booming of more firing. Hard upon it could be heard distant cries that might have been either terror or exultation. They came not only from ahead of her, but also from behind her. Elise twisted this way and that on her sidesaddle, listening, her eyes widening with a terrible fear. Then, with sudden decision, she urged the mare onward though she held her to a walk.

The clearing of the Doucet arpents came into view. There was the Doucets' farmhouse with smoke curling in a blue plume from the mud-and-stick chimney. For an instant the scene seemed peaceful, normal. Then Elise saw the body of Monsieur Doucet sprawled on the high front steps and the mastiff that served as his watchdog lying with blood-wet fur beside him. A fat billow of smoke came from the front windows. From the entrance door a pair of Indians emerged carrying bundles of clothing and sacks of food, one of them with a huge ham strapped to his back. Behind them came a third Indian who pushed a screaming woman with blood running down her face before him and held a wriggling, crying young boy still dressed in his nightgown under his arm. It was Madame Doucet's daughter and six-year-old grandson.

For a stunned instant Elise allowed her mare to continue to walk toward the house. Then, with a gasp so sharp it hurt her throat, she pulled her mount up and around and slammed her heel into the horse's side, kicking her into a gallop. Behind her came a yell. She had been seen. She did not look back. Putting her head down, she leaned over the mare's head, urging her along the track back toward her own home. She scarcely gave a thought to the Indians in pursuit. They were laden with booty and captives and were without mounts. Her every fear was concentrated on the farm she had left, the farm she had worked so hard to keep and make prosper, the place where every single thing she owned or cared for was now endangered.

For there could be no doubt. In spite of the warnings and

rumors, they had been caught unprepared. The attack they had not thought possible had come. It had come not with cries in the dawn but with a trick designed to put French arms into Indian hands. It had come with soft words and promises of meat for the winter, with trickery and guile worthy of the French themselves. The Natchez were rising, carrying the French before them and leaving death behind.

2

MOMENTS LATER, SHE was sitting her horse in front of her own home. There were flames licking out of the window openings and smoke billowing in a fog around it. Of her African servants there was no sign. If they were inside the house, they must be dead, but it was possible that they had been taken captive, depending on the humor of the Indians. Near the shed lay her cow that had been with calf, or what was left of it after it had been butchered hastily. Feathers were scattered around the chicken run as if the poultry had been scooped up. As she sat in frozen horror, she saw a goose come from behind the house, scurrying into low flight as it made toward the woods.

She thought of the food that had been inside the house, the eiderdowns and woven coverlets and all the other comforts that she had made with her own hands here in the wilderness; of her few gowns, the material for which had been brought at great cost from France. Were they gone, taken by the savages? Could she save any of it?

She could not think of what she must do. There was a tight feeling in her throat as if she might scream at any sudden movement or noise. She was grateful for the warmth of the mare under her and for the necessity of controlling the animal that was upset by the smell of smoke and death since it occupied her hands and quivering muscles.

Her mind moved in distraction to the Indians who had accosted her just a short time before. Why had they not attacked her then? She had been unarmed, defenseless, an easy prey for the three of them in spite of the fact that she had been mounted while they had been on foot.

But wait, the shot she had heard must have been a signal. The time had not been right then. How short was the span of moments that had saved her.

On the wind came the faint sound of more gunfire and distant cries. Smoke was rising above the treetops at all points of the compass. It was a concerted attack, then, not just an isolated raid. The men at the fort would fight if they could reach their weapons in time, but how long could they last? There were over two thousand Natchez and of that number probably seven hundred and fifty were seasoned warriors. Of the French there were only seven hundred in all, with less than half of them ready to bear arms. Even if all the able-bodied French men were able to reach the fort, which seemed unlikely, they would be outnumbered two to one. With the element of surprise firmly on the side of the Indians, it was all too likely to be a massacre.

Tears of rage and terror sprang to Elise's eyes, and there rose inside her a corroding bitterness for the ignored warnings. She wiped her face with hard impatience. Crying would not help. Something must be done. She could not sit here on the main road to the fort when at any moment another war party might appear around the bend. There was no safety anywhere, not at the fort, not at any other holding of the French. The only place left was the woods.

With one last look at her house, she clenched her teeth and released her knee from the pommel of the sidesaddle, sliding down. The mare was a scrubby beast, traded from the Spaniards, and she hated to lose her; still, she dropped the reins and gave the animal a hard slap on the rump to send her galloping wildly down the road. A horse was of no use in the thick, encroaching woodland and would be too likely to attract pursuit with its whickering and heavy movements. The cavalier's hat she wore, with its broad brim, would also be a nuisance. She took it off and sent it sailing as close to her own front yard as she could, then she picked up her skirts and ran swiftly toward the woods on the opposite side of the track.

It was colder among the trees and damp. Elise did her best to step on the matted leaves and gnarled roots so as to leave as little trail as she could and to ease herself beneath the saw briers and smilax that hung in wads without snagging her habit and presenting anyone who followed her with bits of velvet. It was not always possible. The falling leaves drifted into her hair and clung to the skin of her face. Long red scratches appeared on her hands and wrists, stinging as if with some poison. She stepped into a hole and wet her shoe and stocking with foul-smelling black water. Her breath rasped in her chest, sending sharp shafts of pain into her lungs and side with every step. Still she pushed on.

At last a huge magnolia tree rose before her. Its evergreen leaves were thick and glossy green on top, rust-brown on the undersides. The massive limbs grew low, twisted and arthritic, resting on the ground to make a pyramid of deep black green. Here was shelter. Elise pushed into the tree, stepping over the limbs and bending over to reach the more open center. There she sank down and put her back to the rough trunk. Drawing up her knees, she clasped them with her arms. She sat for long moments, listening to the stillness. Finally she put down her head and closed her eyes.

It might have been half an hour, it might have been two full hours later, when she heard the blundering crash of footsteps. She tensed, lifting her head and breathing deeply like an animal scenting danger. She came to her knees, parting the branches a minute amount to look in the direction from which the sound came. The first thing she saw was a moving shape, careening, staggering along. It resolved into the thin shape of a man. He wore nothing more than a shirt and breeches, and the linen of his shirt was splotched with blood. His face was white and his eyes staring. It was an instant before Elise recognized him as the teenage boy who was apprenticed to the man who had the cooperage and lived beyond the Doucets.

"Henri!" she called as loudly as she dared, "over here."

He did not seem to hear. She called again, then got to her feet and pushed the limbs aside to wave.

He stopped so abruptly that he fell sprawling, then came to his hands and knees, scrabbling toward her in the fallen magnolia leaves so that they crackled like musket shots. She bent to help him through the limbs. As they reached the center, he fell against her and lay trembling.

"Are you hurt?" she said softly.

"J-j-just a g-graze."

It was difficult to understand his speech through the stuttering and chattering of his teeth brought on by shock. "Are you sure?"

He nodded his head violently. "I w-was in the p-privy. The

Indians killed them all, m'sieu, madame, the t-three little ones. They found the wine and c-cognac or else they would have k-killed me.''

It came out in bits and pieces. The boy had huddled in the privy while his master and his family were killed, had watched them being hacked to pieces through the cracks in its walls, and had seen their house fired. The Indians had saved the spirits and some food and proceeded to have a feast. The sparks from the house had set fire to the roof of the privy and Henri had been forced to emerge. He had run and they had shot at him. A ball had scratched him, but so drunk were the Indians that they had not pursued him when he ran into the woods.

Elise soothed him as best she could, persuading him to let her look at his wound. It was no more serious than he had said; still, he could not stop shaking. He had barely controlled himself to the point where he could sit up with his hands tightly folded between his legs when they heard the woman crying.

The sound was thin and hoarse, like the wailing of a newborn infant and yet fraught with the hopeless grief only heard in the sobbing of women. Henri looked at Elise and there was fear in his face, fear that the sound was a trick, fear that as the woman drew near she might bring the Indians down upon them with the noise she was making. It was easy to recognize the emotions that moved over his thin features for Elise felt them herself. She was torn between a need to make the woman be quiet at all costs and the pricking of compassion that urged her to do what was in her power to aid her.

It was neither one impulse nor the other that won, but a combination of both. Driven by anger and concern, she pushed her way out of the magnolia. She stood, getting her bearings for a moment, but before she could move, Henri was beside her. Her voice was curt as she said, "You stay here."

"I-I can't, not by m-myself."

"There's nothing you can do."

"T-there might be." Though his teeth had stopped chattering, his difficult speech remained.

"You'll be safer," she pointed out with reasonableness that was surprising, considering the state of her nerves.

"I don't c-care."

She could not force him. She gave a curt nod and started off in the direction of the crying.

They came upon the woman suddenly and from the last quar-

ter they expected. It was a moment before Elise realized that the
crying woman had been lost and was wandering in a wide circle.
Hard on that understanding came the knowledge that she also
knew her. Under the wild tangle of her hair, behind the sagging
flesh of her face that seemed to have aged years, the woman was
none other than Madame Doucet.

"Elise!" Madame Doucet cried on a fresh sob and cast herself upon Elise's bosom with no more surprise than if the younger
woman had stepped into her own salon at a time of mourning.

Elise held her, stroking her and murmuring, but the sobs continued. She had forgotten Henri until she felt him clutch her
arm, heard his strangled sound of joy. She looked up then to see
two Frenchmen striding toward them through the trees. One
carried a musket in his hand while the other limped along with
the aid of a stout limb, favoring an ankle that was badly swollen,
perhaps sprained if not broken.

"Shut her up," the armed man rapped out, "else the Natchez
will do it permanently."

"She is too distraught." Elise raised her voice no more than
was necessary to make herself heard over the sobs.

"A slap in the face is what's needed. Here, give her to me."

Elise had seen both of the new arrivals about the fort and, in
the way of all small communities, knew them by repute. The
man with the makeshift crutch was Jean-Paul St. Amant, a man
near thirty whose handsome appearance was considered to be
enhanced by the desolate look in his dark eyes. He had come
upriver to satisfy his curiosity about the country and remained
to become a planter of sorts on family holdings. He was so
obviously unsuited to the undertaking that no one understood
why he stayed, particularly when preferment in New Orleans
would have been made easy by his family connections. The
other man was known as Pascal, a merchant friend of the commandant who supplied the fort by special, and mutually profit-
able, arrangement with Chepart, or so it was whispered. His
thickset body and overbearing manner had so reminded Elise of
her dead husband that she had always avoided him.

Now she took instant dislike to his rough words. Her grasp
on Madame Doucet tightened and she turned her shoulder to the
merchant. "She will calm herself in a few minutes."

"We don't have a few minutes."

"I am as well aware as you, m'sieu, but see no need for
cruelty."

Pascal grabbed the older woman, jerking her free of Elise and swinging her around. He drew back his hand, but the blow never landed. Madame Doucet, her eyes wide and so pale blue they were colorless, stared beyond him with horror growing in her face, then crumpled forward in a faint at their feet.

"Your problem," said a deep voice tinged with derision from just beyond where they stood, "seems to be solved."

Henri drew in a single deep breath and was still. The merchant spat out an oath and raised his musket. Elise swung her head to see a tall man with copper skin and white breechclout and cape and instantly thrust up her arm, flinging the barrel of the merchant's firearm skyward. The Frenchman cursed again, but the expected report did not come; it seemed he, too, had identified the man in front of them in time to keep from pulling the trigger.

He grunted as he lowered his musket. "You were nearly a dead man, Chavalier."

"As you say."

Elise watched the graceful inclination of the head that accompanied the acknowledgment with resentment as rankling as it was amazing. Even more astonishing was her action in preventing injury to the half-breed. It was self-preservation, she told herself, no more and no less. The noise of the shot might have brought the Natchez down on them, and in Reynaud Chavalier could well lie their salvation.

"What brings you here?" the merchant was demanding. "Is your scalping arm tied or could it be the handiwork of your blood brothers turns your stomach?"

"I was following the lady."

Reynaud allowed his gaze to rest on the woman at their feet. If they wanted to think it was this one he meant, he would not enlighten them. In truth, it was the Widow Laffont for whom he had been searching since he had found her hat lying in the mud in front of her burning house. The sight of it there had struck sick pain into the center of his being. For an instant he had wanted to kill his brother, the Great Sun, for leaving him in ignorance of the day of the attack, for letting him lie sleeping while the warriors set off at dawn to station themselves for the slaughter. An instant of reflection had convinced him that the Great Sun might well not have known himself. As the godlike ruler of his tribe, he was not expected to take part in the planning of such exploits, much less direct them. That last was the re-

sponsibility of the second most important man in the tribe, their
uncle, Tattooed Serpent, chief of war.

"For what purpose?"

That was an excellent question. Reynaud flicked a glance
over the face of the young Frenchwoman, who had knelt to take
Madame Doucet's head on her lap. There were traces of tears
on her cheeks, but her self-control was complete. She looked
deathly tired, however, and her features mirrored a haunted fear
that he would give much to banish. At that instant she lifted her
lashes, meeting his gaze, and so much virulent dislike sprang
into her eyes that he felt the muscles of his abdomen tighten
involuntarily as if in anticipation of a blow.

"To keep her from harm," he said slowly.

"You could do that?" It was the man with the crutch who
spoke and the hope that threaded his voice gave it a ragged
sound.

"It's possible."

"How?" the merchant asked, a sneer curling his lip. "By
taking her back to the village to slave for you?"

"There is another way."

Something in the half-breed's tone sent a tremor of uneasiness
over Elise. Or perhaps it was the way his gaze kept returning to
rest on her in impassive speculation. She had had time while
hiding under the magnolia to think about what might be done,
however. She swallowed hard, then spoke from where she knelt.

"If we could know what has happened at the fort, know if
they are holding out there, perhaps we could reach it."

"It has fallen." St. Amant shifted uncomfortably on his
crutch. "Or perhaps it might be best to say it never held. Chepart
is dead. I saw him struck down and dismembered in his own
garden."

She caught her breath at the implication of those stark words.
If the fort had not held, then all was lost. There was scarcely
time to consider it at this moment. "Then we must get away.
With a boat, we could go down the river to New Orleans, give
the alarm."

Reynaud shook his head. "The river will be watched, sentries
posted for miles downstream. It is unlikely that you would get
through. There were six men who took to the river at the first
sign of the attack. Four were killed and the other two are being
pursued even now."

Elise glanced at the others. Their faces were tight and pale, their eyes fixed on Reynaud Chavalier as if he alone could save them.

"You mentioned a way out," St. Amant suggested.

"The nearest place of refuge for you is at the fort at the *Poste de la Saint Jean Baptiste*. I could take you there."

The normal method of reaching this post, located in the country of the Natchitoches Indians, was to travel down the Mississippi to where the Red River flowed into the larger river, then to proceed up the Red to the site of the French post, which had been built on its banks.

"But if we can't go on the river, how—"

"We would have to cross to the west bank after nightfall, then make our way overland using the Indian trails. That's much less dangerous than running the gauntlet down the river."

"Yes," interrupted the merchant, Pascal, his voice harsh. "I seem to have heard a tale or two about these trails. Dangerous, they are, if I remember right, and long and hard."

"Regardless, it appears we have no choice." St. Amant looked at Reynaud, but the other man only returned the Frenchman's gaze without speaking.

The merchant gave a hard nod. He spread his legs and put his fists on his hips. "Name your price, half-breed!"

Until that moment, there had been no thought in Reynaud's mind of profiting by the misfortune of the small band of French; he would have sworn it. Now something in the other man's tone grated on his taut nerves like a flint knife scraping buffalo hide, mingling with the scorn shown him by the Widow Laffont to stir his anger. That they could despise him even while he was offering his help was bad enough, but that they should show it so plainly marked them as arrogant and bigoted ingrates who even in the deadliest of danger could not forget their prejudices. It would be best if their position was brought home in a single, sharp lesson.

Still, he hesitated a moment as the idea took form in his mind. He was not certain whether it was prompted by the need to make these people aware of their dependence upon him, by sheer petty vengeance, or by something more that he did not care to name. Did it matter, in all truth? The impulse was too strong to be denied.

"I have no price," he said slowly. "All I require is the usual services."

"I don't believe I understand." The expression of the merchant who had become their spokesman was wary as he glanced from Reynaud's intent face to the others.

"It is the custom among the Natchez to supply male guests with a woman to see to their needs: to cook for them, to refill their food bowls, and to warm their bed furs on a cold night, whether in the village or on long hunts."

"You are saying that we should supply you with a woman, a Frenchwoman?"

"What objection can there be?" Reynaud asked, one brow raised in polite inquiry. "There is one here who is acceptable to me, a widow not unaware of the ways of men."

"Why, you bastard!"

Reynaud's voice was soft as he spoke. "Is it too much to ask, too great an exchange for your lives?"

Elise stared at Reynaud with the last vestiges of blood draining from her face and congealing in her veins. Madame Doucet stirred and gave a soft moan, but she did not notice. Coldness spread from the center of her being and she could hardly breathe. Her stiff lips formed a single word. "No."

Reynaud expected her swift objection, had set himself to listen to an impassioned appeal. If she had approached him in that vein as a civilized man, if she had asked him to reconsider, then he would have abandoned the suggestion on the instant, with apologies. Instead, he saw the horrified loathing in her face and felt his purpose harden. If she was so ready to think him the complete savage, what had he to lose by acting like one?

"I am to understand you do not think it too much to ask?" His voice carried a hint of steel in its quiet irony. "How generous of you, Madame Laffont. I will accept your sacrifice."

"No!" she cried.

"Wait, Madame Laffont, we must not be too hasty." The merchant's tone was soothing, almost oily, as if he thought her needlessly upset but considered it unwise to disturb her further.

St. Amant, his face pale, looked at her, then away again. "It's a question of—of life or death."

"It's m-monstrous," Henri declared, moving to stand protectively at Elise's left shoulder as he glared at Reynaud. "That you c-can suggest it is beyond belief!"

Indeed, it seemed so to Reynaud, and yet as he stared down at Elise Laffont he felt a tightness in his loins, an urgent need to hold her against him until the frantic disgust on her face turned to soft compliance. He wanted her, had wanted her from the moment her glance had clashed with his across the dining room of Commandant Chepart's house the night before. That instant of self-knowledge played havoc with his resolve.

"He can suggest it," Elise said with venom, "because he is a monster indeed, a vile mongrel lower even than the Natchez who at least act out of righteous anger."

Reynaud's head came up and his features hardened. "One capable of leaving you to meet that anger, if such should be your decision."

"Leave me then! Only take the others!".

"Now how can I do that?" he asked, his voice soft. "Madame Doucet is a worthy woman, but no substitute for someone of your—charms."

Elise clenched her hands upon Madame Doucet's arm and wrist so that the older woman groaned and opened her eyes to stare around in pain and bewilderment. There had been times before in her life when Elise had wanted desperately to strike out at a man, but they were as nothing compared to this moment.

The merchant stepped forward. "She will go with us and she'll be sensible about it; this I will assure you."

Reynaud transferred his gaze to the merchant and so dark with menace was it that the man stumbled backward again. "I want no unwilling woman, nor do I care for a damaged one."

"You think we would—"

"I know not. I can only assume that you judge me by yourselves."

"I'm sure she'll see reason."

"That may be. There are arrangements that must be made. I will return at dusk and will expect an answer then."

Reynaud directed one last glance at Elise where she still knelt at his feet. His features were hard, unreadable. Abruptly he swung around, moving away. Before he had taken a half-dozen steps, he had disappeared into the forest.

Pascal argued with her in the long hours that followed, talking until he was hoarse with the effort to keep his voice down yet to convince her that she was a fool, that what was being asked of her was a mere nothing, a few days of unpleasantness soon over. When his temper rose, St. Amant stepped in to prevent the merchant from becoming abusive. Still, he conquered his own scruples enough to swear that he, St. Amant, would see to it that she was not ill-used, if that was her fear. Also, though the decision was, of course, hers alone to make, he would point out that she held in her hands the lives of four other people. For himself it did not matter, but she must remember that one was a woman like herself, another a young boy. It might well be a mistake to let pride and fear dictate a choice that she could live to regret.

Elise was enough of a realist to recognize that they were right in their way; still, she could not overcome her revulsion. As the time grew shorter and Madame Doucet roused enough to add her tearful entreaties to their arguments, she began to feel the desperation of one cornered, left without a choice.

In the end, it was the thickening pall of smoke, the sound of the drums, the piping of cane flutes, and the drunken shouts of celebration that forced her decision. There could be no doubt that the Indians were in command, that the vast majority, if not all, of the French were dead. There was no possibility of making a foray for food and water to sustain them without the risk of discovery. Every moment they remained where they were only increased the danger of some Natchez warrior walking up to them. If that happened it would mean torture for the men, without doubt, and for herself and Madame Doucet slavery at best. They had to get away and their best hope of doing so successfully was Reynaud Chavalier. As long as he was not before her, as long as she did not think of what she must do to assure his cooperation, she could convince herself that she could go through with it. Somehow. It could not be any worse than the alternative, could it?

When she had given her assent, Elise was left alone, alone with her fears and her memories. She did not want to think about Vincent Laffont, not now, not ever. It was easier to think of France and of her father and their house on the Quai Malaquais.

Her mother had died when she was thirteen, a difficult age to lose one's maternal influence. For a year she and her father had consoled each other, then her father had begun to keep company with a certain Madame Rouquette. The Widow Rouquette had had a child, a boy of eight years with beady eyes, a large moist mouth, and a nature that took pleasure in petty spite. He was the image of his mother. Within weeks, her father and Madame Rouquette had married, and the widow and her son had moved into the house that Elise had still thought of as belonging to her own mother.

The months that followed were miserable. Elise's father was completely under the thumb of his new wife, as much from an addiction to her overripe sensuality as from any overt domination. Her stepmother had disliked Elise on sight, partially because she was a constant reminder of her predecessor, but primarily because Elise, according to her father's will, would inherit two-thirds of the estate on his death, should there be no issue of the new marriage. There had begun a slow campaign to make it seem that it was Elise who resented the new order and in time that was certainly true.

The situation became harder and harder to bear, especially since her father, after a time, ceased to take her part. A month before her fifteenth birthday there had been a terrible quarrel over a lace shawl that had belonged to Elise's mother. Her stepmother had taken up a broom handle to beat Elise and she had wrenched it from the older woman, striking back. The woman had run screaming from the house with blood pouring from a cut on her cheek. She had summoned the *gendarmes* and demanded that Elise be taken away to a house of correction.

The days and weeks had passed. Elise had finally given up hope of being removed from the terrible correction house by her father. All she could think was that her stepmother must have told him she had run away. She hadn't wanted to consider that he would allow her to be kept where she was, without protest, when his word alone would have been enough to secure her freedom. She had refused to think that it might be so.

She had begun to listen to the women who were crowded into the correction house. Their tales were often, or so she suspected, a strange blending of fact and fancy, and yet there was enough horror in them to furnish years of nightmares. A common thread running through them seemed to be the perfidy of men: men who took what they wanted with force or threats, without thought for the damage they caused; men with smooth tongues and consummate guilt who lied and cheated, then left the women behind. Much was made of their cruelty also, of their senseless rages and tortures, both physical and mental. As the stories she heard blended with the pain of her father's betrayal, Elise came to despise the male sex.

Then one day there had been a great bustle. Men had appeared with a proclamation that declared that they had the right to choose from among the correction girls, brides for the colonists of Louisiana. Those chosen would be given a small bundle of clothing, taken to the coast, and put on a ship for that distant colony. Once they had been signed up, there was nothing—no representation from parents or guardians, no bribe or legal maneuver—that could save them from the long journey to the new world. They had a quota to fill and none were exempt, though they preferred young females without vices or diseases. They had chosen a score or more of the women. Elise had been among them.

The journey to the coast had been a trial of endurance. It had taken place in the dead of winter in an open cart. The women had been inadequately clothed, most wore thin summer stuffs, without capes or cloaks. They had been chained together at the waist, herded in and out of ordinaries and inns like cattle with little privacy from the soldiers guarding them while they attended to their physical needs. A fever had struck while they waited at Le Havre for a ship and several of their number had died. Other women had been brought to join the ship: women snatched off the streets and from the farmyards of small villages; women from the prisons of scattered towns, many branded with the fleur-de-lis that marked them murderesses, traitresses. Many more of them had failed to survive the storm-wracked voyage aboard the *Mutine*, and the rest were only half alive when they finally reached port at Mobile.

They had rested for a time, regaining their strength before continuing the voyage to New Orleans. In that city, the women had been taken in by the director of the Company of the Indies, Monsieur Jacques de la Chaise. Their wants had been attended to, and they had been allowed to bathe, to wash their clothing, and to rest for a few days. During this respite, many men had come to stand before the director's house, craning to get a look at them or to approach it with some trumped-up errand. At the end of a week, the women had been put on view at a reception.

The women had been told that they would be able to choose their own life partners from the assembled men without coercion. It had not been that way for Elise. Vincent Laffont had swaggered into the room where the women were standing, looked them over like slaves at a market, and advanced at once upon Elise. He had given her no chance to refuse him, had not bothered to make a formal request for her hand, but had taken her at once to the director where he had made his choice known. Due to the unusual circumstances, the banns had been waived and the ceremony performed within the hour.

Her husband, she had discovered, was a scoundrel. A man twenty years her senior, he was a merchant of sorts, though a more accurate title might well have been smuggler. His authority came directly from the offices of the Company of the Indies in France, as did his backing, so that he was able to circumvent the regulations—the regulations that forbade trade with any except French vessels from French ports—of Governor Etienne de Perier and the Superior Council, and even of the company itself. It was this authority that had also permitted him to take precedence over the other men in his choice of bride. A swaggering man much given to food, drink, and the company of traders who shared his own lack of scruples, Vincent had made a fortune for the company trading with the Spanish and had also gained one for himself.

He had given his bride no time at all to adjust to her new state. He had bedded her within minutes after the toasts to their healths had been drunk. It had been a painful and degrading experience. Vincent had not expected a virgin and so had used her like a common woman of the streets, without preparation or consideration. As she came to know him, Elise was not certain that it would have made any difference had he known it. He had enjoyed her shrinking and cries of anguish, had taken pleasure in forcing himself upon her. The act of sexual coupling had become a thing of horror for her. Long after it had ceased to be actively painful, it had been an invasion of her innermost being that left her sickened, something to be avoided at all costs. The coldness that she had adopted as a defense had only excited him, however. He had cared not at all for her passions, but had delighted in arousing her to anger and defiance just for the amusement of beating her into submission.

He had overreached himself with the company, however, shortly after their marriage. Following an investigation into his affairs, instigated by the director, de la Chaise, his authority to trade was revoked by order from France. His ship and the goods that were on it at the time were impounded and sold, and he narrowly escaped charges of smuggling. He had been allowed to purchase land in the Natchez country near Fort Rosalie, the stockade and settlement named for the wife of the minister of state under Louis XIV, the Comte de Pontchartrain, and had retreated there to nurse his wounds and to plot ways of regaining his lost position.

It was at this time that Elise had begun slowly to lose her fear of the man she had married. She had discovered that, in common with most bullies, he was a coward. So great was the rage that he had inspired with his spiteful comments and careless blows that she had ceased to care what damage he might do to her. She had refused to sleep in the same bed with him, and when he had tried to compel her, she had fought back, kicking, clawing, using whatever weapon came to hand. Once she had poured a pot of boiling sagamite, containing cornmeal, pork fat, ham, and beans, over his head. Another time she had chased him out of the house with an axe. It was after she had crushed three of his fingers with the heavy pestle she used in the pounding trough for turning dried corn kernels into meal that he had brought Little Quail into the house to serve his needs.

Elise had lived for five of the seven years she had been in the colony unmolested by a man. In that time, the abhorrence she felt for the physical act of love had grown rather than subsided. That it threatened her now filled her with as much terror as impotent rage.

Reynaud Chavalier was not the same kind of man that Vincent Laffont had been; she recognized that well enough. He was no braggart, no bully. The half-breed was a man of obvious strength, of implacable will, of deep-running desires that he controlled without effort. It would not be so easy to defeat such a man. There would be no bluster in his anger, no wavering in his determination to subdue her. That he was a half-breed mattered not at all, except that it was his Indian heritage that gave him the stoic hardihood that hid his emotions and made him, therefore, doubly dangerous. To use a man's weakness, one must first find it, and as far as she had been able to tell in her brief acquaintance with Reynaud, he had none. It was these things that frightened her, these that she must add to the illogical terror she felt when she was near him because he was tall, overbearing, and had shown a flicker of interest in her as a woman; because the blood that ran in his veins had a fierce taint; but, most of all, simply because he was a man.

3

B Y THE TIME the early dusk of November deepened into darkness, the small group under the magnolia was thirsty, hungry, and near dagger-drawing with each other from the tight
stretch of their overwrought senses. They were no longer speaking. Elise, driven close to madness by the barrage of angry
demands and strident pleas for her to rescue them with her cooperation, had withdrawn to sit alone with her back to the tree
trunk and her hands clasped between her knees. Madame Doucet, told in a savage undertone to cease her moaning or be strangled, was sitting, staring at nothing, while her hands pulled and
patted her dress as if it was a child's blanket. Exhausted by his
terror of the morning, Henri had fallen into a jerking, twitching
sleep while St. Amant sat rubbing his injured leg and Pascal
strode up and down, ostensibly on watch.

It did nothing for their state, particularly that of Pascal, to
have Reynaud suddenly step up to them from the tree shadows.
The merchant started back with an oath. Recovering, he demanded, "Where the hell have you been?"

Reynaud ignored the question. "We will go now."

"I asked you a question," the merchant said, squaring up to
the half-breed with his musket held in front of him.

Reynaud paused, then looked down at him. When he answered, his voice was deep and deliberate. "Listen and hear me
well. I owe you nothing, not duty, not explanations. I care not
whether you live or die and know no reason why I should. I will
lead you away from my brothers the Natchez for the sake of the
blood of my father and for the favors of the woman I have

requested. As we go you will do as I say, instantly, without question, because your life may depend on it. If you fail, if you seek to put yourself over me, I will leave you behind because you will have become a danger to all. This I promise. Heed me and you will be safe. This I swear. Come with me now if it is still your will, for this is the last time I will tell you.''

''You haven't asked if Madame Laffont agrees to your proposition.''

''She is still here.''

Elise met the gray gaze he directed toward her. Caught in its dark intensity, she could not look away. She had the feeling that Reynaud Chavalier knew how near she had come in the past hours to running away. A half-dozen times she had fought the urge to leap to her feet and flee through the woods, to try to make her way to the river's edge in the frail hope of finding a boat to take her downstream away from the Natchez country. It had not been fear that restrained her so much as the certainty that that way led to death. She did not want to die, though the choice offered to her seemed only marginally better.

Reynaud moved toward her, ducking under the magnolia limb with a graceful twist of his body and leaning over to offer her his hand. She wanted to refuse it; any other time she would have done so instantly. Instead, she stared at him, noting that he had donned more protective clothing, wearing beaded leggings and a heavier, thigh-length cloak of soft buckskin. His crown of feathers and topknot of hair were gone, replaced by a simple queue tied with a leather thong. She felt an odd constraint, as if she were held by the force of his will, while in her head beat the cadence of the words he had spoken to the merchant and the need to know to what extent they applied to her.

She reached up to put her hand in his. The touch, the voluntary contact of her palm with that of this man, sent a shudder along her nerves that spread through her body, lodging in the pit of her stomach. The warmth and strength of his grasp brought the dew of perspiration to her upper lip. There was a tremor in her voice that did not hide the bitterness as she inquired, ''And will I also be safe?''

''None will be safer, since none will be closer.''

He drew her up to stand before him, then reached to steady her as he felt the trembling that shook her. She twitched away from him, turning her back. He stood, staring at her erect head and stiff shoulders, torn between anger and chagrin that she should find him so repulsive and yet more disturbed by the fine edge of panic he had seen in her eyes.

It took the best part of two hours to reach the river. The night was dark, without a moon. They moved with slow care, cutting straight through the woods by some reckoning Reynaud alone knew and avoiding the road. The half-breed scouted ahead every few hundred yards, ranging back to them to urge them forward, directing them with care over slopes littered with limestone shale or around thickets of wild plums. Their progress was slow but without incident.

They found the boat where he had left it covered with underbrush, a heavy craft hollowed from a great log. It appeared to be half full of provisions wrapped in strapped bundles to form packs. Elise was doubtful that it would also carry the six of them, but under Reynaud's direction they were squeezed into it. It sank low in the water, wallowing as he shoved off, then leaped aboard, but once he had settled down and dug in his paddle, setting the beat for St. Amant and Pascal, it bore them well.

The women and Henri were spaced between the men with paddles, Elise sitting just ahead of Reynaud. She leaned forward to get out of his way as he changed his paddle from one side of the boat to the other. She looked back over her shoulder, glancing at his dark form, which moved with what appeared to be effortless ease to send them skimming over the water, before fastening her gaze on the receding shore. The hills and bluffs glowed with fires in the darkness. Back there was all that she owned now, her land, the only place to which she had any ties. She did not know when she would see it again, or if she ever would. She did not know what she would do when she reached Fort Saint Jean Baptiste, how she would live, where she would stay. None of it seemed to matter. The only important thing was getting away, and the price she must pay for that escape.

There was a movement on the bank they had left, then another. ''I think they have seen—'' she began.

A shout of anger rang across the water, followed by a shot and the whistling passage of a musket ball. Reynaud bent harder into his paddle. The others followed suit, grunting with the effort. Another shot exploded, echoing with a muffled booming over the river, reverberating from the wooded shore opposite, so very far away. The ball skipped away over the water on their right. It was followed by another, and yet another.

They were a shifting, uncertain target in the darkness on the river. Though the water was kicked up around them and the black and acrid smoke of spent powder swirled out to meet them, they were not hit. The Indians had the dugout canoes called pirogues by the French, but those that were not beached somewhere up at St. Catherine Creek were being used to harry the two Frenchmen who had fled down the river. Standing on the bank, the Indians fired at nothing, howling in frustration and impotent rage.

As she huddled in front of Reynaud, it came to Elise that his was the most exposed position, there in the stern, that he was in the greatest danger of being hit. As a member of the Sun class and the brother of their king, surely the Natchez would not shoot at him if they knew who he was, but they could not see him in the blackness of the night. He could have called to his Indian brothers and offered up the French settlers as his captives. In such a case, he could still have claimed her favors if that had been his object. That he did not, that he bent with tireless determination to pulling away from shore, served to indicate that he would live up to his sworn word. It only remained for her to live up to hers.

But she had not sworn. Her word had been taken by force, accepted without direct agreement. Could there be any reason to consider herself bound in such a case? If there was some way to remove herself from this obligation, then she had every right to take it, and with honor. Every right.

The Mississippi was wide, more than a mile across. As the boat scraped the mud of the west bank, Pascal hung over the side with his paddle trailing in the water and his breath rasping in his chest from the long strain of fighting the current. St. Amant dropped his paddle in the bottom of the boat and sat slumped, unmoving. It was Henri who scrambled to his feet and leaped out, dragging the heavy craft onto the shore. Reynaud stood, taking Elise's arm and urging her forward. His breathing was deep, but far from labored.

"Must . . . rest," St. Amant said as Elise's skirts brushed against him and he turned his head to see them waiting for him to move.

"There's no time. They may decide to come after us. We must leave no sign that we did not continue down the river."

St. Amant nodded his understanding of Reynaud's words; still, it was a moment before he could find the strength to surge to a standing position and weave his way toward the shore.

Pascal also heaved himself from the boat in time to remove himself from Reynaud and Elise's path. The two men then stood to one side while the half-breed and Henri unloaded the supplies and stacked them in a pile. Reynaud pushed the heavy dugout back into the river's flow, letting the current take it on downstream before he turned to face them.

In an amazingly short span of time, the packs were sorted out and assigned and an order of march established. They all stood waiting a short distance into the encroaching woods while Reynaud obliterated the signs of their landing, then he hefted the heaviest, hide-wrapped load to his back along with his bow and a quiver of arrows and a musket slung from a braided leather strap. He took his place in the lead. In silence they set out, Pascal behind Reynaud as double protection from the front should they run into any trouble, Elise next, with Madame Doucet behind her, followed by St. Amant with his crutch, and Henri bringing up the rear. They had nothing to say and much to think about, all of them. In any case, they were well aware of the need to put as much distance as possible between themselves and the Natchez. If when morning came the Indians did not go chasing their boat down the Mississippi, if instead they searched the riverbank on this side, then it would be just as well if they were as far away as they could be. A party of Natchez warriors would move as swiftly as the flight of an arrow, far faster than their band, slowed by women and a wounded man. Time, then, was their greatest ally.

"Say, half-breed," Pascal called after a time, "what's your brother the Great Sun going to think when he finds out you took off in the middle of their little party?"

"It will not be unusual." The answer was calm, without a trace of apprehension.

"What about when he hears that you showed up at Fort Saint Jean Baptiste with us? That ought to make you a traitor, the way I see it."

"I owe allegiance to none."

Elise heard the firmness of the words, but she could not help remembering that Reynaud had sought to warn Chepart and the French.

Pascal laughed. "Let's hope the Great Sun sees it that way. The way I understand it, your people have no more liking for a turncoat than anybody else."

"I have no people," Reynaud said.

His words echoed in Elise's mind long after the two men ceased to speak. They had been without consciousness or self-pity and yet they touched some fragile cord of response in her. They made Reynaud Chavalier seem less forbidding somehow. Everyone had people. The half-breed's misfortune was that he did not know which were his, the Natchez or the French.

The hours passed. They walked for league upon league, stumbling along with eyes grown accustomed to the darkness and a slowly developing instinct for avoiding the whip of released branches or the dangle of brier vines. They stopped to rest when Madame Doucet sank, groaning, to the ground, but were up again and moving as soon as she was able. Toward dawn, they made a cold camp to slake their thirst and take a bite of food, then sank down to sleep for a few short hours. By the time the sun rose they were moving again.

The day was fine, even a little warm, for the exercise of hard walking. The autumn had been a long one. They had had one or two light frosts, but the days had continued pleasant; cool enough for a fire at night, requiring nothing more than light sleeves during the day. As the hours slipped by, they fell into a routine, learning to place one foot in front of the other without thought. Madame Doucet complained of blisters, sagging under her load until Reynaud relieved her of it and thrust it upon a disgruntled Pascal. Elise, tired of the constant fight to keep her skirts from under her feet, asked Reynaud for a thong, which she tied around her waist and then pulled the hem of her skirts up through it in the front in imitation of the washerwomen of Paris. She was tempted to catch the back hem of her habit skirt and draw it up between her legs, also tucking it in, as was sometimes done, but decided that the bulk of the heavy velvet habit and petticoat she wore under it would make for uncomfortable walking. After sleeping in it on the ground, snatching a hundred small tears in the fabric on briers, and soaking it in the many small streams they were forced to cross, dragging it in the mud hardly mattered.

The air grew warmer as the day advanced. The country they were traveling in was low and swampy with a high canopy of enormous cypress, oak, and maple trees; hickory, sweet gum, ash, bay, dogwood, and a dozen others, all hung with the swaying gray moss the French had named Capuchin's beard. Creeks and branches wound through it in such snakelike curves that they forded the same streams again and again. As perspiration gathered under Elise's hair, trickling down her neck and between her breasts, she came to look forward to wading in the cool water, despite the necessity of pulling her knit stockings and half boots on and off and getting the black alluvial mud between her toes. She considered doing as Pascal and St. Amant did, tramping through the water with her shoes on, but she was afraid that walking in the wet footwear afterward would make the blisters rise quickly on her tender feet. The most bothersome thing was the mosquitoes that hovered in the air under the tall trees of the forest swampland. They were black and vicious, with a keening whine that grated on the nerves like a high-pitched scream.

They had crossed a clear-running creek lined with white sand at the bottom and overhung by dark green moss and ferns that had not yet felt the blight of frost. On the opposite bank they stopped to rest. Elise sat down against a tree and began to dry her feet on the tail of her habit. She shook out a stocking and slipped it over her foot, slapping in idle irritation at a mosquito before smoothing it up over her calf, tying a garter in place, and then rolling the stocking and fastening it over the garter just below her knee. Reaching for her other stocking, she surveyed the hole beginning to show in the heel with rueful dismay. There was nothing to be done except to put it on, however.

She was smoothing it upward with her skirts bunched just above her knees when an odd self-consciousness moved over her. She glanced up to see Reynaud leaning against a tree a short distance away, his gray eyes shuttered as he watched her. His gaze followed the slender turn of her ankle, the gentle swell of her calf. She was still for a moment as she felt the rise of hot color. She did not like the sensation. Setting her teeth, she lowered her eyes and, with a great pretense of unconcern, continued with what she was doing. She was fervently glad when she could roll and knot her stocking above her knee and lower her skirts, however, and there was unnecessary violence in the slap she used to kill the next mosquito that landed on her wrist.

Reynaud pushed away from the tree. He moved to one of the packs that had been piled by the group. Loosening it, he rummaged inside, then stood with a small clay pot in his hand. He came toward her, dropping to one knee as he held out the pot.

"What is it?" Elise asked, making no move to take it.

"Bear grease. It will discourage the mosquitoes."

Elise frowned, wrinkling her nose. "I don't doubt it, but, no, I thank you."

"It isn't as bad as you think."

"I've smelled rancid bear grease before and I don't think it's something I want to put up with all day."

"This is fresh. I'm wearing it now."

His voice was quiet, without inflection, and yet that very lack of expression was both a reminder that she had once accused him of being malodorous and a challenge to her to say the same again. A chill rippled over her skin, followed by a flush so intense that she felt sick with it. Her lips parted as she stared into his eyes, but she could not make a sound.

"In any case," he said easily, "it was not a suggestion, but an order. The medicine woman of the Natchez claims that the bite of the mosquito can cause illness and she may be right."

He dipped one finger into the grease, whitish, semiliquid with the day's warmth, not unlike olive oil, and reached out to draw it down the soft curve of her cheek. She flinched, snapping her head back, her embarrassment turning quickly to defiant anger.

"You can do it, or I will."

The words were no less of a threat for being softly spoken. Elise held his gaze for a moment longer, then reached to snatch the small pot from his hand. He inclined his head, then his lithe muscles flexed as he got to his feet. Moving away, he said over his shoulder, "When you are done, give it to Madame Doucet and the others."

She did not answer, but then he did not expect it. It was an effort not to turn and watch her as she smoothed the bear grease into her skin. He had allowed himself to be distracted by her too often: by the white flash of her calves beneath her tucked-up skirt; by the swing of her hips; by the lift of her breasts as she reached to push a hanging limb aside or stretched aching muscles. He felt torn between the urge to stay at her side helping her over obstacles, as much for the sake of touching her as to aid her, and the necessity to range ahead of the group breaking the trail or to let them pass, lingering behind on the alert for danger. Though she hardly seemed aware that he was there, he knew every moment where she was and what she was doing. And as he kept watch there grew inside him a combination of guilt, barely suppressed lust, and anticipation that curled inside his loins in white-hot heat.

By midafternoon, the sun had vanished behind a solid bank

of clouds and the day had turned sultry. The peculiar feel of the air for that time of year was disturbing; regardless, the spirits of the group rose as the leagues dropped behind them with no sign that they were being pursued. They were tired, however, their footsteps lagging, the packs they carried growing so heavy that they might have been filled with rocks. Madame Doucet turned querulous, forgetting her terror enough to complain in a voice well above a whisper. Henri grumbled also at the chafing of his pack across his shoulders, and St. Amant had found a second forked limb and swung along on a pair of makeshift crutches. Elise was weary beyond thought. She had grown used to the smell of the bear grease, a scent that was not, in truth, unpleasant with its undertone of the herb spikenard. That it was effective she found not at all surprising, though she refused to give Reynaud the satisfaction of knowing it and slapped at a mosquito buzzing around her now and then as a matter of form.

Still, the half-breed led them onward. To Elise he began to seem less than human. He was seldom still, always on guard; even when they stopped to rest he often left them to scout to their rear or swung himself into the highest branches of a tree to scan the country before and behind them. He showed no impatience with their weakness as they flung themselves down on the ground to lie spent and panting, but if he felt any degree of that same fatigue, there was no sign of it. It was maddening and, at the same time, comforting.

It was an hour before dusk when they reached the river. It doubtless had a name on some map drawn by explorers sent out by the company of the Indies in their searches for mines of gold and silver, but what it was Elise neither knew nor cared. Smaller by far that the Father of Waters, the Mississippi, it was still a wide and deep stream. It would require a raft to cross it, and to build it would take more daylight than was left to them. They would make camp for the night and cross in the morning.

The packs were opened, disclosing bed furs of bear and fox, closely woven lengths of cloth, and short-handled axes, as well as sacks of cornmeal and mixed dry sagamite, that universal dish of cornmeal, and chips of dried meat and dried beans. There was a basket of some odd tubers and another of ripe persimmons and also a crock of bear grease, without herbs, for seasoning the food. Included, too, was a pair of sharp knives, an iron pot, and a set of six hand-carved wooden bowls and spoons. Reynaud had spent the time that he had left them alone before their departure well.

Henri gathered wood while they were unpacking and Reynaud kindled a small but hot cook fire. The half-breed leaned over to place at Elise's side a pair of ducks that he had killed in the late afternoon using silent skill with bow and arrow. Detailing Henri to carry water for her, he set St. Amant as guard with the musket, gathered axes and Pascal, and went into the woods.

Elise set Madame Doucet to cleaning the ducks while she mixed the sagamite with water and put it on to simmer in the iron pot. By the time the men had returned, the ducks, basted with bear grease, were roasting on spits that she had cut from stout limbs, the sagamite was sending its rich smell into the air, and the corn cakes lay baking on a pot lid placed among the coals. There had been no difficulty with the food. The French had long since learned to cook as the Indians did, though not all liked it by any means. Elise, tending the meal, watched from the corners of her eyes as Reynaud and Pascal made five tentlike enclosures using the saplings they had brought from the woods. They bent each sapling in a half circle, three per enclosure, then lashed three more lengthwise before covering the frame thus made with cloth.

The enclosures were not large, being slightly wider than a man's shoulders and only high enough for one to creep into them. Their purpose was to offer some protection from the weather, but most of all to prevent sleepers from being eaten alive by mosquitoes. Four of them had been erected near the fire, with a fifth, this one wider at the base than the others, a small distance away. It took no great intelligence to realize that the last was meant for her to share with Reynaud Chavalier.

Elise tried to avoid looking at that shelter set apart. It seemed to her overactive imagination that the others did the same. So scrupulous were they in looking away that their very tact drew attention to it. She felt that they were each thinking of what must take place in it when night drew in, some with pity, some with anger, and some with lascivious interest. The quick glances they divided between the half-breed and herself made that much plain.

Her appetite deserted her and she finally scraped away the food from her bowl into the fire. She thought to while away a little more time before she had to retire for the night by cleaning the iron pot, bowls, and spoons, but Reynaud took them from her. With Henri, he went to the river's edge where he scrubbed the pot with sand and sent the boy back with it filled with water to be heated over the fire. He washed the bowls and spoons, too, rinsing them well. Returning to the fire, he helped Elise dry them and put them away, along with the extra cakes she had made for their breakfast.

Darkness had fallen while they worked. St. Amant had crawled into his shelter, as had Henri and Madame Doucet. Pascal was sitting, puffing on a narrow clay pipe much like the calumets, or peace pipes, of the Indians and staring into the fire. Reynaud closed and strapped the pack with the food in it, then got to his feet, moving to hang it on a tree limb out of reach of nocturnal animals that might be attracted by the smell. He stood for a long moment with his dark gray gaze resting on Elise, then moved away once more, out of the circle of firelight, in the direction of the river.

The pot of water on the fire still simmered. Elise stared at it, feeling the itch of dried perspiration on her skin and the film of bear grease and woodsmoke. She picked up the tail of her habit and folded it into a protective holder against the heat of the pot's bail, then lifted the water, carrying it with her in the direction of the shelter that had been set apart from the others.

Unlike her fellow travelers, she refused to think of what would shortly happen inside the enclosure. Insofar as it was possible, she readied herself for bed exactly as she would have if she had been in the bedchamber of her home that lay smouldering somewhere across the river. Keeping the bulk of the cloth-covered poles between herself and the fire, she removed her habit and petticoat, then, after a moment of hesitation, stripped off her shift. She dipped the shift into the hot water, using it as a bathing cloth, and held it to the soreness of her muscles. When she was done, she rinsed it and hung it to dry across the top of the shelter. Then calmly, without stopping to reason why, she pulled her petticoat and habit back on, ducked into the shelter, and lay down as far to one side of the spread bed furs as she could get.

For some time she lay stiffly, with every muscle taut. By degrees she relaxed as the minutes ticked past. Perhaps this was her shelter alone, perhaps with his Indian blood Reynaud preferred to sleep in the open? Could it be that he had changed his mind in the face of her obvious reluctance? Was it possible for him to be that considerate? She lay for a time listening to the night stillness. There was a rustling sound as a small animal, a raccoon or an opossum, investigated the camp and the quiet clatter of beech leaves still clinging to the tree that spread its limbs above her shelter. Perhaps Reynaud had met with an accident, a panther or a wildcat, or even a surprise attack by pursuing Indians?

Her thoughts were sent scattering like dry leaves before the wind as there came a soft footstep outside and the lifting of the end flap. Her breathing quickened and she felt the leap of her heart before it began to thud against her ribs.

His broad form filled the shelter, a dark shape against the greater darkness, bringing with it the freshness of the night. He was close, so suffocatingly close, as he hovered for an instant above her, then stretched out full length on the furs. She could pretend to be asleep. She could if she could control her breathing. But it was impossible. She heard him shift, turning toward her. She thought he whispered her name, but could not be sure. He pushed himself up onto one elbow and reached out to touch her.

She swallowed a scream. His fingertips brushed her shoulder through her habit sleeve and a shudder ran over her. They trailed across her collarbone to sear the taut line of her neck. She stopped breathing and lay with her eyes tightly closed as waves of tremors wracked her. She wanted to stop them. She wanted to lie with cool hauteur, uncaring of what the half-breed did to her. But she could not. At the edge of sanity, she felt him pause. Endless seconds stretched.

Then with slow deliberation he skimmed his hand downward, touching, clasping the trembling mound of her breast.

Rage exploded inside her. She flung up her arms, knocking his hand away, pushing, clawing at him with a single word bursting from her throat. "No, no, no!"

Swift and hard, his hands found and caught her wrists, pulling them inexorably above her head where he held them with one hand. He found her mouth with the other, stilling her cry. His muscular thigh clamped over her knees, holding them immobile, bearing down until she ceased to move. His hold was firm, inescapable. She felt the brush of a strand of his hair, wet as if he had just come from swimming, as he leaned over her. In the sudden quiet his voice had a harsh, accusing rasp.

"It isn't just me, is it?"

Where the tears came from so soon after her intolerable wrath, she did not know, but they rose in her throat with hurtful pressure, overflowing her eyes and spilling down her face to pool against his restraining hand. He jerked it away with a stifled oath, releasing her in the same movement, pushing from her until he was against the far side of the shelter.

"Why?"

The heat was gone from his tone, leaving confusion and slow-fading tension. She heard it with a relief that she could not acknowledge. Her voice thick with tears, she said, "What does it matter?"

"Someone hurt you, a man, maybe more than one." It was a statement, tentative, but holding the beginning of hard understanding.

"One was enough."

"Your husband?"

"My—husband."

"It is," he said clearly, "an excellent thing that you are a widow."

Surprise stopped the salty flow of her tears. "What?"

"Else someone would have had to make you one."

Someone? Himself? She lay still, intrigued and puzzled by the thought. He shifted and as he lay down his knee brushed her leg. She recoiled, scooting away from him.

He crossed his arms over his chest. His voice was tight once more as he spoke. "You need not fear me. I have no use for a cringing woman in my bed."

The description was hardly flattering. Perhaps that was the reason that she was able to believe him, able to allow her cramped muscles to relax; able, finally, to obey the will of her weary body and drift to sleep.

The soft rumble of distant thunder woke her. She gave a soft moan as she opened her eyes, expecting to see the pale light of dawn. It was still dark. Indeed, so black was the night that she could not see the outline of the man beside her, though she could feel his warmth. Coming awake with a start, she discovered that the reason the temperature of his body was so apparent was because her head was resting on his arm and her hand was lying lax with sleep on his belly.

She smothered a gasp. Contracting stiff muscles, she began to withdraw by degrees. If she could remove herself from him without waking him, all would be well. Wide-eyed in the dark, she inched away.

Lightning flickered, a white glare that illuminated the inside of the shelter. In that instant of light she saw that Reynaud was awake, though lying infinitely still, awake and watching her.

She stopped, her breathing suspended.

"All men are not the same," he said, his voice deep and pensive.

"No?" It was not reluctance to believe so much as it was an inability to do so.

"I don't expect you to accept my word; it's something you will have to discover for yourself."

There was an inflection in the measured reason of his tone that troubled her. "I would rather not."

"You don't have that choice." He raised his hand to capture her fingers that lay slackly against him.

She pulled sharply against his hold. When she could not free herself, she clenched her hand into a fist. "What—what do you mean?"

"We made a bargain and I hold you to it. You will serve me as I—as I desire."

"But you said—" she began in panic.

"And I meant it. I will not touch you."

"I don't understand you!" That was better, she thought as she felt the rise of anger and heard it strengthen her protest.

His chest lifted in a deep breath. "You will touch me."

"I can't!"

"You can. You will, if you and your fellow countrymen want to reach Natchitoches."

She went still. This was not a whim, but some carefully thought-out substitute for what he had originally planned. All the time she had been sleeping, he had been lying there thinking of some way to bend her to his will. If it had been only her own safety at stake, she would have defied him, but she could not take such a risk for the others. It was true that they were not in as great a danger now, on this side of the river; still, there were many leagues of dense forest between here and the post on the Red River, forests that could be traversed only by those who knew the way, those who could follow the cunningly blazed Indian trails. To pit her strength against him would be foolish, as she had already discovered, and even if she should prevail there was nowhere for her to go, no one to whom she could appeal for succor. Pascal and even St. Amant had already made it plain that they expected her to placate the half-breed regardless of the cost. Anger and defiance would not serve her then. She would need something more.

She moistened her lips with the tip of her tongue. "You know that I can't—that I—"

"I know, yes. But how else are you going to learn to trust if you are never near a man, never intimate with one?"

"Trust?" she inquired with cold scorn. "Trust a man who uses blackmail to gain his ends, one who issues the most cruel threats against helpless people? You must think me a fool."

He turned his head. "You prefer to remain a terrified rabbit, cringing when a man comes near you?"

"I am not a rabbit! As for men, I make sure none ever come near."

"Then you are missing the supreme pleasure of life, its most vivid joy."

"The physical use of a woman by a man?" she asked in bitter irony. "I've never found it so."

"The love of a woman and a man together, a sharing, one of the other. It's a different thing, something I would wager you have never had."

For a fleeting instant she was aware of the stir of curiosity. Ruthlessly she subdued it. "And you in your vast experience know it well?"

He did not answer. Instead, he pried open her tight, chilled fingers and, controlling her shrinking, spread them over his chest, holding them there when she would have snatched them away.

Tremors shook her in waves and she closed her eyes, turning her face into the firmness of his shoulder. His hand was warm and strong over hers, the grasp gentle, though inescapable. Slowly her trembling subsided. Her hand warmed against the radiating heat of his body. Beneath her sensitive palm she felt a peculiar throb and realized that it was the beat of his heart. The sensation vibrated along her nerves, a hard jarring that warned her that he was not so undisturbed as he wanted to appear. The knowledge brought an unwilling fascination. Through her mind flitted the words he had spoken earlier. *It isn't just me, is it?*

Was it possible that he had been hurt, in his pride at least, by her rejection of him, first at the soirée and later in the woods? It did not fit the picture she held of his hard indifference and yet he was undeniably affected by her. Could it be, was it possible, that the cause of his disturbance was the simple touch of her hand?

No. She could countenance neither supposition. It must be that the desire he felt for her was stronger than she had any idea that emotion could be for a man. Perhaps he was right, then, perhaps all men were not the same. Maybe she was wrong to judge all men by the vicious demands visited upon her by Vincent Laffont.

Even as she made rational sense of Reynaud's purpose, the sensitive tips of her fingers found the faint ridges of the lines of tattoos that marked his chest. They made a concentric pattern, those lines, like links in a chain design set in rows, one above the other. They had been made by the pricking of some sharp-pointed instrument, like a bone needle, with soot or some dark plant dye rubbed into the injuries and left to heal. Meant not for decoration, but as a proof of manhood, they should have been hideous to her. Somehow they were not. Instead, she wished that it was daylight so that she might see them at this close range. At least he did not have them on his face as many warriors did, particularly across the forehead and bridge of the nose. That much of the appearance of a savage he had forgone.

There was another thing. Unlike Vincent, whose body hair had been as thick as an animal's pelt, or most other men she had seen in their shirtsleeves who seemed to have thick tufts sprouting at their necks, Reynaud's chest was bare. She had noticed the phenomenon among the Indians before and particularly on the half-breed that night at the commandant's house. There was no coarse growth to prevent her from pressing her hand fully against his chest, none to obscure the sculptured molding of the muscles that swathed his rib cage or to disguise their smooth play under his copper-bronze skin.

Once more lightning flared with the roll of thunder close upon it. In its bright light Elise saw something she had overlooked until now. Reynaud, lying so still under her hand, was without a particle of clothing. She jerked away from him as if he had been suddenly transformed to a glowing coal.

He caught her wrist. "What is it?"

"You're naked!"

"What difference does it make?"

"It does, it just does!"

"You have my word," he said, the words rough.

"You—you won't touch me, you promise?" She could not

prevent the question or the catch in her voice as hers were spoken.

"It is a vow, one most sacred, sworn on any saint you please, on the veil of the virgin, the true cross, by the beard of Louis XV, most Christian majesty, by the shadows of the walls of Combourg chateau and my father's tomb—"

"All right," she said to stop the flow of the oath, "I believe you."

"Then place your hand upon me now, of your own will."

It was a demand, but one that also carried a hint of supplication. He released her. She lay unmoving for a long moment, then, with a slow, jerking motion, as if the flesh and tendons she controlled were not her own, she did as he asked.

She placed her spread fingers on his diaphragm, sliding them upward and recognizing, with a familiarity that was oddly shocking, the pound of his heart, the ridges of his muscles, the tracing of his tattoo lines. He did not move and gave no sign of triumph. His breathing was steady, an even rise and fall, and his hands were at his sides. In the glow of lightning that now came with more regularity, she kept her lashes lowered. She did not want to know if he watched her. She was unwilling to risk seeing his nakedness, though it seemed that the flat expanse of his belly with the turgid length of his manhood upon it and the long, well-formed length of his legs were imprinted upon her memory.

After a time, it seemed that lying there pressing against his chest was not enough. She bit the underside of her lip, then she whispered finally, "What shall I do now?"

There was richness and depth to his voice as he replied, "Whatever pleases you," then added as she lifted her hand to move away, "except that."

Her palm brushed across a pap as she settled it upon him again. The flat nipple contracted much like her own and she paused in surprise, returning to probe it delicately with a finger. It hardened still further. Interested in spite of herself, she trailed her hand across to the other. She flicked that one with a fingernail, smiling a little in bemusement as it tightened at once. She circled it then, widening the motion by degrees.

So firm and well hardened were the muscled planes beneath the paps, she found, that a channel was created where his breastbone lay. She followed it like a path to the hollow of his throat, dipping her fingers into that shallow well and sliding upward along the ridge of his Adam's apple to the firm jut of his chin and the cleft that cut into it.

She stopped there, rubbing her knuckles back and forth over the unstubbled smoothness of his face. The Indians did not shave, or so she had been told, but rather pulled the hair out one by one, an operation much less frequent than the daily scraping of whiskers. It appeared to be true.

She thought of the mouth of the man beside her: free from the burning scrape of unshaven beard, the lines of it firm, the surface of his lips smooth, their shape well molded. They were so close to her fingertip. What would it be like to . . .

She shied away from the thought, quickly running the pads of her fingers back down his throat and along his breastbone to the surface of his diaphragm. It was exceedingly hard, even rigid. He seemed to be breathing with shallow movements of the bellows of his lungs. She spread her hand wide, checking that minute rise and fall. How strange that slight motion was, when she had half expected from his stillness to find the deep and regular respiration that precedes sleep.

Like his chest, his diaphragm was wrapped with broad bands of muscle. His navel was a deep indention in the ridges that continued even on his abdomen. Beneath the small sink was a narrow line of downlike hair, and as she trailed down it with one questing fingertip she had a sudden vision of that first time she had seen him: his thighs and calves gleaming in candlelight, free of the hair covering of the Caucasian race, with the smooth athletic grace of some ancient carved statue.

With sudden violence, Reynaud clamped his fingers upon her hand, halting her downward exploration. Before she could move, before she could cry out at his hand grip, he surged up, letting her go even as he left her. There was a rush of wind as he ripped open the end flap of the shelter and glided outside.

It had begun to rain, a slow pattering of drops that must have been falling unnoticed for some minutes. Elise lay listening to it, an incredulous frown gathering between her eyes. He had left her and she was not glad.

The bed furs were warm where he had lain. A chill touched her skin and she shivered. She sat up, staring into the darkness, listening, but she could not tell what Reynaud was doing or where he had gone.

With abrupt decision, she got to her knees and crawled to the end of the shelter. She tugged aside the flap to look out. The night was black and the wind whipped the wetness of rain into her face. Then came the crackle and flash of lightning, ripping across the sky in a jagged tear. It silhouetted the trees in its white glare and was reflected in the spattering rain that sheeted the ground. And it gilded in silver splendor the naked form of the man who stood just outside.

It was Reynaud, with his arms at his sides, his palms turned outward, and his head thrown back. His eyes were closed and his features blank, shut-in, as he lifted his face to the cold autumn rain.

4

ELISE KEPT HER gaze on her feet as she walked. Plodding along behind the squat form of Pascal was fast becoming so ordinary, such a habit, that it did not require her attention. There was an abstracted frown between her brown eyes, and now and then she glanced up to stare past the merchant at the broad back of the half-breed who led them all.

She could not understand Reynaud. The thing he had demanded of her in exchange for her own life and those of the other refugees from Fort Rosalie was barbaric. And yet his behavior, his consideration the night before, was, she had reason to believe, rare even among civilized men. Which was he, then, savage or gentleman?

There was a purpose behind his leniency, this she did not doubt. It was likely that he expected her to be so affected by the proximity of his masculine form that she would succumb to her own curiosity to know how it would feel to have him make love to her. His talk of the joys of such, his taunt about her lack of knowledge of it, pointed toward that end.

He was going to be badly disappointed, of course; still, how many men would have the patience to wait? Most seemed to think that a woman's protests, the barriers she erected, were only there to be swept aside. They took pleasure in thrusting straight toward their goal, caring little for the pain they caused. Some even enjoyed it. Certainly she had expected nothing more from Reynaud. In some peculiar way, his forbearance was more disturbing than if he had forced himself upon her.

Was that strictly true? She herself had been shocked by the

violence of her physical reaction, her total rejection of the nearness of a man. Even now she was embarrassed by her lack of control, by the fact that he had seen her a prey to overwrought sensibilities. She did not know what she would have done if he had exerted himself to take her. She refused to think about it.

Arrogant Indian bastard! she thought in a sudden rush of anger. How dare he think that he could slip beneath her defenses with so paltry a subterfuge? Was she supposed to be impressed with his well-developed muscles or the tattoos that marked his ascent to manhood? Touch him, indeed! The next time she would leave the marks of her nails on his belly. She would make him sorry that he had driven so infamous a bargain with her. She was no giggling Indian maiden, ready to play slap-and-tickle and enjoy a roll in the bed furs. She was Elise Laffont, a widow of property, a Frenchwoman of pride and self-respect. The next time would be different; he would not have everything so much his way. She would conquer her aversion enough to defend herself, enough to set him back on his moccasined heels. He could save his pity for himself, for he would need it when she was through with him.

She lifted her lashes, looking once more to where Reynaud strode at the front of the column. He ducked beneath a tree limb, bending to the side with his heavy pack in a movement that was lithe and smooth in its strength. His breechclout swung and for an instant she caught a glimpse of the copper stretch of his muscled thigh above his leggings before he straightened again. She swallowed with a heated feeling in the pit of her stomach, her mind flashing an instant image of him as he had stood naked in the rain the night before.

She turned swiftly away, giving her head a quick shake to banish the vision. She thought instead of his stealth as he had returned to bed some time later, his intense quiet as he took care not to disturb her. He had fallen asleep immediately, or so it seemed. She had thought to lie wakeful, but it had not been so. Exhaustion had crept upon her moments later and so soundly had she slept that she had not known when the rain stopped, when the dawn came, or when he had left her once again. Good enough; she had certainly not wanted to face him. She would be only too happy not to see him ever again.

"If you please," Madame Doucet called. "I must stop, must rest."

Reynaud strode on without pause. His gaze was alert, probing as he watched the trail ahead, but the tilt of his head was rigid and his manner so aloof it seemed his thoughts were elsewhere.

"M'sieu Reynaud!"

He swung at the despairing call of the older woman, coming to a halt as she repeated her request. A brief gesture indicated a rest stop for them all before he moved on. The men threw themselves down on the ground, but Madame Doucet beckoned to Elise, nodding toward a clump of evergreen myrtle a few yards into the woods.

Elise went with the older woman. A few minutes later, she stepped from the myrtle clump, wandering deeper into the woods and breathing deeply in her relief at being away from the others for even a few short minutes. It was difficult enough to be obliged to keep so close to people whom she barely knew, but the sidelong glances she had received this morning had strained her temper as well. She knew very well what they were all thinking. They wondered what had passed between her and the half-breed the night before, wondered if she had taken pleasure in it and if Reynaud was satisfied with his payment. Doubtless they pictured all manner of cavortings and wearisome frolic in the storm-wracked darkness and were each curious or concerned after their fashion. Elise reached up to jerk a handful of leaves from a beech tree, shredding them as she let them fall.

A shrill, demented scream brought her slewing around. She ran toward the sound, toward where she had left Madame Doucet. The scream came again.

"Indians! *Mon Dieu*, Indians!"

The older woman came running from the myrtles with her hands in the air, her mouth open in a wail, and her eyes wide with terror. Elise caught her and they were both nearly thrown off their feet as Madame Doucet reached out to grab her in a stranglehold.

"What is it? Where are the Indians?"

"I saw him." The woman moaned. "It was horrible, horrible; a face, watching me."

Elise flung a quick look around her, but could see nothing. By that time Pascal and Henri were upon them, shouting, demanding to know what had happened. Elise told them, completing her explanation with her gaze on Reynaud as he arrived from where he had ranged ahead, followed by St. Amant on his crutches.

"Return to the track, all of you," Reynaud ordered. "I will look into it."

With Henri supporting Madame Doucet on the other side, they did as they were bid. They sank down among the bundles they had dropped at the wayside with Elise cradling Madame Doucet in her arms. Henri and St. Amant settled close by, though Pascal, cradling his musket, leaned against a tree on guard. For long moments they were silent, though the older woman continued to sob. After a time her crying turned to words. "Ah, my daughter, my beautiful Annette, gone, gone, gone. And Charles, so sweet, so dear, so little. They will die, I know it. They will die."

"Be still, woman," Pascal grunted. "We will all die if you bring the Indians down on us."

"But you did not see. He cried out and they struck him, my dear little Charles, my only grandson. My daughter, there was blood in her hair. . . . Oh, *mon Dieu, mon Dieu,* I cannot bear it. I cannot."

Elise did her best to comfort the woman, murmuring softly and smoothing away the tears from her cheeks. Henri sidled closer. Keeping his voice low, he asked, "Did you see anything, Madame Laffont?"

She shook her head. "That doesn't mean there was no one there."

Pascal and St. Amant exchanged a long look and St. Amant shrugged. Henri asked, "How could they follow us so far?"

"For all Chavalier's precautions, we are doubtless leaving a trail as obvious as that of a herd of buffalo. We are none of us *coureurs des bois,* used to living in the woods."

"Why didn't they attack then? Why follow and spy on us?" the boy persisted.

"Perhaps out of respect for our guide," St. Amant suggested.

"Or cooperation with him," Pascal said, his lip curled in a sneer.

"What do you mean?" Elise asked.

"He could be playing us along, pretending to lead us until he has what he wants. When he's tired of the game, he'll call in his friends—or kill us himself. Try to, that is." The merchant hefted his musket.

"Don't be ridiculous! We have nothing that he values."

"Oh, no?" The sneer was more pronounced as Pascal allowed his gaze to wander suggestively over Elise.

She lifted a brow, her mouth twisted with derision. "If you refer to me, then I must remind you that it would have been much easier for him to have dispatched you all earlier and taken me prisoner."

"Are you defending that half-breed?"

"I am telling you how I see our situation."

"He must have been something last night if he managed to please our frigid widow."

She stared at the merchant. "What did you say?"

"It was Chepart's name for you. Didn't you know?"

"I should have guessed it," she replied with a snap.

"No Frenchman good enough to thaw you, and now you share the half-breed's furs and seem to be melting. What kind of a fire did he light under you, *ma chère* madame; what kind of instrument did he use to warm you?"

There came a soft sound like a rush of wind and Reynaud stepped among them. When he spoke, there was deadly quiet in his tones. "If you are curious, Pascal, why not ask me?"

Pascal opened his mouth, then as he met the iron-gray gaze of the half-breed, saw the casual placement of a copper hand near the knife in his belt, he faltered. He licked his lips. "It—it's no concern of mine."

"Remember it."

Madame Doucet reached out to pluck at one of Reynaud's leggings as he stood so still beside her. "The—the Indian I saw?"

"Not Natchez, but Tensas."

"That was one of the tribes expected to rise with the people of the Great Sun," Elise said quickly.

"True. But because the Natchez attacked in advance of the chosen day, they are incensed against them instead of the French. The man was a scout only, and harmless."

"You found him, spoke to him?" St. Amant asked.

Reynaud inclined his head in assent. "Briefly."

There was an inflection in his voice that Elise did not understand. Did no one else notice it or was the half-breed so intimidating that they did not dare question him? The insight was vague, no more than a flash of feeling. A moment later, as everyone broke into chatter in their relief, it was forgotten.

The day slipped past in a haze of fatigue. Streams were crossed, fogs of mosquitoes fought with applications of bear grease, and packs shifted and exchanged to redistribute the chafed spots on their backs and shoulders. The stiffness of their muscles faded with their exertion, becoming a deep soreness. Their strides lengthened, developed a regular cadence.

There was no further sign of Indians. The leagues dropped behind them as they threaded the primeval woods, staring up at cypress trees that towered one hundred and fifty feet above them, skirting oaks and hickories so large that three men could barely reach around them and so prodigal with their acorns and nuts that the ground beneath them was ankle deep with the cuttings of squirrels.

Their way was enlivened by the antics of those same small animals, gray squirrels and those with orange-rust tails, squirrels so curious, so seldom hunted that they played tag above them and scolded from the lower limbs of the trees as the column passed underneath. They saw silent files of deer ghosting away from them into the forest or bounding in flight ahead; they had to stop more than once for a family of opossums, known as wood's rats by the French, to waddle out of the way. Once they stood still, holding their breaths for what seemed like hours until a skunk scratching in the leaves had thoroughly searched the area for grubs and beetles and meandered away.

It was while Elise was stepping over a rotted log at the edge of a natural clearing that she rammed the thorn into her foot. The wild plums grew thick there, their quivering leaves turning yellow, their limbs armed with thorns. She did not see the dead limb until she felt the piercing pain. The thorn had sliced through her shoe on the side and ripped out again. She did not want to call attention to such a small thing by asking to stop and the rate of marching that Reynaud set was so brisk that there was no time to look at it and catch up again. By the time they halted once more, she had such a blistered place on her shoulder from her pack that she had not thought of the thorn again. She remembered it only after they had made camp for the night and the evening meal was done.

Still, she sat, so weary that it seemed too much of an effort to take off her shoe and tend to the thorn scratch. She leaned forward with her arms wrapped around her knees, staring into the flames. Madame Doucet retired early, crawling into her enclosure where her muffled sobbing was heard until she had cried herself to sleep. Henri wandered away. Pascal and St. Amant went into the woods and came back again before heading for their small tentlike shelters. In the back of her mind, Elise expected Reynaud to leave as he had the night before; there was a spring only a short distance away that had supplied their water for cooking and would doubtless do the same for those who felt the need of bathing. Her own pot of water sat simmering near the fire even now.

He did not move. He reclined across the fire from her, lying on his side with his weight supported on one elbow. She glanced at him, then at their own shelter that lay in the shadows apart from the others. If he was aware of any strain in the atmosphere, he gave no sign of it. The sharp-edged planes of his face, gilded by the leaping yellow-orange light of the fire that left the hollows in shadow, were schooled to impassivity.

But Reynaud was aware. He watched Elise in the firelight, feeling a slow tightening in his loins as the night drew in. She had rolled up the velvet sleeves of her habit and the flickering light was reflected in a gold sheen from the delicate turnings of her arms. He wanted to reach out, to stroke her skin, to put his finger on the frown between her brows and trail it down the narrow bridge of her nose to the tender softness of her lips. He could not and so he watched the expressions that crossed her face, and he listened.

There was a raccoon in the tree above the shelter he would soon share with the woman across from him. It had been there since they had stopped, dithering about from limb to limb. Soon, when everything was quiet, it would make up its mind to climb down and lumber off into the night. The rustle of cloth told him that Henri was not asleep. The boy was turning restlessly, probably thinking of ways to murder him and rescue Elise. Poor Henri was infatuated. Reynaud was not unfeeling. He would not deliberately exacerbate the boy's natural sense of revulsion at the situation if he could prevent it. The trouble was, he could not. He would have to be careful with Henri. Often such raw emotion was more troublesome than having a rank traitor in the group.

Pascal would also bear watching. He had not cared for being forced to back down, not in front of Elise. His injured pride might demand some recompense. In dealing with him it would be well, Reynaud thought, if he could look beyond his dislike of the man and try to understand the frustration of one whose freedom had been bought and paid for by a woman's favors. Or perhaps he was giving Pascal too much credit. The man might well be as much like the late Commandant Chepart as he seemed, too stupid, too self-centered to feel the obligation. It would make him easier to deal with, if it were so.

St. Amant was a different type altogether. If Reynaud was any judge, there was within him the remnants of an aristocratic background. Many a younger son had come to the Louisiana colony hoping to make his fortune and return in glory to flaunt his wealth at the French court. There had also been any number smuggled out of Europe with the law grasping for their coattails or else sneaking away with the shadow of debts of honor, of one sort or another, hanging over them. That kind often found Louisiana more of a prison than a refuge. And they could be dangerous because they had so little reason to live.

Madame Doucet was a burden, there was no other word for it. She slowed them to less than half their possible pace. Her shock and grief had confused her, troubling her mind to such an extent that her grasp on sanity was far from strong. She must be closely watched if she wasn't to jeopardize all of them. It might be a double benefit to put her under the special charge of Henri, giving her protection and the boy a sense of purpose and responsibility.

Reynaud's gaze narrowed and a slight smile tugged at the corner of his mouth as his thoughts returned to the woman on the other side of the fire. She was making a valiant effort to keep up and was succeeding, though he expected it was pride and anger that sustained her. That the rage he had glimpsed once or twice in her eyes was directed at him he minded not at all; better that than fear. It made him feel sick inside to think of the way she had trembled in his arms the night before. He had tried during the long day to keep himself from thinking of how she must have been mistreated by that bastard of a husband or of the ultimatum he himself had finally given her. He might have been able to feel better about the last if he could be sure that it was concern for her that had driven him to make it instead of the urging of his own base desires.

God guard him, how he wanted her. The lithe grace of her body as she walked, the sheen of the velvet that covered the roundness of her breasts when she turned, the gleam and weight of her hair coiled at the base of her slender neck—any of these things was enough to bring the tightness to his groin. Even the sight of the pale and slender turnings of her ankle and the narrow length of her foot as she removed a shoe and stocking caused him no small amount of distress. It almost seemed that she knew it as she lifted her skirts higher, angling her bare foot to the side to catch the light of the flames.

"What are you doing?"

Elise looked up, startled by the sharpness of his tone. "Trying to see if I have a thorn in my foot."

"You stepped on one?"

"It went into the side of my shoe."

"Let me see." He came upright in a single motion, stepping around the fire, then getting down on one knee beside her.

"I can do it," she said hastily, jerking her foot back as he reached for it.

"I won't hurt you."

"It—it's nothing, just a scratch."

"The thorn may have broken off in it."

His voice was deep and persuasive, but it also carried a hint of steel. She stared at him in indecision. If there was still a piece of thorn in the streak of torn flesh, then it could become septic and cause blood poisoning. Failing that, it could make it hard for her to walk, something she must be able to do at all costs.

"All right then," she said with ill humor as she thrust out her foot, "look at it!"

His warm grasp closed firmly about her ankle, the other hand sliding under the sole of her foot. He was silent, his gaze intent upon the red weal that marred her skin.

"Well?"

"There is a dark spot, probably the thorn. I don't suppose you have a needle?"

"No." Her answer was short.

"I can take it out with my knife point." Ignoring her immediate denial and her attempts to wrench her foot from his hand, he went on, "But I have another bargain for you. I'll remove yours if you will do the same for me."

She was still. "You have a thorn?"

He released her, swinging to show her his right hand. That the skin was not torn was due to its toughness, for the thorn that had been driven into him was thick and vicious. Over an inch in length, it was imbedded in the side between his wrist and little finger. She could see at once that it would be difficult for him to remove it with his left hand.

"I don't know if I can."

"You'll enjoy it," he said with a brief, hard smile.

That was entirely possible. She frowned to cover the thought. "I'll try."

"Good."

He took up her foot again and, almost before she was set, drew his knife and sliced quickly into her foot with the razor-sharp point.

"Ouch," she said on a quickly drawn breath of pain.

"Stop wriggling."

"Just you wait," she said through clenched teeth.

He did not comment. A moment later he removed the knife point and pressed his thumb to the place it had been to stop the tiny trickle of blood. "There's your thorn."

"Let me see," she said darkly, by no means sure there had ever been such a thing.

But it was there, a quarter of an inch long and shining blackly in the firelight as he rubbed it off the knife point into the palm of his hand. When she nodded, he brushed it away and stood. "Don't move. I'll be right back."

She watched him disappear into the woods, moving as if it were broadest daylight. She looked down at her foot, expecting to see a deep slit, but there was only a small, clean cut no deeper than the original scratch. The bleeding had stopped and so had the throbbing that had made her remove her shoe and stocking in the first place.

There was a faint sound, then he dropped down beside her once more. He leaned toward the pot of water that simmered beside the fire and dropped what appeared to be a handful of trash into it. Seeing her puzzled glance, he said, "Red oak, the inner bark, to prevent blood poisoning. You will soak your foot in it."

"That was my bath water!"

"I'll bring more. In the meantime . . ."

He unsheathed his knife once more and presented it to her, then turned his hand so that the right side was uppermost and placed it on her drawn-up knee.

She took the knife gingerly, holding it near the tip as she reached with her left hand to grasp his fingers. Staring at the ridged skin where the thorn lay, she tried to decide the best way

to cut it out. She moistened her lips, catching the inner skin of
the bottom one in her teeth. Where had her anger and thirst for
revenge gone now that she needed them?

She sent a quick glance at Reynaud. He was watching her,
his gray eyes dark and intent. For an instant she felt herself
ensnared, unable to look away. Her heartbeat quickened and she
lowered her lashes swiftly.

If she tried to cut through the tough, hornlike skin that bulged
over the thorn, it would roll from under the blade. She needed
more purchase. She released his fingers to grasp the flesh of his
palm, pinching it to hold it steady. Taking a deep breath, she
touched the knife to his skin, increasing the pressure, harder,
harder, until she saw it break beneath the edge, then she sliced
along the ridge quickly. As the shiny black thorn was exposed,
she dropped the knife and, using her nails, lifted the stiff base
and pulled it from its bed. Blood welled up, dark red and rich,
from the small wound, but she scarcely regarded it. A breathless
gasp very like a laugh escaped her, and holding the thorn in
triumph, she looked up at the half-breed.

It was only then that she realized he had neither moved nor
made a sound. The thorn was no major thing, of course, and yet
most men she had known would have yelped and flinched at the
very least under such minor but rough-and-ready surgery. Vincent had cursed and slapped her when she had been forced to do
any similar thing for him, steadying his nerves when it was over
with a strong tot of cognac. As she met Reynaud's steady gaze
once more, she knew with sudden clarity that he had felt the
pain. It was there within the flesh and nerves and sinews as
surely as in any mortal. It was only that he accepted and sur-
mounted it with impassive resolve, refusing to concede it the
victory over him. And it occurred to her to wonder, since he hid
it so well, what else might lie concealed behind the stern and
implacable mask of his features.

Together they soaked their injuries in the steeped and
steaming tea made with red oak bark and bound them with
strips of soft leather to keep the dirt out. Reynaud brought
more water for her bath, then left her, heading toward the
spring. Elise debated for several minutes over whether to sleep
in her habit again. If she wore only her shift, might he not
take it as an invitation? It did not seem likely, not after what
had passed between them. While she considered it, she let
down her hair and combed it as best she could with her fin-

gers. Her loosened tresses were such a relief that in the end the urge toward comfort won and she crawled into the shelter in her single undergarment.

She need not have worried. She was heavily asleep, lying on her side in the middle of the bed of furs, when Reynaud finally joined her there. He did not touch her, but moved carefully to curl his body around hers in the same position, there being no room in the shelter for him to lie otherwise. As he settled the furs back over them, she sighed and stretched out one leg. The smooth skin of her thigh, where the shift had ridden up, skimmed along his knee. Excitement rippled along his nerves, combined with a peculiar guilt as if he had broken a vow. With a wry shake of his head, he put a careful six inches of distance between them and, with the lines of his face set in determination, closed his eyes.

Elise awoke to an uncomfortable warmth and a feeling of being suffocated. She opened her eyes. The dim gray light of dawn was filtering into the shelter so that she could just make out the support poles. The furs were pulled up, half covering her face. The source of heat was against her back, though there was a heavy weight across her ribs and another resting on her knee and the calf of her leg. It was a moment before she recognized what, or rather who, held her, then a spasm galvanized her muscles and she flung up her arm to throw off the cover, shoving herself away from the man beside her. The enclosure shuddered as she came up against the side. Spinning around, she stared with wide eyes at Reynaud.

He met her gaze, his own cogent and brightly self-derisive. His voice was quiet, with a drawling quality, as he spoke. "Good morning."

She lay back, shutting her eyes tightly as she waited for the tumult of her pulse to steady. She swallowed, raising her eyelids. "Good morning."

With her retreat, there was more room in the bed of furs. He turned onto his back and raised his arms, clenching his fists above his head as he stretched out full length. He relaxed again. "If I trespassed," he said, his tone carefully neutral. "I'm sorry."

She eyes him with suspicion glinting among the rust flecks in her amber-brown eyes. "Are you?"

He turned his head to look at her. "In spirit, at least."

Her hair was straight and fine, spreading around her in a

honey-brown veil that covered her shoulders, coiling to a length that reached well past her waist, lying like silk upon the coarse buffalo fur around them. A soft lock, gently curling at the end, lay upon her left breast. It gleamed with the fast rise and fall of her breathing, drawing attention to the rounded softness it rested on and to the taut peak and dark circle of the aureole that could be seen through the much-washed thinness of her shift.

Elise followed the direction of his wandering gaze. Her stomach muscles tightened. A wary note in her voice, she said, "Hadn't we better get up?"

"It's not quite time."

"But the others will be awake and we may as well—"

"Besides," he interrupted without raising his voice, "we have unfinished business between us."

"You mean—" She stopped, unable to find the right words to say what she thought he meant.

"I do."

"But it's morning!"

"Whoever told you that such things happen only at night?"

"I can't," she said, her tone positive. "Not with you watching me."

"I'll close my eyes."

She balled her fingers into a fist, bringing it down to thump the furs. "Why are you doing this? It can't give you any pleasure."

"Can't it?"

"Only if you enjoy tormenting me!"

"Never that."

"I won't." She refused to meet his eyes and there was a sullen edge to the words.

"Remember the consequences."

"I don't believe you will abandon us, and anyway it doesn't matter. We must be halfway there. We can find our own way."

"Something less than half, and the worst is yet to come. But perhaps you would like me to take the initiative?" He reached out with his left hand to take up that intriguing lock of hair at her breast.

She slapped his hand away and snatched at the tress, throwing it over her shoulder. Her eyes narrowed, she said, "Make me do this and you will regret it."

"Will I?" The words were calm, but there was a hint of doubt in the gray depths of his eyes.

"I'll see to it."

His thick lashes dropped, shielding his expression, "If you mean what I think, I look forward to the attempt."

She would see about that, she told herself grimly. There was scarcely a tremor in her nerves as she shifted closer and reached out to draw the furs down below his waist. The faint rush of his indrawn breath as he felt the touch of her nails on the flat surface of his belly spurred her on and she pressed them into him. But though she wanted to claw at him, she found she could not. Instead, she trailed her nail tips upward, circling his navel, raking gently over his diaphragm and along his breastbone in a titillating threat. She teased his paps and followed his tattoo lines, explored the hollow of his throat and the jutting cleft of his chin.

An idea came to her and she raised herself on one elbow. She leaned over him, allowing her hair to slide forward, cascading over his face and forming a shining tent over his head and shoulders. Smiling slightly, she picked up the end of a tress and brushed it gently, tentatively, over his lips. As they tightened, she did it again more firmly, paying attention to the corners. He did not move, but she plainly felt the muscles of his arm, against which she lay, as they tightened into hard cords. Then, with slow care, she trailed the lock of hair under his nose and across the angle of one cheek, then back under his nose to the other side. She brushed his eyes and the ridges beneath his brows, his forehead and temples, then down to the intricate turnings of the ear next to her.

It was disappointing when he showed so little sign of the distress she was sure he must feel from her unmerciful tickling. She was not deterred, however, but rather spurred on to greater liberties. She inched lower in the bed furs, drawing the soft strands of her hair down so that they spread over his chest. With sweeping motions, she rubbed that silken abrasiveness over him, massaging him with it so that the warmth of his body and her own brought out the scent of violets that still clung to her hair from the soap she had used to wash it last. Lower and lower she moved, her hand pressing along his side, down to his flanks, smoothing over his belly with sure strokes, her face absorbed behind the concealing curtain of hair.

The hardness of his body under her palms, the sense of its

contained strength, which she recognized with her fingertips, pleased her in some deep level in her mind. Without being obvious about it, as if it were incidental to what she was doing to him, she pressed against him, letting the fullness of her breasts brush his arm, grazing his rigid thigh with her own, moving her hips so that the small, firm mound at the apex of her legs touched the knuckles of his lax hand. Somewhere in the center of her being, warm enjoyment grew, opening, spreading like a soothing, exciting opiate.

With her foot she dislodged the buffalo fur, exposing him to the knees. The veiling of hair swirled lower, covering, surrounding, entangling his manhood. She touched it first by accident, her hand sliding along its length, but so instantaneous was its lift and throb that she captured it in a cocoon of hair, kneading. And inside her was an abrupt flush of heat and triumph as she understood that in this at least he could not deny his physical reaction.

He wanted her. His need was strong, incredibly so. But because of his promise he would not take her, would not touch her. It followed then that the worst thing she could do to him at that moment would be to withdraw from him. To leave him there in the throes of unsatisfied arousal. It would hurt her in some strange way, that withdrawal. How much more devastating it would be for him then.

She did it, moving slowly so that her hair trailed over the length of his body with the tickling softness of a lingering caress, so that it was long moments before he knew what she intended, before he could grasp that she would actually go.

By then it was too late. He caught a glimpse of the curve of her hips as she wriggled out of the end flap. He started up, lunging after her, then, with a wrenching effort, stopped himself. He flung himself back down on the furs with one fist thrown across his forehead. As he stared up at the weave of the material of the enclosure, a single refrain ran through his mind: What had he done, with his devil's bargain with the Widow Laffont? What had he done?

"Hey, half-breed, you're going the wrong way!"

It was Pascal who called out to Reynaud, though the decision to confront him had been made by all of them. Henri had first noticed their gradual northerly trend. He had said nothing for a time, thinking that it was caused only by the curves and twists of the trail they followed. Even after he had mentioned it at a rest stop to the others, several hours had passed before they could confirm it with the setting sun. They should have been traveling west and north, and had been before now. For some reason Reynaud was now leading them almost due north.

"You hear me?"

Reynaud had been ranging some two hundred yards ahead. Now he slowed and turned, waiting for them to come even with him. "I hear."

"Well?"

"You are mistaken." The words carried the bite of temper. The half-breed had not been in the best of humors since early morning. It was as if he was holding himself on a short rein and the challenge of the merchant was an added irritant.

The merchant put his hands on his hips and stuck his chin out. "We may not be woods runners, but we know the difference between north and south. You're leading us into the wilderness."

"No. Merely to my home."

"Your home?" St. Amant exclaimed. "But, *mon ami*, what is this? We were to go to the fort on the Red River."

"And so we will, eventually. Nothing was said of going direct."

"But it was understood—"

"By whom? You asked me to guide you and I remember no conditions."

"We must get to the fort," St. Amant said, throwing out his hands. "There are people there who don't yet know of the uprising, the massacre; people with relatives who are now dead. They must be told."

"Or they can be left in happy ignorance a little longer."

"It will seem odd if we tarry on the way."

"Will it? You must blame me then," Reynaud said with a shrug. "I go to my home to make arrangements that are necessary before going on to the fort."

"You can't do this!" Pascal shouted.

"On the contrary, I can."

Elise, watching the arguing men, felt an odd tremor of fear and anger. Was it possible that Reynaud was doing this because of her? Had he taken her claim that she and the others could find their own course as a challenge to be met? Perhaps he thought to take them far out of their way, into the deep forest known only to the Indians and a few intrepid French trappers? They would be at his mercy then.

Reynaud turned his head, meeting her amber gaze. As he saw the accusation there, his features hardened.

"And what are we to do," St. Amant was asking, "while you tend to your arrangements?"

"Do what you like," Reynaud said, his tone abrupt. "You may come with me as my guests, you may wait for me here, or you may go on under your own guidance."

Everyone fell silent. St. Amant looked from Pascal to Elise and away again. Pascal stood, frowning in unaccustomed thought. Madame Doucet was weeping, though more at the loud voices, Elise thought as she tried to comfort her, than from any understanding of the problem they confronted.

Henri stepped forward, his face white and his hands clenched at his sides. His voice shaking, he said, "Y-you are a bastard, Chavalier. Y-you demand and we m-must obey, all of us, e-especially M-madame Laffont. You lead and we m-must follow or risk d-death. You p-play with our lives and souls and d-defy us to stop you. W-what I would not give to s-strike you down, here and n-now."

"I don't doubt it, but I cannot allow you that pleasure. In the meantime, poor Madame Laffont is tending to your charge."

Elise glanced up to find them all watching her. Pascal was scowling, and as her gaze turned in his direction, he gave a small, meaningful jerk of his head toward Reynaud. When she still stared, he did it again and she realized suddenly that the merchant wanted her to reason with the half-breed. That she was expected to have some influence with him after what had occurred between them that morning struck her as funny indeed, but she felt no real inclination to laugh.

She moistened her lips. "M'sieu . . . Reynaud, won't you reconsider? The—the delay may mean the news will arrive before us and it could be weeks before people can be told that we are safe. That would cause much unnecessary grief. Besides, you must realize that we have deep concerns about recovering our property, concerns that must be placed before the governor at New Orleans as soon as some way of reaching that city can be assured."

"Property?" Reynaud asked in scorn.

"It's our livelihood, our only security."

"Your security lies in yourself."

"If you mean my body," she began in tones thick with rage.

"No," he said, making a hard, cutting gesture straight out from his body with his right hand. "No."

She believed him; still, she had not another word to say in appeal. It would, she was sure, be useless. She did not know this man well, but she understood him enough to realize that much.

St. Amant cleared his throat. "I suggest we take a vote."

"We must go with M'sieu Chavalier," Marie Doucet said.

The older woman had understood more than they thought. There was a moment of surprise, then St. Amant, rubbing his chin, agreed. Pascal wanted to go on to the fort, as did Henri. Elise hesitated, uncertain what would be best.

"The choice, it would seem, is yours since the vote is even."

She looked at Reynaud, seeing the grim amusement in his gray eyes as he spoke. For there was an added choice and he knew it well. If she voted that they go on alone, she would be free of him, while if she took the safe course of remaining with him, then she must continue to share his bed and keep their bargain. She opened her mouth.

"This is nonsense," Pascal said. "Women have no vote."

"Nor do striplings," Reynaud said without looking at him, "which would leave you against St. Amant. What say you? Shall I cast the final vote? Or would you prefer to hear from the lady?"

She had decided to cast her lot with Henri and Pascal. Suddenly that seemed a foolhardy thing to do, trusting to a merchant and a boy to find their way through this tangle of trees, vines, and briers that stretched for endless miles. Why should she risk all of their lives out of pique? Far better to allow the half-breed his victory, to endure his company for a while longer, than to court death in this wilderness.

"Enough," Pascal said with a grunt. "This place of yours, Chavalier, how far out of the way is it?"

"A matter of two or three days of travel at our present pace."

"Then let us get started, the sooner to have done."

The amusement vanished from Reynaud's eyes, to be replaced by brooding annoyance as he was cheated of hearing Elise's answer. He shouldered his pack and moved ahead with his long, loping stride, soon outdistancing them. Though he left them a well-marked trail of glaring, resinous blazes cut into the trees to follow, they did not see him again until dark. They came upon him then, outlined against a beacon fire that drew them in, a great leaping blaze that had been kindled beside a river that tasted of salt.

5

THE MOON ROSE low on the horizon: huge, yellow-tinted with shadings of orange, and circled with a blue ring. It had been another warm day and the night was cool, no more. A faint wind stirred the trees, sighing among the thinning branches, and the patter of leaves drifting down was like soft rain. Soon the cold and the frosts would come, but not yet. Not yet. These were the wine-sweet days of the autumn called Indian summer by some. How they lingered this year, and what a cruel jest it was that they did.

Pascal had gone to bed, as had Madame Doucet. St. Amant and Henri sat near the fire, talking in low voices. Reynaud had disappeared soon after they had eaten and had not returned. Despite the tiredness that hung about her like a cloak, Elise could not settle down. The fire was too warm and she was not sleepy enough to retire. She did not care to join the two males in their discussion. St. Amant, for all his gentlemanly reticence, had a cynical edge to his voice that wore on her nerves, especially when he mentioned the half-breed and herself in the same breath. Henri's soft gaze was so doggedly worshipful that it made her uncomfortable, though this afternoon she had seemed to feel reproach when he looked her way.

She sighed, picking at one of the worn, bald spots on her once splendid velvet habit. Why was it so difficult to live with other human beings? Why must they continually appraise each other's actions and stand in judgment of them? Why must there be quarrels and killings? What possessed men to turn and rend others of their kind? Why could there not be tolerance and peace and the cooperation that would bring prosperity to all? Was she so simple that she did not see the reason?

Men, and women, were as God made them, fallible creatures, and yet surely they had the intelligence to see that greed and betrayal, as in the case of the Natchez, led only to hatred and vengeance? How much pain and misery and death would there be before the French could live in peace once more with their former Indian allies? Injuries inflicted, for whatever reason, only brought more revenge in return, creating an endless cycle of bloodletting. Could they not see?

She drew in her breath as a sudden thought struck her. Fine words, but how did they apply to herself? Because of the hurt she had been dealt in the past, she had this morning taken her own minor vengeance and that against a man who refused to defend himself. He had deserved it, perhaps, for the way in which he had compelled her to share his bed, but after his forbearance when he had discovered her revulsion for lovemaking, had it not been a little unworthy?

She had taken unfair advantage of Reynaud Chavalier. Remorse, unwanted and unfamiliar, crept in upon her, a feeling that had been a vague disturbance in the back of her mind all day. The temptation he had presented with his demands that she caress him had been irresistible, but that was no excuse. She had known that he would not retaliate. He had given his word and she trusted him to keep it.

Trust. It was a strange word to apply to the half-breed with his barbaric dress, to the man who had demanded her favors as a right, who had forced her each night to sleep beside him and used blackmail of a most heartless kind to bend her to his will. And yet it was undeniable that she did trust him to keep the vow he had made. She believed implicitly that he would not touch her, had no fear that he would raise a hand against her in anger.

She had no fear.

Staring into the night, Elise examined that curious fact. It was not in her nature to fear many things, of course; thunderstorms and snakes, mice and crawling insects had never held any terrors for her. Her one secret terror, formed by the past few years, had been in being held by a man, subjected to his greater strength and unbridled desires. She had fought it, had fought the men who would treat her so, but it had always been there. With Reynaud Chavalier, it was gone. He had banished it with a few words and with the iron control that governed his every action, a control that had allowed her to accept his word and to depend on it.

Elise had a code that she lived by. It had evolved over the past three years since her husband had died, three years in which she had had to deal with men in a man's world. The basic premise was fairness. In the produce of her farm, she had given good measure and expected the same in return. She had paid a reasonable price without argument for what she bought, but refused to set down a *piastre* more. She sold only healthy animals from her excess stock and any who tried to put a diseased beast off on her received short shrift. When she made a bargain, she kept it, and she expected others to do the same.

She felt now that she had not kept faith with the letter of her bargain with Reynaud. Her code required compensation in some form. That did not mean that she must confess her fault or give recompense in kind. It would be enough that she performed some service for him, a just return, even if only she knew the reason for it.

Where was he? While she had sat thinking, St. Amant and Henri had banked the fire and retreated to their shelters. She knew that Reynaud always made a circuit of their camp before seeking his bed; perhaps that was what he was doing now. It was also possible that he was down at the bayou performing his nightly ablutions.

She got to her feet, stretching cramped muscles. She could hear Pascal snoring and the low moans that Madame Doucet made in her sleep. With the dying of the fire, the moonlight seemed brighter, a white light that washed the color from the night, leaving a landscape of black and silver gray. The woods around her were quieter now, with only a faint, almost secretive rattle caused by falling leaves and the foraging of small nocturnal animals. Then faintly the splash of water came to her.

Without conscious thought she moved toward the sound, skirting the embers of the fire and threading through the trees. She saw first the gleam of moonlight on the bayou. So slow moving was the stream that it seemed still, reflecting the starlit sky and the shafting path of the moon. The trees grew to the edge, hanging over it to make a skirt of black shadow. The water did not appear to be deep, though the banks were high, a mark of the greater flow of the winter and spring rains. It was, however, the glittering streaks, which were the arms of a fast-moving swimmer, that caught and held her attention. Smiling a little in satisfaction that she had found Reynaud, she moved to the water's edge.

Her approach startled a frog and it plopped into the water. Reynaud rolled on his side, looking toward the sound. He saw her there in the shadows and lifted a hand, then began to swim toward her with strong, sure strokes.

"Is something wrong?" he called as he came near.

"No, no, I just . . . wondered where you were."

Not far from where she stood was a slanting shelf in the bank that angled down to the water, a natural path where animals made their way to the water to drink. He started toward it, flinging back his wet hair as he struck bottom and rose to his feet. The copper of his wet skin was silvered by the light of the moon, sculpted in bold angles and hollows. It turned him from a man into a pagan deity, remote, savage, splendid in his nakedness.

He was naked! She had not thought—she had expected he would be wearing his breechclout at least. She looked away and heard his low laugh. Still, from the corner of her eyes, she saw his springing bound as he came up the bank, saw him bend to pick up the scant squares of cloth that made up a major part of his wardrobe. She had seen him unclothed before, and her husband also, of course, though Vincent had been modest, and with reason, of his barrel shape and stocky legs. Regardless, she felt easier when Reynaud had fastened his breechclout around him.

"Don't you find it cold?" she asked, rushing into speech before he could comment. "I mean, with the night so cool and your skin wet?"

"No. The exercise is warming and I'm used to it."

"I believe the Natchez make a great to-do about bathing."

"More so than the French with their powder and perfume and tight velvet coats."

She was reminded forcibly once more of the insult she had given him. The words tight, abrupt, she said, "I must apologize for what I said—that night at the commandant's house. I didn't mean it, at least not in the way it sounded. And—and I know it isn't true."

"A magnificent gesture. I accept it."

The mockery in his tone was not lost upon her. She turned toward him. "Don't you believe me?"

He moved his shoulders in a shrug. "It just strikes me that I am sorrier now than you are."

"I doubt that," she answered, an unspoken acknowledgment that if she had never made light of him then neither of them would be in their present situation. "But when you speak of velvet, I trust you are not thinking of my habit? I am heartily sick of it, but have no alternative."

"You could always dress in the costume of the Natchez women."

"Thank you, no." The women of the Natchez wore no more than a square of woven material wrapped around their lower body and knotted on one hip, leaving their breasts bare. For warmth during this season, they swung a short cape of woven cloth or fur around them.

He moved to lean with one shoulder against a tree beside her. "It would give you ease of movement and be most becoming. I could make one for you from what we have with us."

"You can't be serious."

"Suit yourself."

It was a curious thing how itchy her habit had become since they had begun talking. The need to take it off and never look at it again was strong, but she managed to disregard it. "Besides, though the costumes of your women may be comfortable, I don't know what keeps them, or the men either, from freezing to death."

"It can get a little drafty at times," he said with humor threading his tone, "but the weather is seldom severe and, as with bathing, you get used to it."

"The apparel of the Natchez is even more meager than that of other tribes, I think?"

"A little, perhaps. It may be a matter of tradition. They came here years ago from farther south."

"Did they?" she asked, her tone distracted as she watched water drip from his hair and gather in the hollow of his collarbone before trickling in a silver runnel down his chest.

"The Natchez are different from the Choctaws or Chickasaws. It's a difference you can see in their greater height, their broader foreheads, and especially in their customs. They are the last of what was once a tribe many thousand strong who, like themselves, built and lived on great mounds of earth. According to the ancient words of the tribe, kept by the wisest men, they came from the south, from the lands now claimed by Spain. They are of the same blood as the old mound builders, but arrived much later, at the time the older ones were dying out, between two and three hundred years ago as near as I can determine.''

Elise frowned. "If I remember the teachings of the good sisters concerning the Spanish excursions, that would have been near the time the adventurer Cortez conquered the Aztecs.''

"The Natchez claim to be old enemies of a great tribe with whom they fought many battles. Then one day white men came, as the legends had foretold that they would, moving over the water in 'houses' of wood. The Natchez became allies of the white men against their old foes. But when their enemies were defeated and their leaders dead, the white men turned on the Natchez. They fled, finally coming to rest here. There being no stones to use to build their ceremonial pyramids, they mounded up earth instead, as had their predecessors. Whether the story is true or not, I can't say, for the ancients give no names to the white men who came or to their Indian enemies.''

"And were the white men indeed the followers of Cortez?''

"Some think they were. Others believe they were the soldiers who came with the Spaniard de Soto two centuries ago and that the Indians the Natchez fought were the forest tribes who hunted these lands. The latter story doesn't explain the migration legend, however, nor does it tell why the Natchez build their mounds and worship the sun today, long after such practices have died out in the Mississippi valley.''

"The Natchez are different, yes," Elise mused. "They worship one supreme being whom they embody in the sun, they have a hereditary ruler, and they trace their succession, most realistically, through the female line, thereby allowing women importance. They are eloquent in speech, always treat guests with honor, and are uniformly gentle with children. They are, in short, more civilized than other tribes and many Europeans. And yet they also strangle the wives and servants of their ruler, the Great Sun, on his death, torture and kill captives, and, when provoked, rise and massacre hundreds.''

He was quiet a moment. "You have taken the time to learn something of my mother's people, I see.''

"It would have been difficult not to, living so close.''

"Others have managed not to learn.''

"I was interested. There was much to admire, until—until St. Andrew's Eve.''

"There still is, though who's to say for how long?''

"What do you mean?''

"Can you doubt that the French will retaliate with overwhelming force? Or that the other tribes who were to join the Natchez, being balked of their share of the spoils by an error, will join the French as allies?"

"I suppose so."

They were quiet. Elise reached up to scratch a small itch on her neck at the opening of her habit jacket.

"If you would like to take advantage of the water," he said, his voice laced with quiet humor, "I will stand as your guard."

"I can't swim."

"There's no need. If you stay near the bank it will not be over your head."

The lure of cleanliness, freshness was overpowering. Ordinarily she might not have been so aware of the need; there were people she knew who claimed never to have bathed and who were vociferous in their opinion that the Indian habit was the reason for the high rate of infant mortality among them and the cause of their succumbing in such numbers to mild diseases such as measles. She herself could not bear grime and filled a tub for a complete bath while at home at least twice a week, more often during the summer. But now it was Reynaud's daily ritual, and her own stupid insult of him, that made her aware of her own ripeness.

"You must turn your back," she said finally.

"As you will."

He swung, stepping away a few paces. She stared at his broad form in mistrust for a long moment, then began hurriedly to strip off her habit. Dropping it to the matted leaves that covered the ground and retaining her shift, she hastened down the bank and splashed out into the water.

She drew in her breath with a sound of shock. "It's c-cold!"

"Never mind," he said over his shoulder, "you'll—"

"Get used to it, I know!"

Elise had the uncomfortable feeling that he was laughing at her, but she refused to look at him to find out. Clenching her teeth to prevent their chattering, she waded deeper. After a moment, she discovered that the water, though by no means warm, was not as cool as the air above it. If she moved even farther out, to a point where she could submerge her shoulders, it might even be bearable. Stepping gingerly on the mud bottom with its rotted sticks and limbs, she followed that impulse.

"Wait," he called, "I forgot to give you the soap root!"

"I don't need it!"

"Yes, you do. I'll bring it."

She flung a quick look over her shoulder in time to see him chop at something in his hand, then lay his knife aside with his other clothes. With one hand, he released his breechclout and let it fall before stepping into the water. She slewed around, backing away. "Stop. Go back."

"It's no trouble."

That was not her concern. She felt vulnerable here in the water where she could not maneuver as he could, vulnerable in a way she had never felt on dry land. There was also his state of undress and her own scant covering. They had lain together in their shelter in just that way, but somehow that had been different.

She retreated, the water rising to her breasts, her shoulders, her neck. Her foot came down on something slick and slimy, a rotted log. She stumbled, lost her balance, and sank under the water.

There was a heavy splash and a deep surging in the bayou's flow. Before she could regain her feet, something brushed her side, then Reynaud's strong arm encircled her waist, pulling her upward.

Her head broke the surface and she gasped for breath. The water swirled and she was pulled against the unyielding hardness of his body. For an instant she lay along his long length, her breasts pressing into his chest, her thighs gliding over his heated loins and the ridged muscles of his legs as he stood with feet planted. The agitation of the water moved them gently, one against the other. There was whipcord strength in his grasp, and safety, and in the dark surface of his gray eyes as he gazed down at her was the reflection of the moonlight on the water.

A shiver ran over her that was caused partly by the warmth of his body upon her own cold flesh, by the shadow of an old distaste, and by something more that she could not name. She unclenched her jaws, saying in icy tones, "Thank you. You may release me."

He complied, the movement stiff, almost jerky. "I beg your pardon for the trespass. It seemed . . . necessary."

"By your own admission I was hardly in danger of drowning."

"You went farther than I expected and it isn't always possible to be certain."

His tone was distracted and he did not meet her eyes. His gaze, in fact, was directed somewhere beneath her chin. Elise glanced down. In putting her on her feet again, he had set her nearer the bank, where the water came only halfway up her chest. Her wet shift had sagged at the neckline, twisting around her. The white curves of her breasts gleamed, one of them exposed to the apricot-rose aureole and taut nipple.

"I must thank you then," she said, her voice tight in her throat. She grasped her shift, snatching it around to cover herself before she went on. "I suppose you lost the soap root?"

"No."

He raised his left fist that had been clenched at his side. Opening the fingers, he showed her the tiny bits of root. With his other hand, he scooped up water to sprinkle over them, rubbing his hands together to make lather. She reached out and he carefully transferred the soapy bits to the palm of her hand, smoothing over it with his warm fingers before he let it go.

She looked at him. He stared back, standing unmoving as if he had no intention of returning to the bank. She thought of asking him to go, but there was something about him that made her think better of it. Half turning from him, she worked at the soap root. The memory of her earlier remorse came to her. It was gone now and in its place was an impulse so curious that she was not sure from whence it came.

Still he had not moved. Lowering her lashes as if unaware of his regard, she began to smooth the lather up over her arms and shoulders, lingering over the slender turnings, enjoying the gliding sensation of the rich soap and its raw, fresh smell. She lifted her chin, stroking the curve of her neck, letting her hand slide in a slow circular motion downward to the swells of her breasts. She molded the cloth that covered them, rubbing with unconcern, as if she meant to wash the shift as well as herself. Leaving the lather as it was, she reached up with both hands to apply the suds to her wet hair. Shaking her head back, she worked it through, only half aware of Reynaud now, though she slanted a quick glance at him now and then from slitted eyes.

He shifted to place his hands on his hips, watching her with a brooding look in his eyes. His stance brought an odd *frisson* of fear, but she dismissed it. An idea came to her and she began to turn her back, holding out the hand that contained the root bits, saying, "Would you mind doing—"

She stopped abruptly, appalled at the request she had been

going to make. She snatched back her hand, closing it into a fist
and holding it against her chest as she swung around.

"Second thoughts?" he asked, his voice rough.

"I didn't mean—"

"I think you did. Did you forget you aren't supposed to like
being touched or can I congratulate myself that you no longer
consider me a threat as a man?"

"It isn't—it wasn't—" She stopped, pushing back her hair
with a helpless gesture before she began again. "I wasn't thinking, you must believe me. I was just—"

"You were baiting me again and went too far." The wet
surface of his chest glistened and his nostrils flared as he took a
breath that was bellows deep. "Fair enough. I suppose I should
be flattered that you feel safe enough to try it. But remember
one thing, Elise. I may be no threat, but I am still a man. Bait
me if you will, but never invite me to touch you unless you
mean it. Never."

A cloud drifted across the moon, dimming its light. She could
no longer see his face. The timbre of her voice was strained as
she answered, "No, I won't."

"I think," he said slowly, "that is a promise that deserves a
seal."

"What?"

"You have not yet kissed me. I think it's time."

"Because of what happened?"

"In part, but also because I desire it."

"But it wasn't a part of the bargain!"

"Wasn't it? I don't remember a ban."

"It isn't touching," she protested, "and that was the agreement."

"Isn't it? It would be difficult without."

"You're impossible!"

"And I'm waiting."

"I have soap all over me."

"I don't mind, but rinse if you like."

"You are so kind!" she jeered, though the words sounded
petulant even to her own ears.

"And patient, up to a certain point."

"You won't . . . take over?"

He hesitated for an instant as if there might be a doubt in his
mind, but his voice was firm when he replied. "No."

She owed him a recompense. If she must render a service,

then it would be just as well if it were something he wanted. She was not finished with her bath, however. He must put up with the soap.

She closed the distance between them with slow grace and lifted her arms to slide them around his neck. Rising on tiptoe, she drew down his head and placed her mouth against his. His lips were warm and smooth and vibrant, and though he did not move, they molded infinitesimally to cling to the moist and alive surface of her own. She felt her mouth tingle in response, knew the moment when her heart began to throb in her chest. Briefly she thought of Vincent's fetid kisses that had threatened to devour her and left her lips bruised and cut. This was nothing like that, nothing at all.

With slow, experimental care, she moved her head, brushing her lips over his, feeling the faint ridge that marked their edges, their firm yet tender texture, the deep indentation of their corners. Tactile pleasure caught at her, spiraling downward into the center of her being. Longing, suppressed and denied, gripped her and with a sigh she moved nearer. The slippery surface of her breasts touched his chest, their resilient softness skimming, melting into him. By degrees her lips parted and the warm tip of her tongue found the sensitive line where his lips met and, sweetly, exquisitely probing, ran along it. Their pressure lessened and she found the moist and fragile inner surface, felt the lift of his chest as he drew breath, heard it catch in his throat. He lifted a hand, setting it at her waist under the water. His grasp was firm, as if he would draw her closer to him, then abruptly it fell away.

She lifted her head, and for an instant confusion and loss crowded in upon her. Still, when he did not try to prevent her, she stepped back. He stared at her in the darkness, then, with a movement that roiled the water, swung from her. He lunged for the bank, and though she could not see him without the moonlight, she heard the crackle of the leaves as he found his clothing.

"Don't be long," he said, a terse command. "I'll build up the fire to dry your hair."

Elise wanted to answer, but could not find the words. Thoughtfully she began to rinse away the soap, finishing the peculiar bath since she had begun it. It was an odd thing, but the fire he had promised held little appeal. She was no longer cold.

For all the care she took drying her hair, she might as well not have bothered. Toward dawn of the next morning came another rainstorm, one that settled into a downpour that continued without letup. Reynaud had swung his leather cloak about her as she stepped from the shelter, but it had no hood and her hair was soon soaked. She had worried about what the half-breed would do for protection from the elements, but he had taken out another square of leather and wrapped it around himself, knotting it at his right shoulder to leave his right hand free. It was a style she had often seen on the men of the Natchez, and women, too, when they were working. It seemed to suit him.

Elise did not enjoy the protection of the long cloak alone. She could not leave Madame Doucet to be wet through, so she took her under her arm. They struggled along through the downpour together, slipping and sliding in the wet leaves and mud. It was as well to keep moving. They had little protection in any case, and it not only brought them nearer their destination, but kept them warm as well.

It was a miserable camp that night, with the rain blowing and hissing into the fire even under the protective lean-to of saplings and pine boughs they had constructed. The bedding that was not wet was clammy with damp so that, as tired as they were, no one wanted to leave the fire. Reynaud had killed a pair of squirrels, but even the savory stew Elise had made did little to enliven their spirits. The only blessing was that the mosquitoes were not in evidence. In the end, they simply rolled up in the driest of the bedding and curled around the fire, with the women on the inside slant of the lean-to, away from the sweeping rain.

The day that followed was much like the one before. They started out in a mist that turned to driving rain before the first morning halt, afterward becoming a steady drizzle. It began to seem as if rain was all they had ever known or ever would know. The creeks became deeper as they crossed, the streams wider. The ground, black and rich, was so soggy with moisture that it oozed with every step. Their shoes grew sodden and the skin of their feet turned white, then began to form blisters. They wrapped their feet in rags and limped along, for there was nothing else to be done.

The land had begun to rise. Though barely discernible under the great virgin trees, there were gently rolling hills and ridges along which the Indian track ran to stay as much as possible out of the swampland and creek bottoms. Still they trod on and on, following Reynaud, too tired and dispirited to question where he led. When he said stop, they halted; when he said go, they struggled to their feet and went on. They had ceased to grumble or even to talk among themselves. Madame Doucet still moaned in her sleep and moved her lips as if talking to someone unseen, but she did not falter. Her endurance was amazing, or perhaps it wasn't. The older woman had survived the voyage to the new world and the hardship of making a life in this wild country. She was strong, at least in body. St. Amant struggled along with his crutches, finding it heavy going in the uncertain footing caused by the rain. At first he had complained of cramps in his arms from hitching his sticks along, but no longer. Henri, without Madame Doucet to care for now, walked beside St. Amant, reaching out to steady him when needed. Of them all, Pascal strode out with the most élan. His energy was fed by resentment, Elise thought, for she sometimes saw him staring at Reynaud's back with frustrated fury in his small eyes. She suspected it might be better if he would vent his anger with his customary curses and sneers, but he seemed to be biding his time, doggedly marching, though his back was so stiff it could be seen that he begrudged every step that did not take him to the fort in the Natchitoches country.

Dusk came and still they did not stop. Night fell. An hour passed. They staggered drunkenly as they walked and hardly noticed when the rain finally ceased to fall. At last they came to a clearing. Beside it ran a fair-sized stream. The earth was sandy, a mixture of white, gray, and sooty black. Scattered about were large clay pots, most of them broken. There were a few that were whole and filled with water sitting near a wide flat of sand in the center of which was a bubbling spring. The water of the spring was cold and clear, but with such a strong taste of salt that Henri, the first to dip into it, spat it out again onto the ground.

This then was where the Indians made their salt by letting the water evaporate from the clay pots, leaving the grainy residue behind. It was a neutral ground, open to all without fear of reprisal. They could rest easy.

They dried their bedding around a roaring fire, but did not build the shelters. The air was chill now that the rain had stopped and there were no mosquitoes to be heard. Elise went to bed early, but, despite her exhaustion, could not sleep. She lay with her head on the crook of her arm, staring at the fire where Rey-

naud sat alone. If he did not come to bed, it would be the third
night. She had slept alone after her bath in the bayou, after she
had kissed him. Perhaps he had thought that demand enough,
or possibly he had grown tired of her teasing. It didn't matter,
of course. She was relieved of the strain of wondering what he
might next ask of her. It was only that it would be warmer with
him beside her. It really was turning colder at last. At dusk they
had seen large vees of ducks and geese flying southward, their
numbers so great that they had streaked the sky with geometric
designs. Their honking and calling could still be heard overhead,
a mournful sound in the dark stillness.

Dawn came too soon. The first slanting rays of bright sun-
shine found them on the trail. They pressed forward at a break-
neck pace. There was time lost in the rain that needed to be
made up, but they could not keep up such a scrambling run for
long. The rest periods were much too short and not nearly frequent enough. Elise found herself lagging and looked back to
see their column stretching out longer and longer. She looked
with concern at Madame Doucet hobbling along some distance
behind her; she could hear the labored breathing of the older
woman even above her own. Someone had to complain, persuade Reynaud to slow down. At one time St. Amant could have
been depended on to do that, but now he swung along on his
sticks with his face set in grim lines as he stared at the ground.

Elise turned her face forward. Her mouth tightened and she
lengthened her stride. It did not help. She broke into a trot,
coming up behind Pascal and easing past him. She could see no
sign of Reynaud at first, then around a bend she saw him. She
started to call out, but thought better of it. He might not heed
her in the mood he seemed to be in. With one hand pressed to
the stitch in her side, she redoubled her efforts.

Had he heard her behind him? Seen her? She could not tell,
but she did not seem to be gaining on him at all, though she
could not see that he had increased his speed. Her breathing
became ragged. Now she was running, ducking limbs, her feet
pounding on the spongy ground, her heart jarring with each step.
There was a red haze before her eyes and she could feel the
wetness of tears flowing back into her hair. The knot at the nape
of her neck loosened, uncoiling onto her shoulder. Her skirt
caught on a brier and was torn loose at the waist so that she
tripped on the hem. She fell to one knee, then was up again,
clutching at the torn cloth. Behind her she heard someone call,

but could not stop, could no longer see the others. There was only one important thing, and that was reaching Reynaud, catching his fleeting form, and stopping him.

Then suddenly he halted, his back to her. Her footsteps slowed, thudding, jolting until she came to a walk. Her chest heaving, she came even with him at last. She looked up at him, at his face with its faint smile and his gaze fixed somewhere ahead. Her voice a rasp of sound, she said, "What is it?"

"There. Look."

She followed the direction of his nod. Ahead of them lay a house, a veritable manor of two stories with shade trees around it and an alley of pin oaks leading to the door. Beyond were outbuildings, barns, stables, *pigeonnier*, and slave cabins, and surrounding the whole lay arpent upon arpent of land cleared of trees and broken to the plow. So unexpected was the sight, so different from the endless forest and from the nameless dread that had risen in her mind, that her breath came out in a gasping laugh.

"But where—where are we?"

"Home," he said.

6

"YOU ARE PLEASED, Madame Laffont?"

Elise turned once more before the cheval mirror with its gold-leaf frame. Her hair was dressed in softly rolled curls high on the crown of her head with the front eased into deep waves. Her gown of sea-blue satin, with its scooped neckline, cuffed sleeves to just below the elbow, and full skirt with demitrain, was made lighter in appearance by cream silk gauze ruching at the low neck, gauze undersleeves ending in frills of ruching at the wrist, and an apron of the same material sewn into the waist of the gown. Her waist was made smaller, no great task after the strain of the past week and more, by a boned corset, and her skirt was held out by a petticoat of cream satin quilted over horsehair. By lifting her skirts, she revealed shoes of cream and gold brocade with dainty red heels. The shoes were a bit large, but it scarcely mattered since they were without backs—and considering her blistered heels, that was just as well. At least the place on her foot where the thorn had been removed was scabbed over, nearly healed. She had noticed that Reynaud's similar wound was the same.

Due to the efforts with a needle of the woman who stood behind her, however, the fit of the gown was excellent. Elise picked up a fold of the thick, heavy satin skirt in her fingers. It was of the finest grade, far more expensive than anything she had ever owned. Her father had not been wealthy—far from it—and her clothing had been utilitarian, especially after his second wife had been set in place. Vincent Laffont had been vain of his young wife and had seen to it that she dressed to do him credit, but he had seen no point in paying for extra quality. She was used to the flimsier fabrics of the bourgeoisie; the gown she wore was made of stuffs fit for the aristocracy.

"How could I not be pleased?" she answered. "Though I am still not sure I should accept such lovely things, nor do I understand how Rey—M'sieu Chavalier was able to produce them on short notice."

"He will tell you, I'm sure," replied the woman who served as Reynaud's housekeeper, his cousin Madeleine. The words were polite but without warmth. "If you would care to wait in the salon, it is just through the door."

How very odd it seemed; this luxurious toilette; the French-woman of indeterminate age, rail-thin form, and imperious bear-ing; the rich comfort of the house. Elise could not become used to any of it, though she had been in residence at Reynaud's home for the best part of two days and a night. The first afternoon and night she had slept, as they all had in their exhaustion. It had been midmorning when she awoke in this room with its floor of polished cypress covered with thick woven carpets in rose, cream, and sea blue; its cream-plastered walls and hangings of rose silk drawn back at the windows with tassels; its elegant bed and armoire of carved wood; its dressing table and tall mirror and mantel candelabra of crystal and gilt. She had taken break-fast in bed, sipping rich, sweet chocolate and eating flaky crois-sants. Then had come a hot bath with real milled soap from Paris scented with roses, followed by the surprise of a trio of gowns and a change of underclothing brought in by Madeleine. The time since had been taken up with fittings, with rubbing scented cream into her hands and face, and with the drying, brushing, and arranging of her hair.

"I will do that," Elise answered. Reynaud's relative had un-bent not at all in the time they had spent together. It was as though she used politeness to conceal her disapproval. She seemed to think that Elise was encroaching, a danger of some kind to her cousin. The tone the woman used in speaking of Reynaud was reverential, her attitude protective. It might have been annoying to be cast in the role of a siren if Elise had not known her sojourn in the half-breed's home would be brief; as it was she was bemused by the idea of Reynaud standing in need of protection from anyone.

The house was built solid, four-square, as they had seen as they approached it. The façade was simple, the usual logs and bousillage, though plastered over so finely it might have been white marble. It had wide steps leading up to the main rooms on the second floor, a front door that was inset deep inside a loggia to protect it from the rainy climate, and rounded casements for the shuttered windows that repeated the Italianate arches and columns of the loggia. One of the most amazing things was the glazing of thick glass that filled the window openings.

Inside were wide, well-proportioned rooms, each leading into the great salon that bisected the house from front to back, acting as a hallway. The furnishings had the classic beauty that is the hallmark of taste allied to wealth, though the crystal chandelier, the gold-leaf mirror, the velvet-cushioned settee and chairs, and the jewel-colored wall tapestries in the salon gave an added richness to that reception room.

When Elise entered it was empty. She moved down the long room, enjoying the soft sighing of her skirts around her, pausing now and then to stare up at the tapestries with their idyllic scenes captured in embroidered threads. Candles of myrtle wax burned in the chandelier, in one candelabra set on the fireplace mantel at the end of the room near an ornate clock of ormolu, and in another on what appeared to be a narrow table near the rear windows. As she neared, however, Elise saw that what she had thought to be a table was not one at all but a Flemish harpsichord.

A small chair stood before it. Elise drew it out and sat down, smiling a little to herself as she ran her fingers over the keyboard. She had been taught the rudiments of playing and a few simple pieces. When she had been a girl just entering her teen years, it had been a great joy to make music on the instrument. Slowly, with stiff fingers, she began to search out a melody.

Reynaud heard the music before he stepped into the room. His gray gaze went at once to the tableau in front of the windows. The candlelight was caught in golden radiance in the waves of Elise's hair. It shimmered on the width of her high cheekbones, touched the delicate lobes of her ears, and played on the sweet and generous curves of her mouth. Her hands and arms were models of grace, and the skirts that settled around her made a pool of lambent color.

She was beautiful, truly exquisite. Inside him there rose a fierce need to shield her, to keep her always from hurt, to surround her with joy. But her pride and the guard she had erected around herself against injury prevented it. That knowledge galled him even as he respected it. What a tempting witch she was, sitting there with her arched brows drawn together in concentration. What magic did she possess that made her as desirable fully clothed as hidden behind no more than a veiling of soap and wet cloth? There were facets of her that it might take years to know, some that might never be revealed. She was beginning to prey upon his mind, haunting his dreams with the tender torment of her caresses and the horror in her eyes. That was dangerous, for soon, in a matter of days, he must let her go. There was no other choice.

He took an abrupt step forward, moving toward her. She looked up without recognition though she ceased to play. Lowering her hands, she got to her feet, shaking out her skirts before she summoned a polite smile and faced the man advancing upon her.

He was wearing a coat of ice-blue satin braided with silver that came to his knees, hanging open over a waistcoat of silver-embroidered blue silk and gray satin knee breeches. His clocked stockings were gray and his shoes, set with silver buckles, had high heels that gave him extraordinary stature. His wig was full, curling to his shoulders, its whiteness giving a swarthy look to his features. The jabot at his throat was of Malines lace set with a large diamond, and in his hand he carried a snuffbox of silver and cloisonné.

"I bid you good evening, Madame Laffont." He reached for her hand, bending his head over it in a bow that was a masterpiece of deference and grace before brushing it with his lips.

"I fear, sir, that you have the advantage—" Elise began, then stopped, "Reynaud!"

He straightened, laughter bright in his gray eyes. "My transformation, confess it, is greater than yours. I would have known you anywhere."

"Yes," she said with more frankness than tact. "It is amazing."

"But an improvement, I presume?"

She opened her mouth to answer in the affirmative, then hesitated. He was magnificent as a gentleman of the court, distinctly impressive with his wide shoulders, which needed no padding to ensure the fit of his coat, and his long, well-formed legs displayed in the tight knee breeches that fashion dictated. Yet his facile comments, so courteous and meaningless, grated and he seemed in some strange manner diminished. "I'm not sure."

"Now what displeases you?" He flipped open his snuffbox with one hand and took a pinch. His comment was lightly plaintive, but the expression in his eyes was keen.

"I think I prefer your own hair—even with feathers," she said, the words abrupt.

"Then you shall have it."

As he swung away from her as if he would go that instant to remove his wig, she reached out to catch his arm. "No, no. You—you are truly the gentleman, very handsome. It's only that I was surprised."

He put away his snuffbox and took a handkerchief from his sleeve to wipe his fingers. Smiling down at her, he said, "So I am very handsome, am I?"

"As you well know."

"But I didn't know you had noticed."

She lifted a brow. "Is this a new form of seduction?"

"Not at all. They have been practicing it at court for some years."

"I don't like it."

His mouth twitched. "You didn't care for my rough embraces and now you object to my most polished address. Is there no pleasing you?"

"Apparently not. You should cease trying."

"Now what is this?" he said softly. "I seem to have disturbed you. Tell me how and I will remedy it."

Tell him how? That was the last thing she would do. Her distress was caused by an almost ungovernable urge to unbutton his waistcoat and strip away his lace-cuffed shirt to see if underneath his chest was still marked with the barbaric artwork of his tattoos.

Turning from the candlelight to conceal the high color she could feel spotting her cheekbones, she tried for a light answer. "It's nothing except that everything here is so different from what I expected. Permit me to tell you how beautiful your home is and how grateful I am for your attention to my comfort."

"More flattery? I will be undone."

"No, I am quite sincere. You have created a miracle here in the wilderness. Tell me how it was done, but first tell me how you were able to supply my needs so well as to clothing and—other female necessities."

"There is no mystery to that," he said, taking her hand and placing it on his arm, leading her to the settee. "Everything was left by a former guest."

"How very lucky for me she was so near my size." His answer had been immediate, without evasion, but had it not been a trifle glib? She sent him a quick glance from the corner of her eye.

"Indeed. By the same good fortune she had with her a maid, a most superior woman, who was of a size with Madame Doucet. I fear the garments left by this woman are not the equal of those you wear, being in dull colors, but as Madame is in mourning, perhaps she will not mind."

"There must be a tale that explains why these ladies left behind such fine wearables. So scarce are such in Louisiana that I fear it cannot have been by choice." Clothing was of such value that it was almost never discarded and often figured largely among items of inheritance, with an inventory taken of every piece down to the last handkerchief.

He sent her a quick look, but was rewarded only with her cool profile as she gazed at a marble figurine on the table beside the settee. "I'm afraid it was not. They were carried off by a fever."

"Both?" she inquired with limpid curiosity.

"Both. It was a brief illness. I assure you there is no fear of contagion."

"You reassure me." He was not telling the truth. She knew it, though she could not think why the charade was necessary. She decided to probe deeper. "Do you often have guests here?"

"Not often."

"Occasionally then."

"Yes."

"Are they often female?"

"Sometimes a wife will accompany her husband."

"How very brave of them to venture so far."

"You sound," he said deliberately, "as if you don't believe me."

"Do I?"

"If you are suggesting that the female who left the gown you are wearing behind was a *fille de joie* come to while away my hours of boredom, then you are wrong."

She turned to him with interest. "Now I hadn't thought of

that! Would such a woman venture this far into the wilderness? I would not have expected it, not without ample compensation.''

Reluctant amusement and a certain intrigue shone in his eyes for an instant and were gone. "You don't think that consorting with me at journey's end would have sufficed.''

"I doubt it.''

"You might at least have appeared to consider it.''

"I only meant," she explained kindly, "that a *fille de joie* would expect a monetary reward as well as—''

"Yes?'' he asked softly as she paused.

The door opened at that moment to admit Pascal. He strode into the room, slamming the panel behind him. His stride broke as he saw Reynaud and Elise, but this was not, apparently, the first time he had come upon his host in the dress of a gentleman, for he had no trouble in recognizing him. He ducked a crude bow in Elise's direction, accepted Reynaud's offer of wine, and began to prowl about the room. There had been no providential death to provide him with fresh clothing, for he appeared to be wearing one of Reynaud's coats from the way the sleeves hung over his hands and the waist strained in the back. His own waistcoat and breeches, though refurbished, made a sorry contrast to the rich velvet of the coat and the new stockings that encased his legs.

Elise had little thought to spare for the merchant, however, or for the conversation between the man and Reynaud that ensued. She knew that she had been decoyed away from the issue of where the clothes had come from by a discussion of Reynaud's probable female visitors. Why had he bothered unless the clothes had indeed belonged to his kept mistress? Had he challenged her on that point purely to obscure the truth? It was not a thought that pleased her. She cared not at all if he imported a dozen women to service him, of course she did not, but neither did she relish being led down the garden path. She would like to tear off her gown and fling it in his face, but that might be a spectacle he would enjoy too well. Instead, she sent him a look of such smouldering resentment that he blinked and raised a brow in inquiry.

Dinner was a sumptuous meal compared with the fare that had sustained them during their journey. It was served in lavish style, with damask napery, heavy silver, crystal, and chinaware. There was a footman in well-cut livery behind each chair to see to their individual needs, to offer the succulent meats and rich gravies, to refill the wineglasses, to brush away the crumbs, and to refill the finger bowls with clove-scented water as required.

Marie Doucet sat up straight with a flush of animation on her cheeks. This was her element, this social gathering, and not even the somberness of her gown of gray grisette trimmed with black or her memories could detract entirely from her enjoyment. Watching her, Elise was hopeful that the older woman might regain her equilibrium here away from the reminders of her loss. Hers was not a strong personality, and grief and hardship had come very near to oversetting her reason.

Henri had been placed beside Madame Doucet. How dignified he looked with his hair tied back by a full black ribbon, the down shaved from his face, and an outdated coat, most likely one left from Reynaud's boyhood, stretched over his bony shoulders. As he caught her eye where she sat on Reynaud's right at the head of the table, he gave her a quick smile that also held warm admiration. All of their temperaments, it appeared, had benefited from warm beds and good food.

The table was covered with white damask that was overlaid diagonally by another cloth in an oriental pattern with pagodas and blossoms in red and gold. Near the foot of the table, to the right of Reynaud's cousin Madeleine, St. Amant sat, sipping his wine and tracing the pattern of the cloth with one finger as he waited, with the others, for Madame Doucet to finish spooning up the last of her dessert before beginning on the savories and nuts in front of him. As a small silence fell, he looked up at their host. "A delightful meal, Chavalier. I congratulate you on your cook."

Reynaud inclined his head. "I will convey your compliments to him. I had him from a planter in the Indies, where he was used to a more discerning palate than mine. He will be pleased that you approve."

"You are too modest," St. Amant said. "A cook, like any other human being, does not expend his efforts unless he knows they will be appreciated."

Reynaud did not comment, but sat waiting, his eyes narrowing slightly as if he expected more.

"Your hospitality has been altogether too generous, even overwhelming. I'm sure I speak for all of us when I say that we are most grateful."

"I will be repaid if you enjoy your unavoidable stay with me. I have arranged for a hunting expedition, if that should appeal.

There are abundant deer around us, or bear, if you prefer. The bayou named for the Duc de Maine is near, practically on the doorstep, if fishing is your pleasure. Or, if you have had enough of forests, there are cards, chess, and the use of my library.''

"What more could we want," St. Amant said, his tone dry though his shrug was no more than a quick movement of his shoulders, "except to know when we are to leave here."

"Not an unreasonable request. I wish I could give you a definite answer, but that is impossible. The fact is, I am expecting a visitor, a friend. He may arrive tomorrow or it may be next week. When he has come and gone, then we will leave for the fort."

"Forgive me, m'sieu, for interrupting," Madame Doucet said, her hands going out in a fluttering appeal, "but is this visitor to be an Indian?"

Reynaud turned to her. "I beg your pardon, madame?"

"Is he to be an Indian? I—I ask it because . . . Oh, I know it sounds strange, but I woke at dawn this morning and went to the window. My room looks over the back of the house, you know, and as I stood there I thought I saw an Indian warrior pass into the kitchen building. He was wearing a cloak, one like yours, m'sieu, and though I could not be sure, I thought he was of the Natchez."

There was a brief silence. With a frown between his eyes, Reynaud sent his cousin a quick glance. The others did not look at each other. When Madame Doucet had made just such a claim previously, no one else had seen the Indian. There had been a feeling then that Reynaud had agreed that the Indian was there and had identified him as a Tensas merely to pacify the older woman, to relieve her mind. It was not to be wondered at, this preoccupation of hers with Indian warriors; still, it made them uneasy.

"One of the guards, I don't doubt," Madeleine said, her tone offhand.

Reynaud's face cleared and he sent a wry glance around the table. "Of course, though that may be the wrong term for the men you may see about the place. There are a number of them, some of them of mixed blood like myself, some who have been among the Indians so long they look like savages. They are a rough-and-ready lot: hunters, trappers, traders, coming and going at odd hours, but they provide protection for Madeleine in my absence and are a curb against the defection of the African workers.''

"You relieve my mind," Madame Doucet said with a sigh.

"You might want to watch out for the friend I am to meet here. He was one of these men for some time, though now he is more often gone than not, with his trading.''

"He is half Indian?" the older woman ventured with a return of fear to her eyes.

Reynaud's smile was reassuring. "He was born in France, but he has lived with the Natchez. He was one of the orphan boys sent to live with them before he was twelve, to learn their language in the early days. We grew up together, he and I, being much of an age, but he left the tribe when he reached his majority.''

Madame Doucet nodded as though satisfied. St. Amant allowed a respectful moment of quiet, then reverted to his original topic. "When we do leave for the fort, how long may we expect the trek to take? I have been trying to calculate it myself, and though I grant you that dead reckoning is not my strong point, I have a feeling we are not so far from Fort Saint Jean Baptiste.''

"The Indian trails can be deceiving. It is still a journey of some distance.''

"Yes." Pascal grunted, his tone belligerent with the amount of wine he had drunk and his suspicion of what he obviously considered to be an evasion. "But how far?''

St. Amant sent the merchant a quelling look. "I suppose I was thinking of your proximity to the post. Surely it is the nearest French settlement to you?''

"That is correct.''

"It must have been there that you received and unloaded the furnishings for this house after they had traveled upriver from New Orleans.''

"Quite true, though you would be surprised at how little made that trip. The lumber of the house itself was cut and hewn here where it sits. Artisans skilled in carpentry and the making of fine furniture were brought, the best that New Orleans, Biloxi, Mobile—and Mexico City—had to offer; and other laborers also, though much was done by my own people.''

"You astonish me," St. Amant said politely. "Still there must have been many cartloads of fine goods and the great labor of cutting a road through to the fort?''

"Pack trains, yes, but no carts and so no road," Reynaud

said, then added with a smile, "except, of course, for that which runs along the boundary of my property for my own convenience."

Elise saw Madeleine lift her head to stare at Reynaud with a sharp look in her eyes before the woman lowered her gaze to her plate once more. Elise had little attention to give this byplay, however, as she saw the point St. Amant was trying to make. If there was a cart road, however narrow, then it should be easy to follow. They could dispense with the services of their guide and host. The prospect was too enticing to abandon. She leaned forward. "Even the harpsichord came on horseback?"

"Pulled behind a Spanish mule on a special conveyance," Reynaud answered, his composure unruffled. "You are aware that the Spanish mission of Los Adaes is less than thirty miles from Fort Saint Jean Baptiste? That was a stroke of good fortune, for the Spanish have many more horses and mules and I was able to buy what I needed from them—at a price, of course. Trade between the Spanish and French garrisons is brisk, I'm afraid, this far from either center of government."

"Smuggled goods," Elise said, thinking of Vincent's part in that trade prohibited by the French government.

"It is a matter of survival."

She settled back in her chair, leaving the field to St. Amant. What reason, after all, had Reynaud to conceal from them the existence of a road? The men of their party were hardly congenial and, indeed, barely polite despite the fact that he had tried to save their lives. His bargain with her had sorely tried his patience, netting him more frustration than relief. If he had business at the fort of the Natchitoches country, as he had said, then he could easily make the journey there and back in the time it would take to guide them. In all probability he was as anxious to be rid of them as they were to be gone, only his notions of hospitality, imbued from both the Natchez and his father's family, prevented him from saying so.

The unaccountable low spirits that had settled upon her as the dinner came to an end seemed to be firmly attached. They remained with her through a labored game of piquet in the salon with Reynaud, Madeleine, St. Amant, and Madame Doucet. After a few hands, she excused herself and moved once more to the harpsichord, leaving the three to play on. Henri had wandered away in the direction of the library and had not returned. Pascal, after taking a turn outside, had returned to fling himself down on the settee. He accepted a small glass of liqueur from a servant, then sat, staring at the card players with a sullen expression on his face while he scratched his nose.

Elise, letting her fingers move over the keys of the harpsichord, glanced from Pascal to Reynaud. The contrast between the coarse, sprawling merchant and the half-breed dressed in satin, sitting relaxed at the card table, was marked. Even St. Amant seemed to lack both refinement and force in comparison. Reynaud had the urbane elegance of a courtier without the mincing airs, vicious wit, or condescension of that species. It was ridiculous, even unfair, that he should be able to move so easily between the roles of savage and gentleman. She had thought she was beginning to understand him and now she was no longer sure. Even as she appreciated his chameleonlike facility, she mistrusted it.

I have no people. He had spoken those words on the trail. Had he meant them? Did he really feel no greater loyalty to the people of his father than to those of his mother? If not, then even he did not know which guise was the true one. And if he did not, how could she tell?

She glanced up, startled from her thoughts, as Pascal came to stand in the curve of the narrow instrument. His voice was rough and faintly slurred as he drawled, "Do you know you've been staring at that twice-damned half-breed like a she-cat in heat?"

"Don't be ridiculous!" He was drunk, but his voice was carrying. She sent a quick look to be certain the card players had not heard.

"Oh, no, not I. You're the one. Can it be that that savage bastard has thawed the ice widow? Maybe it was what you needed all along, to be forced to give it up."

"You are insulting," she said, rising to her feet and stepping away from the harpsichord. "I will expect an apology when you are sober."

He reached out to fasten hard, moist fingers on her arm. "If you've started to thaw, maybe I can finish melting you. I'll come to your room in an hour."

She wrenched at her arm in the sudden, frenzied return of her old revulsion, but she could not release herself. "Do," she invited in a hiss, "and I'll kill you."

"I'll wager my welcome will be warm enough when I've got

you under me," he said, his grasp bruising as he jerked her nearer.

"You will lose," came a hard reply from behind them.

Elise was freed abruptly as Reynaud came between them. He took Pascal's wrist, bent, and lifted one hip, and the merchant went flying to land flat on his back on the floor.

Pascal shook his head, raising himself on his elbows. The words thick and shaken, he said, "What kind of Indian trick was that?"

"A wrestler's throw. Shall I demonstrate again?"

The merchant sent him a look of black dislike, but managed to signal that it would not be necessary.

"You will make your regrets for your conduct to Madame Laffont."

Pascal stared at Reynaud with his thick lips folded, but apparently something he saw in the other's face decided him. His gaze wavered and he mumbled an apology.

Reynaud took Elise's cold and trembling fingers and placed them on his arm before turning to his guests. "The evening, my friends, is at an end."

The salon was quiet as he led her away. Only Madeleine followed with quick footsteps as Reynaud pushed open the door of Elise's bedchamber and guided her through. His cousin closed the door behind them and moved to stand nearby, her anxious gaze upon Elise's pale face.

"Cognac," Reynaud said to the woman. When she slipped away to fetch it, he turned Elise toward him. A soft curse left him as he saw the look in her eyes. He made an abortive gesture as if he had meant to take her in his arms, then realized he could not. His voice curt yet quiet, he said, "Hold to me."

It was as if she had not been able to breathe since Pascal had touched her. She heard the command with a sense of limitless release. Sliding her hands inside his coat, she clasped her arms around him and rested her face on the brocade of his waistcoat. Closing her eyes, she let out a deeply held sigh. She felt his cheek against her hair, the delicate touch of his fingers against the back of her gown, settling at her waist. She did not move. They stood thusly until Madeleine returned.

Reynaud stayed to see Elise take the restorative, to watch as she sipped it. Satisfied that she was all right, he let himself out of the room. His cousin, mystified but sympathetic still, bustled around, turning down the bed and laying out a nightgown. Finally she approached and took Elise's glass to set it aside before beginning to unbutton her gown with a competence that did not brook refusal.

The cognac was potent. Elise seemed to have little will of her own left and allowed herself to be turned this way and that. She sat down to have her stockings and shoes removed, stood to have her nightgown slipped over her head, then sat down again to have her hair taken down in front of the dressing table.

As Reynaud's cousin began to draw a brush through her long, honey-brown strands, a thought occurred to Elise. Without pausing to consider it, she spoke. "The women m'sieu brings here to his home, do they stay long?"

"Women, Madame Laffont?"

"The women of a certain kind."

"I don't understand you. There have been few women here, only one or two, and they the wives of the officials who visit from time to time. Sometimes a *coureur de bois* will pay a brief visit in passing, bringing with him his Indian woman, but such do not stay in the house, being uncomfortable in so civilized a place."

Elise suppressed a smile at the pride she heard in the woman's voice. "But the—the lady whose dress I was wearing, what of her?"

"Which one do you speak of, *chère*?"

"The lady who died."

"Ah," the woman said with a slow nod. "Reynaud will have told you of it and I can add no more."

Had his cousin been warned not to speak? If so, it would serve no purpose to tease her. In any case, there was no further opportunity, for the door behind them opened and Reynaud stepped inside.

Madeleine gave a final smoothing to the thick curtain of hair that shimmered around Elise's shoulders, then put down the brush, said good night, and went away. Reynaud reached up to drag off his wig and throw it onto the dressing table as he moved to stand behind her. He watched her in the mirror, his gaze running with a hint of possessiveness over her hair and the low-necked gown of white batiste that she wore. His voice soft, he said, "Charming."

She ignored the comment. "You will be sleeping here?"

"It is the arrangement."

"One you have not taken advantage of since our arrival."

"A sign of my commendable patience. Did it trouble you?"

"Hardly. I merely wondered if the rules had changed."

"No." He smiled at her in the mirror as he shrugged out of his coat and hung it on the back of her chair.

"I wasn't even sure if you used a real bed."

"Occasionally."

He kicked off his shoes with their high heels and rolled down his stockings, removing them. As he straightened and began to unbutton his waistcoat, Elise found that she could not look away until he had stripped it off, revealing the linen shirt underneath. She met his gaze with its trace of quizzical humor in the mirror, then her attention was drawn to his hands as they grasped the fullness of his shirt and pulled it from his breeches. He crossed his arms over his belly and drew the linen garment up and off over his head in a single, fluid movement.

The gray-black lines of his tattoos were there, unchanged, undulating in rows across his chest. Without conscious thought, she turned in her chair and reached out to touch them, tracing their course with her fingertips. He drew in his breath as he accepted her touch, the first she had given that was of her own volition. He stood, unmoving, his eyes darkening to the gray of the night sky; then, slowly, so as to pose no threat by towering over her, he dropped to one knee beside her chair. One strong, brown hand lifted to cover her fingers where they rested on his chest, which swelled as he prepared to speak.

"If I were not forsworn," he said, his voice deep, "I would wrap my hands in the wild silk of your hair and draw you to me, enclosing you in my arms, holding you to me until I could feel the beat of your heart. I would touch your lips with mine, holding their sweet warmth until they opened to me. I would taste the essence of your mouth and probe its source, inviting you with every wile at my command to do the same. I would kiss your forehead, your eyes, the softness of your cheeks, that small seductive hollow behind your ear. Gently I would slide your gown from your shoulders, following its fall with a trail of kisses."

"Please," she whispered, a heated flush rising to her face that was not entirely due to embarrassment. She felt as if every word was a caress, as if each had weight and substance that she could feel against her skin. They seeped inside her, bringing a heaviness to the lower part of her body, a languor that prevented movement.

"Your breasts I would take in my hands, cupping their gentle shape that is both soft and firm, stroking the nipples with finger and tongue until they were tight buds of sweetness. I would press my face into the white flatness of your belly and breathe your scent before searching out those secret places that bring you joy. And when you were ready, when you yearned for me, only then, would I fill you, banishing thought of any other man. I would use the force at my command to your service, your good, bringing to us both that boundless pleasure that is our birthright, our solace, our only certain reward for living. These things I would do, if I were not forsworn."

There rose inside Elise a terrible need to have him do precisely as he had said. Her eyes were wide and her lips parted, but the words that would grant him release from his vow would not come. An odd anguish ran with a shiver along her nerves. Her lashes flickered. Unable to sustain his gaze, she lowered her own to her hand, which was still pressed to him.

He bowed his head and raised his fingertips to his lips, kissing them briefly before placing them in her lap. Rising to his feet with the swift flex of taut muscles, he reached to pinch out the candle flames in the candelabrum on the dressing table.

"Come to bed," he said, his voice weary.

They lay together in the dark with a foot of feather-stuffed mattress between them. Outside could be heard the sighing of the night wind. Now and then the house creaked with the gathering cold. From the salon came the delicate ticking of the ormolu clock. It marked the minutes well and chimed the hours with a soft persistence.

Two hours had passed and most of a third when Elise turned on her side, facing Reynaud. In the shelter they had shared on the trail it had been nearly impossible not to lie against each other. In her exhaustion the night before, she had not missed that closeness, but now she could not seem to rest without it. Casually, as if it were nothing out of the ordinary, she reached out to span the space between them, placing her fingers on the curve of his shoulder. He did not move. He must be asleep. She was glad. She closed her eyes and let her tense muscles relax.

Reynaud, lying on his stomach because it seemed best in his present state of restless arousal, felt that soft touch and was barely able to control a start. Did she know what she was doing or had she turned to him again in her sleep? He was a fool to let it matter. Still, it did. He preferred to think that she knew. It gave him a small measure of peace to pretend that it was so. He slept.

The days continued clear and the sun shone so bright that it dazzled the eyes. As always happened during that season, the earth absorbed the warmth and reflected it back at night so that the air grew mild once more and it began to seem as if winter might be held at bay indefinitely. A week passed, then another, and part of a third went by with hardly a ripple as they all in their various ways absorbed the tranquillity of this backwater. The horror at Fort Rosalie faded until it took on the cast of a bad dream that could be forgotten for hours. The time was full, for Reynaud constantly had some outing or expedition that must be made: a duck shoot; a hunt for the wild pigs he had turned loose in the woods some years before to mate with those left by de Soto during his ill-fated meanderings nearly two hundred years ago; or any of a dozen other challenges to the marksmanship of a man. He offered the stimuli of games, whether it be an Indian form of dicing called "toss corn" where they took turns throwing out a number of kernels with one side painted black to see who could land the most with the black sides uppermost, or a race on scrawny Indian ponies traded from the Caddo, who had them from some tribe on the distant plains of the far west country.

Sometimes Reynaud would take on all comers, one after the other, in a battle with buttoned épées, each man protected by a padded vest; at other times he would spend an idle afternoon trying to show Henri the finer points of wrestling Indian style or fighting with a knife. The activities seemed to provide some outlet for his energy and also for that of his guests, those of the male set, at least.

There was food and wine in constant supply, ready at any hour. The greatest lure to forgetting the passing days was, however, the sybaritic comfort of his home.

The refugees chafed and complained among themselves now and then, especially as the third week began to slip past, but they found Reynaud singularly unapproachable on the subject of their departure and no one was quite impatient enough to force the issue.

Often their host went hunting with the other men, but he was just as likely to send one of the men Madeleine called her guards—dark, silent men proficient in tracking and crack shots with the muskets that were their greatest pride—with them. On those days when he remained behind, he usually sent to the stable to have horses saddled and took Elise riding with him over his lands.

He took her down to the bayou to follow its slow windings between banks of rich, dark soil and its wide turns, which deepened into sunlit pools sheltered by trees and overhung with trailing vines. They visited the swamp nearby where his workers were felling cypress logs for more outbuildings, rode around the fields, and cantered along the cart track that wound from the house past the grist mill and cooperage at the bayou's edge and into the dark, stretching forest once more.

There was pride in the way he pointed out the smokehouse filled with meat, the cribs filled with corn, the pastures where sheep grazed to provide wool for cloth, and the pens where chickens and geese were kept from marauding foxes and weasels. He insisted on showing her the pantry stocked with barrels of cornmeal and nuts; crocks of eggs preserved in grease; smaller barrels called hog's heads filled with rendered bear fat; pots of honey robbed from bee trees in the woods; and containers of jams, jellies, and pickles made by his cousin and the women she supervised. His was a self-sufficient estate, using little from the outside world except the wheat flour, olive oil, wine, and dried exotic fruits he could well have done without.

Elise was warm in her praise, for she was genuinely impressed. She knew well the planning and sheer labor of the owner, as well as the workers, that it took to bring such plenty to so primitive and distant a piece of land. Here a man could live with little contact with the outside world, unheeding of its problems and fears, its greed and betrayal. It seemed an inviting prospect and, remembering the ashes that now drifted over her own holdings, the unlikelihood that she would be able to reclaim them at any time in the near future, and the work it would take to make them prosper again, she envied Reynaud Chavalier with all her heart.

Late one afternoon, they sat their horses on the path that ran past the house and through the fields. Reynaud, squinting against the slanting rays of the setting sun, had been pointing out to Elise the weaving house where the great loom was kept, trying to give her some idea of the size of the wool harvest by calculating the number of bags of wool his cousin had carded and spun the spring before and of how many yards of cloth had been woven for clothing for the slaves.

"I don't think Madeleine likes me very much," Elise said when she had shown herself suitably appreciative.

"Why should you think that?"

"She looks at me as if I were one of the roaches she chases with such passion."

He grinned. "She does hate them, doesn't she? I will have to get a kitten for her when I am in Natchitoches; that should help keep them down."

"Do so and she will worship you more than she does now."

"You exaggerate."

As she saw his smile fade, Elise regretted having spoken. "I believe not, but then it's nothing to do with me."

"Madeleine came with me from France, from Combourg. It may be she has a right to be concerned for my welfare."

"You don't have to explain."

"No, but I would not have you misunderstand. She is like a sister to me, an older and dear sister."

"It's none of my affair, really."

He ignored her protest. "She was living as a poor relation at the chateau, tending to the whims of my father's wife. There had been a scandal years before, something she would never speak of but that left her without prospects. She was kind to me, a stranger to France, and saw to it that I was treated as my father's son rather than as the ignorant savage that I undoubtedly was in many ways. She used to listen when I talked of Louisiana, would sometimes say how exciting it must be to begin a new life in a new country. When I decided to leave Combourg, I asked her to come with me. She agreed. It wasn't my wish that she become my housekeeper, but that is the post she chose for herself and I can't take it from her."

"You might tell her I have no designs upon it."

"I doubt," he said, his voice hard, "that the occasion will arise."

She sent him a perplexed look. "You are certainly testy of late. I meant no harm."

"Did you not? If I could be sure of that, I would feel a great deal easier."

"What do you mean?"

"You so enjoy— Never mind." He looked away abruptly, gathering his reins as if he would leave her.

She put out her hand to catch his arm. "You think I would find fault merely to—to test your temper?"

"And my good intentions."

"That's absurd!"

"Is it? Can you say you have never done so?"

The heat of a flush rose to her face, but her eyes were steady. "Not in some time."

"I wish I could think," he said after a long moment, "that you were so innocent—so without guile."

She drew back her hand. With sudden clarity, she knew that he was speaking of that morning when he had awakened to find her sleeping in the curve of his arm with one leg drawn up over his thighs. His start, though instantly stilled, had roused her and she had disentangled herself with as much dignity as she could muster. It had not been the first time it had happened, though usually it was he who reached out to her.

"And what of you?" she asked, her voice tight.

"Oh, I make no secret of my campaign against your defenses. But if I am guarding mine unnecessarily, I would like to know it."

His last words carried a sting of sarcasm. It was this that prompted her answer. "Why? Are you in danger of surrender?"

"Against an equal force, the best way to lift a siege is to attack."

Swinging the head of his horse around, he rode away from her. She watched him go in some confusion. She had known full well that his temper was thin these last days, had realized something of the cost of his stringent control, but there had always been about him a feeling of hard and limitless purpose. Had she depended too much upon the tempered steel of his will? Had she in her dependence, her need, undermined it? Or was it simply that his invincibility was a myth she had created for herself because she wanted so badly to believe in it?

7

ELISE COULD HAVE let him go. She might have if she had not seen him draw in his horse some distance away beneath the limbs of a spreading tree. He sat for long moments, his gaze on the ground ahead of him. It occurred to her that he might have something more to say. Lifting her reins, she kicked her horse into a walk.

When she was only a few feet from Reynaud, he dismounted, his well-cut doeskin riding breeches clinging to the firm musculature of his thigh as he swung his leg over the saddle. Without glancing in her direction, he began to walk his horse, bending now and then to pick something up from the dry brown leaves that covered the sere and broken grass edging the beaten trail. Elise watched him for a moment, then looked up at the tree above them. It was a wild pecan.

Getting down from her horse, she looped the reins around her wrist and scuffed through the leaves, too, picking up the pecans. They were small and well hidden, but plentiful. Looking for them had a certain fascination, like searching for any hidden thing. Going nutting in the fall had always been one of her favorite chores, that and picking wild berries. She scrubbed the blackened hulls that clung damply to the pecans on the side of her legs with little regard for her habit. Though Madeleine had cleaned the velvet outfit and aired it well, it was so disreputable with its bald spots that it hardly mattered. Elise soon had an overflowing handful that she had to hold against her chest. Whenever she bent to collect another nut, she dropped one or two.

"Here. Allow me." Reynaud took her nuts, adding them to the store he had gathered, which caused his breeches pockets to bulge. "I know where a persimmon tree is, if it appeals?"

It was, perhaps, a peace offering. She agreed, and side by side, with their horses trailing after them, they walked on along the track. It was not far. Their approach frightened away an opossum that had been already foraging among the fallen fruit. The ungainly creature trundled off into the woods with his hairless tail dragging behind him.

It was a marvelous blending of flavors and textures: the crisp, slightly bitter pecans and the soft, mellow ripeness of the orange-fleshed persimmons. Reynaud cleared a place under the tree and they sat with their backs against the trunk, eating. He cracked the pecans in his hands and Elise picked out the meats, each stopping now and then to bite into a persimmon. The seeds were large and slick and they spat them out, but Reynaud cracked one to show her the flower design of the kernel inside. Then they broke open others, each kernel different.

It was a curiously peaceful interlude after their quarrel. At first there was some constraint between them, but it gradually faded away. It returned again once as Elise, instead of handing a nut meat to Reynaud, who had his hands full of cracked pecans, had popped it into his mouth. He had stared at her for a long moment, then lowered his thick lashes and reached to pour the broken shells and nut meats he held into her lap.

What a strange man he was, Elise thought as she busied herself once more. Which was his real personification: the gentle savage or the irascible gentleman? He had abandoned his silks and satins, his wigs and jewels since that first night, opting instead for the casual clothing of a landed squire and his own hair tied back in a queue. She sometimes wondered if this was yet another facet of his character, that of the farmer with pride in his holdings and love for the rich and spreading arpents that had been made fruitful by his labors. She could not be sure, for despite the closeness of his company when they retired for the night after the daylight hours they had spent together, she felt no nearer to understanding him. He could be amazingly perceptive as he had been on the evening when Pascal had tried to lay hands on her. How had he known that what she needed at that moment, that all that she could bear, was his strength to hold onto without the confinement or obligation of being held in return. He could also be extremely obtuse, as in his failure to understand that his cousin Madeleine felt threatened by the presence of another woman in his house and was especially resentful of one who had no legal or moral right to be there.

It had become natural to speak something, if not all, of her thoughts when with Reynaud. Now she said, "This house, the land, do you share it with your brother?"

He shook his head. "No, it's mine alone."

"He is perhaps a half brother then?"

"Not at all. In fact, he is my twin."

She stared at him. "You mean that the ruler of the Natchez now, at this moment, has half-French blood in his veins?"

"You find that so hard to believe?"

"But he allowed the killing of his own people!" So hard were her hands clenched on the pecan she held that she felt the sharp edge of the shell cut her finger.

"It was not his choice; the chief of war decides such matters. But the origin of his blood makes little difference. He was raised as a Natchez and is now the Great Sun. He rides in a litter of state wherever he goes, never touching his foot to the ground. He communes alone with the spirits of the temple, who are symbolized by the three swans that guard the roof. He resides in his house on the highest mound of the village, only slightly lower than the temple itself, with his two wives and his children. And his only concern is for the welfare of his people."

"But you escaped."

"It wasn't a question of escape. My mother, Tattooed Arm, saw the justice of my father's request for one of his sons when he returned to France. Until then she had considered us mirror images, exactly the same—she had long since forgotten which had been born first. But she forced herself to evaluate us for intelligence, strength, independence, confidence, and a hundred other things. She chose."

"She chose your brother to be the Great Sun?"

"In part. Primarily she chose me to go with my father because she thought I would have the best chance to survive the submersion in another culture, to benefit from it, and to return to her. It was later that my brother became the Great Sun on the death of our uncle. The next Great Sun is always the eldest son of the eldest sister of the dead ruler."

"Then if you had not gone to France, you might have been chosen since you and your brother were twins?"

"Yes, I suppose."

"Was it—very difficult, adjusting to life in France among your father's people?"

He leaned his head back against the tree trunk, a faint smile lifting a corner of his mouth. "The hardest thing was learning to pronounce the letter 'r.' There is none in the Natchez language."

Was he telling the truth? She would have liked to probe deeper, but could not find the words to ask if his father's half-Indian bastard had been made welcome or instead had found scorn and rejection. Finally she asked, "Do you regret going?"

"No."

The negative was bald, perhaps out of loyalty to his mother and the choice she had made, perhaps as a defense of his brother who had stayed to preside over the massacre of his father's people. At any rate, she did not doubt it. "It seems odd that your mother was given the choice."

"She was not given it, but rather exercised it as her right."

"I don't understand."

"She is of the Sun class, the ruling class. My father, being a Frenchman, was considered of the Noble class only, which made it proper in the beginning for her to marry him. A Sun cannot marry in their own class, but must find a mate in the lower ranks. Because of this, however, my mother was superior in status to my father, at least by the lights of the Natchez. The decision was her privilege."

The children of a female Sun retained their mother's rank, though the children of a male Sun became Nobles, Elise knew. Therefore Reynaud and his brother were of the Sun class, their rank reckoned through the female line. It often happened that a female Sun would marry a Stinkard, merely to avoid any challenge to her superior standing. The Stinkard husband of a Sun could not sit in her presence, could never walk before her, and must ever obey her commands. Since it was also the custom for the spouses of the Suns to be strangled and buried with them, it sometimes happened that a Stinkard husband outlived a Sun wife and was sacrificed. There had been a great scandal in the Indian villages not so very long before when a Stinkard husband, on the death of his Sun wife, had run away, escaping his fate. The most outraged people in the village had been his own relatives, who would have been exempt from such a death for the rest of their lives if he had taken his rightful place in the funeral procession.

Elise tried to picture Reynaud as a part of such a rite, perhaps as one of the men who held the strangling cord. She could not. Once it would have been easy. Had a change of clothing made so much of a difference in her ideas of him?

"What are you called when you are among the Natchez?"

"My name? I'm known as Hawk-of-the-Night."

"And your brother?"

"Now he is only the Great Sun. Once he was Diving Hawk." He went on before she could comment. "You spoke not so long ago of the cruelty of the Indians, of their habit of torturing prisoners, male ones that is. There is no way to justify such a thing to the European mind and yet the custom serves its purpose. It allows the people of the victorious tribe to see that their foe is not a monster or a devil, but only a man who bleeds and dies as they do, plus it gives an outlet for the terror and horror of war endured by the women and children since they often participate."

"You don't condone it?" she asked, frowning at him.

"But neither do I condemn it as the practice of barbarians. That would be hypocrisy, for the annals of the world are filled with such cruelties. The ancient Phoenicians scalped their dead enemies, and some scholars think the Indians of the southern Americas may have the blood of these seafarers, blown off course long ages ago, in their veins. The hordes of Genghis Kahn and Tamerlane massacred thousands upon thousands and left their skulls to dry in the sun. The Gauls, the Franks, and the Crusaders put whole towns to the sword, not excluding the women and children, while rapine and pillage have often been the order of the day in the wake of such armies."

"That was ages ago!"

"Perhaps, but even now the dungeons of Europe are filled with instruments of torture that are regularly used on the innocent in the sacred name of God or to achieve confessions for crimes as small as the stealing of bread—bread that would have been freely given to the hungry by any Natchez. The difference, you might say, is that the torture is done in concealment, the screams muffled. That is true. But criminals are flogged, branded, and hanged in public execution of sentence. Where then is the dividing line between those of European blood and the barbaric natives of the new world?''

''It—it's just that they derive such inhuman pleasure from it, or so I've been told.''

''They enjoy their triumph, as do we all. Still, they can be just and even humane. The torture of a prisoner can be stopped. There is a way for the man—it is always a man despite the practices of some of the eastern tribes in torturing females and children—to be saved. It requires only a single woman, a widow who has lost her husband in battle. If she will ask for the man to be given to her—as a slave, servant, the husband she has lost, in any way she desires—he will be handed over without question. From that moment he becomes one with the Natchez and is never again an enemy.''

''And he will be trusted not to harm the widow?''

''He will owe her his life and feel the debt to the center of his being. He will not harm her, but is likely to serve her with honor all her days.''

Elise lifted a brow. ''What keeps him from creeping away in the night and going back to his own tribe?''

''Honor and gratitude, most of the time. But if the widow is old, or ugly, then he may disappear one day.''

''And no one minds?'' The lazy humor in his tone gave her a peculiar feeling in the pit of her stomach.

''The widow cries since she usually enjoys owning a slave and now has no one to warm her bed or perform the duties she has assigned. She will have lost great prestige also, for you realize that a male slave is rare; most are women and children.''

''Yes.'' Her voice was subdued as she thought of the French even now serving as slaves at the Natchez village. She thought Reynaud gave a soft exclamation of annoyance with himself, but she could not be sure, for in that moment there came a distant hail from the direction of the house. They swung to look and saw the figure of a man coming toward them.

Reynaud was on his feet instantly, every sense alert. He put his hand out to take her arm, drawing her behind him, but so taut was his stance that she could not be sure he was aware of making that protective gesture.

In any case it was unnecessary.

''*Sacre bleu!*'' the man called as soon as he was close enough to be easily heard. ''What has become of the great warrior that he sits under a tree stuffing himself on persimmons like a 'possum? That I should live to see it! And with a pretty woman beside him? This is a sorry pass, indeed. It makes me want to cry—with envy!''

"Pierre," Reynaud called and strode to meet him. They flung their arms around each other, buffeting each other on the backs and shoulders as they stood in the center of the trail.

Elise moved forward slowly. Reynaud turned, drawing her nearer. "Elise, *ma chère*, permit me to present to you my good friend Pierre Broussard. Pierre, Madame Laffont.''

"*Enchanté* . . . madame?'' Pierre Broussard swept off his hat, revealing fine blond hair worn long around his face in the cavalier style. Of medium height and perhaps a year or two younger than Reynaud, he had an open, merry countenance. He lifted one brow in comical disappointment over her married state as he bowed over her hand.

"I am a widow," Elise said, a smile coming unbidden to her lips. "It is a great pleasure to meet you at last, m'sieu. We have been waiting for you for what seems an age.''

"Waiting? Now how is this? Not even I know where I am going to be next.''

"Oh, but—''

"Shall we go back to the house?'' Reynaud interrupted. "I am sure that you would like a drink to wash the dust of travel from your throat, Pierre, and I have other guests who would like to meet you.''

Did the two men exchange a steady glance over her head? Elise thought so, but when she looked quickly at Reynaud, his face was relaxed in a smile as if his sole thought was of his duties as a host.

Pierre Broussard, the orphaned boy who had been placed with the Natchez to learn their language for the good of the French government, had become a trader. He traveled from New Orleans up the great Mississippi and its tributaries as far as the Illinois country, and fanned out over the myriad Indian trails from the domain of the British on the east to that of the Spanish on the west, and sometime even beyond. In pirogue and on pack animals, he carried rings, boxes, brass wire, needles, awls, bells, combs, scissors, drinking glasses, looking glasses, Flemish knives, woodcutter's knives, hatchets, mattocks, gunscrews, musket-flints, powder and ball, sabers, fusils, shirts, materials such as red and blue limburgs, and, often, bags of salt. He visited the forts, settlements and Indian villages, taking the pelts of beaver, fox, bear, deer, and smaller animals, and also the soft, cured and beaded leather of the Indian women and their decorated and baked pottery and woven baskets in exchange for his wares. Sometimes he traded for the stocky plains ponies with the Caddo farther north or for the horses of Spanish breeding with the Avoyels that lived to the southeast, well below the fort of Saint Jean Baptiste in the lands of the Natchitoches.

His friends were many, for he was well liked, and so he was welcome everywhere. Any chance-met stranger was invited to his fire, given a share of his food. Because of this, he was a repository of information, a traveling crier of the births and deaths, the feuds and scandals of the country. In common with most traders, he could always be depended on to know the latest news.

It was this secondary function that was of interest to the group from Fort Rosalie. The man had hardly been presented in the salon and a glass of wine put into his hand than they crowded around him. Elise was no less interested, though she stood back with an arm across the back of Madame Doucet's chair. The older woman's composure, gained during the last few days, was in jeopardy. She leaned forward with her hands twisting in her lap, her eyes red-rimmed and staring, and her face pale.

"What of Fort Rosalie?" Pascal demanded. "Have you news?"

"The fortification, the houses, all burned. I am told the powder magazine on the side of the bluff made a magnificent explosion, awe-inspiring. As for the settlement, it is no more."

"But the people?" Madame Doucet asked, her voice quavering.

"It is said eight men, perhaps other than yourselves, escaped death in the main attack. Four were killed in their pirogue on the river, two made their way to New Orleans to raise the alarm. These men arrived there in pitiful condition, weak from hunger and exhaustion, their clothing smoked and burned, their faces swollen from mosquito bites. The remaining two, a tailor and a cart driver, were taken prisoners, the first because of his usefulness and the last in order to drive the cart that took the spoils to the village. I regret to be forced to say that all others were killed."

How many men had been at the settlement and the fort? Three hundred, four? Elise thought it nearer to the last number. Dead, all dead. They had known it must be so; still, it was a shock that left them silent for long minutes.

"And the women and children?" The words were little more than a whisper as Marie Doucet stared, trembling, at the French trader.

Pierre frowned, looking down at his glass. "The word is . . . They tell me that some one hundred fifty women and eighty children were taken to the Indian village as slaves."

Two hundred thirty women and children. There had once been a counting at the settlement that had shown some seven hundred souls in residence there. The counting was not exact and yet it appeared that seventy or eighty women and children must have died on the day of the massacre. It seemed to Elise that for an instant she could hear the screams and smell the smoke that had been greasy with the taint of burning flesh.

St. Amant lifted his head from contemplating the wine in his glass and there was a blue line about his mouth. "What will become of them?"

It was a reasonable question. The French, due to the enlightened Indian policy of that wily old campaigner and founder of the colony, Bienville, had suffered little trouble with their Indian allies. Unlike the British Carolina colonies where such things were common, there had been few uprisings and therefore few French prisoners in Indian hands. But Bienville, due to political maneuverings in Paris and the general unproductivity of the colony, had been stripped of his position as governor, and now French women and children were at the mercy of the Natchez. All they had to go on as to their probable treatment were rumors and whispered stories of starvation, beatings, and maimings.

"They will be divided among the families according to rank and position. Young children will usually be allowed to stay with their mothers, though older ones may be separated. Tasks and duties will be assigned—the gathering of firewood, grinding corn, cooking, the cleaning and preparing of furs—whatever is in need of doing. They will be treated well enough—after the first frenzy of victory—so long as they show themselves to be willing and cooperative."

After the first frenzy of victory. That was the dangerous time when tempers and actions were out of control. It did not bear thinking of.

Pierre cleared his throat. His lips tightened as if he would not speak, then he said, "There is another story that came to me. There was a boy of six or seven, a fine lad, who was taken by an Indian family of the Sun class as a playmate for their son. The boys became friends, within days were inseparable. Then the Indian boy caught the measles from the French child. He died. It was decided that the French boy must be sacrificed in order that he continue as playmate to the Sun child in the after-life."

Madame Doucet cried out, her face a mask of sorrow. She rocked back and forth with her arms clasped over her chest as if she feared her heart would burst from her if she did not hold it in. Elise moved to lean over her, putting her arm around the woman's shoulders, though she felt helpless before such grief.

Pascal swore. St. Amant set down his wineglass with fingers that shook. "Something must be done. They must be rescued."

"Indeed," Pierre Broussard said. "Governor Perier has sent a dispatch to France entreating the crown and the West India Company for reinforcements to put down the uprising. In the meantime, he has called for volunteers to join the militia and sent the Sieur de Lery as an emissary to the Choctaws."

"The Choctaws?" Pascal demanded. "There was talk, before the attack, that they were to join with the Natchez against us."

"The rumors were true in part, I think. It was to be a massive bloodletting, one planned in secret councils through the past summer and carefully timed, with every chief receiving a bundle of reeds of equal number, one of which was to be withdrawn at every dawn until the day of the attack. The reeds of the Natchez were tampered with and so they fell on the French early. The Yazoos, who with the Tensas were allies of the Natchez, massacred the French at the small fort in their country also, and in New Orleans there was a revolt of the slaves that is said to have been a part of the conspiracy. But the Choctaws were infuriated that the Natchez acted to remove the element of surprise from their own raids and that they have since refused to share the booty from Fort Rosalie. So the Choctaws will in all likelihood ally themselves with the French against the Natchez. At least that is the purpose of de Lery's expedition."

"So we sent Indians to conquer Indians."

"It seems wise," Pierre said dryly. "It is doubtful that Perier will be able to put more than a few hundred men in the field,

and it is estimated that the Natchez have nearly a thousand warriors even without their allies. We need the Choctaws.''

''The Choctaws are not the equal of the Natchez,'' Pascal
said morosely.

''But there are more of them.''

There was a short silence broken only by the moaning of
Madame Doucet. She drew in a ragged breath, then, with a vast
effort, forced coherent words from her throat. ''Please, m'sieu,
have you been to the village of Natchez? Have you seen perhaps
a young woman with long blond hair and blue eyes in a sweet
face? And a boy of six years, a beautiful child, so husky, so
quick?''

Pierre shook his head. ''I am sorry, madame. I could not go
to the Natchez village, for though I lived with them a dozen
years and more and can call them by name, I am a Frenchman
and am looked on now as an enemy.''

Reynaud had been standing in the shadows as if setting himself apart from the conversation. Now he spoke. ''The revolt of
the slaves in New Orleans. It was serious?''

''It caused a great deal of fright but few casualties. It's left a
bad taste in the mouths of many, however. Our fine Governor
Perier, aghast that such a tragedy should happen during his pe-
riod in office and feeling himself surrounded by enemies, decided to use the incident to ensure that such an alliance of Indians
and slaves never occurs again. He first hanged several of the
ringleaders of the revolt, then he armed a contingent of slaves
and forced them to attack a village of perfectly harmless Chouachas. They put to death seven or eight of their number and
burned the village to the ground.''

''The fool,'' Reynaud said, his tone grating.

''Even so.''

The moans of Madame Doucet had turned to sobs. Elise
thought she had heard more than enough. Gently she urged the
older woman to her feet and led her away. It was a relief to leave
the room. She had also heard as much as she wanted to hear, as
much as she could bear for one evening.

She did not go into the dining room for dinner. Instead, she
made her way to the kitchen where she asked that a tray be
prepared for herself and Madame Doucet. Neither ate a great
deal. The older woman rambled, talking of happier days, of the
charming things her grandson had said and done, of the unruly
way his hair had grown and the tooth he had been going to lose,

speaking of him as of one dead. She worried about her daughter, of how she would endure being a slave, of her weakness caused by her injuries, of her spirit that might lead her to defy her Indian mistress. She was troubled that they might not have enough to eat, that they were cold or unprotected from the weather. When Elise tried to reason with her, saying how unlikely were her fears, she only nodded, then went on monotonously in the same vein. Finally Elise brought her a glass of warm milk laced with cognac. Soothed by the potent drink, worn out by her own fears, she slept at last.

So weary was Elise by then that she wanted nothing more than her own bed. Once there, however, she could not sleep. The words Pierre had spoken echoed in her mind, bringing to vivid life once more the day of the massacre and all that had happened afterward. She lay staring into the darkness, thinking of Reynaud as he had been that day in the woods when he had demanded that she share his bed furs, of him standing naked, bathed in cold rain, of the moonlight on his body as he rose from the bayou.

He was half Natchez, with half the blood of the killers of her friends and neighbors, the men who had struck them down in the mellow light of a cool fall morning and torn the scalps from their heads. He had stood listening to that recital of horrors this evening and his face had shown nothing. Not anger, not disgust, not pity—nothing.

What kind of man was he? This afternoon he had dared to try to explain away the torture of men, had actually compared the exploits in the wars of Europe and the Far East with this dastardly murder of her countrymen. It was sickening.

Yes, sickening. But Governor Perier, a man of breeding and birth, had turned armed slaves loose on a village of innocent people simply because they were of Indian blood and he had a point to make. Ah, God, what horrors men were capable of committing. Turning her face into the pillow, she lay still, trying not to think.

Reynaud did not come to bed. She heard the sounds she had come to recognize as the others going to their bedchambers, readying for bed. Perhaps he and his friend had required some time alone to conduct whatever business it was that brought Pierre—if there was any business at all, which she doubted. There was no way to guess how long they might sit over their wine and discussion. In any case, it did not matter. Resolutely she closed her eyes.

Her slumber was fitful, filled with dreams. Once she woke from a nightmare with her heart pounding and her hair damp with perspiration as if she had been running for miles. She could not quite catch the sense of the dream, nor did she try. She reached out her hand to touch the other side of the bed. It was still empty. She slept again.

When she awakened next, there was daylight in the room, seeping around the curtains with the pale yellow glow that meant that the sun had risen. Elise stretched, then remembered and turned her head. Reynaud lay beside her on his stomach with his head on one arm and the other resting, relaxed, on the mattress. She eased a little higher in the bed, pushing her pillow behind her head, and lay watching him.

His breathing was deep and even. His face was closed in, self-contained, its dark copper-bronze a startling contrast to the white of the embroidered pillowcase. There were fine lines at the corners of his eyes and deeper indentations at the corners of his mouth. His lashes lay thick and black, but somehow ragged in their different lengths, on his cheeks. His hair had loosened from its queue, the dark strands roughened, falling in a deep wave onto his temple. His muscles were relaxed so that the line of his arm and shoulder was smoother than normal.

Slowly she grew aware of the need to touch him. She wanted to trace his brows and the turn of his jaw with her finger, to smooth back his hair, and to lean over to press her lips to the pulse that throbbed in the column of his neck. She would like to push the coverlet aside and run her palm over his shoulder and down his spine, to the small of his back and lower to where the lean contours of his hips rose. The longing inside her was intense, coupled with a tingling fullness in her loins and a swelling in her breasts. She bit her bottom lip and curled her fingers one by one into her fist as if to prevent temptation.

How long had it been since she had done these things? She was not quite sure. He had only requested it of her twice since they had reached his home and even then had stopped her almost before she had begun. At first she had been relieved, but then she had begun to miss that closeness, to yearn for it. It was stupid of her. She had castigated herself, telling herself that it was the reaction of one of those daughters of joy that she had once suspected might have visited him here. It had done no good.

He stirred. Her heart lurched as if it would leap into her throat. She drew back as stealthily as possible and closed her eyes. She must not be caught hanging over him like some lovesick idiot. If he found her so, he would have every right to think she would welcome his advances. Just the thought of such a misunderstanding was enough to bring hectic color to her face. She lay quietly, fiercely concentrating on her breathing in the hope of making it fade.

Then came the rustle of the bedclothes, the creak of the mattress ropes as Reynaud sat up. He was still for a moment and she wondered if he were staring down at her. She realized abruptly that her nightgown was twisted around her, the neckline pulled awkwardly across her chest. So cool was the flesh of her left breast that she had a grim foreboding that it was exposed in its entirety. She dared not move, however.

Reynaud sat, looking down at her. She was so lovely with the flush of sleep on her cheeks, her slender white arms emerging from the lace sleeves of her gown, and the delicate mound of one breast, gently rounded and coral-rose-tipped, revealed where the neckline was awry. He inclined his head, irresistibly drawn to that sweet globe. Then, with neck-wrenching effect, he drew back. No. If she awoke with the sick terror in her eyes that he had seen there once before, he would never be able to forgive himself. He must wait. It was too important to do otherwise. And yet time was growing short.

He eased from the bed and gathered up his clothes. Moving to the door, he let himself out and closed it quietly behind him.

Elise heard him go and for some reason she felt like crying.

She could not sleep again. She got up and dressed in a gown of yellow-and-white-striped challis with a fichu and apron of lace-edged dimity and a small, matching cap to cover her hair. In the dining room she discovered that Reynaud and Pierre had gone riding and the others were not yet up. She drank a cup of chocolate and crumbled a roll in her plate; then, thinking Reynaud and his friend might return before she was finished, she accepted more fresh chocolate. Henri emerged, greeting her with a subdued air, but with every sign of pleasure. She managed to engage him in a discussion of the merits of the life of a trader and even won a smile or two from him, but his heart was not in it.

"What will you do when you reach Fort Saint Jean Baptiste?" she asked.

"I don't know," he burst out. "That's the problem. I have no family, nothing. I know no trade since I was apprenticed so short a time at the cooperage. What am I to do."

"There will be employment of some kind for you. Perhaps someone else will accept you as an apprentice."

"Maybe. I can think of no trade that I would like, though, and some I would hate."

"Such as?"

"Oh, the tanning of hides, for one."

"Not too pleasant," she agreed.

"It smells," he said with simple truth.

"What about as a cobbler or a baker?"

He shook his head. "I like to work out of doors; that much I discovered. If I could get to New Orleans, there would be more opportunities."

"Perhaps you can do that then," Elise said, smiling in an attempt to cheer him.

His expression did not lighten, however.

The direction of Henri's thoughts was caused by his assumption that Pierre was the friend for whom Reynaud had been waiting and that they could now proceed on their journey. After his meeting with Reynaud that she had witnessed, the trader had done nothing to disabuse anyone of the idea. She discovered when she went to visit Madame Doucet that she, too, was laboring under the same conception.

"I don't know if I can go on with the rest of you," the older woman announced.

Her voice was stronger this morning, but her color was still far too white and pasty. She was not alone. Reynaud's cousin Madeleine was with her. His housekeeper and Madame Doucet had struck up a firm friendship, perhaps because the first recognized in the older woman a weaker character, one who was not in any sense a rival. It may also have been, to give the woman her due, that she was drawn to Marie Doucet because she was in need of bolstering and had no self-consciousness about showing it.

"Not go on?" Elise asked as she closed the door behind her. "What do you mean?"

"I feel such a need to go to my poor daughter. She will be

distraught. She did love her son so and for him to die in such a terrible way, I—I fear for her!''

Elise watched as the older woman dabbed her eyes with her handkerchief, mopping up the tears that began to pour from her eyes. "I don't understand. Have you had more news?''

"Oh, Elise, *chère*, it came to me in the night. The child who was killed, it was my own precious sweeting, my grandson. The age is the same and he was such a beautiful child. I know he was chosen by the Sun woman to be her son's playmate. How could it be otherwise?''

"But you don't know; no one has said it.''

"Sometimes we know these things without being told. I feel it here, in my heart.'' She clasped her hand to her chest, then bowed her head to wipe her eyes once more.

Elise exchanged a glance with the housekeeper, who gave a slight shake of her head. Then she moved to sit beside the older woman on the bed, reaching to take one of her hands and holding it firmly in her own. "It may be; we cannot know for sure. But even if it is true, there is nothing you can do. You must go on. The best thing you could do for your daughter is to reach the authorities and urge them to go to the rescue of all the women. They will, anyway, I know, but if they can be hurried by even as much as a day, it may help.''

Madame Doucet blinked, wiped her nose, and looked at Elise. "You are so sensible, *ma chère*, so strong. One has always felt it in you, but never so greatly as now. How lovely it must be always to know what is best to be done, never to know fear. I have never been constructed so.''

Elise drew back a little, staring, but there was no sarcasm in the words. She forced a smile for this woman who had probably never felt more than a slight nervousness at the nearness of a man, something that could strike Elise with stark dread. "Things are not always as they seem. But forget me. You must turn your mind to what you may do among your acquaintances in New Orleans that may be of aid to your daughter and grandson.''

"Were you listening, Elise? He is dead, my beautiful boy, strangled in his tender youth. I hope he did not know what was to be done. I hope he was brave and did not cry. Oh, my boy, my boy, and my poor, poor daughter.''

Madeleine came forward with a cloth scented with lavender

water. Fearing that she was only making matters worse by her attempts to reason with the grieving woman, Elise left the house-keeper in charge and went away.

8

IT CAME TO Elise in the middle of the morning that in a few short days it would be Christmas. So much had happened that she had lost track of the normal march of time. The weather had been so mild, with pleasant days and nights barely cool enough for a fire. Now it was nearly upon them. Christmas. So amazing was the thought that she spoke it aloud as she sat drinking a small glass of tafia with Madame Doucet and Madeleine.

"Yes," Reynaud's cousin said. "It gives me great pleasure that Reynaud is here. He isn't always, though last year he came on Christmas Eve, bringing with him a priest of the Jesuits who was bound on a mission to the Caddo. The holy father gave us a beautiful midnight mass."

"And then," Madame Doucet said, her voice breaking, "It will be New Year's and Epiphany."

New Year's Day was the most festive holiday on the calendar. On the night before there was feasting, merriment, and toasts as the new year arrived; then, on the day itself, gifts were exchanged, with special ones for the children. Young men made visits to all the ladies of their acquaintance, bringing small presents of flowers and candy and always accepting refreshment from the steaming bowl of punch that stood ready. It was not unusual for a popular young man to stagger home, singing, in the dark. Epiphany was a day of visiting friends and relatives, with the roads thronged with carts and people on horseback and with much good food enjoyed by all.

Madeleine reached to pat the older woman's hand. "You must not think of it, *ma chère.*"

"How can I not? Last year we were so happy. I made a small stuffed horse for my little grandson with a mane of twisted yarn. He slept with it always. And my daughter and her husband and my own dear husband were together, and my slave women and I prepared such a meal as you never tasted, so delicious it was."

To give a new direction to her thoughts, Elise said, "I wonder where we will be this year, for New Year's and Epiphany, and even Christmas?"

"You do not expect to be here?" Madeleine asked with a lifted brow. Her manner toward Elise had warmed somewhat, but was still formal.

"I don't really know. We wait on Reynaud," she answered with a small shrug.

"All of you?"

Did the woman expect that she would stay behind? She must not be as much in Reynaud's confidence as Elise had assumed. Had no one told her of the situation? Did she not know why Elise was there, why they were all there? Elise found that it made a difference. What must Madeleine think of her intimacy with Reynaud? She could hardly be blamed for putting the worst construction upon it.

"Yes, certainly," she answered. But if she expected Madeleine to show any sign of relief or even acceptance, she was disappointed.

Just before noon there was some excitement. It was discovered that a panther that had been prowling near the house had carried off a sheep. A tracking party was immediately formed, with much calling of dogs and arguing about the benefits of mounts, as opposed to going on foot, in the swampland where the beast was sure to be heading. All the men joined in, with the exception of St. Amant, who preferred to remain behind reading in the library. He had found an edition of Procopius's *Anecdota*, he said, and could not bear to leave this marvelously scandalous account of the romantic triangle between the Roman emperor Justinian, his prostitute-queen Theodora, and his general Belisarius. So, with a great racket of shouting and baying hounds, the hunting party swept away from the house and quiet descended.

It was some hours later that Elise wandered into the library in search of something to occupy the time until dinner. St. Amant, sitting in a velvet armchair near the window, looked up and nodded at her entrance, then went on reading. She wandered along the shelves, scanning the titles and running her fingers over the leather spines with their embossed designs: thick, heavy tomes; thin ones; short and tall ones; in Greek, Latin, and even English, as well as French. Madeleine saw that they were kept well dusted, but there were a few with spots of mildew on the bindings from the damp climate. She smiled over a copy of Charles Perráult's collection of fairy tales, *Histoires ou contes du temps passé*, with its frontispiece subtitle, *"Contes de ma mère loye"*; it was so incongruous to think of Reynaud having it. She skipped over volumes of Racine and Voltaire to pick up a novel by the Comtesse de La Fayette.

She had turned to go when St. Amant clapped his book closed and got to his feet. He moved to place it on the shelf.

"Don't tell me the scandal has palled," Elise said.

"I've finished it, worst luck."

"Then you can regale me with the details over a cup of chocolate since I don't read Latin."

"That you read at all I find most interesting."

"I was taught as a child by my mother, who had learned from her father. It seems that my grandfather was a scholar who could not bear to see a mind untutored. I later went to convent school. The nuns taught a little history, a little study of the globes, but mostly embroidery, household tasks, music, attention to duty, and piety. They did not allow me to help in my spare time with their correspondence and accounts since I was already corrupted by instruction in those matters."

"That explains your fine grasp of the business of running your farm then." He moved ahead of her to open the door.

"I see that you are walking without a stick," she commented as she passed before him into the salon.

"Yes, my ankle is much better."

Elise put the book she carried down and excused herself, going in search of a servant to bring the chocolate. She looked around for Madeleine or Madame Doucet to invite them to join St. Amant and herself, but they were not to be seen. When she returned, she said, "We seem to be by ourselves. The other ladies must be lying down on their beds for a nap."

"It will be good for Madame Doucet."

Elise nodded. "She dwells too much upon the massacre, though I suppose there is no wondering at it."

"Perhaps we all do that."

"You lost someone perhaps? You never said—"

"No, not in the way you mean. And yet . . . Yes, there was a woman."

"She was killed?"

"I don't know, that's the terrible thing about it. I was not there. I could not reach her."

"I see."

He sent her a wry smile. "I doubt it. She was married to another man."

"Ah," she said after a moment. "Justinian, Theodora, and Belisarius."

"The explanation of my interest? I never thought of it that way. The situation is entirely different, of course."

"You loved her?"

He bowed his head in acknowledgment.

"It must be very painful for you, not knowing."

"Yes," he said, clasping his hands together so tightly that the fingers turned white. "To make matters worse, she was to have a child, my child."

"Oh."

What was there to say to a man when the woman he loved could be dead or a slave to savages who might not consider her awkward condition, a condition that must make any hardship doubly hard to bear?

St. Amant sent her a grim look. "But the most terrible thing of all is this: I find myself praying that neither of the men who escaped to New Orleans was her husband. I pray that he is dead and that she is a captive, for that will mean a slim hope for me where before there was none."

Their chocolate arrived then. When the serving girl had gone, Elise poured, then set a cup before St. Amant. She picked up her own and, keeping her lashes lowered in order to give him time to recover himself, sipped at the hot, sweet brew.

He came to his feet so abruptly that he brushed the table where his cup sat, splashing chocolate into the saucer. "Forgive me, Madame Laffont, for burdening you with my problem. I should not have spoken. I don't believe I feel like chocolate just now. You must excuse me."

"Certainly," Elise murmured. Then, when he was nearly at the door, she called out, "M'sieu St. Amant?"

"Yes, madame?"

"I—I'm sorry, so sorry."

As the door closed behind him, Elise set down her cup. She

should be shocked at the tale she had just been told, she supposed. But somehow she could not be. How much more human it made St. Amant to know that he had his own private torments. They all had them: Madame Doucet and her children; Henri with his fears of the future; and even Pascal with his fury over the loss of his merchandise and worries of starting anew. And herself, especially herself. They were all separate people with their own problems that must be solved, or endured, in their own separate ways. They were eternally alone within themselves; still, the recognition that their worries and heartaches were only a part of the natural condition of human beings made it less of an ordeal.

She picked up her book and opened it to the first page, but could not concentrate. Staring into space, she thought of how little it was possible to know other people and to understand them. Who could have guessed that St. Amant had been hiding such a secret behind his quiet air of a gentleman? There had been no sign. What secrets, then, did others hide? If she had known Vincent better, if she could have discovered what had made him so violent and brutish, could she have changed him? If she knew what Madeleine thought, could she sympathize with her? Could she calm her fears and reassure her so that Reynaud's cousin accepted her? If she looked at the world from Madame Doucet's point of view, tried to feel her sorrow and fear, would she be more tolerant of her incessant moaning and tears and alarms? If she sought the reasons behind Reynaud's forbearance and tried to understand the workings of his heart and mind, could she multiply her trust to the point where she might give herself to him?

It seemed possible, in a distant way, at that moment. But an interest in her fellow human beings was a novel thing for Elise. So much concern looked to be time consuming and perhaps even a drain on her own emotions. She was not certain she was capable of sustaining it. Or if it would be a good idea, even if she could.

The day wore on. The men returned in a great swirling of dogs and dust without a trophy to display, though with a fine plan for setting a trap for the panther with a tethered sheep in a day or two. The men disappeared around the side of the house to put away the dogs. The sun began to drop down in the sky, turning the low-lying clouds to swaths of lavender and rose. The weather had been so warm that there was a shrilling of frogs

coming from the bayou, a plaintive sound on the cool softness
of the air. A moist wind from the south rustled the few leaves
remaining on the trees. The delicious smell of baking ham, coming from the outdoor kitchen, perfumed the air. Elise stepped
out onto the loggia to watch the arrival of the men and stood for
a time, breathing deeply, enjoying the gentle feel of the air on
her skin and steeping in a tenuous peace. What a lovely place
this was, the house Reynaud had built. She had come perilously
close in the last few days to loving it for its beauty and serenity,
for the imagined safety of its seclusion.

As she leaned on the railing, she heard a door slam somewhere. Moments later, she saw Reynaud and Pierre walking
along the track in the direction of the bayou with lengths of
toweling thrown over their shoulders. It made sense that Pierre,
living so long among the Natchez, would have the same habit
of bathing as Reynaud. She watched them, two men of excellent
physical condition and the upright bearing instilled by the Indians. They swung their legs in ground-covering strides, moving
in perfect coordination without wasted motion. Their shoulders
were wide, tapering to narrow hips. Their hair, drawn back and
caught by thongs, shone with health and vigor, glinting in the
last of the sunlight. They were talking quietly, earnestly, making
swift gestures of the kind she had noticed between them the night
before. It was some form of sign language, she supposed, one
they were scarcely aware of using.

For so long she had thought of men, with few exceptions, as
cruel, overbearing, conniving, undependable creatures concerned only with their own ravening appetites. They had seemed
ugly to her, with ungainly bodies affixed with obscene append-
ages. It came as something of a shock to find that she could
enjoy watching the two before her. They seemed unusual in that
moment, touched with a kind of heroic splendor. It was only as
she realized that she had begun to undress them mentally that
she gasped, swung her back to them, and, picking up her skirts,
hurried into the house.

She was in her bedchamber when Pierre returned. She heard
Madeleine scolding him about the mud he had tracked in on his
shoes; heard, too, his laughing apologies; heard the woman ask
about Reynaud only to be told that he was still at the bayou but
would be along shortly. Their voices ceased and the door of the
bedchamber alloted to Pierre slammed shut.

Elise got to her feet and moved into the salon. It was empty once more. She walked out onto the loggia and looked in the direction of the bayou. There was no sign of Reynaud. At the head of the stairs that led to the ground, she paused. It was a beautiful evening, the last there might be for some time if the weather changed. Perhaps she would stroll a little. She had been in the house all day and felt the need of exercise. If she went toward the bayou, she might meet Reynaud. Trailing her hand down the handrail, she descended the stairs with slow, idle steps.

The sun was dropping behind the trees as she left the cart track and started down the winding path that led to the bayou. The light was dim beneath the high cypresses with their drapings of gray Capuchin's beard and she strained her eyes looking ahead of her for some sign of Reynaud. With a little shiver, she thought of the panther they had been tracking. The men had said it would not come again for several days, not after its meal of mutton. She was by no means certain she wanted to rely on their word.

It was possible that she had missed Reynaud, that he had left the bayou close behind Pierre. Perhaps he had not come into the house, but had rounded it instead to attend to some chore among the outbuildings. If she walked on down to the water's edge to see, then she would be sure, but she might also blunder upon him while he was bathing. She had done that once before by accident and he had thought nothing of it. If it happened again, he could be forgiven for thinking that, this time, it was on purpose.

She came to a halt in indecision. Was that likely or was it the prompting of her own guilty conscience? Of course she had no real desire to see him naked—that brief vision earlier had been nothing more than a mental misalignment with no meaning—and he should understand that well enough. The urge to turn back was strong, but, having come this far, it seemed foolish not to go on. Anyway, even if he was still there, she could make certain that he did not see her, couldn't she?

He was there.

He swam up and down, his long arms cleaving the water, his powerful body driving through the sluggish current dark with silt and the constant dripping of tree sap. At the farthest limits of each end of the wide pool made by the bend of the bayou, he turned, traversing the width again and again. There was something dogged about his efforts as if he meant to use the last ounce of his strength, tiring himself completely. His hair, slicked back with water from his forehead, trailed around his shoulders. His face was stern, uncompromising. In his turns, she caught a glimpse of his long length and knew that somewhere on the bank were his clothes, though she stood so far back in the woods that she could not see them.

She backed away, turning slowly. Dry leaves lay in a thick brown coating over the forest floor, drifting into the dim pathway, and she placed her feet with the utmost care to prevent the crunch of them underfoot or perhaps the snapping of twigs hidden under them. She breathed a sigh of relief when she passed behind a large tree that hid her from the bayou, but did not relax her vigilance. With her head down, she picked her way, increasing her pace only when she thought she was half the distance back to the track and well out of hearing.

''Where are you going?''

Her head snapped up. She saw the pulled-back hair, the dark skin, the tattoos. In some recess of her mind she knew him, yet for that instant shock and fear ruled her. Her control broke, and whirling from the man she had been avoiding, the last one she expected to see, a man in the guise of a terrible enemy, she ran.

Surprise held him immobile for an instant, then he came thudding behind her, catching her in a few strides. She tripped, breaking his grasp, then stumbled headlong to fall, rolling in the leaves. Instantly he was beside her. His hands were hard, rough as he pulled her around to face him. There was a frown of concern between his gray eyes as he glanced over her, searching for injury. With gritted teeth, she struck out at him, catching him in the mouth, though he turned his head at the last moment. She felt his lip split under her knuckles and suddenly she felt sick. With a gasping cry, she flung herself into his arms.

A soft sound like a grunt left him as he lost balance, toppling to the side under her unexpected assault. He did not try to catch himself, but held her to him, dragging her across him to lie upon his chest. She buried her face in the hollow of his throat, breathing in his freshness, feeling his still-wet skin warm under her cheek, sensing the water that beaded him soaking into the bodice of her gown. By slow degrees, the thudding of her heart eased. She knew she should get up, but there was something so right in her position that she could not bring herself to move. And then she became aware that he was wearing his breeches. He had not only circled around to scare her to death, but he had had the leisure to preserve his modesty as well.

She pushed against him, half rising, though the grasp of his hands on her arms prevented her from going too far. With a martial light in her eyes, she demanded, "Where did you come from?"

"You know very well."

"I wasn't spying on you, if that's what you think!"

"Then why are you blushing?"

"I'm not!" she cried. "I'm furious because you sneaked around like the savage you are and tried to frighten me out of my skin!"

"And very nearly succeeded."

"You did not. I was only—"

"Embarrassed?"

"Yes, if you must know. I was coming to meet you."

"I'm touched."

Stung by his irony, she tried to wrest herself free. "You're . . . going to be hard, if you don't let me go."

"How interesting," he said, a smile curving his mouth as he surveyed her tousled hair and the hectic rose color that gave such a luminous look to her skin. "Is it a threat or a promise?"

"Neither," she answered, her tone a little breathless as she heard the soft note in his voice, saw the slumberous expression in his gray eyes.

"Kiss me, Elise."

"No."

She tried to draw back against the increasing pressure of his hold, but he would not let her. "Yes."

She was drawn nearer, harder upon him. Her gaze went to the firm contours of his mouth. She could not look away. She tried to shake her head in negation, but as she was brought closer the movement made her lips brush his. That brief, sensitive contact sent a tingling along her nerves that she felt in the lowest reaches of her body. The resistance went out of her muscles. She made a soft sound in her throat that might have been of protest or pleasure as she allowed her mouth to conform to his, felt the curves of her breasts melt into the firmness of his chest. By degrees, she increased the pressure until, suddenly, he winced.

His lip was cut. Remorse gathered with tenderness inside her and she drew back; then, with the tip of her tongue, she soothed that small injury, at the same time moving her mouth back and forth upon his. His lips parted and she followed that lead blindly, tasting the moist sweetness of their underside, the smooth edges of his teeth, touching with hesitant shyness the grainy firmness of his tongue. It moved with gentle twining about hers, then his grasp upon her arms tightened and his tongue stopped.

He had remembered that he must be passive.

Disappointment flooded her, rising to her brain with the intensity caused by weeks of unknowing frustration. She lifted her head, staring down at him. She moistened her lips. "If I asked you, Reynaud, to kiss me—and touch me—just a little—only touch—would you?"

He watched her, his breathing deep. Suspended inside himself with the ache of longing, he, too, felt a desperate need to banish the trace of fear he sensed in her, to give her delight and to find in her slender body and mind his own fierce joy. Finally he said, "If this is a trick, I warn you it's a dangerous one."

"No, no," she murmured, shaking her head, hurt in some strange way by the wariness in his eyes.

"Then I will try. More than that I can't promise."

Once more she lowered her head, but even as their mouths flowed together, his arms crossed behind her back, holding her to him. His hard muscles contracted as he raised himself and turned, placing her gently on her back among the leaves of yellow and gold, red and dry, crackling brown. His hard hand cradled her cheek, his thumb brushing the corner of her mouth as he kissed her chin, the tip of her nose, her forehead. His fingers trailed down the gentle turn of her jaw to the curve of her neck, slipping behind her head where he pushed off her muslin cap and began to hunt for the pins that held the knot of her hair.

"Wait," she whispered in sudden doubt, "this is a mistake."

"No, no," he said, his breath warm on her mouth. "It's only an experiment. If I hurt you, or you are afraid, only tell me."

Her hair loosened as he dropped her pins among the leaves. That freedom from confinement, or perhaps it was his words, affected her with an odd expansion of the spirit. She lifted her hand to his side, spreading the palm on his warm skin and sliding it upward to his neck.

"Beautiful, beautiful," he said as he drew the length of her hair over her shoulder, spreading it so that its honey-brown strands caught the last prismatic shimmering of the twilight. His mouth took hers once more, his tongue stroking the sensitive line where her lips came together until she opened for him, entering to test the fragile inner surface and join with hers in a sinuous twining. Rich and warm was the gratification that welled inside her. With a small, incoherent murmur, she pushed her fingers into the wet, thick vitality of his hair as she moved her lips upon his. She offered her mouth, desire and vulnerability warring in her mind even as she felt a poignant craving for deeper penetration.

She shivered a little as his fingers touched her throat, gliding lower to the neckline of her gown, lingering delicately on the soft swell of her breast just beneath the edge of her fichu. Her breathing quickened as he followed the pointed bodice, bending his head to trace his path with the smooth heat of his lips. He found the fichu's knot and unraveled it with dexterity, spreading the ends to expose the deep décolletage of her gown and the pale rise of her bosom. With closed eyes, he pressed his face to her, inhaling her scent, tasting her skin with the hot tip of his tongue.

Sweet, sweet, as potent as strong wine was the excitement that raced in her veins. Intoxicating. Her limbs were boneless, weightless, and she could not think for the languor that had invaded her brain. She must be drunk or mad to be so affected. Bemused, bewitched with an ancient magic, she allowed him to turn her against him, to release the row of tiny buttons that fastened her gown in the back, to untie her stays and spread them wide. His breath wafted warmly across her shoulder as he drew the sleeve of her gown slowly downward. Her skin glowed with internal heat, pliant, firm, and her body, slipping the bonds of her will, rose slightly toward him as he uncovered one breast. It swelled toward his mouth with arousal, and as he captured the throbbing peak, she caught her breath with the sudden, aching pleasure of it.

She hardly knew when he reached to draw up the hem of her skirt. She felt the draft of cool air and then the firm clasp of his hand upon the knee of her drawn-up leg smoothing the weave of her stocking, probing at the ribboned knot of her garter. He flicked off first one shoe and then the other, kicking them aside.

Disheveled, luminous with desire, she lay with half-closed eyes and waited for what he would do next. Still, it shocked her, that bunching of her petticoats, that daring plundering beneath them as he slid his fingers between her white and trembling thighs. He rested them there, gently squeezing, kneading, and grazing the tender flesh with his thumb. His mouth, his tongue at her breast quieted her alarm with soft circling, massaging, exquisite adhesion. When his hand crept higher, her lashes quivered, but she moved slightly, involuntarily, in accommodation.

She heard the swift inward rush of his breath, felt suddenly the hard pound of his heart as he lay against her. The knowledge that he was not as controlled as he would like to appear to be made her own pulse leap. This was pure arousal, a heated joy totally without the malicious satisfaction she once had known. She lifted the arm that lay beneath him and pressed it to his back, spreading her fingers wide as she felt, in the deepest depths of her, an unfurling, like the opening of a woodland fern in spring.

She wore no undergarment. His broad hand rested on the soft and springy fleece of her, spanning the gentle mound it covered, giving her its warmth and weight. His hand smoothed over her hip to the firm curve underneath, gathering it, holding her with increasing tightness. With quickening senses, she felt the rigid length and heat of him against her other thigh. His eyes were squeezed shut. A tremor ran over his skin. He lifted his head, relaxing as if with an effort.

"Shall I stop?"

It was a moment before she could force words through her throat. "It might be best."

"Oh, without doubt, but is it what you want?"

Her heart was beating so loudly she thought it a miracle he did not hear it and her body was enwrapped in flames. Her eyes lustrous, liquid with passion and pity for his madness, she said, "It isn't what I want."

"Nor I," he whispered as he uncovered her other breast and lowered his gaze to its white-and-coral splendor. "Nor I."

Her need was a vibrant pressure in her throat, her breasts, her thighs. Her skin tingled, rising in gooseflesh as he brought his hand back to the flat of her abdomen. His fingers trailed lower, tangling in the fine curls and slipping into the hollow at the apex of her legs. A spasm tightened the tendons of her thighs, making her clench them on his hand. Gently he moved his palm against her until the tension flowed away. He cupped his hand over her then, pressing firmly, intently, steadily invading. Once more internal muscles closed upon him, then eased, allowing entry.

Never had she known anything except stabbing violation or rough caresses that caused more pain than pleasure in her unaroused state. This careful exploration of her senses was entranc-

ing, a revelation. Rapture, vivid and beguiling, rose inside her.
As she felt the wet and lovely roughness of his tongue on her
breast once more, she moaned and turned her face into her arm.

His hand moved in slow rhythm, its firm heel in direct contact
with the most sensitive area of her body. Her hips lifted in gentle
counterpoint. Waves of pleasure licked over her. Captivated by
the incredible sweetness of it, she soared in voluptuous wonder.

It caught her, the sudden glory, in such surprise that it brought
a strangled cry to her lips. He released her breast to seek her
lips and she pressed her mouth, slanting, searching, to his, tasting the faint salt of his blood, lost in the wondrous rapture of
the senses. She thrust her full breasts against him, wanting to be
held tightly, needing his hardness, his power.

He released her after a moment, but only long enough to strip
off his breeches. He levered himself above her, placing his thigh
between hers, rolling so that she was beneath him. The heated
and pulsating force of him rested against her, gently probing.

"Elise, *ma chère*?"

Her face was flushed with the same delicate color that made
her breasts an opalescent rose and dark coral. She refused to
look at him, refused to think, could not in the lovely ravishment
that held her. She understood the demand and the plea in his
voice, however. Understood and felt its vibration deep within.
There were more things in the world to fear than this, many
more. Above her head the dark limbs of the trees made a fragile
cross-hatching against the gray porcelain bowl of the winter sky.
Warm beside this man, she felt none of its chill, none of its
terror.

"Please," she said.

He might not have heard if he had not been waiting. Still,
faint though it was, he needed no more. With straining sinews
and delicate perception, he eased into her liquid warmth. Her
breath of wonder fanned his cheek. She made a soft sound, then
pressed herself to him with her hands clutching his shoulders
and trembling arms, gripping tighter and tighter, rubbing, grasping, urging him to the turbulent vigor that must surely bring the
return of glory and an ultimate surcease.

"Ah, love," he said the words thick, ragged, shadowed with
laughter, "I should not have swum so long."

He plunged into her as if unable to resist any longer that
perilous temptation. Stalwart, powerful, he held her, thrusting
past old memories, banishing them and bringing new peace,

seeking and finding joy. The surcease, golden and beckoning, touched them. It came.

It was completely dark by the time they reached the house. Candlelight glowed from the windows, casting yellow beams into the night to welcome them. They did not hurry, but strolled with their arms about each other, stopping often to kiss with unappeased hunger. Elise rested her head against Reynaud's shoulder, though now and then she turned to peer into the encroaching blackness of the woods.

"What are you looking for? The panther?"

"Nothing really, only to see if there is anything to be afraid of."

"You think there might be?"

"Not as long as you are here," she answered and was disturbed to discover how true those impulsive words were. She went on, her tone tentative. "It seems strange to have nothing to fear."

"Nothing?"

"At least not at this moment."

"There will be other times, other things. We need fear to encourage caution."

"I don't want to be cautious!" she said with sudden heat.

He smiled down at her. "I hope that in one thing you won't be."

She reached up to draw his mouth down to hers. It was some time before they walked on.

There was only Madeleine and Henri in the salon when they stepped inside it. Reynaud's cousin looked up and saw their rumpled state. Her mouth tightened, but she said nothing, only transferring her gaze to a point just above their heads as she spoke.

"Dinner will be served in half an hour."

"We will take it in our bedchamber." Reynaud's voice was calm, faintly mocking.

The woman lifted her brows. "If you wish it."

"We do. We will now bid you good night. Make our excuses to the others, if you please."

"I will do that."

"Elise?" he prompted.

"Good night," she said, inclining her head to Madeleine and nodding with a quick smile at Henri.

Without waiting for a reply, they whisked themselves from

the room and into the bedchamber they had shared without intimacy until this moment. Quietly they closed the door behind them.

The candles had been lighted in the crystal-and-gilt candelabra on the mantel. Reynaud moved to take a taper from one, using it to light those on the dressing table. Elise turned to face him, suddenly ill at ease with him here in the house in the brightness of the candlelight. A momentary shame for the fervor of her response to him made her movements stiff.

The candle flames were reflected in his eyes as he smiled at her. "I wish I had thought to refuse dinner."

"What?"

"I would like to undress you now, this minute, and begin all over again."

The words seemed to touch some vulnerable place just under her heart. "Would you?"

"I am like a man long thirsty; I can never have enough of you."

When had she last thought of him as unfeeling, without emotion? The idea seemed laughable now. A slow smile curved her mouth. "I'm as bland as water, am I?"

"As necessary."

She heaved a mock sigh. "It is too bad."

He tilted his head, lifting a questioning brow.

"That you didn't refuse dinner, of course!"

He reached her in a bounding stride and picked her up, turning and swinging her so that her skirts flew out around them. Their mouths met as his momentum slowed and finally he set her on her feet.

He bent his neck to rest his forehead on hers. "Ah, but perhaps it's as well. We had better keep up our strength."

"Yes," she murmured, "especially you, after all that swimming."

"Witch," he said, laughing. "It was your fault, you know."

"Mine?" She tried to draw back in umbrage, but he would not let her.

"How else was I to keep a hold on myself unless I was exhausted when I fell into bed with you?"

She played with the opening of his shirt, slipping her fingers inside and rubbing their backs over the smooth hardness of his chest. "Well, in that case—"

He caught her questing hand, lifting it to his lips. "Behave if you want to eat."

"Reynaud?"

"Yes, love?"

She felt the vibration of the word in his chest and she almost let the question forming in her mind go unspoken. She looked up at him, the rust flecks in her amber-brown eyes brilliant. She looked down again. "Would you really have left us behind if I had not agreed to your bargain?"

"The others possibly, never you."

"You would have left them to die?"

Her body stiffened by degrees. Feeling it, his hold tightened. "They would have been no worse off than if I had never seen them. By my offices they escaped; why could they not have done the same thing alone?"

"Some tried and failed, like the four men killed on the river. But you well know that if they had gone on alone, I would have been with them."

"Not if I had kidnapped you."

"You would have done that?"

"Without a qualm, rather than let you risk the mercy of Pascal, who might well have abandoned you if you became a burden, or rather than see you become a slave to someone else if the attempt failed."

"You would have brought me here by force—or perhaps you thought to enslave me yourself at the village of the Natchez?"

He frowned at her rising tone, but answered without evasion. "The village would have done. Except for our bargain and my theft of you and the others who were enemies of the Natchez, I had no need to escape."

"But you said . . . I thought you were going to the Natchitoches country anyway."

He shrugged. "There was no urgency."

She pushed away from him and was momentarily surprised when he let her go. She swung away. "I can't believe what you are saying. You would actually have made me your slave?"

"The idea had a certain appeal."

"I'm sure!" she said with a flashing glance over her shoulder. "But what of Madame Doucet? If I would have been a liability to Pascal and the others, how much more would she have been? Would you have taken her, too?"

"Can you honestly say that she is better here than with her

daughter and grandson? Are you sure her tasks as a slave would have been any more draining on her physical strength than the overland journey here?''

"I couldn't say, never having been a slave," she answered harshly. "But to think that you would abandon your own countrymen—Henri, St. Amant, Pascal—sickens me."

He answered with deliberate quietness. "This is the wilderness. Men are expected to be able to take care of themselves and those who depend on them. Those who can't do that have no business here. As for the men, they came with me, not out of despair at their own chances, but because they recognized that I could give them a better one."

There was a certain truth to his argument. She moved to the candle, cupping her hands around the flame to warm them against the chill that had begun to creep along her veins. "You may be right, I don't know. Still, what of me? If you could so easily have taken me, why the effort of rowing across the river? Why make the journey at all?"

"I had no desire to humble your pride or to have you set yourself forever in opposition to me for possessing you by force."

"Are you sure? I had insulted you."

"And intrigued me with your complexity. You still do."

"How marvelous for you that it wasn't a wasted trip."

Ignoring her brittle sarcasm, he said softly, "And for you."

She turned, her eyes brilliant with accusation. He came toward her with lithe steps, taking her hands and resting them against his chest. When she did not resist, he drew her into his arms.

"Why do this to yourself, *ma chère*?" he said against her hair. "Is it guilt that you gave yourself to me? Do you despise me because I urged your surrender? If it is neither of these, what does the rest matter? I did bring the others here with you. They are alive and well because of you. It is useless to talk of what might have been unless you are content to let doubt rule your life as surely as fear."

She drew back to look up at him with lingering anger on her face. "Must you be so reasonable?"

"Forgive me. It's only my nature."

She sighed, laying her cheek against his chin and closing her eyes. He rocked her gently. Presently she started to speak, stopped, then went on anyway. "What of Fort Saint Jean Baptiste, what of when we get there?"

"We will talk about it soon, in a day or two, when Pierre goes."

She gave a slow nod. The answer told her little, but still she was satisfied. She did not want to think of leaving this place, but neither was she anxious at this moment to delve too deeply into her own desires, her own wishes. They were far too confused.

9

T HE BLOWS ON the door were thunderous in the morning
quiet. They jerked Elise awake and she sat straight up in
the bed. Reynaud, alert, grim, already had his feet on the floor
when the panel burst open and the men poured into the room.

Elise's nightgown had been discarded the night before. She
snatched the sheet and comforter up to cover herself, embarrassed anger rising in her eyes as she stared at Pascal, St. Amant,
and Henri.

"What the devil do you mean by this?" The rage in Reynaud's voice was dangerously quiet.

"You bastard, you half-breed bastard!" Pascal shouted,
shaking a fist. "I could kill you with my bare hands!"

"And I!" St. Amant's face was stern.

Elise stared from one to the other, her gaze coming to rest on
Henri's flushed features and clenched hands, seeing their outrage with a sinking feeling inside. Her first thought was to wonder how they could know. Then it came to her that they could
not, that they considered her fall from virtue assured long before. It was something more serious than the long hours of the
night she had spent locked in passion with Reynaud that had
incensed them.

It had turned colder. Their breaths fogged in the chill air of
the room. Reynaud moved to put on his breeches, then stepped
to the fireplace where he picked up a tinder box and prepared to
kindle the wood left stacked ready to hand. He spoke over his
shoulder.

"If one of you could tell me to what I owe the honor of this dawn visit, it might help me to understand your—displeasure?"

"We've found you out."

"Indeed?"

"We know, because we heard it from your friend, that this house sits less than ten leagues from Fort Saint Jean Baptiste. Ten leagues! That's little more than a good day's journey for us all, less without the women."

There was a movement at the door. Pierre, holding a cup of chocolate as if he had been at the breakfast table, stepped into view. I'm sorry, Reynaud, *mon ami*. I didn't know it was a secret."

"You kept us cooped up here like geese in a pen," Pascal went on. "We could have been at the fort long ago, even in New Orleans by now. Why did you do it? Damn you, why?"

The words were echoed by St. Amant and even by Henri. The younger boy looked at Elise, then quickly away again while the color in his face spread to the tops of his ears.

"Why do you think?"

"I think the reason is right there in bed with you."

"We believe," St. Amant said, "that it was Madame Laffont you were keeping with you; that the rest of us were included willy-nilly."

Elise sat gazing at Reynaud's broad back. Was it true? Had he deliberately misled them? If so, it was not for the sake of enjoying her favors a while longer, as the others seemed to think, but for the express purpose of seducing her to gain those favors at all. She waited for him to deny the accusation. She waited in vain.

The fire caught, crackling as it flared up the chimney, filling the room with the smell of the pine kindling and fresh burning oak. Reynaud turned and set his hands on his hips. "I gave you the option of going on."

St. Amant stepped forward. "But you left us completely in the dark about the distance we must travel because you knew Elise, Madame Laffont, would have gone with us if we had set out. No, you wanted us all here and saw to it that we came. You kept us kicking our heels like fools, dependent on your hospitality while you dallied longer with the woman you had forced to share your bed. By your ruse you had condemned us before our friends as heartless wretches careless of the tragedy at Fort Rosalie and the feelings of those who must want news from there, as sybarites lounging here while everyone thinks we surely perished with our neighbors.''

''No, no, for the last at least I refuse responsibility. I told Commandant St. Denis that all of you were very much alive and were recuperating here with me from your ordeal.''

''You told—'' Pascal began, then drew a deep breath to calm himself before rapping out, ''When?''

''The afternoon of our arrival here I rode to the fort on a fast horse and returned by midafternoon of the next day.'' His tone grave, Reynaud went on to explain. ''It was necessary, you see, to provide Elise with something to wear and I know well a lady there who is near her size, one who enjoys a considerable wardrobe.''

As the magnitude of the perfidy of the half-breed struck them, they were stunned into silence. It lasted only a moment before Pascal began to curse and St. Amant's eyes narrowed to a hard glitter.

Pierre looked from Reynaud to Elise, his gaze lingering with interest on her pale face and white shoulders, on the flowing mane of her honey-brown hair, which spilled over the covers around her. The trader turned to Reynaud, lifting a brow, smiling a little as he wagged his head back and forth in comic disbelief at the predicament of his friend. Reynaud, scowling, merely shrugged.

''Is it true?'' Elise demanded, finding her voice before the others. ''We could have reached the fort in the Natchitoches in a matter of hours if you had loaned us horses and set us on our way?''

There was pain in his eyes as Reynaud looked at her; still, he made no attempt to evade her question. ''It's true.''

Henri had stood, rigid, staring from Elise to Reynaud with as much adolescent jealousy and disillusionment as anger over what had been done. Now he burst into speech. *''Mon D-Dieu,* if no one else will p-punish this b-blackguard, then I w-will!''

St. Amant put his forearm out to block the boy's way. ''Softly, softly. Let us hear this out.''

Elise looked only at Reynaud as if they had not spoken. ''But you must have known we would discover it?''

''Only when it no longer mattered, at least to you.''

''Such as after last evening?''

He made a swift, repudiating gesture. ''No. In a few days, another week.''

When he had tired of her, Elise thought as she stared at him with features turned to stone. He had expected the pleasure of having her to last no longer than that. When it had gone, it would no longer matter what she thought, what any of them thought.

Pascal made a growling sound in his throat. "I say we take it out of his hide."

"No violence before I've finished breakfast, I beg you," Pierre said, waving his cup. "I cannot allow it."

It was a reminder that Reynaud was not without someone to come to his aid, should they decide to trounce him together.

"There is no point," St. Amant agreed. "All that we require is that he take us at once, by the fastest possible means, to our destination."

"You may take yourselves, with my compliments," Reynaud answered, inclining his head.

"You refuse—"

"As you pointed out, it's only ten leagues. It happens there is a cart track right up to the gate of the fort."

"Let me guess," Pascal said with heavy, swaggering sarcasm. "You lied about the road out there, too."

"I'm surprised you didn't think to follow it while out hunting."

"We did, for a way. You told us it only went to the edge of your land. Does that mean your land extends to the fort?"

Reynaud smiled. "Not quite."

"We will leave within the hour," St. Amant said and, with scant civility, bowed and left the room.

Henri began to follow the older man, then stopped and swung back. "M-madame Laffont, y-you will go with us?"

"Yes, I will go."

Pierre stood aside as the others tramped out, then retreated also, his blond lashes tactfully veiling his expression as he closed the door. Elise and Reynaud were left alone in a quiet broken only by the crackle and hiss of the fire. Elise slid from the bed and went to the wardrobe, where she took out her old habit. Flinging it onto the bed, she began to search for her own petticoat and shift.

Reynaud watched her. Torn by the need to explain and an equal need to have her understand his motives without explanation, he allowed himself to be distracted by the pearly sheen of the morning light on the flesh of her hip and thigh, the long slender line of her back as it joined her narrow waist. He could still feel her softness imprinted on his flesh, taste her essence in his mouth. What he would not give to be able to reach out and hold her, to force her to stay. Reason was not nearly so certain a way to keep her with him.

"Elise, listen to me."

She glanced at him, seeing in that brief moment the broad width of his chest with its dark and mysterious lines of tattooing highlighted with burnished copper, the sculptured columns of his legs in his doeskin breeches outlined by the orange yellow glow of the firelight behind him. She looked away again, her face shuttered as she pulled down the shift she had drawn over her head and stepped into her petticoat.

The shrill rasp of a scream cut through the cold air. Elise started before she realized that it was Madame Doucet. Had the older woman seen yet another Indian? That was the only thing that seemed to cause her such horror.

Then came a pounding on the door. It was Pierre's voice that called. "Reynaud, you had better come out here!"

They gathered on the loggia, Elise still tugging at the habit she had donned so hastily. Behind them in the salon could be heard the sobs of Madame Doucet and the soft murmurs of Madeleine. No one took any notice of them. This time the alarm was real. The house was encircled by Natchez warriors: tall, massive men, their faces painted with white and yellow ochre and with leather-and-fur capes swinging from their shoulders. They carried muskets and bows and arrows, but held them at their sides, all in the same stiff position.

Coming straight toward the steps, marching in single file, were ten more warriors, each wearing the crown of swan feathers that marked the men of the Sun class. The man in the lead carried a calumet, holding the great pipe of peace, some four and a half feet long, out at arm's length. A chill morning breeze caught the white eagle feathers with black tips, which hung in a spread fan between the long stem and the bowl, and the brilliance of the rising sun shone on the green iridescence of the duck-neck plumage with which the stem was decorated.

Elise, standing beside Reynaud, heard him give rapid and detailed instructions in an undertone to Pierre concerning the gifts that must be presented on this occasion and the feast of welcome that must be held. The next moment, the procession stopped and the calumet was solemnly presented. With deliberation, Reynaud detached himself from the others and moved down the flight of steps to accept the pipe. There was an exchange of compliments in the swift-moving Natchez tongue.

The Indians, though they were the finest warriors of the Natchez, were not a war party but members of a ceremonial procession, a delegation. They were here, it appeared, to make a request of Reynaud. It also appeared that his answer would have to please them or the delegation might well become a war party.

"It occurs to me," St. Amant said softly, his tone dryly reflective, "that it must have been in truth a Tensas warrior following us across the woodlands, no figment of Madame Doucet's overwrought imagination."

Pascal cursed, but quietly enough not to be heard by their Indian guests. It was an instant longer before Elise remembered. The Indian Madame Doucet had seen that first time, soon after they had crossed the Mississippi, had been identified as being of the Tensas tribe, allies of the Natchez. It would seem that there had never been a time in their travels when they had not been under surveillance. What did it mean? Had Reynaud betrayed them? Had he let them think he was helping them escape, knowing all the time that they were being followed? Or had they been kept in view not because of their importance as possible hostages, but because of the prominence of the half-breed? There was no way of knowing.

"Suppose," Elise said in quiet tones, "the Natchez have come to ask for us?"

"Don't think of it," St. Amant said. "Just don't think of it."

It proved to be excellent advice in the hours that followed.

Plans for departure were postponed by common consent. There was no guarantee that they would be allowed to leave, and even if they were, to go might be considered an act of cowardice, one that would arouse the contempt and the hunting instincts of the Natchez. It might also be looked upon as an insult, which could have the same results. No one cared to run a footrace with the Indians all the way to Fort Saint Jean Baptiste.

Reynaud's servants were thrown into a frenzy of preparation for the feast. As they ran here and there, with a harried Madeleine directing them while consulting a closely written list of food and drink, it seemed churlish not to offer to help. Elise was soon up to her elbows in flour as she oversaw the making of fifty loaves of bread in the outdoor oven. At the same time, as she moved in and out of the kitchen, she kept an eye on the young girl who was basting the whole pig roasting on a spit in the fireplace and the boy who was stirring the huge black pot of deer stew and the even bigger one of sagamite. It was good to stay busy. When she slowed, her thoughts closed in upon her. They were not comfortable ones.

Finally the gargantuan meal was ready. It was served on enormous wooden platters that were set in a circle on the ground around a leaping fire. The eldest of the delegation gave a long speech that was listened to with respect. When he sat down, a signal was given and the eating began. Each man served himself with his knife, placing his selection in a small wooden or clay bowl, sometimes dipping the gravy and beans and corn of the sagamite into it with a horn spoon. For a beverage there was strong tafia, made from fermented molasses flavored with spices. Before many minutes had passed, the voices of the Indians grew noisy and their laughter came with greater frequency.

Elise watched from a window, carefully holding a shutter open a crack to see out. Only the women were excluded from the festivities; even Henri had been persuaded that it was best to behave in a civilized manner, rather like ambassadors sitting down with enemies to discuss terms. It had gone against the grain with the young boy. So great was his dislike and distrust of the prospect that he could scarcely speak for stuttering. Pascal had shown a tendency to glare and St. Amant had been so stiff that Elise feared he was more likely to cause offense than to aid their cause. Now as she watched she saw that all three were eating with every sign of enjoyment, tilting their glasses back as avidly as the rest.

Near the others, Pierre seemed perfectly at ease, joining in the laughter at the jokes, replying with quips that were much appreciated from the guffaws that greeted them. His blond hair gleamed in the light of the fire and he had discarded his coat, waistcoat, and shirt for a leather cape. It was not to be wondered at, naturally. He had been raised with these men and there must be many of their number who had been personal friends. Under the truce of the calumet, they could be so again.

Her gaze sought and found Reynaud. He had gone further in his dress than Pierre, changing to breechclout and cape and drawing his hair back into a knot crowned with swan feathers. He spoke with swift gestures to the oldest of the Natchez, leaning forward with his forearm on his knee as he sat with his forgotten food bowl in his hand. How foreign he looked, how savage once more. She tried to think of lying in his arms, of feeling that barbarically handsome mouth on hers, but she could not.

Or could she? They had come together the night before in a passion that had been wild, unrestrained. How many times? She could not recall. And yet she had responded each time with more elemental desire, had become as savage in her need as she could ever accuse him of being. Half-tamed barbarian that he was, he had not failed her. Could any other man have done the same?

She was free; she knew that. Because of his perseverance, the tender relentlessness of his pursuit, she was no longer trapped by her fear of men. They were male creatures like any other; some good, some bad, able to hurt her only if she let them. She did not think she would cringe inside at the touch of one again. She could even sense in a dim way that at some time in the future she might even let another come close enough to love her. Whether she could bring herself to love him in return was still a matter of some doubt. It was not a question of physical repugnance, however, so much as lack of trust.

She had trusted Reynaud, coming to it slowly, against all odds. He had betrayed her. And it hurt.

Night fell and still the feasting went on. Elise ate with Madame Doucet and Madeleine, picking over the food without appetite. She played the harpsichord while Madeleine sat placidly sewing as if there was nothing out of the ordinary in having such an entertainment in her front yard. Now and then Reynaud's cousin got up and went out to the kitchen to see that the food was replenished, but for the most part her job was done.

Madame Doucet tried to embroider a handkerchief, bungled it, pulled it out a half-dozen times, and finally threw the piece—needles, silks, and all—into a corner. She paced, wringing her hands and, talking, talking of what might happen here, of what had happened at Fort Rosalie, going over and over the death of her husband, the taking of her daughter and grandson. After a time, Elise came to the point where she had to clench her teeth to keep from screaming at the woman. There was no point in it, of course. Madame Doucet could not help this crisis of the nerves anymore than the others and she had, after all, been right about the Indians. One had to give her that. If only she would not go on about it so.

It was nearly midnight when Pierre came to them. His face

was grave, though his eyes were bright and there was a smear of grease beside his mouth. He spoke to them all, but it was Elise's gaze he sought and held. "Reynaud sent me to you."

Ignoring the tightening of the muscles of her stomach, Elise nodded.

"What is it?" Madame Doucet asked, her voice breathless. "What are they going to do with us?"

"You need have no fear, madame. They have come only for Reynaud."

Madeleine sat forward. "What do you mean?"

"There was a skirmish with a French scouting party. The war chief of the Natchez was killed."

"What of the French?" Madame Doucet cried in tones shrill with her annoyance that the death of an Indian should be presented to her.

"Dead, unfortunately. It appears the man who led them was criminally stupid and so failed to take the most obvious precautions against attack."

"But what has this to do with Reynaud?" Elise asked, her own tone impatient.

"Those who have come, this embassy that is outside, are asking that he return to the Grand Village of the Natchez with them to become the next war chief. He is the son of Tattooed Arm, the brother of the Great Sun. It is fitting."

"He has agreed?"

"He feels it would be wrong to refuse. There is need of someone with a cool head now, someone who can talk to the French, make reparations of some kind, reestablish peace. That's if the French will allow it, of course."

"You think they might not?"

"Governor Perier may feel that only revenge in kind will wipe out the dishonor and make it possible for French colonists to feel safe venturing into the wilderness again."

"In that case, what can Reynaud do?"

"If Perier will not listen to the wrongs of the Natchez, if he ignores all appeals for peace, then Reynaud can lead them in such a way that it will make an Indian war too costly to pursue. He hopes that the economics of it will force a compromise."

"But why?" Madame Doucet wailed.

"You must remember that these are his friends, the Natchez gathered outside, the people of his mother. He cannot stand by and watch the hand of France raised against them, not when it was the policies of the present government that brought about the uprising in the first place.''

"Would he lead them in yet another massacre of the French, perhaps in New Orleans itself?'' Elise inquired heatedly.

A shadow passed over the Frenchman's face. "It is sometimes difficult to say what he will do, but I think not. One thing is certain: If he is with the Natchez, the women and children now prisoners will be better treated. That must count for something.''

It occurred to Elise that the French would not be forgiving of a renegade half-breed who led the Natchez against them should the Indians be defeated. What would they do to him if he was captured? What would they not do?

"Yes, oh, yes,'' Madame Doucet was crying in excited anxiety, "let him go then. Let him go at once.''

"He will leave at dawn or as soon thereafter as men who have feasted all night can travel.'' He gave them a comprehensive glance, his manner stiff. "You, Mesdames Laffont and Doucet, with the gentlemen of your party, will be going in quite another direction. Reynaud prefers that you leave before the Natchez set out so that he can see you safely on your way. You are to make yourselves ready.''

He bowed and turned to leave them. Madame Doucet jumped to her feet. "Wait! I don't want—I must, I will go with dear Reynaud!''

Pierre stared at her. "Such a thing is not possible.''

"Don't use that word to me! I will go.''

Madeleine jumped to her feet as the older woman began to beat her fists together. "Don't upset yourself now, madame. To join your loved ones will not help them.''

Reynaud's cousin had seen the point of Madame Doucet's sudden obsession a fraction sooner than Elise, but now she added her own weight to the argument. "It is a long and arduous journey, if you remember, with no way of knowing what will happen at the end. You would not like being a slave yourself.''

"I would not mind, if I could be with my daughter and grandson!'' Madame Doucet's face crumpled and she began to weep.

"You don't know what you are saying. It would not do, truly. Reynaud will do all he can to help them. You must put your faith in him.''

Strange words. Elise could not help recognizing that fact even as she said them, but neither could she deny their force.

"I want to go. I will go. He will let me, you'll see."

Was the woman losing her reason? It did not seem impossible. Shallow, pleasure-loving, with few resources within herself and so an exaggerated dependence on her husband, daughter, and grandchild, Madame Doucet had been cut loose from everything familiar. She had come to rely on Reynaud as he guided them through the wild reaches of this land and also here at his home. How would she react when he refused to indulge her in this new desire of hers?

Elise tried tact, pleading, cajoling, anger, and dire warnings, all to no purpose. Madeleine added her own stringent advice and soothing murmurs. Pierre, after a few moments, cravenly retreated. In the end, Madame Doucet settled the matter by wrenching herself from their grasp and running to the front door. She flung it open, flying down the steps as if she were a girl again.

"Reynaud will let me go with him, I know he will. I'll show you. I'll show you!"

Elise went after her, expecting some kind of explosion when the woman found herself among the Natchez warriors, the men whom she had last seen carrying off what was left of her family. It was a tribute to the strength of the idea that had her in its grip that she hardly seemed to notice them. She ran straight to Reynaud and grasped his arm, pulling at it.

The feast was winding down; the men had eaten their fill. It mattered little now that a woman approached. Elise saw their mild curiosity, their averted faces that allowed Reynaud the privacy to speak to this woman if he so wished. Reynaud himself seemed concerned, but not overly so. He was talking to Madame Doucet with firmness, questioning her.

Elise could do no more. She swung away, going back up the stairs. She was weary from the upsets of the day and the effort to prepare the feast. She had nothing to do to get ready to leave. She would not take the dresses that had been altered for her; let Madeleine launder and reconstruct them or not as Reynaud instructed; it was his decision. She only wanted to take off her habit and fall into bed. It would be as well if she could get a little rest before the long trek tomorrow.

She lay in the dark with her hands behind her head, watching the flickering fire shadows on the walls. The noise of the feast would not let her sleep. The Indians had begun to harangue each other for some incomprehensible reason, making long speeches with shouts that had the sound of victory or congratulations. They chanted now and then and often broke into laughter. It was not extremely loud, but it was constant. It was also unnerving since she did not know what the outcome would be.

She thought of Reynaud out there, enjoying the feast and understanding that babble. He was a part of it. He was the same man who, the night before, had held her and whispered soft words of love that had sounded so right in her own language. The same man that she had lain against and stroked with her fintertips: his shoulders, arms, chest, waist, and thighs, every part of him. Incredible.

Where would he sleep tonight? Would he roll up in his cloak with the rest of his savage friends, sleeping where he dropped? Would he find a pallet in the room with Pierre, resting for the few short hours there would be before daylight? Or might he not expect to share her bed? If it was the last, he was going to be disappointed. She would have nothing more to do with him.

Still, he had been a wondrous lover. Never had she dreamed that she could feel so intensely, that it was possible for there to be such magic in the meshing of two bodies. A sweet and heavy thrill moved over her just at the thought of it. For that part of her incarceration here, she bore him no malice. It was only that his own desires had always been paramount and the means he had used to achieve them could not be justified.

She turned on her stomach with a decided flounce, deliberately thrusting such thoughts from her. She tried instead to think of Fort Saint Jean Baptiste and of what she would do there, of the people she would meet. One of the women who had been on the *Mutine* on the voyage from France, another correction girl, had married a man from the community near the fort. They had been friends during the voyage, though Claudette had been older, nearly nineteen. Her case had been a sad one, for she had been sold into prostitution by an uncle after he had initiated her into the practice himself. Claudette had been overjoyed at the prospect of marrying a kindly, older man and of going to live in the back beyond. She thought that no one would know her past there and she might become respectable.

And what of herself in that small community? Would her intimacy with the half-breed be known? Could Pascal and the others be trusted not to broadcast the details to all and sundry? The morality of the colony was rather loose and accommodating, but there might well be snickers and crude jokes behind her back and problems with other men as a result.

It did not matter. She would take care of the situation as she had always done. The important thing would be to regain her property. The first thing she must do would be to speak to the post commandant, a man named St. Denis. He must help her to get to New Orleans where she could plead her case before the council, or even the governor himself. The Indian war, the prospect of an army being sent to fight the Natchez around the area of her holdings, would make it difficult to return and begin to rebuild for some time, but it must be done eventually. There was nothing else she could do.

She awoke to a touch on her hip. Before she could move, she was caught, turned, and held close against a hard male body beside her under the cover. She stiffened, bracing her arms, trying to push away.

"Lie still," Reynaud whispered. "Just lie still."

Her head was on his shoulder, her forehead pressing into his neck. In a voice of fierce resentment, she said, "Let me go."

He did not answer, but only drew her closer against his long length. He was naked, she discovered, his body cool except for a heated area that rested against her belly with disturbing hardness. He smoothed her loosened hair with gentle strokes and bent his head to inhale its light fragrance, pressing his mouth to the top of her head.

A curious weakness possessed her. She relaxed by degrees. Her anger remained, but it seemed to have no force. A tightness rose in her throat, and she was aghast to realize that the thing she felt most vividly was pain for the way she had been used by this man. He had taken her, bent her to his will with threats and slow cunning, not because he felt anything for her personally, but because she represented a challenge. She had insulted him and he had seen to it that she regretted it by bringing her to accept him in the most intimate manner possible. He had breached her defenses and used her own emotions to force her capitulation.

Her one consolation was that for whatever reason he had begun his siege of her, it had not been a bloodless coup for him. She had not given in easily and his methods had left him open to considerable retaliation. He might care little for her as a person, but he had wanted her desperately toward the end.

Indeed, it would soon be ended. He might not have kept to the letter of their bargain, but it would be finished tomorrow—

or rather today—if their horses were swift enough to carry them to the fort by nightfall. It could be considered that in bringing her to his home, he had merely been seeing to it that she kept to the letter of her own agreement. She had promised to share his bed furs in return for their safe arrival and had known well the meaning of the phrase. Perhaps she could not truly complain.

His hand caressed the curve of her shoulder through the slik of her hair. He pushed his fingers into the thick swath that lay against her neck and lifted a strand, holding its satin smoothness under her chin as he tilted her head back.

His kiss had the sweet potency of the tafia he had been drinking. His mouth was warm with desire, his lips firm and smooth but for the scab of the small split place where she had struck him. Slowly he moved against her, letting her feel his need, inciting her to join him in it.

Against her will, or so it seemed, she returned his pressure. Her hands opened, spreading over the smooth and muscular hardness of his chest and touching gently the faint scars left by his tattooing. It would be for the last time. Never again would she feel his strength, know his tender control. She had thought so blithely of other men, but would there ever really be another who would woo her so sweetly, who would tend her desire before his own, who would or could wait with such iron control and unobtrusive patience until she was ready to receive him? Would there ever again be a man with a body so lean and firm and perfectly formed to fit against, and into, her own?

One last time. What could be the harm of it? It would not hurt her and did he not deserve it? Did she not owe him this? She always paid her debts, so let her pay this one, with sweetness, with some small return of all he had given her. She would be generous, for it was how she felt. She would give herself without reserve as he had given himself to her. She would bring him joy, as a final gift, if she could. It seemed to be what he wanted and, for this moment, what she wanted also. Could it be so wrong, when he was letting her go while he took up the dangerous job of war chief of the Natchez? And even if it was, even if he became the enemy of her people, could it make any difference now?

With tears rising in the back of her throat, she slid her arms around his neck and molded her mouth to his. Urgency like pain burgeoned inside her, swelling her breasts so that it seemed she must feel them naked against him, must press their hardened nipples into his chest. She lifted her knee across his thighs and felt a deep trembling begin inside her as his hand moved to her hip, pushing aside the soft material of her nightgown and drawing it higher.

A soft moan escaped her and she returned to help him drag it up and off over her head. Then they moved together in tender savagery, seeking, searching, so closely held that it seemed their skins must become one, allowing them to merge each into the other. With hands and mouths and poignant longing, they nurtured the unendurable pleasure that held them in its grasp until it seemed that no more could be borne.

Elise aided his entry, enclosing the moist rigidity of him with a gasp and a dissolving sensation that brought the darkness of the night close upon her. He filled her and so exquisite was it that she felt the tears she had been holding back spill hot and salty over her lashes, wetting her face. Then he was above her, plunging, taking her with him into the realm of unforeseen bliss, unimagined rapture.

The last time. She clung to the corded sinews of his arms as she rose against him, feeling the echo of their trembling deep inside. For now, this moment, she was his and he was hers, one, indivisible. It must end, but not now, pray God, not now. It was sweet, so bright. Perfect. A magic blending, merciless in its ecstasy. Fire, driven deep. Brilliant even in the dark; a bursting, glaring glory. She could not bear that it might never come again, she could not bear . . .

When it was over and they lay with bodies entwined, Reynaud rubbed a strand of her hair, which was wet with her tears, in his fingers as he stared with burning eyes into the darkness. He had meant to let her go. He had thought that he could, that it was necessary. No matter. He would hold her, for he knew now, if there had ever been any doubt, that she was his. He would keep her if he had to fight the world. Or Elise herself.

10

"They have gone."

Elise looked at Madeleine over her morning cup of chocolate, a stunned expression gathering in her eyes. "What do you mean, gone?"

"Departed. Left for the fort. At daybreak."

"But how could they go without me? Why wasn't I called?" She set the china cup painted with a pattern of violets carefully to one side, afraid she might drop it or throw it.

The woman's voice was colorless as she answered, but her hands were tightly clasped at her waist. "They were told you had decided to remain behind."

"By whom?"

Madeleine did not answer and in truth there was no need. Who else would dare? Who else could, or would, persuade the others to go on without her? Who else except Reynaud?

"I will kill him." Elise flung back the covers and slid from the bed, heedless of her naked state. With her face set in grim lines, she reached for her habit and underclothing, which she had laid out, and began to struggle into them.

"There is no need to upset yourself. He meant it for the best."

"The best for himself! What am I supposed to do? Stay here patiently waiting for his return from war? He had best not depend on it!"

In the last two days, an unacknowledged truce had been drawn up between her and Reynaud's cousin. The older woman seemed to accept her as a necessary part of Reynaud's comfort while

Elise looked upon the older woman in much the same way. Their basic attitude had become one of mutual respect and tolerance, with tentative friendliness. Now Madeleine frowned, hesitating before she spoke.

"It was too bad of him not to give you the choice, but is it so terrible that he wants you to stay? He needs you and I think the same may also be said of yourself about him."

"I need no one."

"Come, we all need someone."

"I will not be kept here against my will!"

"You cannot go alone."

"I can catch up to the others if I have a fast horse."

"Yes, but will Reynaud give you one?"

"He will or I will steal it!"

She flung herself from the room, buttoning her habit as she went, throwing her hair, which streamed around her back over her shoulder, with a gesture of angry impatience. So incensed was she that she hardly noticed the chill of the morning air or the thick layers of fog that swirled among the trees, obscuring the sun. She saw Reynaud, however, saw his broad shoulders and the billow of his buckskin cape. He was directing the loading of a pack train of five scrubby plains horses. There was a half-dozen Natchez around him, though it appeared that the others had gone. All that was left where the Indians had feasted the night before was a wide circle of bare and beaten ground and a curling wisp of smoke from the blackened coals of the fire.

"Who do you think you are?" she demanded as she neared him. "By what right did you have the others leave me behind?"

He swung on her with his face set in hard lines. His hair was drawn high, dressed with swan's feathers. His cape tie had loosened so that the edges hung open, leaving his chest bare. The thong that held up his breechclout rode low on his hips, exposing the flat surface of his stomach. His leggings clung to his thighs, but left a fair expanse of the copper skin of his hips revealed. In his half-naked hauteur, he seemed suddenly foreign, not at all the same man who had held her the night before. There was about him, too, a hardness of purpose that was daunting.

"You are speaking to me?"

"Of course!" she replied, lifting her chin in defiance.

"Then you will do well to moderate your tone. My warriors have no use for harridans and will not understand if I permit myself to listen to one."

"A harridan? Simply because I object to being kept here against my will?"

"Go into the house. I will talk to you there."

The words were harsh, dismissive. He turned his back, rapping out a trenchant order to an Indian who had stopped to listen to their conversation. It was highly likely that the warrior had understood most of what had been said; the Natchez had been dealing with the French for some thirty years and they had a certain facility for languages, there being so many dialects among the different tribes. Most Indians spoke their own dialect, a portion of that of their near neighbors, plus the Chickasaw that was used universally in a vast area of this southern portion of the continent. But even if he did understand, why should she care?

And yet it was her misfortune that she was able to see Reynaud's point. He was now the war chief and must keep the respect of his men. He could not do that if he was seen to accept the strictures of a woman, no matter how highly regarded females might be among his mother's people. Deference to warriors was a sacred tenet of all the tribes. It boosted the confidence and ensured the courage of the men who would be called upon to risk their lives for the good of their people.

She turned on her heel and stalked back to the house, but there was a dangerous glitter in her eyes and a restrained temper in the quickness of her step.

By the time Reynaud joined her in the salon, Elise had brushed her hair and plaited it, wrapping the braids around her head and fastening them with a few brass pins loaned by Madeleine. She had paced back and forth before the fire, deciding what she wanted to say, pausing now and then to warm her hands. Her lips were thin and her stance militant as she faced him, and there was no warmth in her amber-brown eyes as she watched him come toward her.

"What do you want?" he asked without preamble.

"I want a horse so that I can catch up with the others." She congratulated herself on the calm reason of the request.

"No."

"No?"

"I cannot permit it."

"You cannot keep me here. If you will not permit me to leave now, at once, then I will be gone as soon as you are out of sight!"

"I fear not."

"Wait," she said between clenched teeth, "and you will see."

"You can be sure I will be watching you every moment."

She stared at him with a sudden suspicion forming, looming enormous and dark in her mind. "You mean—"

"Just so."

The magnitude of the betrayal left her speechless for a long instant. He was not going to leave her here. He meant to take her with him to the Natchez village.

"I won't go!"

"You will go. The only question is whether it will be as my companion, free to ride beside me, or bound and led like a slave."

"We struck a bargain; you were to take me with the others to Fort Saint Jean Baptiste! It was understood that I was to be free when your part had been kept. You have twisted the situation to suit yourself well beyond what is acceptable already. You cannot expect to get away with this, too!"

"I assure you I can."

She stared at him straight in the eyes, her own dark with hatred. "You will be sorry."

"Probably."

The dry self-knowledge in the word did nothing to improve her temper. "You are a bastard."

"Enough of one to hold you."

Goaded past all bearing, she drew back her clenched fist and struck out at him. He caught her wrist, twisting it down and behind her back so that she was jerked close against him, her firm curves pressing into the hard planes of his body. The pain in her wrist was sharp, but so great was her rage that she hardly felt it.

"Let me go!" she said on the hiss of an indrawn breath.

His mouth inches from her own, he answered, "Be warned. I will not, and cannot, let you distract me from this point onward. I would advise you to be reasonable. If you do not, whatever happens will be on your own head."

"You listen to me. Our bargain is at an end. From this moment, there will be nothing between us. Lay a finger on me and I will fight you with every ounce of my strength."

"We will see," he answered and released her arm. "Make ready. We leave in a quarter hour."

It was a mistake to have warned him, of course. She realized the full weight of it when she saw her horse on a lead rein fastened to the pommel of Reynaud's Spanish saddle. She stood just inside the doorway, debating the wisdom of trying to sneak out the back, of refusing to set foot out of the house. Neither course seemed likely to win her way to freedom. Without a horse, she could not get far before she was run down, even if she could escape the back way, and if she hid out among the outbuildings it was all too likely that she would be run to earth and hauled out unceremoniously. Remaining inside the house would only be an invitation to Reynaud to come and carry her out and, while he might enjoy the opportunity, she had no wish to give him an excuse to domineer over her.

The only dignified thing left to do was to march out with her head high in the hope that capitulation now would give her breathing space and a chance to get away when his vigilance had relaxed.

At that moment there came the sound of horses' hooves moving at a slow trot. Reynaud rode out from around the hut on a magnificent black horse, a great barb from Barbary by way of Spain and Mexico with flowing mane and tail. On the lead he held in his hand was a cream-colored mare with the delicacy of form that hinted at Arabian bloodlines. He stopped near the mounting block and sat staring at the house with a frown between his eyes. Even as Elise, seeing the maneuver, frowned in her turn, there was the chatter of voices behind her. Madeleine entered the salon, holding what appeared to be a pair of cloaks over her arm and standing aside so that Madame Doucet, attired in a gown of heavy black drouget, could precede her. There was excitement and trepidation in the older woman's face and she turned and embraced Madeleine with fervor, thanking her for her help in a voice thick with tears.

Madame Doucet was to have her wish; she was to return with Reynaud to the Natchez village. She had misjudged him then. The horse on the lead was for the older woman who did not ride well while the Arabian was for her.

Reynaud's consideration was like a slap in the face. It was obvious that he did not doubt his ability to control her movements, even when she was mounted on horseback. The Arabian should be much faster than the plains ponies, faster than the barb over short distances though the larger horse undoubtedly had greater stamina. If she made a run for it, he was certain to catch her if he saw her go. If.

Madame Doucet had accepted a cloak and was out the door. Madeleine stepped closer to drape another cloak of the same dark stuff over Elise's shoulders. She thanked the woman, murmuring a good-by.

Madeleine shook her head. "Thank Reynaud, it was he who sent for them for you and for Marie. It was he who spared the time to guard your comfort, your safety." She hesitated, then went on. "Perhaps now you will think of him, guard him if you can. He will have many enemies."

"Only the French," Elise said bitterly.

"And those who would deny his right to be war chief, those who despise his mixed blood."

"There is nothing I can do."

"You can watch and listen. Sometimes it is enough."

Was it a subterfuge to make her feel concern for him? It would not work, not now, not ever, but Madeleine could not know that. Inclining her head in a motion that could be taken for consent if the other woman so wished, Elise turned away.

She had left her departure too late. Reynaud was advancing on her, climbing the steps with his cape flaring around him and a grim look on his face. Alarmed against her will by the hard purpose she saw in his eyes, Elise put out her hand in a useless attempt to stop him. He caught it, drawing it behind his head and swooping to pick her up. She was lifted high against his chest before he swung around, descending the steps once more. She heard the masculine laughter, saw the Natchez, normally so impassive, weaving in their saddles with their amusement. Color flared into her face.

"Put me down," she said in a furious undertone. Pride and the certain knowledge that it would increase the mirth of the savages prevented her from struggling.

He made no answer, but carried her down the flight of steps to where the horses waited. He shifted her, clasping her rib cage, then threw her up into the saddle. She grabbed the horse's mane as she sought for balance. With flushed cheeks and eyes downcast to hide her enraged embarrassment, she kicked her skirt into place and gathered up her reins. Settled, she sent a fulminating stare at Reynaud to find him already mounted and watching her, his gray eyes assessing.

Their gazes clashed for a long instant. Then he looked past her to where the warriors sat with Madame Doucet and, glancing back, reached out to adjust Elise's cloak, which was twisted over her shoulder. It was as if with that single movement he had marked her as his possession, his alone. She had an insane urge to throw off the cloak in a symbolic rejection of that gesture. She might have, except that on second consideration it seemed as if it might well have been a mark of his protection.

They went from the yard before the house in single file with Reynaud in the lead, Elise behind him, and the others strung out in the rear with Madame Doucet sandwiched between them. It was colder as they turned off from the cart track and entered the woods for the fitful sun scarcely penetrated the dense meshing of limbs overhead. During the time that they had spent at Reynaud's holdings, the leaves had all fallen except for a scattered beech tree or post oak that held on to its fluttering brown covering. In the main, the branches were bare, though clothed by gray rags of Capuchin's beard near the streams where the air was damp. As they rode the hoofbeats were muffled in the thick carpet of leaves, though now and then the rattling of a layer of crisp dry ones seemed deafening in the quiet.

The miles fell away behind them. It was odd to Elise to see how calmly Madame Doucet viewed her escort. It was as if she hardly realized that the men with her were Natchez, that they might have been the very ones who had killed her husband and carried off her daughter and grandson. What curious logic had she used to allay her former fears? Did she trust them not to harm her because Reynaud was with her or was it simply that, having decided to join the other French women and children, she need no longer fear capture?

She hoped that her own demeanor was even close to being as serene. She felt as if her stomach was in knots as every league took her farther away from the fort in the Natchitoches country. Her anger was allied to a bitter frustration that would not leave her no matter how chilled and tired she became.

She had lost so much; family, home, lands, everything she had gained at such cost. Now her self-respect was gone as well because she had surrendered herself to a man who had betrayed her, because she had become to all intents and purposes his slave. Her face bleak, she contemplated the future. By comparison, going to Fort Saint Jean Baptiste had promised limitless opportunities. St. Amant, Henri, and Pascal must be well on their way to the stockade. She regretted that she had been unable to say good-by to them. They were survivors, all of them, and though she could not quite claim them as friends, there was a curious kinship between them that could not be broken. It galled her to consider what they must think of her failure to join them in their trip to the fort.

The weather did not warm, but seemed to grow grayer and colder. A fine mist began to fall. They stopped now and then to rest the horses, but long before Elise was ready, they were in the saddle again, riding onward.

Once during the early afternoon, Reynaud dropped back to join her. He was almost affable, as if happy to be riding toward the village of his mother's people once more. He told her the names of the men with them. There was Path Bear, the largest and most fierce looking, a Sun named for the black bear who refuses always to give way when meeting anyone on a trail, and who was chief of the Flour Village, second village in importance after the Grand Village. There was also Long Neck, Red Fox, Shouting Deer, and Spent Arrow, men of the Noble class, many related in some way to Reynaud. They were as tall and broad as he, but darker of skin. Their shoulders as well as their chests were tattooed; one or two even had lines of geometric designs from cheekbone to cheekbone, and most wore ornaments of shell or rings of steel and gold in their ears. To a man, they were alert, watchful, with a hand always near a weapon, either the muskets across their laps, the bows and quivers of arrows slung over their backs, or the small hatchets at their waists. Their vigilance seemed a threat, one that assured she would never be able to get away from the column.

It was getting on toward late afternoon when her chance came. Reynaud had gone ahead a little way on foot, scouting, as had been his habit before as the others rested. Two of the warriors had stepped a short distance into the woods while the others stood leaning against the trees, talking among themselves, cracking and eating handfuls of pecans that they took from pouches tied to the thongs at their waists. Madame Doucet, rubbing her stiff legs and seat, was walking up and down.

Elise wandered along the faint track in the direction they had come as if stretching her legs, too, stopping now and then to arch her back in a parody of aching muscles, though leading her horse at the same time. Just where the track meandered out of sight, she swerved into the woods as though at the urge of bodily functions.

Once hidden from view, she mounted her horse, urging the mare farther away from the others, though she did not dare kick her into a faster gait for fear of being heard. Then behind her came a call. She had been missed. It might be a few minutes before they came after her. She could not risk having that much time, however. She kicked the mare into a run and, bending low in the saddle to avoid the tree limbs, headed toward the open track. By the time she reached it, she could hear the thud of a single set of hooves thundering after her.

She leaned along her mare's neck, using the ends of the reins as a whip to urge greater speed. She remembered somewhere ahead a point where the path diverged. If she took the wrong fork, would the warrior behind her automatically take the correct one, losing her? Or would she have a better chance of escape if she dismounted, hiding in the woods as she sent the mare on without her?

The cold mist wet her face, streaming back from her eyelids like chilled tears. Her heart was pounding with fear and excitement. Her cloak fluttered and flapped around her, slapping against the straining horse. The sharp hooves of the mare cut into the rich loam of the trail, throwing it up in clods. In Elise's nostrils was the smell of the wet, dank woods, the warm horse, and the damp wool of her cloak. The fork in the path loomed ahead of her. She had not made a decision. Without checking, she took the correct turning, trusting blindly to the Arabian blood of her mount to give her greater speed.

The horse was tired, however. It was not long before she began to flag. Elise rubbed her neck, whispering, urging her onward. It helped, but not for long. The pounding of the hooves behind her grew louder. There was fury in the sound and a threat. She dared to glance back. It was Path Bear who pursued her, riding his spotted plains pony as if they were one in strength and will, ignoring the flecks of foam that flew back from the animal's neck and withers to dry on his body.

Then he was upon her, leaning in, catching her around the waist. His arm closed like a vise around her and she was dragged from the saddle, snatched brutally against him. He reined in his horse to a dancing stop and half dropped, half flung her to the ground. She caught herself on her hands and knees, feeling the sting of sharp limbs and twigs under her palms. She shook her head to clear it, clenching her teeth against the ache in her joints from the jarring fall, trying to catch her breath.

Path Bear spoke, the words harsh, with the sound of command. She looked up, a dazed expression in her eyes, to see that he had dismounted. He was telling her to get up, she thought. She did not like the way he was standing over her, so she pushed herself erect, swaying a little. Her mare had come to a halt a short distance away, standing with her head down and blowing. Instinctively she turned toward her.

The big warrior reached out to catch her arm, his fingers bruising as he jerked her around. She raised her head, giving him a look of cold scorn as she snatched her wrist from his grasp and stepped back. Once more he spoke, then, swinging away from her, he moved to a tree where he broke off a limb as thick as his thumb and studded with twigs and buds. He slashed it through the air once, twice, then turned and started toward Elise.

He was going to beat her. She felt the blood drain from her face as the realization struck her. Did he think she was a slave that he had the right to discipline or was this the treatment meted out to Indian women who caused trouble? It made no difference, she knew, as she backed away from him. The foolhardiness of her actions leaped to her mind. She should have known escape would not be so easy. She should have considered the consequences more thoroughly. Regardless of her error, however, she had no intention of submitting to the drubbing the Indian planned. With grim concentration, she looked around for a weapon.

There it was, a limb of pitch pine, the hardened core of a rotted pine trunk. She scooped it up and, with cold fury in her eyes, stood her ground. Path Bear stopped, a stunned look making his features blank for an instant before rage that she should defy him took its place. He threw his cape off, then advanced upon her, slapping the limp he held into his palm with whistling blows.

Abruptly he lunged, swinging the limb with hard strength toward her shoulders. She thrust her limb up and out with both hands to catch the blow. It sent splinters and bits of rotted wood flying and numbed her arms with its force. It was all she could do to twist low to parry the next blow that was aimed at her knees. Hard and fast they came. Elise stumbled back, panting with the effort to deflect them. There was no doubt that she would be borne down in short order for her hands ached, her shoulders burned, and there were sharp pains in the muscles in her back. First, however, she would strike at least one blow, though she knew beyond doubt that if it landed squarely Path Bear might well kill her.

The warrior drew back for a final effort that he expected to smash though her defense. In that brief moment, the way was open. Since there had been no retaliation from her, he expected none. With both hands on her stick like a staff, she swung to the side and thrust the jagged end straight toward his midsection. Glad triumph sang in her veins as it landed squarely in his solar plexus.

His eyes glazed and the air left him in a grunting rush as he staggered back a step. He looked down to see the ragged injury she had left as her limb skidded along his muscles to tear his skin. Blood rushed to his face, turning it purplish copper. He crouched to attack.

A command rang out, sharp, authoritative, and the black shoulder of the Spanish-bred barb was pushed between them. Reynaud slid down. He looked at Elise, his hard gray gaze running over her as if to check for injuries, but without a shred of softness as he met her look of startled relief. Without a word, he ducked under the head of his horse to confront Path Bear.

So intent had she and the warrior been on their minor battle that they had not heard the arrival of Reynaud and the other Natchez. Elise looked to where the warriors sat their horses with Madame Doucet among them, slumping in the saddle like a sack of cornmeal after the swift ride. The faces of the Indians held judicious patience, though she thought she saw also surprise edged with humor in the glances they exchanged as they looked from the limb she held to the wound on the top of Path Bear's abdomen.

Of the exchange between Reynaud and Path Bear, Elise understood not a word. The Indian's gestures in her direction were violent, accusing. He listened with scant respect to Reynaud, pointing to her once more with an obvious threat. Reynaud side-stepped, blocking the way, his voice firm. Path Bear dropped his stick and shook a fist in Reynaud's face. Reynaud crossed his arms, his words suddenly flat and stern. The other man stood for a long moment, then dropped his gaze, backing away. He turned and with long strides went to his horse, mounting in a single movement. He looked back one last time, then swung his mount's head, going to join the others. He spoke to them and in a body they wheeled and moved away at a walk.

Elise let fall the limb she had been holding and shut her eyes with a trembling sigh. Until that moment she had not known how tightly strung her nerves were. She felt weak suddenly as if she might fall if she tried to move. At the slight sound of rustling leather, she opened her eyes to see Reynaud standing in front of her.

"How good are you at screaming?"

It was not an idle question, she saw that at once from the grim cast of his face. Still, it made no sense. "What?"

"You must be punished. I have made it clear that you are my woman and that privilege belongs to me. As much pleasure as it might give me to turn you over my knee, it seems unjust and should be unnecessary if you can bring yourself to cry out at my command. Now."

At the last word, he swung his hand to slap his open palm against the leather of his Spanish saddle. It cracked in the wooden stillness with the sound of a hard blow. The horse sidled, but did not shift from his position that hid them from the party of warriors.

He reached out to catch her wrist in a hard grasp, pulling her toward him, His voice soft, he said, "Cooperate or I warn you, I'll be forced to pick up Path Bear's stick and lift your skirts—"

"Don't!" she said sharply.

"That's better." He released her. "Now!"

They played out the charade, though Elise turned away from him to lean her head against the warm and quivering flank of the barb. Tears gathered inside her, pressing against her throat. It seemed that she had become abnormally sensitive of late with emotions tearing at her that she had thought suppressed out of existence years ago. She wanted to be self-reliant, but fate had conspired against her, bringing loss and pain, fatigue and disappointment. Nothing happened as she expected or as she planned; everything seemed to show her how ill-equipped she was to protect herself.

The blows had stopped. There was an awkward moment of silence. Reynaud broke it.

"Now if you can bring yourself to appear chastened," he began.

She turned her head swiftly, stung by the jeering note in his voice despite the fact that it seemed directed as much at himself as at her. The tears she had been trying so hard to control rose in her eyes and spilled down her cheeks. With an angry exclamation, she swung from him once more, scrubbing at them with the heel of her hand.

"Why?" she demanded. "Why are you doing this?"

"Call it a personal quirk; I am uncomfortable lifting my hand against a woman."

"No, not that!"

"You mean why am I forcing you to come with me? The answer is simple. I want you."

The words sent a peculiar sensation along her nerves. "It will do you no good."

"That remains to be seen."

"You need not think your—magnanimity this afternoon will make any difference."

"No, I won't. And you need not think that because I have stayed my hand this time that I won't be able to overcome my quirk if it happens again."

She allowed her lip to curl, though he could not see it. "I never doubted that for a moment."

"Good. We understand each other."

Did they? Elise could not be so certain. She mulled over what he had said as she permitted him to mount her on the barb and swing up behind her, leading her mare and riding with her before him like a captive to join the others. Resentment and gratitude warred within her, impeding her efforts to separate her thoughts. She wanted to despise him, but could not. She tried to feel incensed at his expression of desire for her and discovered instead a strange trepidation. She reached for her rage at his high-handed actions, drawing it around her as if for comfort. It was only that she was tired, she told herself, tired of riding, tired of this journeying back and forth, tired of conflict and of being sufficient unto herself. It was only a temporary lapse. Tomorrow would be better; it must be.

Reynaud held her slim and supple body in his arms, feeling the softness of her hips through the habit skirt and cloak shifting against him as the horse moved. He knew when she began to relax, leaning on him, and something tightly held inside himself loosened, began to dissolve. It was all he could do not to rein the barb into the woods and have her then and there, once more naked among the leaves with the salty taste of her tears on her lips. It was not the pride he sensed inside her that prevented him, but the sight of her hands lying with the palms turned upward in her lap. They were slowly becoming a bluish purple from withstanding the blows of Path Bear. She had courage, his prickly love, and strength. He must not destroy either by taking her by force, the only way he could have her now. But there was another reason, too. As much as he needed the sweet surcease to be had in her body, he yearned to know her mind, to seek deep within it and sense a welcome for him there. He wanted to share her thoughts, her dreams, her secrets. He wanted her to come to him with desire, to reach inside him and discover how open he was to her. It could not happen yet, if at all. He concentrated instead on what he would like to do to the great Indian bastard who had caused her bruises. The Natchez did not fight among themselves; no quarrel ever came to blows on pain of banishment. It was a pity.

Elise slept with Madame Doucet when darkness fell. She was not comfortable. The bed furs were chilly and dampish without the intense heat of Reynaud's body to warm them. The older woman twitched and moaned in her sleep, waking Elise times without number. There was no shelter against mosquitoes, for they needed none. The misting rain had stopped; still, its wetness lingered like a heavy dew, turning slowly to frost as the cold of the night deepened. They lay in a circle with their feet toward the ashes where the small fire Reynaud had permitted had burned. If she stretched out her hand, Elise could have touched his furs, but he was not in them. He sat on watch during the darkest hours of the night. It was only toward dawn that she saw him lie down and pull the furs around him. She slept best during the same hours that he used for resting.

The days continued gray and cold. One night it rained and the next morning they crawled from the lean-to they had constructed to find every tree limb, leaf, and blade of grass coated with a glistening shell of ice. The ice crackled around their horses' legs as they crossed streams and sparkled with a brilliance that pierced their eyes as the sun rose high. Numbed by the cold that crept under the cloak and took the feeling from her fingers, Elise ceased to think of escape. The journey became something to be endured: an unending vista of trees and more trees; of countless winding streams that wet her skirts and routed her carefully hoarded warmth; of poor meals of parched corn and dried meat; and of the unending feeling of being watched by the Natchez warriors that plodded behind her. She sometimes noted landmarks: the bayou that tasted of salt where she had swum with Reynaud in the moonlight; the river where they had built a raft for the crossing though they let the horses swim it now; the clearing where Reynaud had stood naked in the rain on that first night. She noted them, but could arouse little more than fleeting recognition, a faint smile of remembrance, so complete was her stupor of exhaustion and depleted emotions.

They came finally to the Mississippi one late afternoon. There were pirogues waiting, the large crafts of the Indians capable of holding sixteen men, along with the warriors to send them lunging over the placid, shining water. The crossing did not take long with the cold northwest wind at their backs. Still, by the time they had reached the eastern shore and brought the horses over by swimming them behind a pirogue, twilight had fallen.

It was just as well. The gentle lavender light softened the edges of the blackened timbers that lay at angles where Fort Rosalie had been and made the sagging barns and outbuildings still standing on a hill here and there, marking where homesteads had been, seem less forlorn. It hid the scattered bones, human and animal, that had been picked clean by buzzards, creeping animals, crows, and the blackbirds of winter. It made the cracked and dented kitchenware, the staved-in barrels, the broken hoops and torn cornhusk dolls, and the scattered bits of clothing that littered the road seem like mere refuse instead of the ruined belongings of the dead and the enslaved.

Madame Doucet sobbed quietly to herself as they passed the place that had been her home. Elise wanted to turn away as they came near her own holdings, but she forced herself instead to look closely. How desolate it was, in the semidarkness, with nothing more than a pile of dead coals and ash where the house and barn had been; the poultry run was empty, the pastures sere and gray. It made her ache for the pride she had taken in her ownership, for the plans for a prosperous future she had nurtured so carefully. She had been so sure of herself, so positive that if she were careful and worked hard enough disaster could never befall her again.

It was fully dark when they saw the light. Shining like a beacon high in the sky, it was the eternal fire kept burning in the Temple of the Sun that crowned the highest mound of the Grand Village. It leaped and wavered, beckoning them with bright orange promises of warmth and food and rest. The pace of the column picked up. The warriors straightened. The smells of woodsmoke and food cooking wafted on the cool air. A messenger had been sent out earlier to announce their coming; they would be expected.

Minutes later they sighted the cook fires of the Great Sun at the apex of the second highest mound and those of the other Sun families lower down, clustered around the mound at ground level. The glow of fires gleamed through cracks in the walls of the huts, through the doors that were opened as people went in and out, watching for them. Then they saw the great bonfire in the middle of the ceremonial ground that marked the center of the village, an enormous blaze that consumed whole trees and sent sparks spinning upward to the heavens. Dogs began to bark. Then came a cry as they were discovered. From every thatched hut and hovel, the Indians poured, shouting to each other, jubilant at the safe return of the men with Reynaud, known as Hawk-of-the-Night, leading them. The column rode into the circle of the light cast by the huge fire and, surrounded by the Natchez, came to a halt.

Hands touched Elise's habit skirt, tugging, pinching, assessing as the faces of their owners turned up to stare at her. Bland, curious, distrustful, disdainful, they pressed in upon her. Ahead of her, Reynaud was being greeted like a conqueror or lost son. Slowly he drew away from her, the distance between them widening. She heard Madame Doucet protesting and turned to see her being pulled from the saddle and tumbled onto the packed earth of the ground. Eager fingers caught at her, too, dragging her down among them. Her hair was touched, pulled. She was pushed this way and that, though she stayed stubbornly on her feet.

Did she imagine it or was there a shouted order from Reynaud? She could not be certain in the cacophony of cries, thudding drums, rattling gourds, and shrilling cane flutes. The women converged on her, giggling, pulling her between them over the ground toward a hut that lay behind the second highest mound. She stumbled on the uneven ground, ducking under a low-hanging tree limb, nearly falling as she was jerked along. In a sudden surge of temper, she struck out at the hands that dragged at her, wrenching back away from them. A big Indian woman who was hauling her by her arm reached out to slap her, a stinging blow, before she grabbed a handful of her loosened hair and pulled her onward.

A massive shape loomed ahead of them, a hut. They ducked to enter through the small door that was no more than four feet tall. Inside, it was seen to be a large structure some thirty feet square with a fire blazing in the center, surrounded with cooking pots, and a small hole, half-covered by a woven cane flap, in the cone-shaped ceiling through which the smoke escaped. The hut had no windows; light was supplied by the fire and by two or three small clay lamps made of open pots with burning wicks floating in herb-scented bear oil and hung in a netting of plaited ropes from the beams. The floors were covered with woven mats. Wide benches piled with furs lined the walls, serving both as beds and for seating. Mercifully, the hut was empty, for the instant she was inside the women began to strip her clothes from her.

She fought them, but she was so outnumbered that it was of no use. In short order, she was naked. They stared at her in frank appraisal as she stood gilded in firelight with strands of her honey-brown hair veiling her pale skin. One woman tweaked the nipple of her breast, then smoothed a hand along her hip, apparently making some disparaging remark at its slenderness compared with her own. The others laughed, then half pushed, half led Elise toward the center sleeping bench. They pressed her down upon it and covered her with furs, then with what appeared to be an admonition to stay where she was, they trooped out and slid the door into place over the opening.

It was warm in the hut, even stifling with the thick pall of smoke that hovered in the peak of the roof. She lay still, feeling her chill flesh absorbing the heat. She stared up at the blackened ceiling; at the undersides of what appeared to be woven cane mats; at an assortment of dried herbs that released their scent in the hot air; and at a motley collection of weapons, animal skins, bear and panther claws, and strips of leather that hung from the beams. What would happen next, she did not know, nor could she summon the will to care. The light from the crude lamps flickered, casting odd shadows on the high walls. The bed furs grew soft in their warmth. She closed her burning eyes.

II

THE WOMAN MOVED about the hut, kindling the fire, starting a pot of corn gruel to boil, bringing in a load of fragrant cedar boughs to place under the benches to repel fleas. Reynaud pretended that she was not there, as he had been taught to do in order to allow her privacy for her tasks while guarding his own, doing it so completely that he was scarcely aware of her presence.

He lay on his side covered to the waist by the bed furs with his head propped on one elbow. A faint smile on his mouth, he watched Elise where she lay between him and the wall. She was turned toward him on her side with only her head and one hand out of the covers. Her eyes were closed and she breathed with the deep and even rhythm of sleep.

There were blue shadows under her eyes, her cheeks were windburned, and her lips dry and slightly cracked from the cold of the days on the trail; still, he thought her lovely. She had not stirred when he joined her in the early morning hours, nor did it seem that she was disturbed by his presence. At least once toward dawn, as he had reached out to her, she had turned without waking him to allow him to fit her into the curve of his body. He found that unconscious acceptance oddly endearing and even promising.

The palm of her hand lying open and lax on the fur was as bruised as the skin under her eyes. Silently he damned once more the man who had harmed her. But he could not escape the fact that a part of the blame was also his. He had been so intent on intimidating her to the point of acquiescing in his scheme for her that he had not thought what effect it might have on the others. They had taken her for a slave, one only incidentally his woman, and Path Bear had behaved accordingly.

It would be useless to deny that he had taken a certain satisfaction in forcing her to do his bidding. That had been before she had risked becoming lost in the forest in order to escape him; before he had seen her valiant efforts to defend herself from his Sun cousin, Path Bear; before he had seen the terror that she tried so bravely to hide as he had spoken of punishment. All he had felt then had been sick self-loathing. Knowing what she had been through with the brutal son of hell to whom she had been married, how could he have exposed her to such a thing again?

It did not bear thinking of. His eyes dark with pain and shame, he leaned to press his lips for a brief instant to the discolored flesh of her hand.

Elise's lashes quivered, fluttered upward. She stared at him for a long moment, aware of a tingling in her palm and a faint soreness, though not of the cause. Abruptly she recoiled from him, coming up against the side of the hut.

"Gloating?" she asked, her voice tight.

He blinked at the accuracy of her insight, but replied with ease, "Why should I do that?"

"I believe you said once that the idea of making me your slave had appeal. You should be happy that you have your wish!"

"I suppose," he said slowly, "that I am, though I prefer not to look at it that way."

She glanced away from the bright light in his gray eyes, her features grim, "What other way is there? I wasn't brought here last night by your women, stripped naked, and put into your bed because I am an honored guest."

"Not my women," he said dryly.

"They obeyed your order."

"I asked them to see to you. Unfortunately, Natchez women have ideas of their own."

"Then you did not expect to find me here?" Color rose in her cheeks as she made a small gesture indicating the bed.

"It was a delightful surprise."

A soft giggling, of mirth suppressed too long, greeted this sally. Hearing it, Elise pushed herself up on an elbow to look over Reynaud's broad shoulder. An Indian woman knelt by the fire less than ten feet away with her hand over her mouth and her black eyes shining with glee. A frown snapped Elise's brows together, then as quickly as it had risen her anger faded. "Little Quail! Is it you?"

Little Quail, the Indian woman who had been sold to her husband as a slave by her parents, the person closest to a companion that she had found in this new world as they had shared the misery of belonging to Vincent Laffont. The Natchez women seldom ventured far from their villages and so Elise had seen the other women only twice since Little Quail had returned to the Natchez after Vincent's death.

"I am sorry, Madame Elise, truly. I tried to be quiet, but it is so funny to think that you did not wish to be in the bed furs of Hawk-of-the-Night, he that most young women would sell themselves to please, and that finding you there this great warrior chief let you sleep!"

Reynaud shifted, turning a lazy grin on the Indian woman. "You have a twisted sense of humor."

"Do I offend you, great one?" she asked, then anxiously repeated the question in the Natchez tongue.

"I may forgive it if you prepare my breakfast well," he answered, stretching.

The woman sent a glance of melting mischief to Elise. "Oh, but how could you not desire to give pleasure to such a generous man?"

"Easily!" Elise snapped. "He is conceited, overbearing, and takes far too much for granted."

"Then you must change him." Little Quail gave a wise nod.

"I fear the effort is beyond me. But, tell me, have you been well?"

"For myself, yes. The last time you saw me, it was as a wife; now I am a widow."

Elise remembered with a faint shudder speaking to Little Quail's husband the morning of the massacre, remembered her conviction that he had meant to be the one to kill her or perhaps take her prisoner. "A widow? How did it come about?"

"He met his death in battle as he would have wished, dying with the great warrior chief that Hawk-of-the-Night must replace."

Elise sat up straighter, clutching the black bear fur to her chest. "I am sad for your sadness."

"It is over," Little Quail answered, her tone subdued.

There was stoic endurance on the young woman's square, piquant features and also a hint of reserve. It seemed as well to change the subject.

"I saw none of the French women and children when we arrived last night. I must ask you if they are all right? Have they been well treated?"

Little Quail looked away as if it was necessary to stir the pot of gruel. "They are well enough, those who are willing to work. It has not been good, I fear, with those who are used to being idle. For a woman of the Natchez, a willingness to work is the greatest virtue. There is no excuse for shirking."

It was easy for Elise to imagine some of the women she had known finding the life of Indian women hard. Like so many of the French, the women had been led to believe the tales of riches pouring from the ground here in the Louisiana country, tales of the great wealth that could be amassed with little effort. They had expected a place where they would need to do little except to spend the treasure that would pour into their laps. Finding the promises false, they had sunk into indolence, anyway, their greatest exertion being to harry their few slaves to perform the tasks necessary for their comfort. Such idleness, along with their lack of physical strength, their pride and stubbornness, would doubtless have brought the scorn of the Indian women down upon them.

"There was news of a young boy who was said to have been killed in the funeral rites for a Sun child," she ventured.

"Yes, one was so honored."

"Was it perhaps the grandson of my neighbor you may remember, Madame Doucet?"

"I could not say," Little Quail answered hurriedly. "I did not hear the name."

Elise asked after the African slaves of the French community and learned that many had been sold, her own among them, following the attack by the slaves of New Orleans on the Chouachas Indians at Perier's instigation. Some had gone to the Spanish, some to the Carolina English by way of the Chickasaws and the Creeks, some to the Tensas who would trade them in New Orleans. Then they spoke of other things, of the warming of the day as the sun rose higher, of Elise's thankfulness of finding Little Quail there.

"I came because I wished to welcome you," the young woman said with a shy smile, "and because Hawk-of-the-Night has no woman to cook for him and I knew you would be very tired after the long journey. Later, if you wish, I will show you the Natchez way of preparing food and furs and all the other things you must know."

The words had an ominous sound, as if Little Quail expected her stay among them to be long. "That . . . is very good of you."

"It is only to repay your kindness when I was sold by my father into your home."

"Then I thank you," Elise answered and refused to look at Reynaud, who lay quietly listening to the exchange.

The gruel, seasoned with bear fat and honey, was delicious, or else Elise was hungry. Little Quail served it to Elise and Reynaud where they sat on the sleeping bench. When her bowl was empty, Elise looked around for her clothes, preparing to rise. Her habit had disappeared, however, and in its place was a pile of folded cloth. Soft, finely woven, the material, when shaken out, was squares made of swansdown dyed rust-red. The large square was to be tied on the right hip as a skirt, with the smaller square serving as a top covering if tied on the shoulder. There was also a cape of cured and bleached doeskin embroidered with red and black beads. To complete the costume was a pair of moccasins with beaded toes and ties at the ankles to keep them snugly on the feet.

"Where are my things?" Elise asked, her tone sharp.

"Gone." There was complete unconcern in Little Quail's answer.

"Gone?"

"Burned."

"What!"

"You could not want to wear anything so soiled?"

The woman's expression held surprise and a certain flashing mischief that the man beside her seemed to share. Remembering Reynaud's attempt once before to persuade her to wear Indian dress, Elise rounded on him. "You did this!"

"I might have if I had thought of it, but no. I had nothing to do with it."

"I can't wear those!" Elise gestured with one outflung hand toward the squares of leather.

"It's easy, once you have the knack of it. Little Quail will show you how—unless, of course, you prefer to stay here in the bed furs with me."

She threw him a scathing look, then reached out slowly to take up the soft swansdown squares.

If it had not been for the fear of sending Little Quail into gales of laughter and the certainty of Reynaud making some snide comment, Elise would have asked him to leave the hut while she dealt with the unfamiliar costume or to at least turn his head. As it was, she did her best to ignore him as the Indian women seemed to do so well. It was not easy, not while he lay with his hands locked behind his head watching with an interest so unabashed that it appeared he was laying claim to the right to view her in any state of dress or undress. He found her self-consciousness amusing, she thought, and did everything in his power to heighten it. He surveyed the rose-coral-tipped globes of her breasts, as she turned this way and that way trying to tie the strange skirt, with a proprietorial appreciation and allowed a spark of heat to smoulder at the back of his eyes as he caught a glimpse of the long white length of her thigh that was exposed at the side when it was knotted.

From outside the door of the hut, which was a simple panel that slid back and forth between posts to open and close, came a quiet greeting. Reynaud looked away reluctantly from Elise as she flung her cape around her. He pushed himself erect with a bed fur over his lap, but made no other effort toward dressing before he called out his permission to enter. The panel eased open and a young man stepped inside.

"Magani," he said with a swift gesture of his right hand, a request to speak.

"St. Cosme!" Reynaud sat up straighter, reaching out his own hand as he added the greeting, *"Tachete-cabanacte."*

The two men clasped wrists, then Reynaud turned to Elise. "I present my half brother, St. Cosme, named, in case you are curious, for the French priest who baptised him at the time of his birth. St. Cosme, this lady is Madame Elise Laffont."

Younger than Reynaud and the Great Sun, the man before her had the same handsome features and grave, yet polished, manner. He inclined his head, smiling, before he turned back to his half brother. "I come on a matter of importance."

"Speak as you will," Reynaud answered, indicating that he should be seated.

His half brother dropped down onto the foot of the bench on which Reynaud reclined. Little Quail hurried to offer refreshment, which the visitor accepted, tasting the hot herb drink at once so as not to offend her. Then as was the custom, since he was the guest and it was his duty to speak first, he began to deliver what sounded like a carefully rehearsed message.

Elise could not follow all of it, but thought it was a matter of a council. Little Quail stood still, her eyes wide. Reynaud listened carefully, then signified his agreement to some request. His half brother rose shortly thereafter and took his leave. Reynaud, stepping out of the bed furs with smooth economy of motion and total lack of concern for his nakedness, began to get dressed.

"What is it?" Elise asked.

"Nothing that need be of concern to you," he answered.

She was doubtful that he told her the truth, but since it seemed likely the matter was one that concerned his new position as war chief, she did not question him further. She did not care to become involved in an argument in front of Little Quail.

When he was ready, he moved toward her, reaching out to grasp her forearms. Before she could free herself, he brushed the firm warmth of his lips lightly across her forehead. He released her, inclined his head, and swung away, letting himself out of the hut.

Elise looked at Little Quail in brief puzzlement. The woman was fussing with the fire, however, her attention upon her task without concern for the affairs of men. Trying to shake off the peculiar feeling that something was not quite right, Elise joined her.

Little Quail began at once to instruct her. The tasks were not difficult to follow. The French had adopted so many of the Indian ways, Indian foods, and methods of preparations, that there was little difference in cooking except in the utensils used. The Indians used many kinds of containers. There were tightly woven baskets of many shapes and sizes to hold everything from nuts and berries to fish; pottery ranging from bowls large enough to hold bushels of corn, to fat bottles bigger than gallon jugs, from small bowls that served as drinking glasses, to tiny bottles that were used for weaned babies. Most of the pottery was of a golden brown clay excised with a swirling design of parallel lines that had the look of sea waves, though there were also pieces colored with orange-red ochre. The pots used for cooking over the fire were often of clay, or so Little Quail said. The food in them was cooked not by setting the pot over the heat, but by heating clean rocks, which were then dropped into the pot to bring the contents to a boil. In Reynaud's hut, however, the pots were of iron, as they were in the huts of all the wealthier Indians thanks to the traders like Pierre.

Among Elise's neighbors, there had been some who scorned to use wild meat, preferring the rancid salt pork that came in barrels from France, and who subsisted on a diet of white flour and dried beans instead of using the maize, squash, and sweet potatoes of the Indians. Elise had always considered them to be fools, especially when the fall storms made the arrival of the supply ships uncertain and these same people began to look pinched with hunger. Now more than ever it was good that she was familiar with such changes in diet since it seemed that henceforth, as on the trail, it would be a part of her duties to cook for Reynaud.

She toyed with the idea of refusing, if only to discover once and for all whether or not she was truly a slave. But there seemed little point. She preferred not to challenge Little Quail's friendship in such a way or to waste her energy defying Reynaud on such an unimportant point. She herself had to eat and if she did not cook at his fire, then she would have to go begging at the cook fires of others, which would do little for her dignity.

She could refuse to share his hut, of course, demanding to be allowed to join the other Frenchwomen instead. But as awkward as it might be to live in close quarters with Reynaud, it would be infinitely harder to live and work with a strange family of Indians, as she might be forced to do if she left his protection. No, the privacy of his hut was much better, even if it did mean having to serve him.

As she watched Little Quail making corn cakes, patting them into shape, and setting them to cook on the bottom of an iron pot smeared with hot bear grease, she flirted with the idea of escape. The more she studied the problem, however, the less likely the chances of success seemed. Here in the Grand Village she was surrounded by watchful Natchez. Even if she could get away without being seen, it was forty leagues to Fort Saint Jean Baptiste and more than ninety leagues to New Orleans by the way of the great river. They were long leagues swarming with potentially hostile Indians and wild animals, leagues of treacherous water, swamps, and dark woods. She hoped that she did not lack initiative, but this obstacle of combined distance and danger seemed insurmountable. It was better to be a slave to Reynaud than to be dead. She contemplated that truth and found it grimly amusing. What was not funny at all was the question of how she was to refrain from sharing his bed furs as well as his hut and cook fire. She would discover an answer, however. She would indeed.

The village seemed quiet as the morning advanced. Little Quail remarked upon it after a time. She thought the cause might be the arrival of a new trader or perhaps even a visit from the Englishmen of Carolina offering a bounty for slaves and French scalps. It was the fear that it might be news of more casualties in the war with the French, however, that finally caused the young Indian woman to leave the hut to look into the matter. It seemed that there were hunting parties out and bands sent to discover the intentions of the Choctaws, Tunicas, and Natchi-toches.

When Little Quail did not return after an hour, Elise grew worried. It was probably that any disaster that struck the Natchez would affect the French being held by them, including herself. Reynaud's absence did not concern her. It was not unusual for him to be gone for hours at a time, without explanation.

She thought of going out herself to see what was happening, but she was not certain how she would be greeted by the people in the village. Nor was she happy at the prospect of going abroad in her scanty costume. It had a most insubstantial feel, as if she were dressed for bed, and was not only as drafty as Reynaud had once claimed, but was also apt to flap about her in such a way that large portions of her anatomy were exposed when she least expected it. She was not a puritan by any means, but it was disconcerting to say the least to look down and discover that her top square of material had twisted to reveal a breast or that her skirt had slipped scandalously low on her hips.

She was very near to braving all obstacles, however, when the door of the hut was thrown open. A young French girl with a scared look on her face stepped inside without ceremony or permission. Drawing herself up, she said in breathless tones, "My mistress comes."

An Indian woman moved into view. Tall, handsome in a majestic fashion, she strode forward with a cape made of a red trader's blanket swirling around her and her arms, clasped with silver bracelets, crossed over her chest. She dismissed her servant with a brief gesture and entered the hut to confront Elise alone.

Elise searched her brain for the correct phrase of welcome, finding it at last. When no reply was forthcoming, she began to offer refreshment.

"Thank you, no," the Indian woman stated in a hard voice. "I wanted only to see the woman for whom my son must face death."

Elise stared at the other woman with the color draining from her face. There could be only one explanation. "You mean Reynaud?

"Is there another who must risk so much?"

"I don't—" Elise stopped, then went on in a different vein. "You must be Tattooed Arm."

"I am she."

This was the woman who had exposed the plot of the Natchez to the French. The woman who had loved a Frenchman and was mother to the Great Sun, as well as to Reynaud. "I don't understand what you mean. I've done nothing to endanger your son."

"You live."

Elise was silent for a stunned instant in the face of such a pronouncement. When she found her breath, she said, "Yes, but surely—"

"Tomorrow at sunrise he will run the gauntlet for your sake."

"For me? But why?"

"He has been accused in council by Path Bear, the son of my youngest brother and a woman of common blood. Path Bear claims that the new war chief of the Natchez loves the French too well, that he is a traitor to our people. This was said because he aided in the escape of a number of French people and did this out of desire for you, a Frenchwoman. For you he tarried far from here when my people had need of him, causing much inconvenience when it was confirmed by the elders that he was the proper choice as war chief. Finally, he challenged Path Bear before his fellow warriors over the trifling matter of a few blows for you and would have committed the crime of engaging in combat with him had not a cooler head, that of Path Bear himself, prevailed."

"You believe all that?" Elise demanded.

"It is so. Reynaud has admitted it as the truth."

"But you make it sound so much worse than it was!" She

stared at the woman, hating the calm pronouncements she was making, her stomach knotted with apprehension.

"It is serious enough so that a test of his resolve, his loyalty toward his people is necessary."

"First you say your people and now you say his. You ask too much of a man who is neither Natchez nor French, but of the blood of both. You are forcing him to choose and it isn't fair!"

"He has already chosen or he would not be here."

"Then why?"

"He must be certain in his heart, and we can be no less so. Lives, many lives, may depend on it."

"It must be stopped! You could do it; you could go to the Great Sun. He could order it stopped."

"He will not. The accusations have been made and must be answered. The elders have decided. My son, both my sons, know the old men are wise. It must be the gauntlet."

Elise sent her a fierce glare. "Then if nothing can be done, why did you come to me? Why were you so anxious to tell me?"

"I wanted to see if you were a woman of feeling. I wanted to see if my son deserves the office he has been chosen to fill."

"I don't understand how—"

Tattooed Arm stopped her with an upraised hand. "My son is wise. I am satisfied."

She was gone before Elise could form an answer. She started after the woman, her thoughts in turmoil. Had Reynaud known what he was to face when he had left the hut that morning? Had he guessed? She thought that he might have, and the remembrance of his light kiss, his swift but calm departure, brought the ache of pain to the region of her heart.

The gauntlet. It was as much a punishment as a test, one usually reserved for male prisoners, to inflict pain while discovering their levels of endurance. They could say what they pleased about loyalty and Reynaud's liking for the French, but she saw clearly that he would be running the gauntlet because of Path Bear's pride. The warrior had been incensed at being reprimanded because of a slave. He was not concerned for Reynaud's fitness as war chief so much as for revenge. What would happen, as Reynaud ran the gauntlet, was that he would receive, many times over, the blows that had been meant for her.

Little Quail returned. Her manner was constrained as she spoke of the test that was to come. Elise had the feeling that she blamed her for it, though it might have been nothing more than her own guilt that made her think so. Feeling the need to speak of it, to exorcise some of her angry fear over what was to happen, Elise told the other woman what had happened on the trail and of her distrust of Path Bear.

The young Indian woman nodded when she had finished. "You may be right. Path Bear is not well liked. His mother was a Commoner, a Stinkard who married a Sun, Reynaud's uncle. So strong-willed was she that she dominated her husband, though she was of inferior birth. Her husband tired of her and went away as an emissary to the Chicksaw, a mission that has taken several years. Some say he has another wife and children in that tribe and will not be coming back."

"I see, but what has this to do with Path Bear?"

"I am coming to that; you must be patient," Little Quail answered with a shake of her head. "With her husband gone from her influence, the mother of Path Bear, called Red Deer, pushed her Stinkard son to the front in the councils. With her behind him, he usurped the position of chief in the Flour Village, taking it as his right. He was confirmed in it by the council and the Great Sun because of his strength and ferocity in battle and because he has the blood of Suns in his veins. But there are those who say it was a mistake, for it was Path Bear, chief of Flour Village, who spoke loudest in the council against the French. It was he who urged the war of annihilation known as Blood Vengeance against them."

"Then he is responsible for the massacre," Elise said.

"It was he who put the idea into the head of the old war chief, yes. And once it was done, his power was great. He hoped to be chosen as the new war chief because of this and because Hawk-of-the-Night was far away. But the people, especially the women, had become wary of his bloodthirsty ways and so the elders sent to ask the brother of the Great Sun to accept the duty and the honor of becoming chief of war, in keeping with the ancient tradition."

"Then Path Bear has more than one reason to resent Reynaud."

Little Quail inclined her head in agreement. "But it goes deeper still. Even in childhood Path Bear tried always to surpass Hawk-of-the-Night, for being a Sun and the faster runner, the best shot with musket and bow and arrow, the most fortunate hunter, Hawk-of-the-Night was everything Path Bear most wanted to be."

"If Reynaud should die . . ." Elise said softly, speaking her fear aloud.

"He will not die, but neither must he show doubt or pain."

"When will it be held, this running of the gauntlet?"

"Tomorrow," Little Quail said, pity in her voice as she watched Elise. "At dawn."

By degrees, they began to regain their old footing. Elise asked the other woman to call her by her given name without the title of respect that had become a habit while Little Quail had been a slave to her house. Little Quail, in her kindness, offered to show Elise around the village to make her known to people and also to give her something to think about other than what would happen the next day. Together, they plaited Elise's hair in a single long braid down her back in the manner of the Natchez women. After adjusting Elise's cloak and retying her skirt for greater security, the young Indian woman led her out of the hut.

They strolled beneath the trees, skirting the foot of the mound of the Great Sun with the thirty-foot walls of his house towering above them. It was built like the others, with thick logs set upright in the earth and the corner logs left as trees that were bent toward the center and fastened together to form the roof. These logs were covered with woven cane mats that were then plastered with mud, while the roof was thatched with the covering mats. The house of the Great Sun was different only in that it was larger and had higher walls, with a second room that was used to store the excess corn and food stores, stores that would be parceled out during the winter to anyone in need.

Looking back to where the house given to Reynaud lay in the morning shadow of the mound of the Great Sun, Elise saw that, though not as large as the house of his brother, his home was larger than any other in the village. It was also newer. She realized abruptly that this was because it had been built especially for the new war chief on top of the ashes of the house of the old one. She had not thought of it until now, but there was little doubt that the bones of the last war chief lay beneath the floor she had walked on that morning.

She turned to Little Quail. "How long is it since the death of the old war chief in battle?"

"Not long. His bones were picked clean and buried only a few days before the delegation left the village to go to Hawk-of-the-Night."

The woman's voice was so quiet that Elise felt a quick remorse. Impulsively she said, "Forgive me. For a moment I forgot that this was also the time of your husband's death. If I caused you pain by speaking of it, I am sorry."

"You must not be. He is gone and I am not sad."

It was true that she did not look the grieving widow, but the Indians did not believe in long periods of mourning. Three days were given over to intense outpourings of sorrow and then it was done. Life went on. "You miss him, I'm sure."

"Perhaps," the woman said with a Gallic shrug learned during her days with the French.

"You had no children."

"No. I made certain of it."

"You what?"

Little Quail sent her a surprised glance at the sharpness of her tone. "I chewed the leaves that rid my body of the flesh of his flesh, for I did not wish to bring it to fruit. Would you not have done the same?"

Thinking of Vincent Laffont, Elise said, "Possibly, if I could."

"Surely you could have done so!"

"The leaves are not known among the French."

The woman stopped. "But you have so much knowledge. Surely this, being so important to women, is known to you."

"No."

"How strange. What do you do?"

"There are ways, instruments, but it is dangerous. Usually we do nothing."

Little Quail shook her head in amazement. "But you have no child of your husband."

"He was incapable, I believe, or possibly I am."

"It may be he was, for I had no need to chew the leaves while with him."

It was a relief to hear her say it. Elise had sometimes wondered why she had never conceived in the early days. She had thought that perhaps her body itself had cast off her husband's seed so greatly had she despised everything about him. Nature was not always so accommodating, however.

"In truth," Little Quail went on, "the death of my husband saved me trouble. I was near to putting him from my house."

Once more there was surprise in Elise's eyes as she looked at her. "You could have done that?"

"Most certainly. Oh, I know that the house belongs to the

man among the French, but it is otherwise with us. Here the house, the cooking pots and vessels, the furs and leatherwork, the land we plant all belong to the women. A man owns his weapons, the clothing he wears, and perhaps a horse if he has used furs to trade for it.''

"And you would have been allowed to put him out? There is no law that would compel you to let him return?"

"None. I alone decide."

"But if you had had children, they would have gone with him?"

"My children? Would I not have been their mother, she who carried them under her heart, bore them in pain, and cared for them in their helpless days? Does a fawn follow its father? Does the small opossum cling to its father's tail? Does the bear cub recognize the one who sired it? No! Why should they have gone with him?"

"He might have wished to know them, to help rear them."

"Children are watched and reared by all. There would have been no hindrance."

It was said that children of the Natchez were never struck and seldom spoken to in anger. They were welcome at every fire and in every hut and were taught with gentle words and demonstrations by whoever was near when a lesson was needed. As a result, they grew up confident, fearless, and certain within themselves. It would be interesting to see if it was true.

In the bright light of day, Elise was able to see more clearly than she had the night before that the village was built in a straggling circle. In the center was the mound of the Great Sun with his house facing south and with the open plaza, a large, flat area of beaten earth, in front of and below it. There was a ball game, using a sphere of leather-wrapped moss, in progress on this meeting ground of the village at the moment, with much shouting and yelling among the adolescent boys and girls who played.

On the other side of the plaza, facing the mound of the Great Sun, was the temple mound. The temple itself was the most imposing building in the village, built of enormous logs in a large square, with an antechamber facing east to prevent the uninitiated from seeing inside. Outside the temple the eternal fire burned between posts that were carved at the top in the likenesses of eagles. The most curious feature, however, was the ridgepole of the temple, where the carved images of wild white swans in flight were attached.

Directly behind the mound of the Great Sun lay yet another mound. This was, according to Little Quail, the old temple mound, abandoned in some forgotten year because the waterway that ran swiftly alongside the village, called St. Catherine Creek by the French, had encroached upon it. There was a fairly open space in front of it that had been the plaza in the old days, but it was now covered with huts. The huts also spread to the edge of the creek and on one side of the plaza and for some distance on the other.

"Where do you live?" Elise asked Little Quail.

"My hut is over there, with the Honored People."

The Honored People were those who had won advancement due to brave deeds or unselfish service. They were a special class ranked below the Sun and Nobles, but above the Commoners, or Stinkards.

Elise looked at the indicated round building with a conical roof. It was small but comfortable. A number of others were set close around it, with a space of tree-shaded earth between it and the larger huts nearer the mound of the Great Sun.

"And who lives there?" Elise asked, indicating the larger dwellings.

"The Nobles in the nearer huts and the Suns living closest to the Great Sun. The Commoners live over there, farthest from him. Perhaps I should tell you that my husband was a Commoner, or more accurately, a Stinkard."

Her attention caught by Little Quail's tone, Elise turned to look at her. "That makes a difference."

"Yes, of course. It is forbidden to marry one's own class. If I had been chosen by a Noble, I would have had to obey my husband and wait on his pleasure more closely. By marrying into the class under me, I kept my privileges and possessions."

"I see. In either case, your children would have remained Honored People, following your station."

"You have it right, though if I had been so honored as to marry into the Sun class, my children would have been Nobles."

"But your possessions?"

"They would still have been mine, always supposing that I was not so overwhelmed by my royal relatives that I was persuaded to give them up. If they were not needed, then most likely I would have given them to my daughter as a dowry."

"And in any case they would have descended to your children on your death?"

"This is so. Your inheritance is different, I know, by way of the father. But how unreasonable it is! Every child knows its mother, but who can say without doubt who his father may be?"

"Just so," Elise said with a wry smile. "But among the men of the Natchez there are some, particularly the Great Sun, who have more than one wife. How can this be, if women are free to leave a marriage at will?"

"Most often it is the Suns who have a second or third wife. It is the honor, the hope of advancement for the children, the family, you see, that makes a woman accept such a position. And then there are times when many men are killed in war so that there are more women than there are men of an age to be husbands. Besides, it is not always a cause for jealousy if a man takes another wife. It is done often because the first is pregnant and no longer wishes to please him in the bed furs. Sometimes a woman will suggest that he take another wife because she wants to avoid all possibility of pregnancy while nursing her baby. Though the leaves can be used, it will weaken her and perhaps cause her milk to cease flowing. And if, when her child is weaned, she is unable to live with the second wife, then she can leave, taking her child and the possessions she brought with her."

Elise nodded, mulling over the curious arrangement of the Natchez, and they walked on. They passed a large house set up on piles, the wood of which was polished to a satin gleam. There was a ladder lying on the ground beside it, and as they drew even a woman picked it up, set it against the door, and climbed up into the house. Glancing in, Elise saw her shaking out a coverlet that was unmistakably of French design. Behind the woman could also be seen piles of clothing, stacks of dishes, the legs of chairs, the solid bulk of marriage chests, and even what appeared to be the black snout of a cannon. The house was a storeroom for the booty that had been taken from Fort Rosalie and the houses of the French, and the slickly polished piles were to keep rats and mice from climbing up to damage the goods. Elise closed her eyes, turning quickly away.

They stepped around a pair of young girls playing at something like pick-up-sticks in the middle of the path. From a nearby doorway, two slightly older sisters looked up from where they were taking turns grinding corn to call a greeting. A dark-eyed cherub, wearing only a cloak about his shoulders and moccasins on his tiny feet, toddled from around the hut and stood rocking on his feet in front of them. Proud in his plump, copper nakedness, crowing with glee, he grinned up at them. His eyes were black and his hair fine and straight. Elise, staring down at him, felt an odd pain under her heart. Little Quail bent to scoop the boy up, rubbing her nose against his smaller one. A white-haired woman rounded the hut with hurried steps, dragging a half-scraped deer hide. She laughed toothlessly, scolding without heat as she saw the boy in Little Quail's arms. Greeting them, she began to talk, her wary gaze touching Elise now and then, but always returning to Little Quail.

Elise looked away. She had the uncomfortable feeling, as the old woman let out a cackle of mirth, that she was the subject of conversation. It made her uncomfortable that she could not fully understand, though otherwise she found that she didn't mind. She thought idly that she must begin to improve her Natchez if she wasn't to feel left out.

A flicker of movement caught her gaze and she looked toward the back of the hut. It was a dark column of flies that had attracted her attention, flies buzzing around the viscera of the deer the old woman had been cleaning. They had been disturbed by the approach of a warrior. His movements, stealthy, too hurried, made her watch him as she waited for Little Quail to finish talking. With his knife tip, the man raked an intestine from the pile of refuse, slitting it and spilling the contents on the ground. He took a pair of what appeared to be stout supple canes from under his arm and rubbed them in the entrails and their spilled contents. Satisfied, he glanced quickly around, turned, and walked away.

He had not recognized her in her Indian clothing or had perhaps taken her for a French slave of no importance, but Elise had known him instantly. What he was doing, whether it was some Indian trick or merely an unsavory habit, she did not know, but she was certain that the warrior had been Path Bear.

They walked on after a few minutes. Picking up their conversation, Little Quail said, "You spoke of the Great Sun and his wives. The poor man has been much too busy. Both his first wife and his second are now pregnant and will have nothing to do with him. It may be he will soon be looking for another."

"Perhaps his gaze will light on you?"

Little Quail laughed softly, but did not deny the possibility.

"If it did, would you wed him, despite the danger?"

"Danger?"

"Of being strangled should he die before you."

"The Great Sun lives long, in most cases. He does not go to war and his house stands high, where it is cool and healthful."

"Still, I would think he would have trouble finding a wife. It would seem more likely that he would take a mistress like our own King Louis."

"A mistress! Never!" Little Quail exclaimed.

"What would be wrong with that?"

"It isn't done."

"Oh, come, it's well known that such things happen a great deal in the village."

"Well known by whom?"

"We heard it constantly at the fort and I myself knew several men who enjoyed visits from Indian woman who also had husbands and children here."

A smug smile curved the mouth of the Indian woman. "Indian women. That's different."

"What do you mean, different?"

"There is nothing unusual in the activities outside marriage, or otherwise, of women. It is our privilege. But men are required to be faithful. An Indian man discovered in the arms of another woman can be put to death on the order of his wife."

"You don't mean it."

"But I do."

"And—and not the other way around?"

"Why should it be so merely because that is the way of it among the French? The women of the Natchez are not so bound. It is our right to take as many gallants as may please us regardless of the protests of our husbands."

"Surely they would divorce you for it."

"No, why? It would be to lose everything for the man while his wife would lose nothing. In any case, it is not possible. Divorce is a thing of women."

Elise stared at her with her mouth open, then gave her head a shake as if to clear her thoughts. "I don't understand. If women are so powerful, then how does it happen that they are given to men visitors, such as the French? I know this happens because Reynaud mentioned it himself."

"This is a matter of courtesy, but it requires the woman's approval. It is seldom withheld, for according to the wise men it brings new blood into the tribe, and anyway we females are curious about men who are strangers. Don't you find it do yourself?"

Thinking of Reynaud and the way she had reached out to touch his tattoos on that first night, Elise felt the color rise to her cheekbones. Her answer was barely audible. "I suppose."

There was the smell of woodsmoke and cooking food on the air. In nearly every hut at least one pot, if not two or three, bubbled near the fire. At some there were men gathered to eat, for except on feast days there were no regular mealtimes; each person ate as he grew hungry and found food prepared. A part of the delicious aroma on the air, however, came from the smoking racks. It was a good day for smoking meat, being dry, cool, and bright, and there were strips of deer, bear, opossum, and even the tail of an alligator hanging over the slow-burning fires.

Adding to the smoke was a great fire inside a small hut. The door stood open for ventilation and inside could be seen what appeared to be large rocks being baked. Elise nodded in that direction, asking what the purpose might be.

"The sweat hut," Little Quail said, the words clipped.

"Oh, a kind of steam bath," Elise said, having some faint remembrance of hearing it spoken of by that name.

"Water is poured on the hot rocks to make steam, yes. It is used to relieve extreme fatigue or as a purification ritual. It is being prepared now for Hawk-of-the-Night."

"I see." She had not realized it would be turned into a ceremony, this running of the gauntlet. It made it seem worse somehow, more dangerous.

"He will fast during the day, then spend several hours in the sweat hut this evening. Afterward, still fasting, he will wait out the night in the temple."

Elise swung to face the other woman, putting out a hand to stop her. "Won't that make him weak?"

"It will focus his mind fully on what will happen and how he must withstand it."

"Is there anything I can do to help?"

"You have done enough." The young woman turned her face away.

"What is it?" Elise asked. "What have I done?"

"Nothing."

"Little Quail, please!"

The other woman swung back to meet her gaze, her dark brown eyes steady. "Very well. I said before that Hawk-of-the-Night would not die, but I fear for him, I do fear for him. Path Bear wanted to be war chief, expected to be war chief, but the women influenced the wise men in the council of elders and they chose the brother of the Great Sun. Path Bear was sent instead to fetch the man who has always been his rival, has always been a better warrior, a better man, though he is but half Natchez. You gave Path Bear the excuse he needed to bring down the man who was chosen above him. He will do everything in his power to see that Hawk-of-the-Night does not recover from the gauntlet. At this time my people do not need cunning and bravado but a man of intelligence and daring and steadfast purpose. Without him, we may be doomed. If Hawk-of-the-Night dies, it will be upon your head, as the fate of the Natchez will be upon your head."

"I didn't know it would come to this."

"You are not of the Natchez or you would have thought."

"No," Elise said, a hard note in her voice, "I am not of the Natchez."

They stood staring at each other with the distrust, absent until now, of enemies. A chill breeze flapped Elise's skirt, exposing one leg to the thigh; she scarcely noticed and did not feel the rise of gooseflesh on her naked skin due to the greater chill inside her. Around her the Indians went about their tasks, chopping wood, grinding tools, and sharpening weapons, calling to each other and the omnipresent dogs, yelling in play. Nothing had changed, and yet she was suddenly aware of being French and among foes, in a way she never had before.

"Elise! Oh, Elise!"

She swung around at the sound of her name. Running toward her, stumbling over her ragged skirts and with her hair straggling around her face, was Madame Doucet. The woman threw herself on Elise, clutching her arms and sobbing.

Elise caught her, holding her with compassion. "What is it? Tell me."

"My little Charles! I knew, I knew it. It was he they killed. It was he they strangled, cruel monsters that they are; strangled in his youth, ah, *mon Dieu*, so young, so young. And for nothing. Nothing. I told you! I did tell you how it would be. I knew. Somehow I knew."

"Calm yourself, I beg you." Elise patted her shoulder, tears rising to her own eyes for the woman's grief and for the terrible picture she painted with her incoherent words that somehow became mixed with a deep and private desolation Elise did not care to examine. She drew a deep breath, saying, "Think of your daughter."

"Yes." Madame Doucet drew back. "I must be strong. My poor daughter, to lose her child and in such a way. I fear for her. She isn't strong and she has been working so hard, so hard. I must help her. She needs me. But, oh, Elise, my poor little grandson. He was alive, had survived that terrible massacre, and they killed him. They killed him! Murderers, oh, they are cruel murderers."

It seemed at that moment that Madame Doucet was right. What had either of them to do with such people? Why should she care for their approval or feel guilt at their anger? What did it matter that tomorrow one of them would be whipped for her sake? If Reynaud had not held her against her will, there would be no need. She was French. She belonged with her people. She turned to Little Quail.

"Is there any reason why I should not visit with Madame Doucet's daughter and perhaps some of the others?"

"None that I know of."

"Then I will thank you for your kindness this morning and bid you good day."

Despite her defiance, the visit was not a success. Madame Doucet's daughter was ill with grief and an infection in her head wound that she had refused to have treated by the Indians. She was hardly aware of where she was, much less of who had come to see her. Filthy, rail-thin from lack of nourishment, she lay on a bench in a small hut set off by itself among the Stinkards. Off and on through the afternoon, some of the other Frenchwomen came to visit and to speak to Elise. There was an odd constraint about them, however, as if they did not trust her. They knew she had been with Reynaud, knew something of the circumstances. Still, their resentment that she was wandering around the Indian village free and unencumbered, that she was dressed as an Indian and ensconced among the Suns, that her shining hair hung down her back while theirs had been shorn to indicate their slavery, was an obvious and solid thing. They seemed to think that she had betrayed them in some way, and though they did not want to antagonize her for fear that she might be able to harm them or else in the hope that she could help them if she chose, they saw no reason to treat her as one of them, the slaves of the Natchez.

It seemed that like Reynaud she, too, had no people.

12

THE VILLAGE WAS awake and stirring early. The buzz of voices, mingling with the barking of dogs, the dry rattling of shaken gourds, and the tooting of cane whistles, echoed around the hut where Elise lay staring with wide and burning eyes into the smoke-darkened dome of the ceiling. She had slept little.

After a time, she got up. Wrapping her cloak around her, she kindled a fire, then stood shivering beside it for some time before she got dressed. She wondered what Reynaud was doing, how he was feeling. Did he dread the coming ordeal as much as she did? Or was he resigned to it, even, perhaps, looking forward to the test of his powers, uplifted by his fast and temple vigil?

She would not watch; she could not bear to watch. There was no reason why she should. She was not a savage, used to such sights; why shouldn't she be upset at the thought of seeing a man whipped? She would stay quietly in the hut until it was over. Perhaps she should spend the time preparing to care for the injuries Reynaud would receive; it was possible that she owed him that service for her part in this terrible ordeal. She had learned a great deal about the Indian ways with herbs from Little Quail in the time the woman had spent with her and there were many of the necessary herbs close to hand, hanging from the ceiling beams.

It was easy enough to make a resolution; the trick was in keeping it. When the rise of the voices from the direction of the plaza indicated that the gauntlet was ready and that Reynaud had appeared outside the temple, she could not remain inside the hut. It seemed cowardly to stay there in hiding.

The sun was brilliant as she stepped out of the artificial darkness of the hut. It shone with feeble warmth on the crowd gathered around the plaza, catching the sheen of a patch of beading on leather here, the gleam of the sharp edge of a hatchet or knife there. Children darted, dogs leaped and barked, women sat talking, men stood about with their capes flapping as they made quick gestures in conversation. They paid scant attention to the men drawn up in a double line in the center of the plaza, each with a stripped cane pole some four feet long in his hand. Warriors all, these men who stood waiting; they were the stoutest and strongest of the tribe.

Turning away quickly, Elise saw that most of the Suns had chosen to watch the impending event from the slopes of the mound of the Great Sun. The height gave them a much better view than being at ground level. There were even a few elderly people who had been carried from the huts to a place on the mound to watch. Carefully tended, these respected ones sat waiting for the excitement to begin. Elise moved around to the front side of the mound and climbed a few feet up the slope to be able to see above the crowd.

There was a small commotion from the large house of the Great Sun above her. Turning her head, Elise saw Reynaud's brother emerge from his dwelling and seat himself on a chair that had been brought out for him. An ornate piece of furniture, heavily carved and gilded with a seat of silk upholstery, it would not have looked out of place at Versailles. The Great Sun settled into his chair and adjusted his cloak and breechclout of woven swansdown which were dyed the deep sable-black color only he was allowed to wear. Turning to the man at his side, who might have been a temple caretaker of some kind, he spoke a few words, then lifted his feathered scepter in a signal that the trial, for that was what it was in effect, could begin.

Drums boomed, a rolling, measured sound coming from the huge, baked earthenware pots with leather stretched over their mouths and filled with water to give them different tones. The Indians gathered around the plaza grew quiet.

From the great temple on its mound directly in front of where Elise stood, Reynaud emerged. His breechclout was of white leather and his cape of spun and woven swansdown. The swan feathers of his small crown lifted gently in the rise of the morning breeze. The sun glinted with blue light on his hair and slid along the planes of his chest with a gleam of red bronze. His face was calm and his bearing upright. Step by slow step, in time with the slow cadence of the drums, he descended the long ramp leading from the mound to the plaza.

At the foot of the mound, he stopped. The drums began a soft roll. Women came forward to take Reynaud's cape. They led him to the head of the double line of warriors. He stood for a long moment. Elise thought that he drew a deep breath, allowing his glance to move over the crowd. It came to rest on the place where she stood for a long moment, though his face was without expression. His gaze moved on, lifting to find his brother on his gilded chair. He lifted one arm in a brief salute, then nodded his readiness.

The drums fell silent. Cane whistles shrilled in a single dissonant note, then stopped abruptly. Reynaud took a deep breath, then stepped forward. The first cane was raised. Whining, keening, it fell.

The running of the gauntlet was not unusual in the armies of Europe. Had the custom been brought to the new world by the expeditions of the Spanish and French over the last two hundred years or had it been noted and exported to Europe along with the exotic plants of America? There were differences in the way it was carried out, or so Elise thought, from what she had heard. In most European armies, the man who was to be punished was led at a slow march by a soldier carrying a musket with bayonet affixed. The man could not run forward to avoid the blows without impaling himself and so could only writhe in agony under the slow and repeated blows. There was no soldier, no bayonet, to ensure fortitude here with the Natchez. She expected to see Reynaud run and twist, dodging the flailing canes. He did not.

With set face and slow strides, he moved down the gauntlet, flinching slightly in a muscular reaction under the most severe cuts, expelling his breath in a hollow sound that was not quite a grunt at others. The red of stripes appeared on his back, crisscrossed. As other blows landed in the same place, the skin broke and blood began to trickle. Still he walked on, sometimes wavering a little from the force of the blows, but without breaking stride.

The heavy, meaty whacks of the striking canes sent a shiver along Elise's nerves. She wanted to cover her ears, to run, to hide, but some greater compulsion held her where she stood.

She was shivering, her palms sweating though the tips of her fingers were icy, as cold as her lips were as she raised her hands to them to hold back the cry of protest that rose inside her. She could not interfere, she must not interfere; and yet the need to do so was so great it was like a bursting pain inside her. She wanted to look away, but could not.

Then she saw Path Bear near the end of the gauntlet. He held his cane ready, a gloating look on his square face in contrast to the stern and implacable expressions of the others. Elise's eyes widened as she saw the stout cane in his hand. It was one of those she had seen him with the day before, one he had trailed through the viscera of the deer. It was well known that such excrement could cause corruption in open injuries, even poisoning of the blood that could lead to death. A terrible suspicion rose inside her. If she had only known the purpose of the canes! Now it was too late, for at that moment the cane Path Bear held descended, wielded with every ounce of his hard strength. In the same motion, the warrior jabbed, twisting it into the worst of the mass of oozing stripes that marked Reynaud's back. Reynaud faltered, wincing, but did not stop. Another blow. Another. A final one.

It was over.

A great shout of acclamation went up from the crowd. They surged forward, gathering around Reynaud, praising and congratulating, though none touched him. Above Elise, the Great Sun came to his feet and gestured. Reynaud turned toward his brother, moving slowly to the mound and its sloping incline where the Great Sun stood waiting. At the foot of it, he swayed, then caught himself. His face was pale, Elise saw, as if only now the pain of what he had endured was making itself felt. His face grim, he straightened his shoulders and lifted his foot to take the first step upward.

Placing one foot before the other, he climbed, coming nearer and nearer to where Elise stood. She let her hands fall to her sides, unwilling to let him see that she had been concerned for him, that she wanted to help him. Unconsciously she stood taller, lifting her chin. As he came even, his dark gaze searched for and found her. She forced her stiff lips into a smile, holding his gaze without evasion, without a flicker of the sympathy she felt on her face.

Then he was past, reaching to take the hand of his brother held out to him. The Great Sun drew him to stand beside him in front of the thronelike chair he had occupied. In a voice deep and stentorian, the Great Sun spoke.

"My people," he said, his words rolling away to echo among the trees, "I present to you your new chief of war, known among you as Hawk-of-the-Night. From this day he shall be called by the name borne proudly by those of his calling who have gone before. I bid you to accept this man, henceforth known as Tattooed Serpent, for his courage and honor. I command you to follow always where he leads, for in his hands lies the fate of the Natchez. With him we shall find victory or death!"

The cries and shouts rose, a throbbing joyous noise. Giving orders for a day of rest, games, and feasting, their leader turned back toward his house taking Reynaud with him.

Immediately there was a surge of women up the incline, many of them carrying small pots of herbs and unguent. Seeing Little Quail among them, Elise swung away, leaping down from the mound and running into Reynaud's hut. Coming out a moment later, she held a small clay pot that contained her own concoction of herbs and bear grease for the remedy of cuts and bruises.

She felt a little foolish joining the other women who crowded around the door of the Great Sun's house, but that did not make her less determined. What had happened was not really her fault; she knew that. That did not keep her from feeling guilty or from wishing to expiate that guilt in some way. It was reason enough for aiding Reynaud, the only reason.

They made way for her, the Common women who were outside along with a few Noble women. Inside the doorway, she paused. The house of the Great Sun, though larger and with the storeroom to one side, was not so very different from Reynaud's. Built of the same logs and mud plaster, it had the same sleeping benches around the walls with the same baskets and pots stored beneath them, the same herbs and antlers hanging from the ceiling. It boasted a table that, like the gilt chair, was probably a gift from the French, as was a blue velvet coat that hung on a peg. Otherwise, the main difference was that it had two fires and two sets of cooking utensils, one arrangement for each of the Great Sun's two wives. The smells of smoke and roasting meat filled the air along with the aroma of baking corn cakes. There were a number of women working busily around the edges of the fire, but more of them were clustered around the sleeping bench at the rear of the room where Reynaud could just be glimpsed in the center of them.

Elise approached rather diffidently. She touched one woman on the shoulder, indicating with a word or two and a smile that she wished to come closer to the injured man. The woman shrugged her off, turning her back. Elise tried again, thinking that she had been misunderstood. This time she showed the woman her pot of medicine. The woman, perhaps a Sun, said something that sounded more than a little rude and once more swung away. Elise saw Little Quail standing to one side. She called to her, but the woman, seeing what Elise wanted at a glance, only shook her head. Elise stood frowning, wondering if Reynaud would beckon her forward if he saw her or if he would prefer to be tended by these other women. Certainly she heard no protests from him.

Might it not be just as well if she went away, leaving him to be cared for by others of his kind? But, no, the women did not know what Path Bear had done. They might not be thorough enough, might even press the tainted matter into the wounds if they used a washing motion. She could not leave it as it was.

Once more she tapped the Sun woman on the shoulder. The woman turned around with her hands on her hips and, seeing Elise, gave her a shove. Incensed at the deliberate rudeness, Elise shoved back. The woman reached for the long braid of Elise's hair and suddenly Elise remembered the night when she had arrived, remembered being hauled into Reynaud's hut by her hair. The face of this woman seemed familiar, connected with the humiliation of that moment. Elise slapped her hand aside with such force that the print of her fingers was left on the woman's arm. Another Sun woman turned and then another. The first one began to screech.

In a body the women attacked, pulling and clawing at Elise. They tugged her this way and that, wrenching at her cape, pulling it off over her head along with the shorter square that covered her breasts. Her pot of medicine fell to the floor with the heavy thud of breaking pottery. Elise kicked out and had the fierce satisfaction of seeing one of the women fly backward to sprawl on the beaten floor. She heard Little Quail calling her name, thought the woman had run toward her trying to come to her side. She could not see.

Elise caught the wrist of the first woman as she once more grasped her hair and, twisting it, shoved her into two others who were clawing at her arms. More women ringed her. Hands reached, grabbing and hustling her toward the door. She felt the knot of her skirt loosen, felt the square cloth give way to be trampled underfoot. Setting her feet, she jerked against those who held her, flinging those clinging to her right arm away long enough to double her fist and smash it into the faces of the two who held her left wrist. As one of the women howled, bringing her hand up to her bloodied nose, gladness burgeoned inside Elise. It was short-lived though, as they descended on her once more.

A roared command, repeated above the hubbub, penetrated to the mass of brawling women. Instantly Elise was released, falling to her knees on the floor. The Indian women backed away, leaving her alone, naked in the center of their circle with her breasts heaving from her struggles and her hair in disarray around her flushed face.

The man sitting on the bench, the one she had taken for Reynaud, was the Great Sun. His eyes were wide as they moved over her and he drew in his breath in a gasp of startled pleasure.

Reynaud lay on the bench on his stomach while his mother washed the blood from his back and cleansed the stripes and the gouge that Path Bear had opened with a piece of soft leather dipped in hot water in which herbs had been steeped. He uttered a soft oath as he saw Elise. He tried to get to his feet, but his brother reached out to touch his arm, waving him back into place. Rising, the Indian monarch paced majestically to where Elise knelt.

The Great Sun reached down, offering his hand. Elise, now profoundly aware of her state of undress, hesitated. There seemed no possibility of refusal, however, any more than there would have been if the man before her had been Louis of France. She put her fingers into his hand and rose to her feet with as much grace as she could summon. The chief of the Natchez allowed his gaze to wander down her slender form, resting here and there in an appreciation that seemed half carnal, half bemused. There was a trace of regret in his voice as he said, "You, I take it, are Elise, the woman of my brother."

"I am Elise, yes, your majesty."

He gave a nod, then, still holding her hand, turned to the Indian women. A hard edge entered his voice as he spoke, castigating them for fighting like children who had not learned their manners and telling them, when they would have protested, that Elise was a guest, one dear to their new war chief, one who must be honored in all things. He felt shame for their behavior;

therefore he dismissed them from his house and did not wish to see their faces until he had sent them a direct invitation.

When they had gone, he turned and executed a passable bow. "In what way, Madame Elise, may those of my house serve you?"

"I—I only wished to tend Reynaud."

"Indeed?" He turned toward his mother. "Maman?"

The woman stared at her, her strong features shuttered and her eyes dark with swift thought. Abruptly she nodded.

"Tend him you shall," the Great Sun said, his mouth curving into a smile of utter charm. Elise, watching him, was caught suddenly by his resemblance to Reynaud. They were, in truth, twins, with the same eyes, the same hair, the same body structure. The only obvious difference was that the Natchez chief was tattooed not only on his chest, but on his shoulders and, as a mark of great distinction, on his knees as well.

Looking away from the blatant flattery of his gaze, she said, "If I could cover myself first . . . "

He pursed his lips, sending a glance to his brother's scowling expression and from him to his own two wives who squatted at their fires, watching, the only women left other than Tattooed Arm and Little Quail. Turning back, he sighed. "If you must."

Elise released herself and leaned over to take up her skirt, settling it around her with her lips tightly pressed together. She had come to help; a simple thing, really. Why had she been attacked, mocked, and finally left naked, displayed to all? When she thought of her position as a respectable landowner not so long ago, one who ordered her own days and nights, who made her own decisions and was answerable to none, her resentment was so great that she wondered how she could contain it.

Little Quail brought her her short cape that, tied onto one shoulder, covered her breasts. Her longer outer cloak was hung on a peg. Tattooed Arm rose from the bench beside her son, indicating with a courteous gesture for Elise to be seated there.

Elise glanced at Reynaud. Seeing the sympathy and understanding mirrored in his face, a faint flush rose to her cheekbones. She turned to his mother. "I would not take your place."

"I give it to you," Tattooed Arm replied.

"But the medicine I brought is gone." Already one of the wives of the Great Sun was busy gathering up the broken pottery, scooping up the spilled herbs and bear fat with a piece of the pot.

"I have more. Wait and I will bring it," Little Quail said and turned swiftly away, bending her head to pass through the open doorway.

After everything that had happened, not just here in the house of the Great Sun, but her estrangement from Little Quail, the coolness of the Frenchwomen, the trial by pain that Reynaud had been forced to undergo because of her, she felt odd about approaching him. Why it should be so she was not certain, but it was as if a distance had been placed between them. It seemed as if the very nature of the Indian village made him a stranger again, a different man from the one she had known at his own home near the Bayou Duc du Maine.

She looked at him. Her voice stiff, she said, "You will permit me?"

His eyes lighted with warm amusement. "I would be flattered. In fact, I welcome the attention from you, as you well know."

She moved forward and seated herself beside him on the bench. With a touch on his shoulder to indicate that she wanted him to turn his back more toward her, she leaned over to look at his injuries.

She was prepared, or so she had thought. Still, she had to swallow hard against the sickness as she saw the lacerated condition of his back. The skin around the livid red stripes was beginning to turn purple in great blotches with bruising. Some of the places where he had been struck were ragged cuts; others ran together into a mass of torn flesh, particularly between his shoulders where Path Bear had jabbed his cane. Tattooed Arm had cleaned the area well, and most of the bleeding had stopped, but Reynaud was going to feel the effects of the beating he had received for a long time.

"If only I had a little cognac to use," Elise murmured to herself.

"Cognac?" the Great Sun inquired, his tone doubtful.

"I have seen it used on wounds. It seems to help the healing."

"I may have a dram or two."

"Humph," his mother snorted and the Great Sun sent her an injured glance before turning to instruct one of his wives, the one who was less obviously pregnant, to fetch the brandy.

Elise scarcely noticed the byplay. She had dipped the leather into the pot of warm herb water Tattooed Arm had been using, pressing it to a still oozing gash.

The brandy was brought, just a few inches left in a stoneware bottle. The Great Sun looked at it regretfully, then handed it to Elise. "It might be of greater use to let my brother drink it."

Reynaud shook his head. "I don't think that would be wise, as empty as my stomach is just now."

"We will remedy that as soon as you are trussed up."

"Could you hur-hurry," he said, catching his breath in the middle as Elise poured the brandy onto his back.

By the time Little Quail had returned, Elise was ready for the ointment. She spread it on liberally, then covered his back with strips of woven mulberry cloth, binding them into place with longer pieces that encircled his body.

They ate then, Reynaud moving gingerly into a sitting position. They were joined by others: an elderly man who appeared to be the father of one of the Great Sun's wives; a pair of elderly women, one of whom Elise had met the day before tending the little boy. They were apparently the aunts of Tattooed Arm. The small bronze cherub himself was brought in and introduced as the child of the Great Sun. All were most solicitous of Reynaud, offering him tidbits of meat and bread and pressing strong broth upon him to give him strength. Even the boy, whose name was Small Owl, seemed to realize that something was wrong, for he climbed very carefully up to lean on Reynaud's shoulder and reached to nuzzle his lean cheek with a small nose.

Reynaud ate ravenously and with enjoyment, trading quips with the older women, joking with his brother, playing with the child. In a short while, however, he grew quiet. Glancing at him, Elise saw him sway, catch himself, then inch back to rest against the wall of the house. As she looked at him more closely, she saw that there were the dark shadows of weariness under his eyes and his face appeared drawn.

Why shouldn't he be exhausted? He had kept watch, seldom sleeping, all that long journey from his home, had stayed up half the night they had arrived for the obligatory feast, then had spent last night keeping vigil at the temple. He had eaten nothing for more than thirty-six hours, then had undergone severe punishment. The wonder was that he was able to retain his senses at all.

Reaching out, she touched his arm. "Lie down. Sleep."

Beyond him there was a stir. The Great Sun had moved to his side. "Yes, sleep. This I command."

Reynaud looked at her and none other. His eyes were dark, glazed with weariness and pain, but without subterfuge. "Lie with me, Elise."

It was a powerful appeal in his present state, with the press of self-blame upon her shoulders. And yet she had sworn that she would not return to his bed. He was no danger to her now, it was true, but if she went to him voluntarily now, would he accept her refusal later?

She drew a deep breath. "I would only disturb you."

"I missed you last night and all the other nights on the trail."

"I told you before, our bargain is ended. I am no longer compelled to—to be your companion of the bed furs."

"We will argue about that another time. For now, only come."

He held out his hand. Behind Elise, Tattooed Arm spoke. "Do as he asks."

"I can't."

The Great Sun moved to stand over her. "Must I command this also? It is no great sacrifice, Frenchwoman."

Wasn't it? What of her pride and self-respect? What of her future?

"Elise, please—"

Reynaud's gray eyes were dark, his face pale. The hand that he held out to her had a faint tremor. It was compassion that made Elise take a stiff step forward, reaching out to him. Compassion and the order of his brother. Nothing more.

Ignoring the stares and whispers, she moved to lie on the bench beside him, taking the space nearest the wall and drawing him against her. She covered him with a bed fur, cushioning his back with a part of its softness. With a hard constriction around her heart, she saw that before she had lowered her own head to the straw-stuffed pillow he was already asleep. There seemed nothing to do but attempt the same.

It was dark when she awoke. She was pressed against the wall of the house with the upright logs jammed into her back. It was hot, suffocatingly so. There was a rough muttering in her ears. She pushed at the heavy weight that held her, raising herself to one elbow.

The coals of the dying fire gave a red gleam to the dark. In their light she could see the sleeping forms of the others along the benches in the house of the Great Sun. Beside her, Reynaud said something deep in his throat. She understood it so little that a sudden fear sprang into her mind. Lifting her hand, she placed it on his forehead.

He was burning with fever, his skin holding an intense dry heat that made her jerk her hand away in consternation. She scrambled upright, crawling over him to get off the bench, then sitting back down beside him on its edge. She felt him again, then sat with her hand cradling his face, trying to think

Cool water, that was what she needed. She must bathe his body in it, then see to the preparation of an infusion of willow bark. She would need help. Looking around at the sleeping forms, she bit her lip in indecision. Should she wake someone? And if so, who? She considered a moment longer, then as Reynaud began to speak hoarsely in delirium once more, she rose with sudden energy and moved to put her hand on his mother's shoulder.

The hours passed. Morning came and still Reynaud did not know them. His fever rose and fell according to their ministrations but did not break. Somewhere around noon, they removed his bandaging and used the water in which red oak bark had been steeped to wash his wounds once more, allowing the water to stand in the worst of the gashes. If it made any difference, they could not tell. An ancient crone, the oldest woman of the tribe who kept the secrets of the plants, brought an evil-smelling brew that she insisted he drink at sunup, midday, sundown, and midnight. They spooned it into him with some difficulty, but could see no results.

People began to gather outside the house. Elise could hear them talking among themselves while now and then a woman would wail as if in grief. When Little Quail entered the house once more, well after night had fallen, Elise looked up from where she was wringing out a cloth.

"What is all the commotion? One would think they expect him to die."

"They fear he may."

"They needn't make it so obvious! What if Reynaud heard them?"

The Indian woman shook her head. "He would understand their fears."

"But I thought Indians were stoical about such things? That they hardly grieved at a death."

The woman gave her a strange look. "It is useful to grieve aloud before death so that the one who must depart will know he is loved, don't you think? And Hawk-of-the-Night, now Tattooed Serpent, is much loved. Besides, he is a Sun and the great war chief."

"You have a point, but as for the other, what difference—Oh! I see."

As a high-ranking Sun, if Reynaud died there would be many who would be chosen to die with him, to go with him and serve him in the hereafter. There would be more ceremonial stranglings before the temple. Since he had been raised to the position of war chief, there would presumably be many more to honor his newly acquired rank. If she were his wife, even she—But, no, she would not consider it.

"There is another thing. Four years ago, when the old Tattooed Serpent, the man who was war chief before the last one, died, there was much terror because he, too, had been the brother of the Great Sun. So strong was the love of the brothers, one for the other, that our supreme ruler had sworn a blood oath that he would follow Tattooed Serpent in death. This would have meant many more ritual deaths, to number perhaps a hundred. It was prevented by a Frenchman who sat with the Great Sun through the night following the death. In the end, of course, the Great Sun met death, anyway; of grief, some say, and the dishonor of breaking his word. Now the people fear that because of the birth tie between the man who is now the Great Sun and Hawk-of-the-Night, the new Tattooed Serpent, he, too, may decide to destroy himself."

"Surely not?"

"Who can say? It isn't often that two who come from the same womb are suffered to live. One is usually destroyed, as with all others that are malformed. It was the French father who saved the second-born, claiming that there was one child for the Natchez and one for his people. Still, it is this tie that causes the greatest fear now."

Elise stared at the other woman, absorbing what had been said without surprise, rather as if she had lost the capability of feeling such a thing. Finally she said in firm tones, "No matter. Reynaud is not going to die."

"If only it could be certain," Little Quail said, her face anxious as she came to stand and look down at Reynaud where he tossed restlessly on the bench.

"I will make it certain. I won't let Path Bear win."

"What do you mean?"

Little Quail had been in and out of the house all day bringing whatever was needed, helping to turn Reynaud and to restrain him, seeing to Small Owl. Without the necessity of spoken words, the two women had put aside their differences. In many ways, they had regained the closeness that had existed between them when they had been united against the petty tyranny of Vincent Laffont.

Now Elise said, "Did I not tell you? I thought I had spoken of it; it's been so strong in my mind. It was like this."

The face of Little Quail was grim when Elise had finished. She swung away, calling to Tattooed Arm to listen to the tale. The other women gathered near, exclaiming, looking from one to the other as the Indian woman told of Path Bear's vicious trick.

Tattooed Arm was silent for long moments when Little Quail fell silent. Her face was grim, etched in sorrow and implacability. She turned at last to the oldest woman among them. "Grandmother," she said, giving the ancient one the honorary title, "what say you?"

It was some time before the toothless woman spoke, but no one was impatient, no one hurried her. Finally, her ancient features drawn with grief, the woman looked up from her contemplation of the floor. "Path Bear has shown himself unworthy," she said. "Let it be banishment."

The others nodded in slow agreement. From one to the other the single word ran, a sentence, a curse. *"Banishment. Banishment. Banishment."*

It did not sound like a harsh decree. The banishment, according to Little Quail, was only from the Grand Village, not from the tribe itself. Path Bear would still hold his office as chief of the Flour Village, still take part in the feasts and dances and be allowed to fight as a warrior. But the decree meant the end of his ambitions, for it was at Grand Village that the council of elders met to plan for the planting and the harvest, for the hunting and the wars. It was there that the Great Sun held his court and dispensed honors and favors. Path Bear was condemned to stay as he was, a small chieftain who could never again influence the decisions that meant famine or prosperity, life or death, in the tribe. He was finished.

The wives of the Great Sun looked at each other, then the

youngest slipped from the house. The voices outside increased in volume, with a sharp note of outrage rising above them now and then.

Time passed as Elise and the others worked on Reynaud. It was perhaps an hour later when a hail came. Since the request for entry had been made in a female voice, the eldest wife of the Great Sun called out to bid the woman inside. The door slid open and a woman stepped into the house.

It was the mother of Path Bear, the woman known as Red Deer, who had attacked Elise. A massive woman, her heavy features hinted at mixed blood, perhaps of Natchez and Tioux. She had come to plead for her son before Tattooed Arm and the Great Sun.

The Great Sun was at the temple and Tattooed Arm refused to go with Red Deer to him or to send him a message to let him know that the other woman was there. She heard Path Bear's mother out in silence, never turning from her though the woman gestured wildly in the direction of Elise and Reynaud, lying on the bench. Finally Red Deer ran dry of words. Tattooed Arm raised her arm and began to speak, the phrases smooth and eloquent as they fell from her lips.

Elise could not understand what she was saying, but the import was obvious. There would be no repeal of the sentence. When she ceased to speak, the mother of Path Bear turned away. Her bearing was erect and there was venom in the look she cast at Elise, but on her face were stamped the lines of defeat and broken grief.

The judgment of Path Bear had been quick and without formality, but it was no less effective for all that. There was no one who would carry out the sentence, no armed men who would escort Path Bear from the village, but if he did not go he would be treated as one dead. No one would speak to him or acknowledge his presence. His friends would look through him as if he did not exist. The women in particular would ignore him, speaking of him in his hearing as a worthless one whose absence made life better. Few could tolerate such ostracism for long. Often suicide was the result of so great a disgrace. Sometimes, rather than try to live under such a decree, the person faded away into the woods. Of these, some joined other tribes; most were never heard from again.

The night passed with little change. Elise searched her mind for some other concoction, some other method of treatment they had not yet used. She had heard of pouring brandy into the wounds and then lighting it to cauterize them, but she could not bring herself to believe that the added shock and pain would not override any benefit. Some people swore that pieces of bread tied to the injury and left to moulder away into crumbs were helpful, but she had no wheat bread to use. There were powders used by surgeons aboard naval vessels that were much touted by the surgeons themselves, but Elise had grave doubts that they were any more efficacious than the herbs that had already been applied.

Toward dawn, Tattooed Arm rose and, ordering Elise to bed, took her place. As much as Elise would have liked to refuse, she could not summon the effort. She was weary unto death, tired out with the worry as much as the physical exertion of caring for Reynaud through the long hours since his fever had started.

She was awakened when the sun was high by shouts and cries coming up from the village plaza. Thinking it was only some kind of game, she did not look out, but struggled up and righted her clothing, then went to check on Reynaud. Finding him much the same with Little Quail now on guard, she moved with stiff steps to wash her face with warm water from a clay pot. She stopped long enough to rescue a puppy from Small Owl, who was dragging it around by its tail, though she knew with wry certainty that the poor little animal would probably wind up in a cooking pot soon enough.

She sat down and took the laughing child into her lap, washing his face while she scrubbed her own, playing with him, enjoying his chortling and his attempts to talk as a relief from her own distress. She felt no self-consciousness about her actions; it was something she saw everyone in the house do a half-dozen times a day, this gentle caressing of the baby boy. He was constantly underfoot, into everything, and had to be continuously moved out of the way, out of the supplies, out of danger of the fire. He was never shouted at, never slapped, but was always given some toy or utensil or bit of food to distract him. By the same token he was never allowed to disturb Reynaud or his father or to impede the progress of the tasks that were being done.

Behind her, Little Quail spoke quietly to Tattooed Arm, then came to Elise's side. They were both in need of the freshness of bathing, she said. Would Elise care to come with her to the creek?

A short time later as they made their way across the plaza toward the creek, a woman stopped them. A scouting party had come across a French expedition that had been reconnoitering to the south. They had killed five of the French and captured two others, one of whom had been tortured on the spot. The other man had been brought to the Grand Village. She did not know his name, but he was said to be a trader. The woman thought it a good thing that the warriors should have something to shout and dance about to take their minds from the worry about what the French might be planning and about the matter of Path Bear.

There was nothing Elise could do for the captured man. With an effort, she tried to close her mind to what was going to take place. She and Little Quail did not tarry long with the woman, but continued toward the water. Elise was silent as they walked, wondering who the Frenchman might be, if it was someone she knew or if it was simply a man who had been doing his duty as a soldier. The Indians, she had discovered, had little respect for the regular French army, considering the men as little better in battle than the greenest of young warriors. They reserved their admiration for the militia, the colonist volunteers who had learned to fight in the Indian fashion, shooting from cover instead of marching in battle formation to their deaths.

On the banks of the running stream, they untied the squares of cloth and leather that covered them and struck out into the water. Its chill brought yelps and gasps from them, but after a moment that cold freshness gave them the vigor to stage a water fight and that activity soon warmed their blood.

Downstream some distance from where they had entered the water was another woman who had just given birth that day. She was washing her newborn infant as well as herself. Elise had heard it said that this practice contributed to the high infant mortality among the Indians but that the women could not be persuaded to discontinue a habit that was of such long standing, considering cleanliness more important. In the same way, the children who ran high fevers with the white man's diseases of measles and colds also came to bathe, bringing on the pneumonia that often led to death. It was true that the survivors of the rigors of daily bathing were strong and healthy—so rare was it to see an Indian who was crippled or disfigured, other than with battle scars, that it was not unusual for Indian youths who first saw the scars of chickenpox or smallpox on them to do away with themselves out of horror.

There were no men in evidence. They bathed at a different place, Little Quail said. It was not that their mutual nakedness was an embarrassment; no, not at all. Boys and girls up to the age of puberty swam and bathed together as a matter of course. It was simply that it was deemed more likely that there would be less time wasted, time that should be applied to tasks, if dalliance between the sexes during the ritual of bathing was controlled. Elise, remembering a certain night some weeks before, found the argument reasonable.

Her step as well as her spirits were lighter when they started back toward the house on the mound. She and Little Quail were chattering, sharing a comb of carved wood as they walked. She looked up as they crossed the plaza, noticing a group of men to one side where a pair of posts stood, set into the ground with another across the top of the first two rather like a gateway. Her mind registered what they were doing and she looked away sharply, falling silent. An instant later, she came to an abrupt halt. She whirled around.

The Indian men were tying a Frenchman to the upright posts, making ready to torture him. He was naked, spread-eagled between the posts with his wrists being fastened at the two top corners and his ankles at the bottom ones. His head hung forward on his chest. His soft hair shone golden blond in the morning sunlight, lifting lightly in the breeze. There were marks of blows on the white skin of his body and traces of blood where his bonds had cut into him. One warrior stepped up behind him, prodding him with the tip of his knife. He made not a sound, but his head came up and he stared across the beaten ground of the plaza at Elise.

"It's Pierre!" she said, her voice breathless with disbelief.

"So it is," Little Quail agreed indifferently. "For a Frenchman once of the Natchez, he has been very stupid. He should never have returned."

13

"YOU MUST DO it—please, Little Quail, I beg you!"
"If I ask for this man, then I am responsible for him always."

"But you are a widow, you have no man to bring you meat or to clear the fields for you before you plant."

"I have suitors enough to do these things." The Indian woman gave a proud toss of her head.

"Yes, suitors always pulling at you, entreating you to let them share your bed furs, snatching at you in the woods."

"You are mistaken. They do not snatch and grab as do the men of your race. With us, no man touches a woman in passion unless he is invited. It is a mark of a warrior that he has complete control of his desires."

Elise stared at her in amazement, but remembering the delicacy with which Reynaud had approached her, she could not doubt that what the Indian woman said was true. "But—but they do entreat you and attempt to entice you into the woods, for I have seen them."

"Yes, there is that. But I alone decide who will come to me and when, as do all girls as they reach womanhood. For this we are called harlots by the religious fathers in their black robes while the Indian men who refrain from women are called upright and extremely moral! They don't understand that a man is expected to be able to ignore the promptings of his male needs while a woman has the right to satisfy her curiosity about men, even the one she will marry, before she is wedded for life. Our marriages are much happier than those of the French."

214

"Sometimes, but not always. You were not happy with your Indian husband."

"He could never forget that I had been a slave to a white man."

"Now here is a white man who, if you wish it, will be a slave to you. You could at least take him into your hut! He could speak both your own language and French with you and would be there to warm you when the north wind blows."

"But, Elise, he is a traitor, an enemy!"

"How so? He left the Natchez to trade goods throughout the wilderness, not to join the French. He went well before St. Andrew's Eve, months ago, even years for all I know. To this day there is nothing that can be said against him. He has not informed the French concerning the Natchez, has not joined the military expedition they are gathering to send against you. He was only with the reconnoitering party because he had heard of Reynaud's running of the gauntlet and feared for him. How can he be an enemy?"

"He is French."

"So am I!"

"Yes."

The argument had been going on for what seemed like an eternity to Elise. Her great fear was that some time before the torture ended they would scalp Pierre. It sometimes happened. When she had first remembered the custom Reynaud had told her about so many weeks ago, that of stopping the torture of a prisoner if he was requested by a widow, it had seemed the perfect answer to how to save the Frenchman. She had not expected Little Quail to be so reluctant.

She took a deep breath, trying for patience. "He is a close friend to Reynaud; you know this. Can you think that Reynaud would not do everything in his power to free him if he were able? Don't you know that he will be sick with grief if he discovers that Pierre died here in this village while he lay unconscious? Only think of how grateful he will be when he learns you saved him."

"I want no man."

Elise had first gone to Tattooed Arm. Reynaud's mother considered the matter of torturing the Frenchman a thing of men; she could not interfere. Only the war chief or the Great Sun had the power to forbid it. Elise had then asked Reynaud's brother to intercede, but he did not feel that it was fitting. There was suspicion on every side that he, as well as the new Tattooed Serpent, loved the French too well. It was best for him to remain aloof from this problem of the trader.

Elise tried again, catching the Indian woman's arm, giving it a shake. "Don't you remember when he lived among you, Little Quail? You were children together, boy and girl; have you no memories of how he was then? No affection from that time?"

The Indian woman frowned. Slowly she said, "He did carry water for me from the stream once when I sprained my wrist. And he gave me ten blue-jay feathers and ten blue beads to decorate a pair of moccasins."

"You see?"

"He helped me to hide a fat white puppy that my grandmother wanted to cook. And he didn't laugh with the others when she found it later."

"He is the same now as he was then, a kind and generous man, one concerned for those he loves; he must be or else he would not be here. He came because he heard what had happened to Reynaud, I know it."

"He was called Hair-of-the-Sun when he came because it was as pale as sunbeams, a color so fine and bright such as we had never seen."

"It may be a little darker now, but it is still different from most men, certainly different from the hair of Natchez men," Elise suggested.

"Yes. To touch it would be very nice."

"If they don't cut it off and his scalp with it! Oh, Little Quail, please!"

"He is counted a Noble among us, and when last he came had many rich trade goods."

Elise made no answer, afraid that one more word might prejudice her case. Silence fell. The Indian woman sat with a look of deep consideration on her face. Abruptly she stood. Her tone brisk with determination, she gave her decision.

"Very well."

Elise gave her no time to change her mind, but took her hand and dragged her to the plaza. A fire had been lit near where Pierre hung between the upright poles. The torture had begun, for already there were several livid burns on his body, though like the people among whom he had grown to adulthood, he had not made a sound.

Now that she had made up her mind, Little Quail seemed to

accept the drama of the moment with aplomb. Her head held high and her hands swinging freely at her sides, she marched toward the men gathered around the prisoner. Stopping before Pierre, she looked at him searchingly, her appraisal as thorough as if she had been going to buy him, not even excepting that portion of his anatomy that proclaimed him a man.

The warriors gathered around Pierre swung to face her, a few annoyed by her presence, one or two hiding smiles, most showing expressions of polite inquiry. Little Quail stared at them without discomfiture.

"I have come," she said clearly, "to claim this man. By the right of a widow who has lost her mate on the field of battle, I demand him as a replacement, to become one with me, henceforth flesh of my flesh, blood of my blood."

Elise, hanging back, saw Pierre raise his head to look at the Indian woman. There was in his clear blue eyes as they rested on Little Quail equal parts of gratitude and disbelief and something more that made Elise shiver in the cool morning wind.

The same warriors who had so callously spread-eagled Pierre between the posts for torture now cut him down with care, covered him with a blanket, and carried him to the hut of Little Quail. Then the Indian woman ordered them out and they went sheepishly, though once beyond the door their quick comments and smothered laughter could be heard.

Elise put wood on the cooking fire and set water to heat before inspecting the pots clustered nearby for food suitable for an injured man. There was a thin meat stew in one and she drew it nearer to the flames. Little Quail glanced at what she was doing, then filled a small pottery bottle with water and took it to where Pierre lay on the sleeping bench.

"Would you like to drink?" she asked, her tone abrupt.

A wry smile lighted his pale face. "Above all else."

It was likely that he had been force-marched for miles from the place where he had been captured to the village and that he had not tasted water since he was taken. That Little Quail had divined his most pressing need was an indication of her concern.

Pierre tried to push himself to a sitting position, but he wavered and fell back in weakness caused by shock from the torture he had endured. Surprise flashed across his features.

The Indian woman bent swiftly to lift his head and with her aid he made the effort once more, grimacing a little as he shifted to one elbow in order to take the water bottle.

"Your wounds pain you," Little Quail said, her voice quieter, softer. "We will tend them soon."

"You are . . . kind, and I have not yet thanked you."

Little Quail drew back. "It is Elise whom you should thank. She is the one who begged that I claim you."

"Then I do so most sincerely," Pierre said, inclining his head with a look of gratitude toward Elise, though his gaze returned almost immediately to the Indian woman.

They bathed him, cleaned his burns, and spread them and his bruises with a healing balm. He made no complaint beyond declaring that they were fiends who meant to tickle him to death, a more terrible torture than that devised by the warriors, though in the next breath he extolled their gentleness. He assured them most solemnly that he was able to bathe himself, that only laziness and the great pleasure he took in having two lovely women do it prevented him, but he propped himself against the hut wall for support even as he spoke.

Once his hand accidentally brushed Little Quail's breast as she leaned over him. She recoiled so abruptly that mischief leaped into his eyes. From that moment on he took delight in allowing his hand to rest on her hip or thigh or along her neck at every opportunity. Flustered and uncertain, Little Quail glared at him, but he managed each time to look innocent. Weak he might be, but there was nothing wrong with his spirit.

Finally their patient lay clean and comfortable, with the lines of pain about his eyes slowly fading and the color returning to his face from the rich broth he had drunk. He had fallen silent, letting his eyes close. Little Quail, sitting beside him, reached out as if drawn to smooth the strands of his hair that lay soft and shining, touched with gold, on his forehead. Alert at once, he caught her hand, carrying it to his lips as he lifted his lashes to gaze up at her.

"You do care for me," he said, his voice low. "Admit it."

"I told you—"

"You told me who bid you to save me, but not why you agreed."

"I—someone had to do it since Hawk-of-the-Night could not."

"What?"

When he had heard what had happened to Reynaud, Pierre lay stroking the back of Little Quail's hand, which she had neglected to remove from his grasp. After a long moment, he said, "It is good that I came."

"Good that you were captured and nearly killed?" Little Quail scowled at him.

"Good that I am here when Reynaud may have need of me," he answered, smiling. "But I don't regret the capture since it brought me to you."

"You are delirious," she snapped, jerking her hand away, "or else mad."

"You were always most disagreeable when you felt the deepest," Pierre said. "I remember once when I gave you a few blue beads and feathers. You kicked me in the shins."

"I did not!"

"But you did, I remember distinctly."

"So do I remember and—"

"Ah, you do love me!"

Little Quail jumped to her feet, turning from him, then swinging back again. "I knew how it would be! I knew that you would think I desired you to distraction because I chose to keep your body from torture and your hair from hanging on a warrior's belt by bringing you into my hut. Conceited man! I only pitied you."

"Pity being halfway to love, I will accept that," he said quickly. "I have thought of you often, Little Quail, since we were children together. I saw you growing up sweet and dear, but before I knew it you were sold as a slave and afterward taken to wife. Did you ever think of me?"

She stared at him. When he reached for her hand once more, she permitted him to take it. At last she answered, "Sometimes."

"In what way? I ask because I am intrigued by the words you spoke when you claimed me. 'Flesh of my flesh,' you said. What did it mean?"

The dusky red of a blush rose to Little Quail's face. "They were but words."

"Oh, no, that I cannot accept. You must tell me." He drew her nearer and pressed his lips into the palm of her hand.

"You—you need not make love to me with pretty words and gestures just because I saved your life."

"Not even if it pleases me beyond dreaming? Not even if it is but a reflection of the worship I feel this moment for you?"

"You are weak and—and must not tire yourself."

"I grow stronger every moment, but it would be a great help if you would come to me, for now."

"Conceit, to think that I would," Little Quail said, but the words were no more than a whisper.

Elise cleared her throat to relieve the tightness gathered there. "I should be going. I've been too long away from Reynaud."

Pierre and Little Quail did not answer, nor was there any sign that they knew when she left the hut.

Elise longed to be able to tell Reynaud what had happened. There was no one else who would feel the same about it, who would appreciate how she felt. He remained unconscious, however, lying still and pale in the stuffy warmth of the house, with all the turmoil of the family of the Great Sun going unheeded around him.

She would have liked to remove him to his own hut. It had been discouraged, if not precisely forbidden. His mother and brother were concerned for him, and did not trust her to care for him alone. This mistrust was not spoken aloud, but the implication could not be missed.

She had tried instead to let some fresh air into the large house, and more light, by leaving the door partially open.

One of the elderly aunts closed the door at once, shivering in her cloak, which dragged on the ground, so bent was she with arthritis. Elise had decided at length to leave it, considering it all to the good that no one had yet suggested taking him in his feverish condition to the creek to bathe.

Night came again. Quiet descended in the Great Sun's house as one by one the family sought their benches. Elise sat on an overturned pot beside Reynaud, leaning with her back against the edge of the bench, staring at the dying fire. She thought of Pierre and Little Quail, wondering how they were adapting to each other.

Elise let her mind wander back to New Orleans and Fort Saint Jean Baptiste. What were the French doing now? How was the expedition against the Natchez proceeding? When could they expect to hear from it, see it? She tried to figure out the days and realized that Christmas had passed while they were on the trail and that it was now the new year of 1730.

Another year. It hardly mattered. Here among the Natchez spring was the time of renewal. That seemed natural and right, like reckoning a child's lineage through its mother or marking time by the phases of the moon so that a year had thirteen equal months and a woman's cycle was easy to count.

Her own time was almost on her again, delayed somewhat by the exertions of the past weeks. She could feel it coming, however. She had been afraid that she would have to apply to Little Quail for some of her herbs, but no. It was her time that made her feel so torpid this evening, so depressed and yet on edge. Combined with the emotional upset of the morning spent arguing for Pierre's life and her weariness, it was no wonder that she was ready to jump out of her skin or to dissolve into tears. She had nearly succumbed to the last earlier in the evening as she tried to spoon the medicine into Reynaud, only to have it spill from the corner of his mouth again and again.

She turned to look at him. His lips had begun to crack with dryness and the bones of his face had become more prominent. There were hollows under his eyes, and on his cheeks and chin was the dark shadow of beard stubble, so long had it been since he had had the opportunity to pull them out. It was a strong face, one to trust. Even lost in unconsciousness, he had such presence, as if at any moment he would rise and make his opinions known. She thought of him dying, of simply ceasing to be, and it did not seem possible.

With one finger she reached out, tracing the edges of his lips with the tip, drawing it across the lower one that was so rough now when it had once been smooth and warm against her mouth. Would she ever feel it like that again? Did she want to? Her head felt light at the idea and she could not bring herself to come to grips with the question. She moved her hand to brush back the rough, black silk of his hair, a fullness gathering in her throat.

"Reynaud," she whispered, "Hawk-of-the-Night, Tattooed Serpent, don't die. Please don't die."

There was no sound from the man who lay there, no movement except for the slow rise and fall of his chest. After a time, because her eyes were burning from the smoke of the sinking fire and she felt so peculiar, she leaned over to put her head down on his shoulder.

A croaking noise dragged her back to awareness. She sat up suddenly, castigating herself for falling asleep even as she tried to bring order to her dull senses. The side of her face was hot and damp and she lifted a hand to feel the moisture there.

"Elise, love," Reynaud repeated, his voice a rasp of sound, "could I have a drink of water?"

She drew in her breath on a gasp, springing up. He was awake, himself again. His fever had broken, for perspiration stood out on his forehead, trickling into his hair and gathering in the sunken hollows under his eyes.

"Yes, oh, yes, of course."

Whirling to where the water was kept in a clay pot covered by a square of leather, she poured some into the wooden bowl and brought it carefully back to him. She lifted his head on her arm and held it to his lips. He brought up his own hand to steady it, drinking thirstily.

"More?" he asked when it was gone. "I'd get it myself, but I'm as weak as a baby wood rat and stiff beyond belief."

"No, no, I'll get it." She felt as if she were disoriented, as if she had been awakened from a nightmare or was still dreaming.

When she had brought it, he took a swallow, then looked at her over the rim of the bowl. "I have a terrible taste in my mouth."

A wavering smile slowly curved her mouth at his querulous tone. "It's the medicine."

"I don't think I want any more."

"No," she said, a quaver in her voice. Then there were tears swelling in her eyes, spilling down her cheeks, and dripping onto her arm that held him.

Concern gathered on his features, darkening his eyes. "What is wrong?"

"Nothing," she said, smiling, shaking her head so that the tears sparkled in the dim light. "Nothing, now."

The days sped by. Dark clouds moved in from the southeast and rain fell with unrelenting steadiness until the sides of the mounds ran with water and the village plaza was a lake of mud. Reynaud mended rapidly, though by no means as fast as he wished. He was, for the most part, a good patient, but he was inclined to move too quickly, pulling the scabs forming on his sore back, and to carp at the smell of the ointment Elise and Tattooed Arm used daily. He chafed at the enforced inactivity after the first few days of extreme weakness had passed; that was until he discovered that Little Quail had been teaching Elise a few more words of Natchez and took over the lessons himself.

The results often set the Indian woman to giggling so that she had to hold her sides. Not only were the forms of address and expressions of politeness different according to whether one was speaking to a Sun or a member of the other classes, but men pronounced the words with a much harder and shorter sound than did the women. Just as Frenchmen, who often learned the language from the women they lived with, were thought effeminate by the Natchez men, so Elise sounded masculine no matter how hard she tried to do otherwise. She made swift progress, however, and there was one excellent effect. When she spoke to Small Owl, warning him away from the fire, from a hot pot, or from squatting in the middle of the floor to do his acts of nature, he paid her the same instant attention that he gave to his father and Reynaud.

Pierre's visits also served to make the time go by for Reynaud. Their talk was sometimes grave, involving maps and plans drawn on pieces of bleached leather. Often it had a distinctly ribald sound as they put their heads together, watching Elise and Little Quail busy at the fire. It had been the Frenchman, putting in an appearance on the morning of the day Reynaud had regained consciousness, who had told his friend of his capture and of Elise's part in gaining his release. Pierre's expression of gratitude and pledge of eternal friendship to her had been moving.

Later, when Pierre and Little Quail had gone, Reynaud called her to him, taking her hand. "You hold Pierre's life in this small hand, *ma chère*. Do you know it?"

"You both make too much of nothing." She tried to draw away from him, keeping her lashes lowered.

"Because I am more thankful than I can say that you had the wisdom and the concern to suggest to Little Quail the means of saving him."

"Anyone else would have done the same in my place."

"I doubt it. There are many other Frenchwomen in the village and none raised a hand to help him, some out of ignorance, some certainly out of fear for themselves."

"My position is different."

"Because you are different and I praise whatever gods there may be for it."

He lifted her hand to his lips, pressing them to her palm. Elise, meeting the dark intensity of his eyes, felt a quiet singing inside her, though her knees, unaccountably, seemed inclined to bend like boiled grass.

Pierre did not appear to find the duties assigned to him by Little Quail at all onerous. As for Little Quail, she had taken to wearing an old pair of moccasins sewn with blue beads and blue-jay feathers and lost no opportunity for touching her Frenchman when she could find an excuse to come near enough. It was a good thing, too, that Reynaud was better, for the young Indian woman was seldom at the Great Sun's house anymore, preferring to spend the time alone with Pierre in her own hut.

It might have been Elise's intervention for Pierre or it may have been her habit of stopping to lend a hand when she saw a French woman or child at a heavy task, but the manner in which the French slaves looked upon her seemed to undergo a subtle change. They were less wary of her, more friendly. They accepted the food she was able to bring them and the Indian-style clothing that she gathered to replace their own, which were falling into rags. More than once she received their fervent thanks for coming to their aid with her new knowledge of the Natchez language, helping them out of difficulties in understanding and carrying out their tasks.

One afternoon Reynaud rubbed a hand over his beard, wincing at the rasping sound it made. He cocked an eye at Elise, who was pitting persimmons, helping the first wife of the Great Sun make persimmon bread that would be used in the spring and summer to control dysentery and other such diseases.

"I don't suppose," he said in cajoling tones, "that you would have time to help me look a little more presentable?"

"You mean find you something to use to pull your whiskers?" She knew very well that he wanted her to do it for him; he had become most adept at persuading anyone who happened to be near to serve him. She fully intended to give the beard pulling a try, but she thought it just as well not to make it too easy for him.

"I suppose," he said, suppressing a sigh. "There should be a pair of tweezers and a piece of looking glass in my hut."

The tweezers was long and sharply pointed, of the kind used by surgeons, and had its own satin-lined case. When she had returned to his brother's house with it, Elise took it out and handed it to Reynaud. In dulcet tones she asked, "Shall I hold the looking glass for you?"

He lifted his gaze to give her a brief glance. "Please."

She watched carefully as he began to draw out the blue-black hairs one by one. There seemed no particular method to it except to begin in one place and proceed steadily until the area was cleared. He used quick but steady movements, pulling in the direction the hair grew; whether from stoic acceptance or simply from being used to it, he seemed to feel no unusual discomfort.

When he stopped for a moment, rubbing at a spot the size of a *piastre* that he had cleared on his chin to see if there were remaining whiskers, she held out her hand for the tweezers. "Shall I?"

His mouth curved into a smile of perfect charm. "If you would."

She sat down on the bench and he shifted around until he could place his head in her lap. There was a lighted bowl lamp hanging above them and she moved so that her own shadow was not thrown across his face. Gripping the tweezers, she set the pincer points around a whisker, squeezed them shut, and pulled. The whisker came out easily. She could not prevent herself from touching the vacant spot, rubbing it gently to take away the sting she knew he must have felt. After a moment, she continued.

She became aware as she reached his underlip that he was smiling. She transferred her gaze to his eyes. "What's so funny?"

"You are. You are so determined, so serious." He would never tell her so, but it was the contrast between her single-mindedness and the sight he had of her left breast, disclosed under the open edge of her short, shoulder-tied cloak as she leaned over him, that caused his amusement. White, tilted, coral-rose-tipped, softly inviting, the gentle globe was half concealed, half revealed by her every movement. He only hoped that she did not discover its exposure.

"I don't like hurting you," she answered.

"No? I would have thought that not long ago nothing would have pleased you more."

She was silent a moment. "That was then."

His eyes narrowed, though not entirely against the pain of the hair she yanked out. "Why should now be any different?"

"I don't know," she said, repeating in Natchez, *"noco."*

"That word," he pointed out, "means 'I cannot tell,' not exactly the same thing."

"Surely you know what I mean; it's just that things have changed."

"Because I'm lying flat on my back?" he asked, the words dangerously quiet.

"I don't pity you, if that's what you mean."

"Don't you?"

"Not anymore."

"Tell me you don't despise me either," he recommended dryly.

"Nor that." As surprise widened his eyes and took speech from him, she went on. "But I do resent being brought here against my will. I resent being forced into your bed, both the first time and yet again, in a different way, here. I resent being made to feel that should you fail to recover it will be on my head."

"I am going to recover," he interrupted.

"Yes," she said, her tone abrupt as she allowed herself the briefest of surveys of his long body, particularly of the area covered by his breechclout, "I think you are."

Reynaud watched the pink color that invaded her face with interest and could not restrain himself from a quick glance to see if it was also evident beneath her cloak. It was, if a man looked close enough, a fascinating discovery. He flexed his knee to bring a bearskin within the reach of his hand and drew it over his lower body, unwilling to allow her to see how such a revelation, and the things she had said, affected him.

"Are you cold?" she asked, her tone dulcet.

"Not at all," he said in perfect truth, "not now."

He mulled over her words, watching her face as she bent over him. That he had not pressed her was partly out of a disinclination to disturb the tenuous sense of communication that existed between them and partly because he did not care to have his brother or his family as witnesses to the quarrel between himself and this woman. They would settle their differences sometime, somewhere; he would see to that. But for now, it was too soon. She needed time—and so did he. Though his need of her was unappeased, a curled knot of hunger inside of him, he was not altogether sure that he would be able to do much about it, even if an opportunity presented itself. The infection and fever had left him far below his usual strength. No, it was better to enjoy her nearness, her touch, her warmth and occasional concern without pressing for more. Yet.

He moved his shoulders a little, feeling the curves of her thighs under him, their softness that was also firm. If he closed his eyes, he could remember how they had felt that night beneath his own, between them, over them. He caught his breath.

"Does it hurt, lying on your back?" she asked, frowning a little as she hovered above him with the tweezers in her hand.

His eyes flew open. For a moment, he could not speak, then in strained tones he said, "No, it—it's just that the bandages seem to be pulling a little, sticking to the stripes."

"Would you like me to loosen them? I would be very gentle."

He would have liked to say that she could do anything she pleased, gentle or not. That would, however, be far from wise. Stifling a sigh of regret, he said, "No, it's all right."

Slowly Reynaud grew stronger. The gray days of winter with their bone-chilling dampness and frequent icy rains slipped past. One morning Reynaud left the hut in the dawn gloom to go to the river to bathe. When the watery sun broke through the clouds a day or two later, he called a meeting of the council. Before another week had passed, he was leaving the house every day, supervising the cutting of logs for the construction of a pair of defensive palisades to be built a short distance below the Grand Village, one on either side of St. Catherine Creek. The land was higher there where the bluffs rose above the winding waterway. Defense would be easier since the enemy would have to approach uphill and could attack only on three sides. It would also not be necessary to take in so great an area as would have been necessary if they had elected to build the stockade completely around the great mounds.

The weather cleared, the days grew warmer, the sun became brighter. Elise went inside one morning, stepping into the dim house. It should have been empty, for the other women were out and about, visiting, working. She saw the form of a man slumped over on the sleeping bench where she always lay with Reynaud and went quickly forward without giving her eyes a chance to adjust to the light. She put her hand on his shoulder, bending over him.

"Reynaud, are you all right?"

He turned and she saw that it was the Great Sun. He caught her hand, tugging on it so that she fell across him. "Elise," he said, his words thick and his breath smelling of brandy, "you came to me."

"No, you mistake—" she said, pushing at him, trying to regain her feet.

"I've thought of this often," he went on, refusing to release her. "I see no reason why you should not prefer me to my brother. I want you, Elise. I want you to stay here with me, as my wife."

She became still in sheer surprise. "You can't mean it."

"I do, I assure you."

"I've given you no reason to suppose that I would agree!"

"Not until now," he answered simply.

"I thought you were Reynaud!" It was uncanny, listening to him, seeing him lying there in the gloom. They were so very alike. His words were only slightly slurred, though she thought he was drunker than he seemed.

"Did you?"

"You must believe that I did!"

"I am sorry. Then you won't consider becoming my wife?"

"Your third wife?" she inquired dryly. "One more subject to be garroted if you should die? I must decline the honor!"

He pursed his lips. "But if I were not the Great Sun?"

"You would still be Reynaud's brother."

"And your devoted admirer. You are fair to look upon, Elise."

"And you are a husband twice over and a father."

"What difference does that make? I would not neglect you, as does my brother, no matter how many wives I might have."

She flushed scarlet, though with angry mortification and embarrassment that he had noticed the lack of intimacy between her and Reynaud, had watched and perhaps listened for it. She would not discuss it, however. "Let me go, if you please."

"No, do you really wish it? This is so pleasant and I could make you happy, for an hour or two."

Elise was suddenly aware of the press of her hip against him and the softness of her breasts resting against his chest. She wrenched herself back from him, trying once more to stand.

"Don't fight me. I won't hurt you, I promise. I only await your invitation to take you."

"You'll wait a long time," she said through her teeth. "Let go, or Great Sun or no, I will not be responsible for the consequences."

"You must love my brother very much."

Once more she was still, staring at him as her mind suspended thought. It could not be true. Abruptly she shook her head. "I certainly don't love you!"

He released her on a sigh and, as she sprang to her feet,

clasped his hands on his chest and closed his eyes. She could not tell if he had lost consciousness or was only protecting his male pride by pretending, giving her a chance to escape. She did not wait to see, but swung around and left him there.

Elise told no one of the misunderstanding with the Great Sun. Who was there to tell? And what could she say? Little Quail would doubtless think her stupid for not falling in with the desires of one who was nearly a deity in her view. If Reynaud knew it might cause trouble between his brother and himself— or else he might discover some peculiar custom that would compel him to step aside for his ruler. Since nothing had happened, or was likely to happen, between herself and the Great Sun, speaking of it seemed a greater risk than keeping silent.

The fortifications progressed with amazing speed. Reynaud drove the warriors as if to make up for the time he had been ill, but he drove himself as well. He left the house every morning before first light and did not return until well after dark. His every meal was taken standing, in common with the other warriors. Elise seldom saw Reynaud during the daylight hours unless she joined the women who carried the food and drink out to them. She was awake some nights when he came to the sleeping bench, but though he was now very near complete recovery, he still did not touch her other than to draw her close for their mutual comfort on the narrow bench.

She told herself that he was exhausted by his labors so soon after his illness, that he had other and more pressing things on his mind than continuing her interrupted education in the delights of physical love. But she was not convinced.

Her concern might have been fostered by the comments regarding his lack of interest made by his brother, the Great Sun, but that was only a part of it. The truth was that having been pushed into his bed once more, compelled to sleep at his side, she was haunted by a mounting need to discover if the sensations she remembered feeling had been real or some trick of the night and the moment. That was disturbing enough, but worse still was the regret that touched her now and then for the way in which she and Reynaud Chavalier had met and the wish that they could have known each other at another time, in some other place.

It was raining again, a cold and steady downpour, on a morning some weeks after work on the palisades had begun when

Elise set out to take a hot herb drink and packet of food to Reynaud. She picked her way across the plaza and past the temple mound, holding an umbrella made of the tail feathers of wild turkeys over her head and wishing she had greased the leather of her moccasins better as waterproofing. The slope that led to the first fort had been churned into mud as the logs for one of the palisades were dragged into place. With the gray sky and the rising wall of the fort, which cut off the light, it was very dark inside. The gradually closing circle of logs was somehow forbidding, a constant reminder of the reckoning that must come. The French were gathering an army, or so said the whispers that seemed to come to the village on the winter wind. They were only waiting for spring to attack, for the good weather that would allow them to move their batteries of cannon and loads of heavy ammunition, along with the men who would destroy the Natchez, up the river.

She stopped near to where the work on the palisade wall was going forth and stood watching. Two deep trenches some three feet apart had been dug all around the perimeter of the site. Great peeled logs from eight to ten inches in diameter were being brought in and placed upright in both trenches, then the area around the logs was packed with earth to hold them in place. The dirt dug from the trenches was being used to fill the space between the two log walls, forming a thick single wall designed to repel the heaviest cannon fire. It was hard, back-breaking work, felling the logs and dragging them to the fort, some with the stolen oxen of the French, some mainly by human strength. The raising of the logs and plumbing them in the trenches, holding them upright long enough to pack them in place, required many hands and complete cooperation. It was the work of men, but many of the Common women and older children had been pressed into service gathering the earth in baskets, carrying it to fill in between the walls, and treading it to pack it down. The last job was one familiar to all since it was the method used to build the mounds that were a part of their culture.

At regular intervals in the wall, small, semicircular bastions had been built just large enough for a pair of men to stand and fire down at attackers. Two of the bastions were being reinforced and made larger for use as gun platforms with the cannons taken from Fort Rosalie. Around the top of the wall was the scaffolding of the walkway where more defenders would stand. When finished, it would be an impressive accomplishment considering the tools and materials the Indians had to work with.

Though many of the tribes had a long history of building palisades for defense in their wars against each other, they were seldom as large or as massively built as those going up at St. Catherine Creek. Much of the credit for the architecture, planning, and organization belonged to Reynaud. Searching for him with her eyes, Elise saw him standing on a section of scaffolding, pointing at a rough plan in his hand as he explained what he wanted done. Keeping a wary eye out for swinging logs and slung baskets of dirt, she made her way toward him.

He was wet, soaked from the rain, his hair plastered to his head, though he scarcely seemed to notice it. He thanked her with a warm smile for the things she had brought. As she stood waiting while he ate and drank in order to take away the utensils, she nodded toward the wall. "It's progressing well."

"Yes. The Natchez have always been good at working."

"Will it be finished in time?"

He looked about him with narrowed eyes. "We must hope so."

"Do you think there will be room enough for everyone?" she asked. Though the Grand Village, home of the Great Sun, was foremost among the Natchez, there were scattered along St. Catherine Creek between it and the river five other villages, small clusters of huts that held families all related in some manner. The combined numbers from the villages added up to the two thousand Indians reported as the population of the Natchez.

"There must be enough."

"You are not expecting a long siege, I think."

With so many inside the two forts, the supplies of food would not last long even if they were supplemented. The work of adding to them was certainly going on, she realized, for she had seen many hunting parties going out lately and much activity around the smoke fires. The women were also busy making new pottery jars and weaving food baskets to carry the supplies from the storehouse. As for water, a group of warriors were digging a well inside each log enclosure.

"We can last longer than the French, if it comes to that. They will have to bring every morsel they eat with them, except for what they get by hunting; and once the connonade begins that will be little enough."

Reynaud stepped away from her to call out a suggestion to a

group of warriors setting yet another post. As he straightened, rainwater ran from his hair, trickling down his back. He reached up, bending his arm to slip his hand under his cape and rubbing his back as he turned.

"What is it?" Elise asked.

"What? Oh, my back? The few scabs right in the middle itch damnably, that's all."

"Can I help?"

He looked at her, the old warmth kindling, rising in his dark eyes along with an odd quirk of humor that might have been the recollection of a private joke. "Would you?"

"If I could." She returned his gaze without evasion, though she could feel the heat of a faint flush on her cheekbones.

It was a moment before he spoke, then he said, "I just may let you later."

The question of exactly what he had meant plagued her as she moved through the still-falling rain back toward the mound of the Great Sun. Were his words as straightforward as they seemed or had there been some meaning she had failed to catch? They had spoken in Natchez as had become their habit of late. She was fairly fluent now, but there were still many times when she felt that she had failed to catch the nuance of a phrase, the complete meaning of a quick jest.

"Elise! Madame Laffont!"

The call came from behind her. She turned quickly, alarmed by the grief and fear in the tone. It was one of the young French-women. She was running to catch up with her, her face contorted with tears. As she jolted to a stop in front of her, Elise caught the woman's hands, holding them tightly.

"What is it? Tell me!"

"It's poor Madame Doucet. Her daughter, may *le bon Dieu* rest her soul, passed from this life during the night. Now Madame Doucet sits in the hut holding her, refusing to let any touch her. She is mad in her grief, quite mad. She cries and speaks to her dead daughter and will let none come near to prepare the body for burial."

"I understand," Elise said.

It was not unexpected. The last time she had visited the hut where the two women stayed, the daughter had been nothing but skin and bones, refusing to eat, willing herself to die. She had been a frivolous young woman like her mother, given to gossiping about the latest fashions, adorning herself with silks and satins at the expense of her husband's holdings. It was amazing what strength of purpose such women could show even if it was often misdirected.

"You must come and talk to Madame Doucet. She will listen to you, if to no one else."

It was an appeal that could not be ignored. Elise, in her concern for the woman with whom she had shared so much, had no such intention. Calling to a small Indian girl about nine or ten, she sent the child with the food utensils to the Great Sun's house while she herself turned away to go to Madame Doucet.

The hut was dark and noisome, little more than a hovel. The fire had been allowed to go out and there were no lamps hanging from the beams. The wooden bowls and pottery dishes of many meals were scattered here and there with the food congealed and moldy in most and the rest unscrubbed. There were no mats on the hard dirt floor and the rain had poured in at the smoke vent in the roof, puddling among the wet ashes and charred ends of wood and making the footing as slippery with mud as a pigsty.

Before she had taken a step inside, Elise turned and gave instructions for firewood and hot water for cleaning to be brought. She moved forward into the gloom, then found her way by the light falling through the open doorway.

"Madame Doucet? I have come to talk to you."

"Ah, Elise, grieve with me, for I am losing her."

The voice came from the farthest corner. As Elise's eyes adjusted to the dimness, she saw the older woman sitting on a bench with her back against the wall and her daughter clasped in her arms. Babbling, brushing back the dead woman's hair, she begged Elise for advice on how to restore her daughter to health, asking her to look at how thin she was, how pale. It was a litany of fear and horror and unacknowledged mourning. The older woman was dressed in the rags to which she clung as being civilized clothing and her once gray-blond hair had turned white.

On her knees beside Marie Doucet, Elise reached out to touch the woman's hand. "I fear, madame, that it is too late. She is gone."

"No, no. She cannot be gone, not when I have found her again. Save her, Elise, save her."

"I would if I could, but I have not the power. Come, let me take her and see that she is laid to rest."

"No! They shan't throw her to the animals. They do that, you know. They take them into the woods and leave them, the slaves, the Common people. There are no ceremonies, no companions for them, no great fires to lift their spirits to the sun.''

It was true, in its way. The burials were simple, a quiet place in the woods, a few favorite possessions placed with them in a shallow, unmarked grave. It was different for the upper class, who were placed first in coffins of bark above ground where their spirits were supplied with food and water until the flesh fell away from the bones. They were then buried in the earth floors of their houses, which were set on fire above them, with the exception of their rulers, the Great Suns, whose bones were kept in baskets in the temple. But, in truth, what difference did it make in the end?

''You agree then that she is no more,'' Elise said quietly. ''Tell me how you would wish her to be buried and I will see to it.''

It was not quite as simple as that, but in the end it was agreed. Madame Doucet allowed her daughter to be taken away, not because she was convinced that it would be all right as much as because she was too exhausted to resist any longer.

It was the Frenchwomen who bathed the body and laid it out in the few pieces of what they called decent clothing left among them. They carried the body to the woods and dug the grave in the wet and muddy earth with digging sticks and clay scoops, then made a cross of limbs lashed together with leather strips. Elise said a prayer as they knelt, speaking in the purest French, then they sang a quiet song that Madame Doucet had requested, one that she had sung in a nursery in France many years before. A few tears were shed, but not many. Most of them had cried so much that they no longer had any tears to spare.

There were tasks to be done, meals to be prepared, and children to be seen after. The women straggled back to the camp in silence, dispersing to the huts to which they had been assigned. Elise returned to Madame Doucet's hut and set to work, sweeping, shaking out bedding, letting in air while a hearty meal cooked on the fire. She talked in normal tones all the while to the older woman, telling her of the burial that she had refused to attend, talking of the progress of the palisades, giving her the news that had been brought by visiting warriors—anything, everything. She bathed Madame Doucet and wrapped her in a clean blanket while she rinsed out her clothing and hung it out to dry. Then she placed food in her frail hands and stood over her while she ate. And through her mind as a constant refrain ran her pity for the plight of the French.

They had lost everything, these women: men; homes; livelihood; often children, especially boys grown to young manhood. They were forced to live in what they considered to be squalor, doing manual labor such as many had not done in years and had thought never to do again, serving as slaves to people they were certain were beneath them. Most of the women had not been molested due to the strict control and moral conduct of Natchez men and the fact that those same men considered the Frenchwomen unclean because they did not bathe every day. A few had excited the lascivious curiosity of their owners, however. It was impossible to say how many, for most would not admit to it, but the one or two who had done so lived in shame. Many of the women had received kicks and blows, though not to excess, usually because of their hauteur and refusal to work. They had learned to live with the fact that they could be beaten at will, but there were many who had been so injured in their self-esteem that they would never recover.

They called the Natchez cruel beasts, these women, and constantly recounted the scenes of horror that lived in their dreams: the shooting down of their men; the slashing of their throats with knives and crushing of their skulls with hatchets; the slaughter of pets and farm animals; the burning of houses that contained family treasures brought with such care and pride from France. Elise could not but agree and yet she was torn.

Little Quail was a Natchez and that wild blood ran in Reynaud's veins. She had watched Small Owl and the Great Sun and his wives and their aunts and uncles, had heard them laugh and seen their affection for one another, and she knew they were not monsters. She had passed the temple and seen the guardians of the flame standing watch two by two throughout the march of the days, and she saw their steadfastness of purpose. She had talked to the women, and she knew that they exclaimed in horror at the way the French sometimes slapped and beat their children; the way the French, instead of tormenting their enemies, used the scourge, the branding iron, the rack, the stake, and the burning fagots on their own people.

Who was right? Were the customs of either defensible? Or was the only thing that mattered the might of the arms and the will of the soldiers that both would bring to the meeting that must come?

It was late, well into the afternoon, when Elise left Madame Doucet. The rain had stopped and a watery sun was slanting through the trees. She stood for a moment, enjoying the faint warmth of it on her face; then, feeling in need of a bath after her labors, she turned toward the creek. She lingered in the water, swimming up and down as she had learned to do in order to warm her blood in the frigid stream. After a time, she treaded water, listening. The men had stopped working, for she could no longer hear the sounds of axes and adzes or the shouts and grunts of effort. They would be coming to bathe soon, passing nearby. A few were already in the water above where she had been, or so she thought, from the sounds of splashing.

She waded from the creek, dried herself on her damp cloak, and donned her clothing. She had left the umbrella of turkey tails in Madame Doucet's hut, she realized; she must go by and pick it up before going home since it belonged to the Great Sun's second wife.

The detour made her late, for Madame Doucet was crying and had to be comforted and settled for the night. The lavender light of dusk was settling over the village when she left the hut again. It seemed odd after the rain, but the air felt warmer, caressing her skin, as if it had come from the south. Its dampness brought out the smells of wet earth and resin from the palisade across the way. Mingling with them were the heavy smokiness of cooking fires and the rich aroma of the evening meal that sat ready at every hearth. The thought of food made Elise realize that she had not eaten since early morning and her footsteps quickened.

He came at her from behind the trees, which during summer shaded the huts of the Nobles. He was not alone, but had two or three other men at his back. Swooping down upon her, he caught her up in his arms and began to run, rounding the mound that held the home of the Great Sun. He covered the ground with swift strides so that her breath was jolted from her and her arms around his neck tightened in reaction.

Above them on the mound, the women of the Great Sun emerged, screaming and calling. Behind them came Reynaud's half brother, St. Cosme, and the old uncle of the Great Sun's first wife, their hatchets in their hands. The Great Sun himself came out, shaking his fist, brandishing his bow and arrows as he ran down the slope with the others in pursuit, though he made no attempt to fit one to the other.

Reynaud ducked into his own hut and put her on her feet. He left his friends outside, Pierre among them, along with his relatives and a gathering of elders. Pulling the door into place and pinning it closed, he swung around to face her.

Outside, the yelling and protests had stopped as abruptly as they had begun. Elise, with a curious rising sensation in her chest, guessed the meaning of the small drama that had been played out; still, she had a role of her own.

Drawing herself up, making her voice as frigid as she was able, she said, "Would you care to tell me the meaning of this charade?"

A smile widened Reynaud's mouth and there was a bright light in his dark gray eyes as he came toward her, though when he spoke his voice was quiet.

"It means you are my wife."

14

"Your wife? I don't remember being asked!"
        "If I had asked, would you have agreed?" He
stepped in front of her, his hands on his hips.

"Who can say now?"

"You could, if you would," he answered, though without
anger. "But it hardly matters. This marriage is not binding on
you."

"What?"

"Unless, of course, you wish it."

"Then why—"

"It is my brother's command."

She stared at him, her excitement fading to be replaced by
wrath. "You mean this farce was at the order of his royal majesty the Great Sun?"

He held her gaze for a long moment before he made an abrupt
gesture. "Not entirely. It is also what I want. I am bound to you
beyond severance, by the sound of your voice, the wild-honey
color of your hair, the vivid life in your eyes. The taste and
touch of you haunts me, and all that will content me is to be
with you. The small ceremony of capture just played out, along
with the questions we must answer soon before the elders, only
makes it public. I love you, Elise."

How long had it been since she had heard those words? Not
since her mother had died. Rich and deep, they echoed in her
mind, bringing such disturbance inside her that her hands trembled. A tightness deep inside her ballooned, then gave way, and
she was assaulted by a sudden need to fling herself upon him,

to become lost in him. Her chest hurt with the burgeoning pain of it. She clenched her hands into fists, standing rigid.

"I don't believe you!"

"Try," he advised, his tone dry, before he went on. "I don't require that you return the feeling, only that you allow me to give you the protection of my rank and title. Since I am a Sun, I cannot be put aside when a woman wishes, as other men of the Natchez can be, but I swear that when this is over, you have only to ask and you will be free."

Her amber eyes were stony as she stared at him. "Suppose I say I want my freedom now?"

"That isn't possible."

"No? Why?"

"The decree has been handed down. We are to marry to show that it was not my preference for the French but for you, a Frenchwoman, that prompted my desertion of the Natchez. And, more than that, because I want you."

"So much for love." Her laugh was forced.

"Do you doubt me?" he asked, his voice suddenly rough. "Shall I prove it?"

She stood her ground. "By force?"

He stopped, the muscles of his face going taut. "How can you think it?"

Assailed suddenly by the memory of all that had passed between them, she looked away from him. There was a constriction in her throat as she said, "I don't."

He reached out to touch her cheek with work-roughened fingers. "That is something. Can you not trust me in this matter of the wedding also?"

"You tricked me before when you arranged it so that I became your slave."

"Not this time."

"You—you have said what must be, what you want, but you have not asked me what I want."

He trailed one finger to her chin, pressing it upward so that she had to meet his dark gaze. "What is it you want, Elise?"

The warmth of his touch, his nearness sent a small shiver along her nerves that seemed to lodge in the lower part of her body. Her lips parted, but no words came.

When she did not speak, he said softly, "Is it so hard to say? Shall I help you? You despise me, what I am and what I have done, and yet you respond to me. If it were not for pride and fear—"

"I am not afraid of you!" she cried in distress, wrenching away from him.

"Not of me, but of what may happen if you admit to desire, if you allow yourself to come close, to accept what I offer you."

"You leave me so little choice." The words should have been a shout, but were instead a whisper.

"That is so."

"There—there is no reason for this."

"The Great Sun thinks otherwise. He considers it best, for both of us as well as for the Natchez."

She spun back to face him. "He what?"

"My brother," Reynaud said, his gaze intent upon her flushed face, "thinks we are suited, as do I."

What had been said between the two men? She wished she knew. "I—I don't know what to think."

"Don't, then, only feel."

"If—if I agree, I will make you miserable."

"No. I intend to safeguard my own happiness by assuring yours in all things. Shall I bid the others enter now?"

What might she have said to his proposal if she had not known it was his brother's idea, if he had not been so quick to reassure her that it was not binding? She was not sure, and yet in her mind lingered the memory of the Great Sun hinting that she was in love with his brother. Was she? No. It was impossible. What she felt was a natural attraction to the man who had brought her release from her fear of physical love. Attraction. Desire. That was all. But they were powerful emotions, for she trembled inside with them.

Did she consent to the marriage? She did not remember it. Regardless, the audience waiting outside crowded into the hut. The women took Elise aside where they combed her hair and braided it with blue beads and freshwater pearls. They released the knots of her skirt and cape, whisking them away and replacing them with others of soft, white doeskin sewn with more blue beads and pearls. Kneeling before her, Tattooed Arm put her gift of soft, white slipperlike moccasins, also beaded, onto Elise's feet. A small branch of laurel was placed in her left hand and a sheaf of maize in her right, representing fidelity and fecundity.

Across the room, Reynaud was being dressed in like fashion.

He wore his cape and breechclout of woven swansdown, and braided in his hair was a tuft of red swan feathers and a sprig of oak leaves. The first signified that he was no longer free, the second showed that he would not fear going into the forest, but would supply his wife with all the game they would require. In his hand he held his bow and arrow as symbols of his vow to protect and defend his new wife.

Elise and Reynaud stood before the elders and answered the questions that were put to them. Afterward a bride gift exchanged hands, only a token since she had no family there to receive it, though Little Quail and the wives of the Great Sun acted the role as they had in the protesting of her ritual capture.

Then came the moment when the maize was taken from her and Reynaud clasped her right hand. His voice deep, he asked, "Do you want me as your husband?"

Elise, staring into the gray darkness of his eyes, answered, repeating after Little Quail in the Natchez tongue the proper reply: "I want it very much and I am happy. Love me as much as I love you! I do not love and will never love anyone except you."

Reynaud, watching her face and hearing the softly spoken words, wondered how much she understood of what she said. For a fleeting moment, the wish that he had conducted this affair differently came to him. And yet there had been so little time. He had what he wanted; he must be content. His voice steady, he repeated the simple vow.

There was more: a threat of banishment from the family if they did not live together in peace and happiness. Then came the small feast spread by the women and the dancing. Elise did not remember what she ate or who had danced. She only knew that Reynaud sat beside her, holding her hands in his warm grasp.

Finally it was done; the last, toothless old woman, smiling hugely, was helped out the door. Pierre and Little Quail wandered off with their arms about each other. The voices of their well-wishers faded into the night.

The hut suddenly seemed huge. In the silence could be heard the distant call of an owl, the peeping of frogs hatched in the wet, warming weather in preparation for spring, the lonely sound of a cane whistle played in a minor key. Reynaud stepped around to extinguish the swaying lamps, to bank the fire. Elise, in elaborate housewifely concern, moved to test the bed furs and the fresh matting of straw that they covered.

She wished with an abrupt, fierce longing that this was a true wedding, her first and therefore her first wedding night. She wished that she could have had something pretty to wear like the soft nightgown that had been left behind at Reynaud's house. It would have been so lovely if she had had the trousseau that other women had to celebrate their nuptials: the daintily embroidered underclothing, the demure but enticing nightgowns. It was not that she cared overmuch for such things; it was only that she would have wished to have some appearance of a bride.

Reynaud came to stand behind her, drawing her back to lean against him. One hand cradled her arm while the other gently held her rib cage just under her breast with his thumb grazing its softness. Against her ear, he murmured, "Tired, *untsaya athlu*?"

Wife of my heart. "No. Are you?" After all, he had been working on the wall since early morning.

"No."

His voice vibrated in his chest against her. He released her rib cage to lift his hand to her cheek, turning her head and bending to lower his mouth to hers. Warm and sweet was his kiss, with an undercurrent of swift exhilaration.

Desire, love, duty—which of these compelled either of them? Did it matter so long as the blood ran warm and turbulent in their veins and they were alone together in the night? Elise relaxed against Reynaud with a sigh, letting her anger and her reluctance go.

She raised her hand, tangling her fingers in his thick hair, drawing his head down so that her mouth burned with the pressure. His tongue touched hers, faintly rough against the infinite sensitivity of her own. She met it, teasing, softly caressing, shamelessly inviting his deeper penetration.

He drew in his breath, raising his head to look at her. She gazed back, her amber-brown eyes liquid with desire in the dim, fire-lit hut.

"Elise," he whispered.

The dark fire of answering passion leaped into his eyes. His fingers sought the knot of her short shoulder cape, untying it with practiced ease before searching out the fastening of her skirt low on her hip. As he loosened it and let it fall, she turned in the circle of his arms to find and release the leather thong that held up his breechclout.

Together they stood, their bodies bronze and cream, gilded, enameled by the play of gold-and-blue firelight on their skin. As shameless as pagans, they observed each other. "You are so beautiful," he whispered, touching the back of one finger to the curve of her jaw, the turn of her arm, the flat of her stomach.

She rested her fingers on the muscled width of his shoulders, trailing them upward along the column of his neck to touch lightly the high cheekbones of his face. "As are you."

Drawn irresistibly, they moved against each other pressing close, breast to breast, thigh against thigh, mouth to mouth. His arms tightened until she could scarcely breathe. She clasped her arms closer around his neck, molding herself to him, driving her body against his until she could feel the taut nipples of her breasts digging into him. She moved her lips on his with a sound like a sob deep in her throat; he drew in his breath, brushing a hand lower down her back to hold her to the pulsing heat of his loins.

Spark and tinder, they caught flame, straining closer still, their mouths slanting, devouring. It was a consuming conflagration that made them sway, absorbed and absorbing, unable to think of anything except the urgency of the need that gripped them.

He stepped over to the bench, putting a knee on it, carrying her locked in his arms as he sank down upon it. He rolled to his side, burying his face in her neck to breath in the scent of her. His hand smoothed the curve of her hip, the slender turn of her waist, sliding upward to her breast. His thumb brushed the trembling peak before he bent his head to take it into the warm adhesion of his mouth.

She moved nearer, offering herself without restraint. His fingers pressed into her, holding her still. He lifted his head with a groan of despair. "Elise, I need you so. . . . If you don't—if you encourage me too much, I won't be able to wait."

"Don't, then," she whispered and opened her thighs, pressing upon the firm and heated length of him.

With a twist of his hips, he accepted her invitation, plunging deep. Moist and resilient, she felt that sudden entry with an internal shiver of ecstasy that radiated upward to the surface of her skin in a prickling of gooseflesh. Warm and liquid, she moved to accommodate his quick, hard thrusts, accepting, returning, giving. Her heartbeat quickened, beginning to pound as she felt his hand upon her, his fingers touching her where their bodies were joined, increasing her pleasure.

She wanted, needed, to take him deeper still. With their legs entwined, she let him press her to her back. Her hands swept over him, taking delight in the power of his corded muscles and sinews. She felt the ridges of the scars on his back. An empathetic pain for them filled her and she wrapped herself closer in an agony of full and tender yearning.

Together they strove, reaching for, coming near to, the instant of perfect communion. It beckoned, a bright and silent explosion of purest pleasure. Elise sensed its approach, its imminent contact. Closer it came. Closer still.

"Love me, Reynaud," she whispered, recognizing her deepest need. And knowing he would not fail, she let the terrible joy of it take her, trembling, into the brightness.

Had he heard her soft plea? The night was long and filled with love in all its many aspects, soft and hard, tender and violent, and yet when morning came Elise could not be certain. There was warmth in his eyes and in his touch. He watched her with a smile playing about his mouth as she prepared a sketchy breakfast with only her skirt knotted around her hips in the fashion of the Indian women on rising. He pretended to help her comb her hair and braid it for the opportunity of touching the silken strands. He was more hindrance than help though as he insisted on spreading them over her breasts and searching for the nipples with his tongue through the fine and shining filaments of her tresses. He watched her from under his lashes as he made ready to go out to work on the wall. But he said nothing.

He was at the door, ready to pull it open through its supports, when he turned back. "Tell me something."

"Certainly, if I can." She gave him a smile over her shoulder as she tied her short cape into place.

"You accepted my offer of marriage, but refused my brother's. Why?"

She sent him an incredulous look. "You know of it?"

"I know. Why did you refuse?"

"I hardly know your brother!"

"But he is the Great Sun."

"Am I supposed to be impressed? All that means to me is

that I would have the honor of being strangled third in line if he should die.''

"The same could be applied to me, only you would be first.'' He watched her with a tight feeling in his chest. What had he expected her to say? That was a foolish question; he had wanted her to repeat the words she had whispered the night before. He wanted to know that she needed him, that her whispered cry had not been the result of nothing more than gratitude, mere bed-fur affection. He should have known better.

"Then I will have to take care that nothing happens to you, won't I?" she said, retaining her smile with an effort. It was unthinkable that he could die. He was far too alive.

"You need not worry. If I am killed, I—"

"Don't say that!" she interrupted, her tone sharp.

He went on as if she had not spoken. "I want you to go at once to Pierre; at once, you understand. He will take you to Fort Saint Jean Baptiste or to New Orleans if the way is clear enough. You can depend on him to protect you."

She looked at him, her throat so tight it ached. After a moment, she said, "I appreciate your thoughtfulness, but I would rather not think of it."

"You must. As much pleasure as it might give me to think of you as my companion in the afterworld, I can't bear the thought of your death on my head. You will do as I say."

Because it seemed that he would not stir from where he stood until she agreed, she forced herself to nod. Satisfied, he turned away.

"Wait!"

He swung back, lifting a brow in inquiry.

"Who told you that your brother had proposed to me?"

"The Great Sun himself," he answered, his voice dry.

"What else did he say?"

"That he had also offered you the joys of his sleeping bench and that you had refused, violently. I believe he was complaining."

"And nothing else?" Such as the belief that she was in love with Reynaud?

"What more could there be?"

"That—that he was the worse for drink at the time and had no liking for my answers."

"He didn't hurt you?"

"No, nor did he come close. It was just . . . embarrassing."

Laughter sprang into his eyes. "For my brother also. It isn't something that has happened to him often, being refused. I will see you at noon."

He turned once more and left the hut, sliding the door shut behind him.

Elise stood staring in front of her, the smaller matter of the Great Sun already forgotten as her mind dwelled on the arrangement Reynaud had made for her in the event of his death. Death. It had been near them in the night. Fear of it might well have been the basis of their desperate need for each other. It must come, as surely as spring would bring the French. Many would die and who more likely than the man who would lead the Natchez into battle? The French would not spare him; in fact, it was likely that they would want him dead above all.

The more she tried to push such thoughts from her mind, the more firmly entrenched they became. It was a relief then when, in the middle of the morning, a knock came on the door.

She opened the panel to discover a Frenchwoman standing outside. She thought at once of Madame Doucet, but there was no immediate message of trouble from that quarter. Instead, the young woman, extremely fair of hair and skin and far gone in pregnancy, stood silently. There was hesitancy in her manner and she twisted her hands in the grimy apron she had used to cover her stomach, which was escaping the bounds of her faded, bedraggled gown.

"Won't you come in?" Elise said, at a loss.

The woman gave a hunted look around her, then stepped inside, moving into the center of the room. She watched Elise with an intensity that was unnerving. Elise offered her refreshment and invited her to sit. The woman refused anything to drink, but sat down on the edge of a bench.

Elise was quiet. After a moment she realized that she had become so accustomed to the ways of the Natchez that she waited as they did for her guest to speak. Collecting her best hostess manner, she asked, "Is there something I can do for you?"

The woman looked up, then down at her hands again. She licked her lips which were pale, almost colorless. "Is it true . . . Can you tell me . . . That is, I have heard that you were rescued from the massacre by Reynaud Chavalier and—and some others. Is this . . . Can this be true?"

"In a manner of speaking, yes,"

"They say that there were three men saved, three who are now alive."

"Yes?"

"Was one of them—could one of them have been Jean-Paul St. Amant?"

"Oh," Elise said in sudden enlightenment, "you are his *chère amie!*"

The woman jumped up in agitation. "I was never his mistress, never! It wasn't like that; it wasn't like that at all!"

"No, of course not," Elise said soothingly, cursing herself for her impulsive outburst. "Come, sit back down."

"We were in love," the woman said, her face twisting as she sank back down, her voice breaking into a sob. "We were in love."

"I know. St. Amant told me." She reached out to put her arm around the thin, shaking shoulders of the other woman who turned, clinging to her and crying as if her heart would break.

When St. Amant had spoken to her of the woman he loved, she had never thought that she would find her. In the press of other things, she had forgotten the woman's existence and had not troubled to inquire about her. She could not have done so in any case since St. Amant, with gentlemanly reticence, had not told her the woman's name. She could hardly have gone among the captives asking for the married woman who had indulged in an affair with the Frenchman.

Elise began to talk, speaking of St. Amant's fear for the woman he loved, of his concern for her condition and how capture might affect her, of his confession that he had prayed she had been freed of her husband by the atrocities of the Natchez. Slowly the woman quieted, then straightened.

"You are too kind," she said, wiping her face. "I—I have been under such strain; the child, you know, and—and my husband dead. And thinking St. Amant dead with the others. I—will be better now."

Elise stared into the pale blue eyes of the woman, seeing such stalwart courage there that she felt somehow inadequate. "Is there something I can do to help you?"

"You have already done that; you have given me hope."

Elise reached out to take her arm, turning it to the light where the yellow and blue marks of both old and new bruises marred the fine white flesh. Gently she said, "There must be something more."

Her name was Helene and she was a slave to Red Deer, the mother of Path Bear. It had taken her so long to hear of Elise's story and to find the opportunity to speak to her because she was seldom allowed out of her mistress's hut, was rarely able to speak to her own kind. She was given an endless series of tasks from dawn to dusk and was beaten if she did not finish them; she was sometimes struck or jerked here and there if she failed to understand instructions instantly or got in the way with her clumsy movements. It was as if she had become a scapegoat for the woman's rage over the banishment of her son brought about by another Frenchwoman.

As the story came out in bits and pieces, Elise felt an enormous guilt. She did not know what she could have done to prevent the mistreatment of Helene, but it seemed that there must be something to be done to relieve it now. It would take time to make any change, however. Though it was hard to be forced to stand aside and to permit Helene to go back to Path Bear's mother, for the moment Elise could do nothing else.

As soon as she had seen Helene back to her hut, Elise went in search of Reynaud. He could not be found, however. He had gone into the woods to choose more trees for the wall. She turned instead toward the house of the Great Sun. She doubted that it would do any good to lay such a problem before the ruler himself; doubtless he would consider it trivial, beneath his attention, even if he was not out of charity with her for refusing him. She would ask for Tattooed Arm.

The mother of Reynaud entertained her graciously, listened with interest and every expression of concern, but gave her little support. The Frenchwoman was the property of Red Deer. How she was treated was no concern of anyone else. It was a great pity that she was being abused, but the one most likely to be able to help her was the slave herself. If she could best her mistress, then that, too, would not be the concern of anyone. There would be no reprisal. The woman's condition made it unlikely, but not impossible, if she chose her weapon well.

Elise tried to imagine Helene taking up a chunk of wood or stone bottle and defending herself. The girl had courage, but it was of a quiet, enduring kind. She would be no match for the mother of Path Bear. Soon, in a matter of days, her child would be born and what would become of her then?

Later that night when Reynaud returned, she spoke to him. He went at once to visit Red Deer, planning to present her with an offer to buy the Frenchwoman. He cautioned Elise not to depend on an acceptance, however. It was just as well that she listened to him. The refusal came within the hour.

Elise did not give up. She spoke to Little Quail, urging her to join her in visiting Helene to see that she was all right. She did the same with the Frenchwomen, knowing that it would be more difficult for them, but feeling that their numbers and their interest would make a difference, perhaps keep up Helene's spirits, if nothing else.

On a morning five days later, such small matters lost their importance. The Natchez woke to find sixteen hundred Choctaw warriors, allies of the French and painted for battle, encamped outside the wall.

A council of the elders was held with the Suns, male and female, sitting behind them, listening. Elise, by virtue of being the wife of the war chief, was given a place. She listened as Reynaud urged caution, suggesting delay by any means until the walls of their forts were completed. The Choctaws were there because they knew the French were coming. They had joined forces with the white men because they wanted vengeance against the Natchez for putting forward the day of the attack on Fort Rosalie, thereby depriving them of booty. If they could be fobbed off with a portion of the spoils taken from the French, even given some of the French slaves, they might be satisfied. It was possible that they might even go away without a blow being struck. If not, then at least the Natchez would have gained time and readiness.

Accordingly, a delegation was sent with a beautiful calumet, one covered with feathers and wrapped in spirals of polished copper wire. The warriors, led by the eldest men of the Natchez, were arrayed in their finest and most impressive costumes, with swansdown capes floating about their shoulders and swan plumes nodding in crowns above their heads. The sun shone down upon them, gleaming on their spendor, shining with a copper sheen on straight broad backs and wide shoulders. Reynaud was among them.

Would the embassy be accepted or would it be rejected, the members killed or maimed, except for a messenger sent to dictate terms? The tension of the waiting to find out gripped the village. When an hour had passed with no word, Elise had a visitor.

Tattooed Arm gave no hint of the anxiety that she must have felt as she sat placidly sipping at herb tea. She spoke of generalities for a time, of the warming days, of the wild onions coming up again, of the swelling buds on the trees and the haze of green grass in sheltered spots. After a time, she fell silent. When she spoke again, it was on something entirely different, perhaps a little closer to her concern.

"It was wise of the women to choose Reynaud as war chief over Path Bear. He is using the weapons of his father's people against them. All may yet be well over this accursed affair of the massacre."

"We must hope so," Elise answered politely. "But I have heard before that he was the choice of the women. How can this be? I thought the position was more or less hereditary, that it was merely confirmed by the council of elders."

"This is true in part, but the council could reject him and choose another in his place if they thought him unworthy. It is in the evaluation of those young men who might be eligible that the women play their part."

"I see," Elise said and truthfully thought she did.

"My son is a warrior, yes, but he does not glorify war. He is wise as well as strong; he prefers to be gentle when there is a choice between persuasion and force. He was tested in this, as was Path Bear, when he was a young man and has now borne out the test."

"Tested? How was that?" It was well to keep some conversation going. Tattooed Arm seemed to need to talk and she herself did not want to be alone with her own fears.

"Where else but in the bed furs? It is there that men reveal themselves. My son had strength, but it was held in reserve. He exercised patience and consideration always. He sought to guide and protect, not to dominate. In the beginning, you see, that was the purpose of a war chief, to protect. No man was ever chosen who would use his strength to gain what he wanted, who would stoop to base trickery to have a woman, or who would callously leave her immediately after he had her."

Elise lowered her lashes. "In this test of Reynaud, were there . . . many woman?"

"It was a most thorough test."

That explained a great deal. "He was aware of it, that he was being judged?"

"No, never. It would not then have been a true evaluation, would it? He was merely surrounded with females who invited his attention."

"I see. And was the Great Sun also tested in this way?"

"Indeed, for as a man uses a woman, so will he rule."

"And St. Cosme?"

"Even my third son, for should either of the first two die, he must take their place until the daughter of my sister can provide sons to carry on the line, it being that I have no daughters myself."

Elise did not like the tenor of this line of conversation. Changing the subject, at least in part, she said, "The women of the Natchez have a great deal of influence and freedom, more than other Indian women or so I believe. How does that happen?"

"We are closer to the ancient times, the times before war."

"Is that what you meant by saying 'in the beginning'?"

The Indian woman was silent, staring into space for long moments. Finally she began to speak. "According to the ancient words, kept not by the guardians of the temple but by the oldest women, the Natchez in the beginning, long before we came to this place, were children of the moon. Women, the givers of life, the tillers of the fertile soil who made it give forth food, ruled. The council was a council of women, the ruler not one, but a trio of women: mother, daughter, and granddaughter. It was this trio who once blessed the marriage unions of men and women without the nonsense of capture, which is a mockery of the woman being stolen from her people. Women, in the ancient days, gave themselves freely without fear, for men, needing women and holding them sacred, courted their pleasure.

"Men, worshippers of the life-force, of the moon that in its waxing and waning controlled the periods of flow for the waters of the land as well as for women, the moon that is like the round belly of the pregnant female, were content to be ruled. They hunted to provide food, cleared the land to be planted, shared the houses of the women, and protected her and her children. All lived in prosperity and peace. So it was for generations beyond counting.

"Then came from the east a tribe who wanted our rich lands. They sought to take them by force, killing our people. The men were invited to join the council since it was their strength that would be needed to repel the foe. Little by little they became important. The woman and mother was set aside as ruler. A man was set in their place as every part of life, the planting and gathering of food, the safe-guarding of the children, became the province of men because of the dangers of war.

"The guardians of the temple say that a white man and woman came down from the sun and dwelled among our people, bringing the worship of the sun. They claim this pair sired the race of Suns and gave us a command to be kind and generous to one another. But the women say that the sun became supreme because no battles are fought in darkness and because the hard brightness of the sun is the opposite of the gentle light of the moon. The women who were the priestesses of the moon were pushed out to make way for the stronger sun worshippers and men took over the tending of the temple. They stole the eternal flame, once the symbol of the safety of the hearth fire, claiming that it had been brought down to them by a man and woman who came from the sun itself, that bad fortune would befall the tribe if it ever went out. They said that no woman could be trusted to give up her freedom to tend the fire, though women have tended fire from the beginning of time. In truth, they want no woman to have that responsibility, for it implies leadership. The changes have been swift, compared to the countless years that had gone before.

"Now the men seek to keep women from the council; they hold meetings they consider important in secret, as was done when it was decided to strike at the French. They do this because they know the women would not agree, would counsel patience instead of attack. Soon, if we survive as a tribe, they will want to own the land and the huts, the cooking pots and even the children of our bodies. They will want to control us as the French do their women. Then will we be lost, indeed, for what will be their purpose except war, constant war? They cannot give life, only take it; that is their power. Without the use of this power, they must lose it. The role of women would become supreme again. The tribe would then revert to the women and this they will not allow."

Women, always the givers of life, in spite of war and the cruelty it brought, the loss and the pain. It seemed right, somehow, that it was at that moment, as Tattooed Arm ceased to speak, that Elise heard Helene calling.

She jumped to her feet, running to the door that stood open

to the fresh air of the day and the warmth of the afternoon. The pale-haired Frenchwoman, clasping her stomach, gasping, awkwardly trod the last steps to the hut, stumbling and staggering as she came toward Elise. She fell into her arms, her face contorted.

"The baby," Helene cried. "The baby!"

15

IT WAS A beautiful child, a girl. The labor was neither long nor particularly hard. According to Tattooed Arm, it was normal for the first child of a healthy woman, even if she was French.

Elise was grateful for the older woman's presence, grateful that she had stayed to help, that she had sent for the medicine woman who was also the midwife. Childbirth was something Elise had no experience with, though she thought she could manage the next time if there was a next time. The moment of birth had been one of such pain and stress, and yet such joy. It had been a small moment of glory.

Tattooed Arm had cleared the breathing passages of the child while the midwife worked on the mother. Then the Indian woman had given the baby girl to Elise, for she had other tasks waiting at her own house and had delayed long enough. It was Elise who, when Tattooed Arm and the midwife had gone, had bathed the tiny girl-child and soothed her until she slept. Helene had looked at her daughter, smiled, and fallen also into the sleep of exhaustion.

Many of the Sun women, having heard the cries of birth, had come to look at the new French child. They had made quiet noises, touched the small pink fingers as if there had never been such a baby before. They had brought small gifts: carved wooden animals, soft doeskin and mulberry cloth wrappings, rattles of small gourds. They had seemed uneasy that the child had not been bound immediately to a cradle board that would give her the handsome, flat contour of the head so admired among them, but they were willing to allow that the French were different. Of course it would be necessary, they seemed to think, when the mother returned to work; how else was she to carry a helpless infant about with her and still have her hands free for tasks?

No sooner had the last of these visitors left than the door was thrown open once more. Elise looked up to see Red Deer in the opening. The woman surveyed the sleeping mother and the child that Elise held. She folded her arms, her face set in rage.

"I had been told that my runaway slave was here. That you could be so stupid as to shelter her, I could not believe."

Elise carefully put the baby down on the sleeping bench before rising to face the woman. "If you speak of Helene, she is indeed here. As you must see, she was in the extremity of labor and needed help, something it seems she was unlikely to receive from you."

"For such useless a one, what should I do? It was my misfortune to be alloted a woman too far in pregnancy to abort so that I have had to put up with her weakness. It will be better now that she is rid of the baby. She will work much better."

"She will have to nurse her and care for her," Elise pointed out. "Perhaps it would better if she remained here in the house of the war chief since she will be of so little use for months to come."

The woman gave a rude snort. "She will regain her usefulness soon enough without the baby."

"Without— What do you mean?"

"Such a pale and weak thing as she must have brought forth will be better exposed in the woods."

Horror moved over Elise as she stared at the other woman. She had known that such things were done to newborns who were abnormal, but there was nothing wrong with Helene's child, nothing at all. Instinctively she stepped in front of the sleeping baby. Her voice hard, she said, "No."

The mother of Path Bear laughed. "The child is my slave to do with as I will."

"You will not touch it."

"Who will stop me?" The woman put her hands on her hips.

Helene, waking at the sound of their voices, began to cry with a hopeless, animal sound. Elise looked with loathing at the Indian woman, then stepped to where Reynaud's musket hung on pegs over the sleeping bench. With it in her hands, she turned to face Red Deer.

"I will stop you," Elise said, her voice quiet. "I will stop you for now. You are a despicable woman who should have been banished with your son. I want you to leave this hut. If you return again, ever, I will not hesitate to kill you."

"I won't leave without my slave. The Frenchwoman must get up and come with me."

The words were assured, but the woman had taken a step back toward the door. Elise shook her head. "She stays here. Get out."

The woman blinked at the masculine tone of command, then recovered to glare at Elise with hatred as she moved backward. "This won't be the end of it, you'll see! I'll go to the council."

"You do that."

"I'll make such a noise that all my friends will come with me and take her away."

"Will they? When they discover what you mean to do? I will tell them, you know, and I will make sure they know you could not recover your property by yourself. They will laugh at you instead of help you."

"No matter what happens, my vengeance will fall on you!" the woman screamed and, turning, ran from the hut.

After much discussion they called the baby Jeanne. It was a common name, one that could be added to at a later time. Elise knew that Helene was thinking of the time when she might possibly be reunited with St. Amant and so applauded the suggestion as extremely sensible. If it encouraged Helene to dream of the future, so much the better.

It was late, well into the night, when the decision was made, the baby given her first feeding, and mother and child settled once more. The day had been so busy that Elise had had little time to worry. But now as silence fell once more and the darkness of midnight crept close without Reynaud's return, her fears grew.

She stood for a long time at the door of the hut, staring into the night. Finally she stepped outside, walking to the foot of the mound of the Great Sun where she began to climb the sloping side. Near the top, she stopped. From where she stood, she could see the Choctaw camp. Fires still glowed there and the small figures of men could be seen passing back and forth in front of the flames. What were they celebrating? Was it a feast of mutual agreement or one of victory over the emissaries of the Natchez?

Frustrated by not knowing, hoping to be able to identify Reynaud in the distance, Elise stood staring for long minutes. The night wind lifted her skirt and blew tendrils of her hair around her face. Its breath was cool and she turned her shoulder cape to the front, holding it close around her and wrapping her arms in its width. Overhead the moon was on the wane. It shed its light onto the village, silvering the roofs and leaving the crooked paths between the huts in shadow. Away to the left were the Indian forts. The pointed ends of the logs that formed the walls had the look of blunt spears.

How long she stood there, she did not know. But after a time there was a stirring in the Choctaw camp. Men detached themselves from the fires and turned toward the sleeping Natchez village. A small party, they dispersed as they reached the outer fringe of houses, treading quietly, almost stealthily. Several turned toward the mound of the Great Sun.

Elise watched them come. One, ahead of the others, looked up. The moonlight gleamed on the copper features of the man for whom she had been waiting. She did not pause, did not stop to think. Swift and sure, she ran down the slope with her short cape flying out behind her. Her face bright with welcome and relief, she met Reynaud at the foot of the mound and flung herself into his arms. He caught her, whirling with her, pressing her to him. The other men of the Sun class averted their faces, moving around them.

A chuckle shook Reynaud as he held her close so that the cool globes of her breasts were pressed to his chest. ''As shameless as a Natchez woman.''

Elise suddenly remembered that she had twisted her cape around and that her breasts were bare. Rather than withdrawing in confusion, she only turned her upper body from side to side, rubbing gently against him.

He caught his breath, then leaned down to slip an arm under her knees, lifting her against his chest. Setting his mouth to hers, sure of foot from long practice, he carried her to his hut.

At the doorway, he ducked inside, threading his way with her through the dimness illuminated only by the coals of the fire to their sleeping bench. He placed her on it, then stripped off his clothes and joined her there.

Elise thought of Helene, lying in the darkness at the end of the room. It did not seem to matter. She freed herself from her clothes and flung them aside, turning against Reynaud with blind need. They flowed together with curves and hollows matched and interlocking, legs entwined. Mouth to mouth, they tasted the essence of each other, and with their hands, they alternately teased and held, pleased and clasped close. Finally he drew her to lie on top of him, leaving it to her to take him inside her when she would, to set the depth and pace of their joining. But in the end it was his tireless strength and his hands upon her that brought surcease to them and vanquished fear once more.

Their breathing had slowed though they still lay with bodies enmeshed when the sound came. Rasping, imperious, it was as demanding as only a newborn dares to be.

"What in the name of all that's holy is that?" Reynaud asked, starting up to one elbow.

"A baby, of course!"

Elise rolled off him, then flung herself back across his chest to pick up her skirt, which had landed on the floor beside the bench. Pushing herself to a sitting position, she began to hunt for the ends she normally knotted.

"What do you mean, of course? There was no baby when I left unless—"

"It belongs to Helene."

"I should have known," he said in resignation.

She went still. "Do you mind that they are here? She's such a small baby; she will be no trouble. Helene was in labor and had nowhere else to go. Now Red Deer means to expose the little one in the woods as if it were malformed so that Helene will be free to work. I can't let that happen."

He lifted a hand to her lips. "Never mind. You can have a hundred babies and mothers if it pleases you. This house is now yours."

"But it was built for the war chief."

"I only reside here. It was waiting for you."

Her mind was tangled in a confusion of French and Natchez traditions. "It is you who must defend it."

"I defend those in it, not the house. It has no importance to me except as a shelter for the one who dwells in it."

The baby had been lying with her mother. Helene must have awakened and given her a breast, for the angry wailing had ceased, turning to small, grunting, gratified sounds.

"You are too generous," she said softly.

"Because I give you what is yours by right? Hardly."

As a Natchez, he undoubtedly felt that the hut was hers, but would he be so generous with the lands he held as a Frenchman? It was not likely.

Almost as if he divined the trend of her thoughts, he went on, "There is nothing that I hold that is not now yours."

"Also nothing that would not quickly become yours again if I should decide not to be your wife."

"I have no way to convince you otherwise, if you think that, for I would not risk losing you only to prove it."

The coolness of his tone sent a chill over her. She had no wish to question his word. What difference did it make in any case so long as Helene was permitted to stay? "Shall I thank you then," she asked in a rallying tone, "or is it unnecessary?"

"That depends on what form it takes," he said and reached out to draw her down beside him, setting his mouth to hers.

They were still wakeful, however, when the tiny noises of the baby's feeding had died away. Elise asked about the embassy to the Choctaws and learned that it had been a qualified success. The Choctaws had a long list of demands, but they were far more concerned with gain than with fighting the Natchez. It seemed obvious that they could be propitiated by small concessions long enough for the walls of the forts to be finished. The Natchez had only to gather up some of the spoils taken from the French, turning over a portion—a few bales of silk, a handful of tools, a few slaves—every few days. In that way, an attack could be put off indefinitely.

Elise listened closely as she lay with her head pillowed on his shoulder. She was relieved that there would be no need to defend the village against a mass rush of the Choctaws, but her mind was on other things. "Would it be possible for Helene and her baby, and perhaps Madame Doucet, to be among the slaves to be transferred?"

"Possibly, but I don't advise it," he said, his voice grave. "The Choctaws are allies of the French, but that doesn't mean that any captives they hold will be turned over to the French the minute they come into view. It's far more likely that the Choctaws will hold them for ransom as a means of increasing their profit from the massacre."

"They wouldn't!"

"I assure you they would. In the meantime, the slaves would only change masters, working for the Choctaws instead of the Natchez. Since the Choctaws are living off the land while camped outside the village, the slaves will be better fed and better housed where they are, certainly they will not have to work any harder.''

"How will you choose who to send to them then?"

"It would be best to send the strongest and healthiest, but it may be that we will give the Frenchwomen the facts and see if there are volunteers. It's always possible that the French will pay a ransom without delay, though I will be surprised if they even get here in less than another month.''

"Why then have the Choctaws come so early?" Her hand lay relaxed upon his chest. She spread her fingers, lightly touching the lines of his tattoos, where there were the ridges of tiny scars to guide her.

"For exactly what they will get: a share of the spoils."

"But I thought it was revenge they wanted."

"To them, taking a large part of the booty that the Natchez captured is revenge of a sort. It's a mistake to think of Indians making war in the same way the white man does.''

"Oh?"

"For instance, Indians never attack against overwhelming odds, over open ground, or against a position obviously well guarded. So far as they are concerned, doing so is not bravery; it's stupidity. They will die readily enough for good reason, but they value life too much to throw it away. Besides, among the Natchez the war chief is obliged to pay the families a sum of money for every warrior he fails to bring back from a battle. That discourages ordering senseless attacks.''

"You will have to pay for every man killed under you? Can you do that?"

"I must.''

Elise paused in her explorations of his chest with the tip of her index finger resting on the tight button of one of his paps. "It certainly seems a sensible way of waging war.''

"Only against people who have the same standards."

"What do you mean?"

"It's seldom that the Natchez, or most Indians, kill women and children; they will do it, but usually only if they get in the way or endanger them in some way, such as attacking them or slowing down a march or crying so as to attract the enemy. A part of this is for the sake of the labor of such captives, naturally, but it is also because of the care they have for their own women and children. It has happened that the British have put whole villages to the sword, however, and I fear that the French will use cannons against the forts we are building. If that happens, I'm not sure how the Natchez will accept it. A man of the Natchez would rather die than submit to slavery, but he will also become a slave before he will let his women and children be killed."

"It isn't much of a choice," Elise said, her voice thin, her movements stilled.

He took a deep breath and let it out slowly. "No."

There was silence for some time. Sleep did not come, however. Finally Elise said, "If a war chief must pay for the men killed under him, then it's no wonder the Suns are chosen. No one else could afford it."

"It's true that a war chief seldom gets to keep his spoils."

"On the other hand, I understand there are criteria for the job that are more important." She trailed her fingers slowly down his breastbone to his navel, pausing there to delve into that hollow.

"Such as?" he inquired. He bent to brush his lips over the top of her head.

"That of the women."

"I don't think I understand."

"Don't you?" she asked, smiling a little to herself. "But you passed the tests with such ease."

"Tests?"

"Perhaps I shouldn't tell you." She trailed her fingers lower over the hard flat muscles of his abdomen, following the thin line of hair to where it widened into a triangle. Gently, caressingly, she touched the smooth, warm length of his manhood.

"Witch," he murmured.

Easing lower on the bench, she asked, "Do you really want to know?"

"No . . . yes."

"It seems," she said, brushing the flat of his stomach with her lips, "that men sometimes use the same tactics with women that they do in battle."

"Profound," he answered breathlessly. "Who says so?"

"Your mother. The test then, you see, is how a man behaves in . . . intimate moments."

"I think I see." His voice was rich if uneven with the laughter that made the muscles of his abdomen ripple under her mouth as he went on, "Will it damage my reputation beyond repair and lose me my office if I surrender now?"

* * *

The days of the month of grace went by swiftly. Hunting parties were sent out more often than before and ranged farther, even across the Mississippi River. The fires that dried the meat burned constantly. The women searched for fresh spring greens and roots, cooking these rather than using the stores of corn. They also sought and preserved supplies of certain herbs that would be needed in case of battle injuries. Water was brought from the creek and stored in special huts inside the forts, the pottery jars stacked one on top of the other to the ceiling, while the wells, though producing water, were deepened still farther. For protection from the weather, a series of huts were built inside the forts so that each stockade took on the appearance of a new, though more crowded, village. In the center of the larger main fort on the west bank of the creek, a small mound had been constructed to hold the larger house of the Great Sun and his family.

As the days grew warmer, the children were allowed out of the village to play in the woods, but were closely watched. Older boys were cautioned not to stray too far away and to listen always for the call to return. The women fretted that the fields were not prepared for planting, that the weather would grow too hot before they could put their seeds of maize, pumpkin, squash, and bean into the ground. None dared to think that they might not plant at all near the Grand Village that year, or if they thought it, did not say it aloud.

There was some concern over a hunting party of four men and two women that did not return. Men were sent out to look for them. They returned with a tale of capture by the Tunica Indians on the west side of the river, a tribe related to the Choctaws and so allied now with the French. An embassy was sent to the Tunica chief, but the old man who led the tribe said that he had already sent the Natchez men and women to the great white chief, Governor Perier, in New Orleans.

The delegations to the Choctaw encampment were frequent. A few of the captive women were given into the care of the French allies, but, as Reynaud had predicted, they only exchanged one kind of slavery for another and with less protection from the elements. A few tools, bolts of cloth, looking glasses, crystal glasses, and brass teapots changed hands, along with a portion of the gold taken from the French. The Natchez also provided a feast of smoked pork, venison, and sagamite. In return for their generosity, they gained time, the most valuable thing they could get at the moment.

The forts were completed. They had no large gates since there were no wheeled vehicles to go in and out. Instead, there was only once place in each encircling wall, not much wider than the shoulders of a man, where the ends overlapped each other, creating an entranceway. Such a stockade could be easily defended since attackers could only enter single file, and if the opening was rushed, it would only admit one man at a time into the interior of the fort.

Suddenly it was March. The trees burst into new growth, their tender leaves like a green haze seen through the gray branches of the forest. The sweet scent of yellow jasmine floated on the warm breeze along with the delicate and delectable fragrance of wild pink azaleas near the water. Dogwoods opened their white bracts, looking like earthbound white clouds, and near St. Catherine's Creek the jack-in-the-pulpits and violets sprang forth in profusion.

One evening at twilight, Reynaud ducked into the hut. In his hand he carried a branch of wild azaleas, the delicate pink flowers contrasting oddly with the copper strength of his work-roughened fingers. He came to Elise and, breaking off a stem of flowers, pushed them into place over her ear. She smiled up at him, engulfed in their scent and a sudden heart-stopping wave of pleasure. He took her in his arm and held her close for a long moment, resting his cheek on the top of her head, and she clasped her arms around his waist, holding tightly in a formless anxiety and an emotion she could not name.

Finally he released her, stepping back. His eyes were dark and desolate as he spoke. "The French are here. They landed this afternoon and are camped now on the ruins of Fort Rosalie."

The French did not advance at once on the village. They rested at their leisure, cleaning their equipment, organizing, building crude scaling ladders and waiting for the remainder of their force to travel upriver. They were under the command of the king's lieutenant, the Chevalier de Loubois. It was expected, due to the deliberation of the French, that the chevalier would send to ask for a meeting with the Great Sun and perhaps make some attempt to win the freedom of the captives. He did not.

The Natchez did not wait. By the morning of the third day, the Indian population of the countryside, swarming in from the outer villages, had emptied into the two defensive stockades. The Grand Village stood empty. The doors of the huts gaped open and the cook fires were cold. So complete was the removal to the forts that even the sacred eternal fire had been transferred to a small temple inside the larger palisade. Nothing stirred, no sound was heard except for the cawing of a crow as it lighted on the carved back of one of the wild swans on the temple roof. Looking back at the village, Elise thought it appeared deserted, with the desolate look of some place where a plague had come taking everyone in death.

On the fifth day after the troops from new Orleans had landed, they came into sight. Whether from spite or merely strategy, they set up their position on the site of the Grand Village. They swarmed over the place, stabling their horses in the huts, pulling down walls, and cutting down the ancient shade trees for firewood. The Chevalier de Loubois made his quarters in the temple and placed his largest cannon on the lower slope of this sacred mound. A flagpole was raised on which snapped and fluttered the fleur-de-lis of France. Drums rolled. Bugles blew. Night fell.

Where the news came from, none could say. It might have originated with the French themselves, might have been told to the Choctaws, who could have passed it to some of the Natchez from the outlying villages as they made their way into the forts. It spread swiftly in the crowded streets where several families now occupied every newly built hut. It was Madame Doucet who recounted it to Elise, laughing in wild, high-pitched glee that was painful to hear. It appeared that the party of Natchez hunters who had been sent to New Orleans by the Tunicas were dead, executed by the French. Governor Perier himself had given the order and it had been carried out. The four men and two women of the Natchez had been burned at the stake.

There were few who slept that night. Men prowled the ramparts, the curious as well as those on guard. Most of them carried muskets, arms bought with furs from traders or looted from Fort Rosalie. Powder and ball had been issued earlier in the day from a store kept in a hut built near the well in case of fire. Some of those less edgy sat carefully painting their faces and bodies with stripes of red, yellow, and white.

The number of warriors within the wall was difficult to tell, but it was above four hundred, perhaps nearer to five. The remaining two to three hundred fighting men were in the other fort across the creek where the people from the smaller, outlying villages were concentrated. Elise had heard that Path Bear was commanding the warriors of this second fort in his capacity as chief of the second largest village and therefore third most important man behind the Great Sun and Reynaud. The total number of armed men in both forts far outnumbered the French gathered outside. But the French had at their backs the Choctaws, so their combined strength was more than twice as great.

In the main fort, the small plaza left open in front of the house of the Great Sun, was a seething mass of confusion as people sought to find shelter for themselves, their dogs, chickens, pigs, and other belongings. Women called back and forth, children screamed, animals barked and cackled and squealed. Dust rose thickly in the air, mixing with the smoke and cooking fires to hang in a pall that was held in by the upright logs of the wall.

A plan for the accommodation of everyone had been drawn up, but persuading several hundred tired and frightened women and children to follow it was not easy. Class lines had to be followed, this was paramount. There was little outright squabbling, but a great deal of stubborn insistence on privilege and precedence. Reynaud was everywhere, ordering loose animals penned, settling disputes over who was to live with whom, picking up a crying child and carrying him around on his shoulder. St. Cosme served as his aide, carrying orders and suggestions back and forth between Reynaud and the Great Sun.

Elise directed people here and there and helped with bundles. When she had a spare moment, she spoke to the Frenchwomen, answering their questions about what was happening as best she could. Their greatest fear was that if the French attacked there would be reprisals against them. Elise was doubtful of it happening. To the Natchez mind, the captives had become a part of the tribe, especially after the passage of so many months. It was impossible to say what might be done in the heat of anger, of course, or if the fight went against the Indians.

To one side of the small plaza, an array of food and drink had been set out, and it was here that the Great Sun presided from his throne chair, which had been brought down from his house for that purpose. He issued decrees and sent runners here and there, acting with surprising dispatch to bring order out of the chaos. It was noticeable, however, that none of the refugees were directed to his own abode on its small mound.

As the night wore on, the din subsided. The last wooden bowl was emptied and the scraps thrown out to be scrabbled over by flapping chickens and charging pigs. The Great Sun ascended to his house. The winding alleyways between the houses were cleared. The only sounds heard from the huts were the rasp of a snore from an elder or the fretful cry of a child. The night wind blew, whining over the enclosing palisade. Now and then a dog growled, jealous of his new territory, then lapsed into silence. The forms of sleeping men rolled in their capes were everywhere, particularly against the foundation of the wall and near the entrance to the stockade. Elise, standing in the doorway of the hut she shared with Helene and her child, watched as the high-riding, three-quarter moon went behind a cloud, leaving the village in darkness. She shivered.

Reynaud, moving to stand behind her, drew her against him. He bent to nuzzle the turn of her neck, the sensitive place behind her ear. His breath was warm against her cheek as he spoke. "It will be morning soon and there is nothing to be done except wait. Come to the bed furs."

He made love to her with tenderness and power, giving of his strength, accepting hers. It was as if he sought forgetfulness in her, a refuge from his terrible responsibility, if only for a brief hour. They clung together in the darkness, their bodies entwined, their eyes tightly closed; afraid but unrelentingly valiant.

He was gone when Elise stirred and sat up, wide awake, as dawn brought gray light into the hut. The morning was quiet, filled with a waiting stillness unbroken even by the calls of birds. At the far end of the room, Helene turned over with a rustle of furs. Seeing Elise sitting upright, listening, she pushed up on one elbow.

"What is it?" the other woman said.

"I don't—"

Elise's words were lost in the booming of muskets and the hoarse shouts of charging men. The noise, rising from the defenders inside as well as the troops outside the enclosing wall, was deafening. It was an attack. The first round in the siege had begun.

Elise threw back the bearskin that covered her and jumped up, snatching her skirt and jerking it around her. The baby was crying, startled by the racket, and Helene was trying to quiet her. Sending them no more than a quick glance, wrapping her cape around her as she went, Elise ran to the door and pushed it aside to look out.

Already there was a heavy cloud of acrid blue-gray powder smoke swirling within the stockade. Through it could be seen the men on the wall, firing down at the advancing French, moving back and forth in squads as first one position and then another was pressed hard. The injured were being let down to the ground where they lay in the way. Women ran here and there, shouting to be heard. Children cried. A pair of horses had broken their tethers and they galloped back and forth across the village circle with keening pigs running from under their flying hooves and dogs barking at their heels.

Elise ran to a section of the palisade that was not under attack. She climbed the ladder that led to the walkway, running along it until she could see and yet not be in the way.

Beyond the wall, the orderly ranks of the French came on, firing, dropping to one knee to reload as the next row fired above them, closing together where the injured fell behind. Here and there were details with scaling ladders, but few were able to get them in place and those that did were repelled with ferocity. To the rear of the French lines could be seen the Choctaws drawn up in firing ranks. They did not advance, however, but stayed well back out of range. The result was that their fire was dropping short of the Natchez on the wall and was actually in danger of falling among the French.

But the French forces were taking a toll. Farther around the fort, near the front section where the brunt of the attack was being directed, a warrior yelled and reeled back with blood streaming down his face. Another keeled silently off the walkway, falling to the ground to lie unmoving.

Elise whirled back toward the ladder, descending to the ground once more. The stickiness of resin from the logs on which she had been standing made her realize that her feet were bare and she ran toward the hut.

On her knees searching for her moccasins under the sleeping bench, she told Helene what was taking place to the best of her understanding. Then slipping on her footwear, fastening her heavy outdoor cape on her shoulder as she ran, she left the hut and stepped into the chaos of the fortified village. The first person she saw was Little Quail. The woman shouted that someone was needed to move the dead and injured out of the way. In no time they had gathered a group of stout females and headed toward the wall.

For the next hour, there were only bodies, the smell of gunpowder, the boom of firing and clatter of balls hitting the thick wall, the smell of blood and sweat, and more bodies. The dead were laid out in the shade of a great oak. A hut was designated as a hospital and the injured were led or carried there. Elise swabbed wounds and bound them with strips of leather, with mulberry cloth and pieces torn from the linen shirts and the silk and satin dresses looted from the French. Few of the injured men could be persuaded to stay away from the wall and those few only if they were too weak to stand. As soon as their injuries were bound so that the pouring blood was no longer troublesome with its slipperiness, they returned to defend the village.

Pausing now and then in her task, Elise watched the fighting on the wall and particularly at the channellike gate into the fort. With Reynaud leading them, the Natchez warriors repelled the French again and again. Their strength was fiendish, inhuman, as if they drew on reservoirs of power and courage unknown to the French. They were fighting for their lives, to keep from becoming vassals, the slaves, of their enemy, fighting to protect their women and children. Still, there was something more. Was it because they were less civilized, more nearly savage? Was it because they feared death less, having no true belief in an avenging God and the fires of hell despite years of exposure to such religious doctrines? Or was it simply that they clung to life more fiercely in their natural reverence for its sweetness?

So little did it seem that the Natchez could ever be driven from their fortified position that Elise, during a lull in the fighting when she brought water to Reynaud, spoke of it to him.

"If you win, you and the Natchez, if the French sue for peace, will you consider giving up the French captives in exchange for being left alone?"

"If that is made a condition, you mean?" he asked, watching as he swirled the water in the wooden bowl she had given him.

"Yes, I suppose."

"Why do you ask?"

She tipped her head toward the warriors around her. "They fight so well, without tiring or feeling pain, almost as if they weren't quite human."

"Don't be fooled. They tire as any man does and feel the

pain they won't show. The French are the brave men here, marching again and again into our fire."

"I thought you considered that stupid."

He shrugged. "A man can be stupid and courageous at the same time. I expect that if I were on the other side, I would find many among the men out there to call heroic."

She nodded her understanding of his argument, but went on with her own line of thought. "The Choctaws are little help to the French or so it appears to me. If the French should lose, things will change."

"In what way?"

"The women will remain captives, for one thing. If they have to stay here, I don't know how they will take it."

"They will adjust, if it should happen."

"Will they? I doubt it, not when their people are so close. Nor will the French forget them, not so many."

He nodded. "No doubt you're right. It would be best to let them go. But whether the council will agree to it, I don't know."

"And what of us? What will we do?"

He looked at her swiftly. "Us?"

"I assumed . . . That is, we are married. Would we stay here?" The heat of a flush rose to her cheeks, but she would not look away from his dark gaze. Let him think what he pleased.

"You said 'them' when you spoke of the French; you don't consider yourself a Frenchwoman now? You would not want to go with the others back to New Orleans?"

"I'm not sure what I am. I . . . suppose I will go with them if it is necessary."

"It will not be," he said, returning the bowl to her fingers and closing his own around hers as she took it. "When it is finished here, I will go back to my house on the Bayou Duc de Maine. You may come with me if you choose."

How far away it seemed now, that house, and Madeleine. Like a dream. Would she ever see it again? Would she feel its serenity around her or walk through its rooms on a warm summer day when everything was quiet and clean and without danger? Would she have children who would play there and grow tall and straight and wise, afraid of no man? It was a dream, in truth. No more.

At that moment Pierre shouted from farther down the wall. A new attack was being mounted. "Go," Reynaud said, spinning her around and giving her a quick push. She turned back to press a hard kiss to Reynaud's powder-blackened mouth and scrambled down from the ladder to the ground, sloshing water as she went.

She stopped to look in at the hospital hut, giving water to several men, speaking to Little Quail who sat with a fan made of turkey tail feathers in her hand, fanning flies away from the face of a dying boy. Returning to the well for more water, Elise heard musket balls whistling through the limbs of the tree that overhung it. One hit the trunk and dropped clattering down through the branches to fall near her feet. She had become so used to such things in the last hours that she hardly noticed.

If I were on the other side . . . Reynaud's words returned to trouble her. In this fight, was he still torn between loyalties? She had thought that such doubts were over since he had become the war chief. She had known that he searched for some way to bring about an honorable peace between the Indians and the French, but she had thought it was for the sake of the Natchez, his chosen people. His method of going about it, that of making their suppression too costly for the French, would not be popular with the government in New Orleans. They would hardly understand a policy that allowed him to lead the Indians that were killing French soldiers. No doubt they would call him a renegade, a traitor. If he was taken, it was unlikely that Governor Perier would be any more lenient with him than he had been with the Natchez he had burned at the stake.

Gradually the attack slowed. The shooting died away to a scattered shot here and there, then ceased altogether. The fort had held; the French had been beaten off. They were retreating back to their positions. A shout of jubilation went up, then another. Dazed men climbed down from the wall. They exchanged tales of moments of danger, of fear and of victory. They were amazed at the mechanical soldiering, at the French marching into the mouths of their guns, astonished that the French had launched an offensive against so impregnable a stronghold as the one they had built, but they were also proud that they had turned them back.

The relief the Natchez felt was transformed into something near merriment. As the hours passed, turning into days with no renewal of the attack, the Indians inside the walls feasted, traded back and forth, and visited among each other as if the purpose of the gathering was purely social. Some of the younger men got drunk and chased each other naked through the village. Others organized a series of games, one a form of ball game where each of two teams tried to prevent the other from touching the house of the Great Sun with a ball made of stuffed leather. Another game, played with poles and a stone, was called chunkey. In it two men used stout sticks eight feet long and a round, flat stone an inch thick and three inches in diameter. One warrior rolled the stone and threw his stick at the same time, while the second warrior, standing ready, also threw his stick. The one whose stick landed touching the rock, or nearest to it, earned one point and also the right to throw the rock the next time. The competition was keen and there was some wagering, but not to excess.

Outside the wall, the French regrouped. The days without fighting stretched into a week and still all was quiet. Reynaud, who spent much of his time on the wall, watched in grim silence, ignoring the games and trading, the feasting and visiting that went on behind him. The French were too quiet, he said, hardly firing a shot except to return fire against them or to cover themselves. Their energy was being used to dig trenches that would afford them protection from which to fire upon the fort or to make a surprise sally. Reynaud had also seen more heavy artillery being assembled and brought up to be set in place closer to the wall. It was inevitable that they would soon receive heavy fire.

He was right. By the next morning, the guns had been brought to bear. The siege began again in earnest.

16

THE FIRST TREMENDOUS explosion of gunpowder and shot directed against the fort shocked the Natchez into silence. The children who cried were hushed; the women looked at each other with wide, frightened eyes; the men ran for the wall to look. Many reached it in time to reel back from the impact of the second barrage. But the thick wall they had spent so much time and labor building held. The logs trembled and dirt sifted between them; fires flared and had to be put out with jars of water passed hand to hand, but the palisade stood upright and solid, a strong barrier between them and the French. It was a tribute of no mean sort to Reynaud's engineering skill and also to his ability as a leader of men.

It was the noise that was demoralizing. The thunder of the concussions as the guns were fired shook the air and made the ground tremble. It rolled in upon them in waves along with the thick blue-black smoke that caught in their throats. It made the dogs cower and run in crazed circles and sent the children under the sleeping benches. At first the men and women flinched involuntarily, but gradually they became accustomed to the sound and treated it with apparent contempt, though they often turned to stare in the direction of the firing.

The hardest thing for the Indians to understand was not the siege itself, but the fact that the French would fire upon the village while their own captive women and children were inside. What madmen were they to endanger them in such a way? If they had so little concern, then their attack was one of deepest blood vengeance and they would surely not stop until every Natchez were dead.

It seemed so, indeed. Day after day the booming of the guns continued. A gray-black pall of smoke covered the sky. Fires broke out as pieces of shot caught in the cane-thatched roofs. The French gunners, finding the wall unbreachable, raised the elevation of the guns and began to fire into the stockade and at the house of the Great Sun on its small mound. Reynaud's brother, fearing for the safety of his wives who were both now large with pregnancy, ordered his family down into the town, but he refused to leave his own house. The new small temple received a direct hit that caved in one wall. A guardian of the temple fire was killed and the other man on duty was wounded. It was feared that the eternal fire would go out, but the next set of guardians marched to take their places, tending the fire in defiance of the French guns.

The nerves of everyone inside the fort grew taut. Tempers flared. Quarrels broke out over nothing. The crowded conditions, the slowly increasing dirt and stench, the gathering refuse and excrement of humans and animals, which could not be disposed of, were as intolerable to the Natchez as the bombardment. Flies buzzed everywhere. Buzzards circled overhead. Fleas hopped and jumped in every hut, infesting the bed furs. The levels of the water wells dropped as the women fought to stay clean and the water was used to wet down the thatch as well as put out the fires that started.

The French women and children fared the same as the Indians, though their spirits were buoyed by the hope of rescue. They gathered together to pray at every spare moment, keeping to themselves as much as possible. There had been a time when it had seemed that they could possibly be assimilated into the tribe, but the presence of the French outside made them sharply aware of who they were and where they had come from, emphasizing the differences between them and the Natchez instead of the similarities. The Indians seemed to feel it also, for they were sharper with them and stricter than they had been since the early days of capture.

A pair of field cannons taken from Fort Rosalie were mounted with great effort and finally brought into action. The first time they were fired created great panic among the French, who had not expected such retaliation. Unfortunately, the Indian warriors, in their enthusiasm, were to liberal in their use of powder. Late one afternoon, one of the pieces recoiled with such force that it broke its mounting and crashed to the ground, maiming half the gun crew. The barrel of the other overheated from the constant firing and, when swabbed out with water, cracked open. The first gun was remounted, but it fell silent within a few hours as the last of the powder and shot was used up. Further ransacking of the supplies brought from the village storehouse brought to light enough ammunition for another day, but that was all.

Elise found the conditions of the siege as wearing as any. She had grown fond of Helene, but at the same time living in close quarters with her was a burden. She longed to be alone, without the constant need to be pleasant to the woman, to explain what was happening and quiet her alarms, to sympathize. The crying of the baby, which time and again dragged her from a tired sleep, was an irritant, especially since quiet for sleeping was so rare.

She sometimes thought that if Helene had not been there Reynaud might have come to the hut more often. There was nothing to prove it, however. He was needed, in constant demand. When he managed to make it to the hut, it was to fall into a stupor of exhaustion. He liked to have her lie beside him even so; still, it seemed that the closeness they had known so briefly was fading. There were lines of fatigue in Reynaud's face and he seldom stayed to talk once he awoke, but returned at once to his post. Sometimes he would hold her achingly tight or make love to her as if he feared it might be the last time. Bit by bit as the siege continued, she, too, became afraid that the passion and the joy were gone forever and that time was running out.

Like the other Frenchwomen, Elise was made more aware of her nationality every day. It was not a conscious process, not her own choice; it simply happened. With the exception of Little Quail, the Indian women withdrew, treating her as they did the others. Feeling isolated, she responded in the same way. She spent more and more time with her own countrywomen, trying to see to it that they had their share of the food and water, that their injuries were treated and their burdens made less heavy. It was not easy, for they had the task of disposing of the refuse that littered the village: shoveling up the gnawed bones, vegetable scraps, and the dung; burying everything, as well as the animals killed by the scattered firing. They had to sweep up the torn and tattered clothing, the broken pottery. They also had to see to it that the rats, growing more fearless daily, did not get into the stores and that the dogs, going unfed, did not dig up the shallow-buried bodies of the dead. Lower than the Stinkards, they were watched and resented and scorned.

Returning to the hut one day, Elise found Helene gone, though the baby lay asleep on a pallet of furs on the floor. Elise turned back to look for the woman. She found her near the gate. Helene was coming toward her, her face swollen and red-splotched with weeping, wet with her tears. Without a word, she went into Elise's arms. Elise held her for a moment, then, when her own anxiety made it imperative, caught her arms, holding her from her.

"Helene, what is it? Tell me!"

The woman clenched her hands together, raising eyes that were drowned in pain, yet luminous with joy. "I saw him, Elise. I saw him."

"Who?"

"Jean-Paul! He's here. And I can't bear it!"

St. Amant, here. He had made it to Fort Saint Jean Baptiste then, with the others. Elise had not realized how worried she had been about them all until she felt the relief of knowing that he and Henri, and yes, even Pascal, were safe. St. Amant must have gone on to New Orleans and, learning of the expedition to the Natchez country, joined it.

"Don't you realize what this means?" she said, giving Helene a shake. "It means he cares for you, enough to come after you."

"But if he should be killed, what then? Reynaud has taught the Natchez to shoot too well. They defend every attempt to rush the gate and inflict such wounds, so much damage, so desperately do they fight. I'm so afraid, Elise, so afraid."

Elise stared at her, her lips pale and her eyes haunted. "We all are."

"You, too? But you seem so brave, so much in control of yourself."

Elise had thought that Helene might find her concern for Reynaud disgusting, a betrayal. Instead, it had aroused her compassion. She seemed to feel that Elise's affair with the half-breed was no simple misalliance, but a tragedy. For herself and St. Amant she clung to hope, regardless of the circumstances, but for Elise's relationship with Reynaud she had none. Some things by their very nature carried the seeds of their doom in their beginning, she said sorrowfully. This was one.

Head lice appeared among the children, both Indian and French, and were fought by careful inspection and removal and drenches of steeped herbs. The dogs disappeared from the alleyways into the cooking pots. Then it rained for three days, washing refuse through the village, which ran into the wells, and afterward a fever broke out among the people spreading faster than a windswept fire. But it was the low levels of those wells and the swiftly emptying pots in the storehouse that caused the council to he held.

Everyone in the village knew it. Elise attended with the rest but sat well out of hearing range. It seemed best not to draw too much attention to herself; the Natchez blamed the French women and children for causing the fever that had forced so many of their number to take to their benches, as they blamed them for so many diseases and with good reason. Elise wished that she could be close enough to hear Reynaud, for she knew he was to speak. But she depended on word of mouth, filtering back through the crowd, to tell her what was said.

His voice, deep and rich as he spoke the flowing Natchez tongue with its many courtesies and sonorous phrasing, came to her. It struck a chord deep inside so that she listened to its timbre without thought for the meaning of the words, without trying to see him above the others. She had heard his voice in laughter and in passion and in love, and she would never forget the sound of it, never. How much she owed him and how little he had been repaid. But she had such memories as few women ever knew, such sweet, vital memories. She would hold them to her when she was old, taking them out one by one, holding them to the light to admire their flash and color. That first night on the trail when he had stood naked in the rain. The time she had seen him cast in silver with the moonlight on the bayou and had joined him there in the water. That evening of lavender-gray twilight when they had made love in the woods. The dusky afternoon when he had stolen her as his wife. A handful of memories. Her only regret was that there were not more.

The speaker changed. An elderly man stood, shouting his rage, shaking his fist in the direction of the French. When he sat down, another rose, speaking in measured tones. When this man sat down in his turn, there was silence.

Listening to the conversation around her, Elise understood that Reynaud had suggested they fight on, that the French were as bad off as they were. He said that the soldiers, many of whom were colonists with duties and obligations back in New Orleans, would soon grow tired of wasting powder and shot on a fortress they could not take. If they were patient, the French would send officers to talk of peace on Natchez terms. The elderly man who had spoken first had disagreed. He was enraged at the protracted siege, claiming that Reynaud would have the Natchez fight like the French instead of in their traditional way. He urged that they creep out at night and surround the French, killing them as they slept. The last man to speak disagreed with both. He feared that they would all die of disease and thirst where they were. The fever had weakened the warriors so that there were not enough fit to man the wall or to make a successful attack. He demanded that an embassy be sent to the French to sue for peace and arrange a meeting for the discussion of terms.

The argument, shifting first one way, then another, continued far into the night. They could scarcely hold the wall for lack of able-bodied warriors, nor could they agree on an attack for the same reason. On the other hand, so vicious was the French offensive that it was feared they would slaughter a peace delegation before its members could speak. There were those who wanted to burn two of the Frenchwomen as a warning to the French of what would happen if they continued and also in retaliation for the Natchez who had been put to the stake by Governor Perier. The suggestion was shouted down, but the threat of it left an uneasy feeling in the air.

At last Tattooed Arm got to her feet. She spoke with quiet conviction, finally putting forth a proposal that caused silence to descend.

"What was it?" Elise leaned forward to ask Little Quail who was sitting a couple of rows in front of her.

"The mother of the Great Sun has suggested that a Frenchwoman be sent to speak for us with the commandant of the French."

"Any such woman would be likely to tell the commandant to level the village."

"Most would do that," Little Quail agreed. "Most, but not you, I think."

"No, but then it seems unlikely that the warriors of the Natchez would hide behind the skirts of a woman."

Little Quail frowned. "They would not look at it that way. The matter is delicate and also out of the ordinary. Who better than a woman, keeper of the peace and preserver of life, to represent them? A Frenchwoman who will come to no harm?"

"Reynaud will not allow it."

"He must if it is the decision of the council. If this was a party of warriors away from the village, it would be different: his word would be supreme, even before that of the Great Sun. But here the fate of everyone must be decided and so the council will prevail."

The elders conferred among themselves. The Great Sun was consulted, then he motioned Reynaud to him. Finally a pronouncement was made. While it was being spoken, Reynaud stood scanning those gathered on the outskirts of the council. He moved toward Elise, threading his way, coming to her as if he had known where she was sitting all along. When he stopped before her, he reached down his hand to help her to her feet.

"Come, my love," he said, his eyes steel gray, mirroring the angry reluctance that gripped him. "You have been chosen."

When morning came, Tattooed Arm, Little Quail, and Helene arrayed Elise in finest style. A gown of snuff brown velvet trimmed with lace and gold braid was brought from the storeroom for her use. Over it went a long cloak of woven swansdown, soft white with swirling designs of gold and red dyed in the soft and floating material. Her hair was braided and coiled on top of her head and held by shell combs. Necklaces of freshwater pearls were placed around her neck and earrings of gold purloined from the French were hung in her ears. No shoes could be found to fit her and so she wore her white wedding moccasins on her feet.

In the little time left, Reynaud, the Great Sun, and Tattooed Arm coached her on what she was to say. From the top of the stockade a white cloth was waved as a sign of truce. Cane whistles shrilled. Drums beat. The narrow barricade at the fort's opening was pulled aside.

At the last minute, Reynaud blocked her way. His gaze moved over her as she stood so straight in her dignity before him. Her skin was touched lightly with gold from exposure to the sun these last weeks, but was flawless in its texture. Her hair shone in the first sunlight of the day; her amber-brown eyes were steady. She was beautiful in that moment, a woman of purpose and courage. He reached out to take her hand, carrying it to his lips.

"I'm not sure I can let you go," he said quietly.

She met his eyes, searching their dark depths, noting the strain in his face and the exhaustion, noting also a burn across his shoulder where a brand from a blazing house he had been helping to extinguish had struck him. "I will return."

"Will you? What if the French won't permit it?"

"They must if they are to save the others."

"They might prefer to take them by force. There is that risk."

"The council has decided. I must go—for all of us, your people and mine."

"If you don't return—"

Her grip on his hand tightened. "Yes?"

Light flared in his eyes, then died away to stark pain. "You will remain in my heart always."

The French would let her return. They must and yet his words brought a tight knot of anguish to her throat. Before she could speak, however, the cane whistles shrilled again, drowning sound. Beyond the entrance of the fort could be seen the blue of uniform jackets as a French contingent formed to meet whoever might be emerging from the fort. They must not be kept waiting. With tears making her vision swim, she freed her hand and turned away. Alone, with the soft breeze catching her cloak and blowing its light weight around her so that it gleamed like gossamer in the sun, she moved from the fort.

The king's lieutenant, the Chevalier de Loubois, was polite. His distaste as his gaze rested on her Indian cloak was obvious; still, he led her to his command tent and seated her on a stool. Refreshments were brought. A number of the other officers and men had gathered round. Among them was St. Amant and Elise nodded to him with a smile of recognition. Loubois sipped his wine, lounging at his ease on his camp chair, then, with sudden impatience, bid her to state her purpose in coming.

Elise drew a deep breath. "I have been directed to say to you: The Natchez have lived long and prospered in this land. When the French came here because there were too many men in their own country, the Natchez said to them, 'Welcome, there is land enough for all.' When the winters were long and food scarce, they divided what they had with the French, leaving their bellies less full so that the French could live. Often when the floating houses, the ships that brought the food of the French did not come, the Natchez took the soldiers of the French into their villages; they fed them, housed them, and their women made them at ease, taking pleasure with them as friends.

"In return, the French gave the Natchez the white man's diseases. They treated them as slaves, taking from them what they did not give freely, beating them. The French would say that they gave guns and blankets. But what need had the Natchez for guns when their bows and arrows brought them all they could eat? What need was there for blankets when the furs of the animals were warm, when the women of the Natchez could make fine mantles of feathers and the fibers of the mulberry tree?

"Now in the last harvest season, the commandant at Fort Rosalie demanded the lands of the Natchez were they have lived for years beyond memory of the eldest man, the best and richest lands of the children of the sun. Were the Natchez to die without the corn standing ready to harvest, to die of moving in the winter season of cold and hardship so that the commandant might have what he wanted of them? The path of friendship does not require such a sacrifice, only the path of war. The Natchez therefore took the path of war. Commandant Chepart is dead and they have retrieved the value of all they had given to the French who came to the Natchez. They wish now only to live alone, at peace, without communication with the French. They will give up the French women and children they hold in return for your given word that they will be allowed to live unmolested by either the French or their enemies the Choctaws. In token of this pledge, they request that you withdraw a distance of at least three leagues from the fort at which time they will release the captives."

The Chevalier de Loubois stared at her, leaning forward with his arm braced on one leg. His face was rigid, unyielding. When he spoke, it was as if he had heard nothing of what she had said except the offer of the return of the prisoners.

"In your opinion, Madame Laffont, how much longer can the Natchez hold out?"

"I couldn't say," she answered, her features stiff.

"Can't or won't? You see, I have heard of your affair with Reynaud Chavalier, of his gallant rescue of yourself. The man is the lowest form of life in this colony, a half-breed traitor. You owe him nothing. You lived through the massacre, have seen the Natchez at close quarters, are fully aware of the treatment of the French prisoners. You have information that is valuable to us. If you have any feeling for your country or your countrymen, you will tell us what we need to know.''

"I am not a military man," she answered slowly, feeling her way. "What do I know of the ability of men to hold out during a siege?"

"I spoke not of their morale, but of their food supplies. Are they plentiful? How much do they have stored? What of water? What are their thoughts concerning the guns of the French?"

"The food seems adequate, also the water. They have not yet begun to ration it." It was true only in the strictest sense. The water was rationed for everything except drinking and putting out fires. The lack of bathing was almost as great a hardship, but the king's lieutenant need not know that.

"What of the guns?"

"They seem to be doing little damage."

"Yes, yes," the chevalier said, rubbing his hands together, directing his gaze toward the ground before he looked up again. "Why then this offer? We were most surprised to see a flag of truce."

"I think that they truly wish to live in peace. They feel the massacre was a blow struck in retaliation for all that Chepart had done against them. It was a blood vengeance brought on the commandant's head by his own actions. It is done now and honor is satisfied. They feel that your presence here is for the sake of the women and children. They will give them to you if you will leave them alone. If you take the prisoners and go away, then you will have nothing to fear from them."

"That is childish reasoning! The Natchez have killed hundreds of our people. Governor Perier has sent to France for reinforcements, guns, supplies to put down a major uprising of the Indians. They will be here in a few months' time."

"Are you saying, Chevalier de Loubois, that because the governor has sent for more troops from the Company of the Indies he cannot now settle this matter of the Indians peaceably and without further bloodshed?"

"You have no idea what you are talking about."

"Indeed? To me it sounded remarkably as if the governor would prefer continued Indian trouble because otherwise he is going to appear like the boy who cried wolf."

"That is not at all the case," he snapped.

"Then if peace is important to Governor Perier and the company, I don't see how you can afford to ignore this appeal, particularly as it may be the only opportunity you will have to secure the release of the captives unharmed."

"What do you mean?" he asked sharply.

"The French women and children share the danger of the Indians and the hardships of the siege. How will you answer to the governor and the people of New Orleans if they die before you subdue the Natchez?"

"That will not happen."

"I assure you, Chevalier, that much though you despise the Indians in that fort over there, if you press them, if you force them into a corner, they will die to the last man before they will surrender. If you harm their women and children further, there will be no fury to compare with theirs."

"Are you saying that they will harm the captives?"

"It isn't impossible. Governor Perier burned the Natchez women."

He stared at her with an arrested look in his eyes before he put his hands on his knees and pushed to his feet. His manner was abrupt as he spoke. "I will have to think on this. I will rejoin you in an hour."

St. Amant moved at once to her side, refilling her wineglass that she had hardly touched. Picking it up, placing it in her hand, he said, "Drink this. I believe you need it."

"Yes, thank you," she answered distractedly. As he complimented her on her appearance, she only shook her head as if the words were meaningless, which indeed they were.

"And the other women, how do they fare?"

She sent him a straight look, giving him her attention with an effort. "Much as you might expect. But are you sure that is your true interest, the other women, or is there one in particular who concerns you?"

"Elise," he breathed, "you have seen her?"

"Just this morning."

"And? And?" he asked in impatience as he leaned over her.

Elise relented with a smile. "She is very well, indeed. You have a beautiful daughter who keeps the village awake with her demands."

He closed his eyes and there was a rim of moisture clinging to the base of his lashes.

"I have a message for you also," Elise went on. "She saw

you, you know. She sends her love and her prayers that you will take care.''

"Ah, Elise, I could kiss you!''

"You had best not. Your Helene may be watching or Reynaud.''

"Ah, yes, Chavalier. I'm sorry if Loubois was unpleasant about him. I tried to tell everyone that you were abducted, separated from us against your will. It was Pascal who in his cups suggested otherwise. Henri has threatened to challenge him to a duel.''

"You must not let him!''

"Oh, Pascal would not meet him. He laughs at the boy's insults, saying he was too smitten with calf love for you to believe a word against you.''

"Perhaps they will not come together often enough for there to be trouble.''

"The community around the fort in the Natchitoches country is a small one, but St. Denis is looking after the boy.''

"They are still there?''

"Assuredly. The place is more of a wilderness than Natchez, with better opportunities for smuggling with the Spanish at Los Adaes; why should Pascal not wish to remain? As for Henri, as I said, Commandant St. Denis has taken him in charge, given him work.''

They spoke of other things, of the baby and how it was born, of how Helene was living and the conditions of the siege, though Elise was hardly more forthcoming about the latter than she had been with the chevalier.

Toward the end of the hour, she sent St. Amant a quick glance. "What do you think of Loubois? If he gives his word, will he honor it?''

"You mean, will he roll up his tent and march away to his waiting ship when he has the captives safe? He must, if he gives his word.''

"You think so? There are many who feel that a man's word given to a savage is no word at all, especially if given under duress.''

St. Amant lifted a brow. "You have grown cynical.''

"Cautious, perhaps, but then I have always been that. But Loubois strikes me as an ambitious man. Would it not be a feather in his cap if he were to secure the women and children, then turn and annihilate the Natchez when they have lowered their guard?''

"He could prove the extent of the Indian problem, thereby giving Perier justification for his alarm, and at the same time save the company the expense of sending out men and arms to put down the uprising.'' With a thoughtful frown on his face, St. Amant nodded. "It is possible.''

"Probable?''

"I would not like to think so,'' he answered, his tone grave.

Behind them, the chevalier approached. He moved to bow to Elise. "My apologies for keeping you waiting, madame. It was most important that my decision not be made in haste since so much is at stake.''

"I understand,'' she murmured, risking a glance at St. Amant. The smoothness of the king's lieutenant's tone appeared to strike him as odd also, for he was frowning.

"I agree to the terms you have presented. We will withdraw a short distance so that the women and children can be released. Then in return for the release of the captives taken during the massacre at Fort Rosalie, the Natchez may live unmolested.''

"You will smoke a pipe of peace with them?''

"Yes.''

"And the Choctaws will not be permitted to enter the fort of the Natchez?''

"They will not.''

"Their warriors will leave with you when you go?''

"They will.''

There was something here that she did not like, but she could not quite put her finger on it. She stood staring at the king's lieutenant, trying to think of something she could say to bind the man to his given word. There was nothing.

The chevalier put his hands behind him, rocking back on the heels of his boots. "There is a condition.''

"Yes, what is it?'' she inquired sharply.

"Simply this. The Natchez must burn this fort they have constructed to the ground in earnest of their wish for peace.''

To burn the fort would leave them virtually defenseless against a surprise attack. "I cannot answer for them, but I will carry word of this condition to the Great Sun and to his brother, Reynaud, chief of the warriors.''

Loubois lifted a brow. "You will return? I thought perhaps

you would write out a message. You could then stay with us in safety."

"It's kind of you to suggest it, but they will be expecting me."

"Are you certain we can't persuade you?" St. Amant added his weight to the proposal.

"No. I must go back."

"As you will." The commandant of the French expedition bowed. "In the meantime, while we await our answer, we will prepare to receive the captives."

It was a dismissal. Elise, feeling unaccountably as if she had been manipulated rather than having won a victory, began the short walk back to the fort.

The council of elders that ensued was one of angry and acrimonious wrangling. The older men did not trust the French. The white officer had given in too easily, they said. More, if the Choctaws were not to be allowed into the fort, why were they gathering in ranks outside? Could the French be so without intelligence as to allow the captives to be received by the Choctaws? They would not be turned over to their own people without the payment of a large ransom, in such a case. If that happened, the French would then blame the Natchez, and might that not be used as an excuse to negate the terms of the peace? They would not deliver the captives.

They must deliver the captives, said the younger faction. To fail when they had promised would also negate the peace. The French, with the Choctaws, would fall on them in a pitched fight and what then? They were not as strong as they had been, not since the fever. If the French and the Choctaws overran the fort, there would be a massacre and it was doubtful that their women and children would escape.

Reynaud, after listening closely to Elise and questioning her with care, recommended yet another course. He suggested that they wait until morning to send the pipe of peace, the calumet. There was no reason to hurry their capitulation. There was less chance of making a mistake if they did not rush into anything. Let the French withdraw, as they were already beginning to do. True, the Natchez must release the captives since they had given their word, but they need not destroy the fort until the French and the Choctaws were gone, not if they stipulated this safeguard as a part of the agreement. Then, if the French failed to lift the siege, the Natchez would at least not have the captives to worry about or to feed.

The Great Sun, listening, watching, said nothing. He heard them out, just as he had heard Elise out as she told Reynaud everything that had occurred at the French encampment. It was not, Elise thought as she studied him, because he had nothing to impart to the discussion, but because he wanted to hear all the arguments before stating his own views, before ordering a course of action. If the council could not agree, could not make a recommendation, the decision would rest with him.

"Elise!"

The quiet call came from behind her. She turned from where she had been watching the proceedings of the council at the outer edge of the crowd to see Helene beckoning to her. Rising, she joined the Frenchwoman out of hearing distance of the important meeting.

"What is it?"

"Is it true that we are to be released? Oh, tell me it's true!"

"I don't know. It appears so."

"When?" Helene demanded, catching her arm.

"Perhaps this afternoon, perhaps tomorrow."

"The rumors said so, but I could not believe them. And Jean-Paul, you saw him, you gave him my message?"

Elise reassured her, telling her word for word what had been said, describing to her how St. Amant had looked, how he had reacted to the news that he had a daughter.

Helene scrubbed her eyes with the heel of her hand, then gave Elise a quick hug. "What a fool I am to cry over good news. But I must run and tell the others. There are such rumors flying you would not believe. They will be so happy, so happy."

The council droned on. Noon came and a meal was served to the members. The people privileged to watch came and went. Outside the wall, Loubois joined the Choctaws, pacing up and down, staring at the fort. After a time he went away, then as the sun began to coast down the sky in the west, he returned.

Elise, her legs and back stiff from sitting, left her post. She walked to the hut, looking inside for Helene. It seemed she had not been there in some time. The fire had died away to coals and ash and the pots left simmering around its verge were cold, the bear grease seasoning congealing on their contents. The baby was gone, too, and the furs where she usually lay were cold.

A peculiar fear gripped Elise. She swung out from the hut, skirting the small mound of the Great Sun and avoiding the plaza. She turned toward the huts of the Commoners where the French captives usually met.

She found Helene and the baby among the other captives in a crowd under the smoke-blackened limbs touched with the tender new green of a sweet gum tree. They surged around her, pleading, demanding, so that a passing Natchez woman laughed to hear their ill-mannered babble as they all tried to talk at once.

They had been told that they would be released, but the day was coming to an end and still the order did not come. The French were withdrawing, except for a token detail, and also many of the Choctaws. Was it all a lie? Were they to be kept forever by the Natchez? Had their country and the Company of the Indies abandoned them?

"We don't ask for much," said one woman, twisting her hands, "only the courtesy of being told what is to become of us."

"I wish I knew," Elise said helplessly.

"The Natchez!" another woman said and spat.

"The soldiers of the company!" said another and repeated the action.

Helene, with the baby in a wood frame on her back, looked at Elise and lifted her shoulders in a gesture of impatience. "We are pawns, are we not? You who carry the messages, we who wait and wonder how long we are to be slaves."

"If we were men," said the first woman who had spat, "we could say to the devil with them all. We could pick up arms and fight our way out."

"If we were men," someone echoed.

"If we were men," said another, "we would be dead."

Still, they turned almost as one to stare at the entranceway. It stood open, though closely guarded. Through it could be seen the French officers and the single rank of Choctaws, waiting to receive them. Out there were their countrymen, come to rescue them, men who spoke their language, had the same memories and tastes, habits and illusions. All that separated them was a little space, a few yards of ground. The only things that stood between them and freedom were a dozen warriors armed with muskets.

The warriors were guarding against the French coming in, not the women going out. Would they shoot at them, seek to kill unarmed women and children? They had killed many such during the massacre, but that had been while they were in the grip of blood frenzy. Now the captives were considered a part of the Natchez and as such to be protected. Or were they?

"They said we could go," Helene whispered. "They said we could if the French agreed to leave them alone. The French agreed. Why are they keeping us?"

"It's cruel, the waiting," another said.

It was cruel, indeed, bartering with human lives, with the helpless who had never harmed either side. What had women and children to do with war? It was, as Tattooed Arm said, a thing of men. They made the rules and set the penalties; they killed and met death in return. Why should these agreements they made between them be binding upon those who had no say in the proceedings, those who created life but seldom ever took it?

"So close to being free, so close."

"If there was someone to go first, I would follow."

"And I. I also. And I." The voices were quiet but determined.

Helene turned, her pale blue eyes shining. "Elise could do it. Who else better?"

Elise heard their voices as from a great distance. Would this be a betrayal? Would it? Like these women, she had been brought here against her will. Like them, she had lived with a master, done his bidding. But, oh, it was different, so different. Still, had Reynaud not said that the Natchez must let the captives go? Hadn't he said that even in the event that the French did not keep their word, the village would be better off without them? Where then was the betrayal?

It would be in leaving him.

The pain ran deep and straight, lodging in her heart. How could she leave him? How could she?

There was a gasp from among the women. They turned to stare. Elise swung around to see what had disturbed them. Strutting toward them was an Indian woman. So close was she that she must have heard what they had said. On her broad face was a sneer and in her eyes was the sharp gleam of triumph. It was Red Deer, the mother of Path Bear.

"So, French slaves, you wish to leave us? No more than we

wish to have you gone. I am sent to tell you, woman of the new Tattooed Serpent, that you are to go once more to the French soldiers. You are to take these miserable excuses for females and their puling offspring with you, and you are to say to the lieutenant of the king that the Natchez will not deal with them more this day. We will send a pipe of peace in the morning and then this matter will be settled.''

"You were sent? Why you? Why did Reynaud not come to tell me?''

"He did not wish to give himself the pain of seeing you. When you take the women and the message, you are not to come back.''

"Not to— But I don't understand.''

"Don't you? It is what he wishes.''

Around her the Frenchwomen were laughing, crying, shouting with joy. Hands reached out to Elise, hugging, patting, urging her toward the gate. She could not think, could hardly breathe for the weight that had settled upon her. Reynaud was sending her away. Did he really want her to go? Was he tired of her despite his words earlier in the day? Or had some news come, some message or rumor that made him think it was too dangerous for her to stay, that it would be better for her to go?

She made a valiant effort to gather her wits. "Is—is everyone here? Does everyone have everything?''

A dry laugh ran over the group at that. Someone ran to bring back the few who had wandered away, to gather children who were playing not far off. There were a few women who were ill, but they were brought out from the huts where they lay, helped along by friends. Among them was Madame Doucet, though she looked bewildered, even terrified, and kept asking over and over where they were going.

Finally Helene called out, "We are all here. Let us go before they change their minds again.''

With her eyes dazed, but her head high, Elise began to walk toward the gate. It seemed so far away now, so very far. Her knees were weak with a tendency to tremble. She clasped her hands together at her waist. Her cloak swung around her and her skirt brushed with a regular rhythm against the calves of her legs. The women behind her shuffled along. They talked among themselves, but their voices were subdued. The closer they came to the open gateway, the quieter they became.

The warriors on guard saw them coming. They stood

straighter, holding their weapons ready. Scowling, one spoke to a younger man and the other loped off in the direction of the council in the center of the village. Elise hesitated. Had the guards not been informed that they were leaving? Why were they blocking the way? Perhaps it was sham, a mock show put on for the sake of the French and the Choctaws who waited? At the last moment, the guards would step aside and let them pass. She walked on.

The distance to the gate was narrowing. Twenty feet, fifteen. The guards were bringing their muskets up. Their faces were set, steady. At least two of them had their sights trained on her breast. She thought of Red Deer, of her triumph. Was it possible that the woman had lied? Was her hatred so strong that she would arrange the death of a dozen or more women for the sake of seeing Elise among them?

There was a flash of movement on her right. It was Reynaud, brought by the younger warrior, coming on the run. He stopped as he saw her, saw what was happening. His face hardened, setting like a death mask. Elise, watching, knew finally what she should have guessed all along, might have if there had been time. He had never sent a message, had never authorized the release of the captives, had never wanted her to leave him and not return. She met his blank gaze across the stretch of dirt that separated them and knew the things she had been told were lies. But she knew also that he thought she was leaving of her own free will, going to join her countrymen. She saw the moment when he accepted the knowledge, saw his hand clench, saw the blood leave his face.

Still, the women crowded behind her, forcing her to walk on, forcing her nearer and nearer the aimed muskets. She scarcely noticed. She felt as if her heart would burst with the pain inside her, as if molten tears were forcing themselves up into the back of her nose, searing her throat, taking her breath away. He thought she had betrayed him and the love they had shared. He must think it had been a farce, her response to him, that she had pretended in order to take him off guard. He could not know how she had burned to his touch, how she had come to long for his kisses, for she had never told him. Now she never would.

"Let them go."

The warriors lowered their muskets and stepped aside. Elise and the captives of the Natchez walked in single file out of the fort of the Natchez and into the yellow blaze of the setting sun. Elise, her eyes filled with tears, saw its brightness, but not its glory.

17

THE FRENCH WOMEN and children were welcomed by the army with shouts and embraces and even a few tears. Many of the volunteers were brothers, uncles, cousins or more distant relations. Tales of the massacre had to be told, the terrible stories of how and where men had died and also the few women who had fallen with them. The days of the imprisonment were recounted with the hands of the women often going to their shorn hair, the most visible symbol of their captivity and enslavement to those they called savages. Children were petted and hugged, given treats of hard candy or allowed to play with pipes and uncharged muskets.

The reunion of St. Amant and Helene, the hesitant way they approached each other and then the crushing force as they met and clung together, brought the salty moisture to Elise's eyes before she turned away. It was at that moment that she saw the king's lieutenant, Loubois, coming to greet her.

He had heard of how she had led the women to safety. She was a heroine and he would not fail to spread her fame in New Orleans. He honored her for her bravery and revered her for the way she had held up under the adverse conditions in which she had been forced to live. She need not fear that those who had oppressed her would go unpunished.

"What do you mean?" she asked, frowning. "The terms of the agreement call for the French to leave the Natchez in peace on the release of the women and children."

"A bagatelle, this agreement," he said with an airy wave of his hand. "How can we be held to terms extracted by threats?

We would have promised anything in order to prevent these savages from burning their French captives.''

"You gave your word. It is a question of honor."

"What do the Natchez, who fell on the people of Fort Rosalie and slaughtered them like swine, know of honor? Besides, it is the explicit order of Governor Perier that these savages know the full weight of the anger of Louis of France. They must be punished so severely that they will never commit such an atrocity again.''

"But you can't do that! It isn't right!" Elise was oblivious of the heads turning in her direction.

The expedition commander reached out to touch her shoulder. "You are overwrought and no wonder. Don't trouble your head over matters beyond your understanding, Madame Laffont. Leave it to the military men whose business it is to pursue these matters.''

The man bowed and walked away. Elise, staring after him, knew that the council of elders had been right to be so distrustful. She would not have believed it if she had not heard it herself, but the French had no intention of honoring the terms of the truce. There could be no doubt that they would attack again; the only question was when. It was some consolation that Reynaud could be depended upon to be ready.

Still, the French and their Indian allies had withdrawn as far as the river, where their supply ship was anchored. A series of lean-to shelters had been thrown up in orderly rows on the bluff near where Fort Rosalie had stood and on the surrounding hillsides. Built of saplings and cane thatching, they gave some protection from the weather. A number of them were assigned to the women and children, and blankets and clothing, soap and cooking utensils were issued. The shelters they had been given, however, built with the labor of the Choctaws, were near the camp of the Indians. Armed warriors patrolled the area, standing guard. As the day advanced, it became obvious that they considered the Frenchwomen in some sense their hostages. They brought game and corn to them, but when the women tried to leave the area to fetch water and firewood, they were either prevented from leaving or else had to suffer an escort on their errands.

The virtual imprisonment came as no surprise to Elise. After Reynaud's warnings, she had expected no less. Still, she saw with some surprise that the women accepted the restriction of their movements with good grace. At least the Choctaws could be considered friendly, they thought, and they had every faith that the king's lieutenant would secure their release, seeing to it that they were soon on their way to New Orleans.

For herself, Elise trusted the Choctaws so little that she resented every indication of confinement. The Choctaws were neither as tall nor as clean as the Natchez. Their clothing consisted of a queer combination of discarded or traded French finery and animal skins. Their camp was scattered with broken tools and pottery, French as well as Indian, and with the bones of past meals. The warrior who dogged her footsteps as she moved here and there had a pockmarked face and skin that was a dingy gray color due to the habit, one he had in common with the rest of his tribe, of standing in the smoke of the campfire to warm himself. She treated him with scant courtesy, exploding into sharp words in the Chickasaw lingua franca every time he tried to bar her way. It did not help to realize that a major part of her irritation was caused by worry: worry about the status of the women; worry about the Natchez still in the fort and the imminent French renewal of the attack upon them; worry about the look she had seen in Reynaud's eyes as she had left the Indian fort that the French were calling *Fort de Valeur*, fort of valor.

She stayed close to the other women, translating so that they could express their needs, trying to settle the inevitable disputes that arose over who would share the shelters, finding places for the more than three dozen children who appeared to be orphans. Several hours had passed before she realized that she had not seen Madame Doucet placed in a shelter. She began to look for her and, when she could not find her, searched out the young girl she remembered who had been helping the older woman.

"Oh, Elise," the girl cried, "I am so sorry, but what could I do? It was at the gate when the Indians were about to fire on us. Madame jerked away from us and turned and ran back into the fort. We were afraid to cry out; we tried to call to you, but you did not hear, and then we were too frightened to call again for fear of causing the warriors to shoot us all. We did not dare run after her, for we might have been caught and prevented from leaving. Don't blame us, please! We could not help it, truly we could not!"

"No, of course not," Elise said, her tone dull. It was she who should have heard, who should have gone after Madame Doucet. She might have if she had not been so concerned with her own problems. But, no, she had been in such fear of what her half-breed lover would think of her that she had abandoned a helpless woman, one who had depended on her. The guilt of it twisted inside her like a sickness. What more she could have done, she did not know, but she could have at least tried.

What would become of Madame Doucet now? Would the French, when they learned she was still in the possession of the Natchez, demand that she be released? If the Natchez refused, would the army attempt to rescue her at the risk of more lives or would they leave her for her fate, preferring to secure those so nearly in their hands?

She was able to gain few satisfactory answers. The Choctaw warrior who guarded her would not permit her to go to the French, and when she sent a message, it was a young sergeant who came to her to discover what she wanted. He was all concern and went away at once to tell those in command of the loss of Madame Doucet. The hours passed without word, however, and there had still been none when darkness fell.

Elise shared a shelter with Helene and her baby and four of the orphans. The two women prepared an evening meal of roast duck and sagamite. Before the last bite was eaten, the children were asleep and Helene was yawning. It was natural after the excitement of the day and in the first sense of safety they had been able to feel in months. As soon as the food bowls were cleaned and the food covered, they lay down without bothering to undress and rolled up in their blankets.

Elise could not sleep. She lay staring into the dying flames of the fire. Outside, the camp grew quiet except for an occasional burst of laughter from the direction of the French bivouac. Again and again, she wrenched her mind from the memory of her last sight of Reynaud. It hurt so much to remember that she concentrated instead on the pain of having left Madame Doucet behind.

The bond she had felt with the older woman was hard to explain. Madame Doucet had been a foolish woman, frivolous, vain, with few inner resources. Still, there had been no malice in her. She might have been petty, but was never mean. More, Marie Doucet had loved sincerely and with all her heart. Her home and family had meant everything to her and without them she had lost her reason to live. Perhaps it was the last that endeared her to Elise? She, too, had lost everything and though something tough and stubborn inside her would not let her give up, she had known the fear of being alone, at the mercy of the world. Or maybe it was even simpler than that, maybe it was just that they had been through so much together.

She was haunted by a vision of the older woman, left alone with the Natchez, unable to work, half mad with grief. Who would take care of her? Would she die of starvation shut away in her hut? Would the Natchez turn her out into the woods to fend for herself? Or would they, in that same cruel kindness that they were known sometimes to practice toward injured humans, in the same way the French used it toward injured animals, kill Madame Doucet to put her out of her misery?

It did not bear thinking of. It seemed that nothing did. The night wind whistled in around the loose mat of cane that leaned against the opening of their shelter as a door. The cane leaves that covered it rustled as if whispering to themselves. Elise pulled her blanket higher, covering her head. Closing her eyes tightly, she tried to sleep.

The sound of the wind woke her. From a distant soft whine, it became something immediate, brushing her face and stirring her hair where she had thrown back the blanket in her sleep. For an instant, she thought the flimsy door had blown down as she opened her eyes and saw a rectangle of deep gray in the darkness. Then her scalp prickled and gooseflesh ran along her arms. There was someone in the shelter, a looming presence above her. She turned her head a fraction and saw the shadow of a man between her and the door.

She rolled, flinging herself away. In that same instant he moved. Hard hands caught her, one clamping over her mouth, the other gripping her shoulder. She struck out at him, reaching to claw at his wrist near her face. She heard a soft imprecation, then his weight descended upon her, stilling her movement. The planes and ridges of the body were familiar as was the faint male scent. She drew in her breath and was aware abruptly of the wild and shuddering beat of her heart.

"I'm not going to hurt you," Reynaud said.

She nodded, a weak movement of her head. Before she could relax, he shifted from her and pushed upright, releasing her mouth, drawing her with him. He thrust a hand beneath her knees and clamped an arm across her back, then surged to his feet with lithe strength. Elise snatched a hold around his neck as he swung around toward the door and ducked through the opening. A moment later they were out in the chill dark night.

"What are you doing? How did—" Elise began in low tones.

"Not now."

The words were short, firm. They were a reminder that he was among enemies. If discovered, he would be killed, perhaps on the instant, probably at leisure, truce or no truce. Explanations would have to wait.

"Put me down, I can walk," she whispered.

He paid no attention. It was probable, she recognized belatedly, that he could move much more quietly, even with her weight, than she could.

Reynaud quartered the night with his eyes, searching, listening for danger. For himself it mattered little, but he preferred not to brand Elise a traitor also, not if he could help it. He had done enough in that direction and would do no more. He was prepared to claim that he was abducting her, if caught, which was true enough. Her cooperation was unexpected; he would not have been surprised if she had kicked and screamed.

Her weight was little enough, but the soft resilience of her breasts and hips against him, the silken feel of her hair cascading over his arm was a definite distraction. Perhaps he should let her walk; but, no, it would not do for her to be seen aiding her escape in any way. He would give her that protection while he could; it was all that he could do.

Reynaud ghosted past the lean-to shelters of the other women, stepping within a few feet of a Choctaw hut. He skirted a sentry, then stood stiff and silent in the shadow of a live oak while another passed them. The canvas tents of the French glimmered palely in the darkness while the coals shone with a dull red gleam in a bed of ashes before the command post. With silent tread, he weaved among them, at last reaching the outside edge of the encampment. Still he did not release her, but picked up the pace to a lope. His strides easy, his breathing even, Reynaud left the French army and their Choctaw allies behind, heading toward the river.

Like all bodies of water in the darkness, the Mississippi

seemed to gather and reflect the faintest trace of radiance in the sky, appearing lighter. The large pirogue that lay waiting at the river's edge, the bundle in the stern and the man who stood beside it were silhouetted against the lightness. Pierre moved forward.

"*Mon Dieu*, my friend, you were gone forever."

"I'm here now."

"You have Elise?"

"Obviously. Let us go."

Pierre replied something that ended, "—as cranky as a bear with a sore foot."

"I have little to celebrate," Reynaud said in clipped tones.

"You are alive, my friend," Pierre said and, turning away, stepped into the boat, moving to sit near Little Quail who huddled there.

Reynaud set Elise on her feet, then took her arm, ready to hand her into the pirogue. She pulled back against his grasp, not enough to free herself, but enough to gain his attention.

"Where are we going?"

"We had a bargain; I was to take you to the fort in the Natchitoches country."

The coldness of his tone chilled her, but she persevered. "What of the Natchez, your position as war chief?"

"The Natchez have gone."

"What?"

"Gone, into the night with everything they own, pot, pail, and piglet. They want only to live in peace and so will leave this area where they have lived for countless years and seek asylum west of the Mississippi. They will fight no more, so they will no longer need a war chief."

She swallowed. "Because of me, because I led the captives out of the fort and took away their bargaining power?"

"Because they distrust the French."

"With reason," she said, looking away.

"It is no surprise, not after thirty years and more of broken promises."

"Reynaud—" Pierre said, a warning inflection in his voice.

"Yes," he answered, flicking a look at his friend before looking back to Elise. "Will you come or would you prefer that I take you back to your people?"

"Why did you take me from them if you are only going to deposit me at Fort Saint Jean Baptiste now?"

"I keep my word and, besides, I—I watched you in the hands of the Choctaws tonight, saw you moving about their camp, a prisoner. I didn't like it. An agreement will be reached on a ransom, but it may take days, weeks."

That was not what he had started to say; she was sure of it. This was no time to press it, however. "I don't like to leave the others, Helene—and everyone. Or Madame Doucet. Did you know—"

"Yes, I know," he said and, bending, lifted her once more and walked into the water, setting her down in the bottom of the boat on a bundle of fur. He pushed off the heavy craft, then leaped into it at the stern, taking up a paddle to guide it into the river channel.

She was grateful to him. Duty, responsibility, even when she could do nothing, was a paralyzing thing. She had wanted to go, had been glad to see the pirogue, to know that there would be days with him ahead of her. And yet she had not been able to bring herself to leave without a word or thought for the rest of the women. Would he understand her gratitude, did he know it without being told? She suspected he might. She was a fallible human being; there were things she could not help, things she could not change. She had done the best she could and now could do no more. It was a relief that she would not have to try and so she sat in the boat and slowly bowed her head, resting her face in her hands.

Their progress was swift. Sunrise found them far downriver. The bright rays slanted across the water from a pink-lined horizon, penetrating the gray mists that rose from the water in soft, diffused shafts. Reynaud and Pierre paddled on, bending, straightening, dipping into the water with tireless rhythm.

The river was swollen from the recent rains and the beginning of snow melt from higher up the Mississippi valley. The water was swift-moving, heavy with silt, and churning with bits of bark and leaves and the trunks of uprooted trees. The mist beaded on their clothing and the wind across the water was chill, so that the sun felt good.

Elise, sitting in the bottom of the boat, turned to watch the unrelenting movements of Reynaud's upper body as he and Pierre thrust the boat through the water and wondered how he could keep to such a pace. In his endurance, he seemed more than human, just as he had in those far-off weeks immediately

after the massacre. His silence, the withdrawal she sensed in
him, added to the impression. The need to explain, to banish
the constraint between them was an ache inside her and yet she
could not bring herself to broach the subject of how and why
she had left him in front of Pierre and Little Quail. She could
not begin to guess how he might react, what they might need to
say. The matter was far too personal, though the other pair would
be, she was certain, the most discreet of audiences.

An opportunity to speak to Reynaud alone came when finally
in midmorning they pulled into the bank to stretch their legs,
rest, and eat a cold breakfast. Little Quail and Pierre moved off
into the woods while Reynaud lifted a bundle from the pirogue
and began to unwrap it. Elise came up to help him, and shoulder
to shoulder they spread out the wide cowhide that would serve
as their table and took corn cakes and meat from the flat, woven
baskets it had protected.

Elise paused in the act of pulling the corncob stopper from a
clay water bottle. She took a deep breath, glancing at his averted
face from under her lashes, then plunged into what she wanted
to say.

"About the way I left the fort yesterday—"

"There's no need to speak of it. You did what you had to
do."

"No, it wasn't like that," she said earnestly, her hands white
at the knuckles on the water bottle. In words that tumbled and
halted and went jerkily on, she told him what had happened. He
paused in what he was doing to watch her, listening closely, but
there was nothing in his face to show that the story gave him
joy or even satisfaction. Finally she trailed off into silence.

Reynaud felt something hard and defensive inside him dissolve and yet he would not admit to belief. It could well be that
Elise only thought her actions had been prompted by Red Deer.
Perhaps her mind had seized upon the stratagem, using it as an
excuse to do what she had wanted to do all along, to rejoin her
own people. Even so, he wanted her. The need to reach out, to
catch her close to him and press his face against her soft skin,
to breathe her fragrance and lose himself in her was so powerful
that he had to steel every muscle to prevent himself from acting
on it. But the sight of her among the Frenchwomen yesterday
morning and the way she looked at this moment with her hair
on top of her head and her body concealed under the rich velvet
of her French gown was enough to tell him that he must use

control. She was a Frenchwoman. He was a half-breed traitor in flight from the French army. For them there was no hope.

"Reynaud—"

"Leave it, Elise."

"But don't you believe me?"

He stared at her, his eyes dark, and a muscle corded in his jaw. Abruptly he surged to his feet and, turning on his heel, strode away from her into the woods. Nor did he turn back or give any sign that he had heard, when she called after him.

To reach the *Poste de la Saint Jean Baptiste*, named for the patron saint of Bienville, who had founded New Orleans and been governor of the Louisiana colony for so many years, they had to descend the Mississippi to the mouth of the Red River, then travel up the Red to the country of the Natchitoches. The post and fort commanded by St. Denis lay on an island formed as the channel of the Red River separated into two sections. It was not an arduous trip in normal times, being traveled in a matter of days, but these times were not normal.

Twice during that day, they sighted Indians along the river bank, Choctaws and Tunicas by their dress. The hair and clothing of Reynaud, Pierre, and Little Quail just as surely marked them as Natchez, with Elise having the appearance of a French captive. They were hailed both times and the second time, when they failed to reply to an invitation to draw into shore to talk, they were fired upon. The shots flew wide and they were soon out of range, but it was an indication of the temper of the country.

Still, the twisting river miles dropped away behind them. Now and then they were able to cut miles from the distance they had to travel by taking the cross channels formed by the high water. The mists of morning lifted and the sky turned blue and clear. They saw deer drinking at the river's edge and buzzards circling, heard the cracked calls of blue jays and the clear whistles of cardinals. There were wild plum thickets in bloom with the fine white petals floating in the water. The rose-red and purple mantles of swamp maples and redbuds were reflected in the current while the tangles of vines that twisted and trailed down from the trees were turning green with new growth. Passing the still water that extended into dead sloughs, they surprised the sunning blackish-green mud turtles so that they plopped from their logs one after the other.

The sun reached its zenith and began its downward plunge.

The afternoon sped away behind them, and as the twilight deepened, the gurgle and rush of the water, the quiet splash of the paddles seemed to grow louder.

Pierre, in the rear of the pirogue, called out, "Shall we stop for the night?"

Reynaud paddled on for two more strokes, then as if rousing himself from some dark reverie, he stopped with visible effort, nodded, and began to pull for shore.

They bathed, Reynaud and Pierre going a short way downstream, Elise and Little Quail remaining near the pirogue. The water was cold but refreshing, a boon to muscles stiff from sitting so long. To Elise it seemed to take her fatigue and wash it away downstream. Depression had gradually settled upon her during the day as she had accepted Reynaud's silence, the fact that he did not seem to believe what she had said, and also the curious, anticlimactic ending of the meeting between the Natchez and the French expeditionary force. The river also took some of that depression away.

Little Quail, treading water, blew at a wisp of dark hair that persisted in falling into her eyes, smiling at Elise beside her. She slapped water at Elise and they indulged in a mock battle that served to warm them and work off some of their tension. Elise, blinded by water and exhausted by the game, plunged away from the Indian woman and, as her feet struck bottom, waded to shore. Little Quail came after her, giggling as she reached for a piece of leather with which to dry herself. Her humor faded slowly and she turned toward Elise.

"I don't think I have ever said to you how much I am grateful that you asked me to save Pierre that day."

"It was a good thing that you did."

"For him, yes, but also for myself. I love him, Elise, as I have never loved before."

Elise sent the woman a smiling look. "Indeed?"

"Ah! You know it is true. But I wished to say thank you in case there was not another chance."

"Not another chance?" Elise asked slowly, her smile fading.

"We know not what we will find at the French fort. It may be the commandant will not accept me. He is known to be a wise and generous man, one who ignores the quarrels of New Orleans and the orders that come from there if it so pleases him. Pierre is well known to him, of course, and it will be understood that he had to fight alongside the Natchez after he was captured, but that does not mean he will wish to have us at his post.''

''And if he will not, what then?'' Elise asked, frowning.

''It is agreed between us that we will go into the woods or perhaps to the Spanish at Los Adaes. Pierre will resume his trading and I will travel with him.''

Elise flicked the water from her skin and began to get back into her petticoats and gown. With her head down so that she need not look at the Indian woman, she asked, ''And what of Reynaud? Has he said what he will do?''

''No. It is not quite the same with him, you see. He was not captured like Pierre, but led the Natchez of his own will. He is half French and a man of property, but this will not be forgiven. When he has taken you to the fort, he will perhaps remain with us or he may rejoin the Natchez. I don't know.''

There was no time for more. The voices of the men, talking a little above normal to warn of their approach, were heard and the two women hurried to finish dressing.

They lighted a small fire, carefully shielded in a scooped-out pit, to heat their evening meat and warming drinks with which to wash it down. While Elise and Little Quail busied themselves around the coals, the two men constructed the usual shelters of saplings bent in a half circle over the bed furs and covered with cloth. Watching their work with quick, surreptitious glances, Elise saw that they were making only two, each of a width for two people. The sight brought back a wave of memories. It also brought an odd hope and an excitement that she suppressed as firmly as any Natchez woman.

Reynaud tried to send Pierre to sleep while he took the first watch. His friend refused and in the end they flipped a coin. The watch was Pierre's and he took a musket and moved to squat beneath a tree in the darkness some distance from the fire. Elise crawled into the shelter and, thinking wryly of how easy it had been to get out of her Natchez costume, began to take off her velvet gown. She could hear the quiet murmur of the voices of Reynaud and Pierre as, naked, she slid under the furs. After a time, they stopped.

She was relaxed and warm, but wide awake in spite of her long day, when Reynaud slipped into the shelter. His movements were stealthy as if he preferred not to wake her or feared that he might. She spoke then, as much because the words could

not be kept inside any longer as to save him the trouble of being
so quiet.

"You didn't answer my question this morning. Didn't you
believe what I said?"

"How can I?" he answered when he had thrown aside his
breechclout and lain down facing her with the furs over the lower
part of his body. "I had told you that I loved you. Why would
I send you away?"

"I thought—it might be out of nobility."

He laughed. "You misjudge me."

"Do I? I think not."

"If you had known me as well as you think, then you would
not have doubted me."

"I . . . My doubt was for the—the madness of this war, the
betrayal it might bring."

There was no relenting in his tone as he answered. "You
should have known I would never willingly have let you go."

"Not even for my own good?"

"No, not even for that."

She pushed up to rest on one elbow, facing him in the darkness. "And yet you are taking me to Fort Saint Jean Baptiste
after which you will disappear into the wilderness."

"Who told you— Ah, Little Quail."

"It's true, isn't it?"

"You would expect me to throw myself on the tender mercy
of the French for your sake?" The dryness in his tone had a
forced sound.

I would expect you to take me with you. The words rang in
her mind though she did not speak them. With them rose such
anguish that she thought she could not bear it. When had she
come to love him like this? When?

"We—we are married," she began.

"After the fashion of the Natchez, without the blessing of a
priest. It means nothing."

"Does it mean nothing to you?"

He ignored the question. "I am half French and half Natchez.
In peace it did not matter, but now we are at war, one with the
other. I left the French for the people of my mother and there is
no ceremony, no test of the gauntlet, that will return me to a
state of grace in this colony. I have no rights. I am an enemy
and the reasons matter not a whit. St. Denis may receive me for

the sake of friendship in other days, but it will be for a few hours only. After that, what is there for me but the woods?''

"And what about me?"

"You were born to the security of property and the benefits of civilization. It was wrong of me to take you from them. It would be wronger still to keep you away longer."

"Once again you leave me little choice," she whispered.

"What?"

"It could be that I—prefer to remain with you."

He stiffened beside her in the dimness. It was long moments before he spoke and then his words were strained. "The inclination will pass. What you feel is only gratitude because I have protected you and perhaps because I—"

"—taught me to love"

"—allowed you to set free your natural desires."

There had been pain in his words; she would have sworn to it. Were the arguments he had brought forth meant to convince her or only himself? It mattered little since she could not seem to reach him with words alone. Instead she stretched out her hand to touch him, trailing her fingertips along his forearm to the hard planes of his chest. "You think all I feel for you is gratitude and desire?"

"I know it," he answered, his voice deep and rough, "but for now, as in the past, it is enough."

He drew her to him, holding her tightly, molding her to the long, hard length of his body as if he could absorb that essence of her through the thin satin of her skin. She clung to him in the anguish of fear for what he meant to do in the days ahead, for what would become of her without him, for the price that might be asked of them from an unforgiving world. Once before she had known the distress of thinking that their night together might be the last. Now the feeling returned a thousandfold. She wanted to take him inside herself, deeply, indelibly. She wanted to feel his strength plunging into her and, in returning it, know that they were linked, inseparable, two parts of a whole.

The need inside them was a spreading flame bright-edged with desperation. Fear for what the days to come might bring fed their desire, and the pain of a parting that seemed to be hurtling toward them gave it strength. Trembling, their eyes tightly closed, they sought in each other the ageless affirmation of life and the boon of momentary forgetfulness. They found both in the fierce and unmeasured rhythms of the passion that joined them, but though they lay with bodies closely entwined and panting breaths mingling as their mouths clung, they could not hold on to them.

Eight days later they reached Fort Saint Jean Baptiste. They knew they were coming near after they passed the *Poste des Rapides*, portaging around the rapids in the early morning without raising an alarm from the small garrison of the post. They entered the Natchitoches country, coming upon the cleared lands of the outlying settlement and the cabins with smoke trailing away from the mud-daubed chimneys. Finally they rounded a bend and saw the fort lying before them.

It was built in a rectangle with jutting, diamond-shaped bastions at three corners and at the fourth a rectangular one. The palisade was massive, but not as thick as that of the Natchez, primarily because it was not expected to withstand cannon fire. There was no sign of alarm; the gates stood open and people moved in and out freely. There was, however, a full complement of men on watch on the parapets.

By the time the pirogue had pulled into the landing and they had stepped on shore, a squad of soldiers had advanced to the gates and stood ready to meet them. A tall, handsome man with a soldier's bearing and an air of authority moved to take his place in front of the squad.

Reynaud, his movements fluid and his back straight despite days bent over a paddle, strode toward the gate. Pierre fell into step at his side and Elise, with Little Quail, followed. Elise's attention was on the officer who waited. He had to be the commandant here, Louis Antoine Juchereau de St. Denis.

St. Denis was reputed to be an intelligent man and a fair one, a man who paid only as much attention to the dictates from New Orleans as was necessary. Rather than adhere to a ruinous policy of trading exclusively with faraway France, he turned a blind eye to commerce with the Spanish at the fort of Los Adaes less than sixty leagues away to the increased profit of the colonists in his jurisdiction. It was not surprising, perhaps, since he had been a trader before being named commandant. Much good had come from his close ties with the Spaniards, including his marriage to his beautiful wife Manuela, who had been the granddaughter of the commandant of the Spanish Presidio San Juan Bautista. His policy toward the Natchitoches, Caddo, and Adaes Indians was fair and openhanded, and his grasp of the conflicting and shifting loyalties of the tribes was firm. The result was stability in this section of the colony. St. Denis enjoyed somewhat despotic power, due to the distance to the center of government, and was known to be unconventional. And yet he was also a faithful servant of his king.

How would he receive them, given his character and his duties? That was the question.

There might have been a snapped order to fire, a command for immediate arrest, or, at the very least, a refusal to allow them to set foot in the fort or to remain in the surrounding country. Instead, St. Denis returned Reynaud's bow with a grave inclination of his head.

"My apologies," Reynaud said, "for what must be an unwelcome visit. I ask only a small indulgence: a few minutes of your time."

St. Denis's eyes were narrowed as he studied them. Finally he asked, "You have come from the Natchez country?"

"Yes. We have news of what has taken place there if you care to hear it."

"I've heard of the expedition, as who hasn't? I have also had a dispatch warning us, quite unnecessarily, to hold ourselves ready in case of trouble. I had heard, too, that you had joined the Natchez. I can only assume that there has been a defeat."

Reynaud inclined his head in agreement. "Of a kind."

"Your presence is not, I take it, an indication that we should prepare to fight to the death?"

"Hardly."

"Then come inside to my quarters," St. Denis invited, adding with a faint smile, "I have an obligation to hear all reports that might aid in our defense."

The commandant's office, which also served as his living quarters, was directly in front of the gate, just forward of the center of the compound. To the right lay a long, low building that served as a barracks, with a separate dining hall at one end and a guardhouse at the other. Near the left rear bastion was a small building set with a steeple that marked it as a church. It, along with another one-room cabin that served as lodging for the itinerant priest, made a protective bulwark between a small powder house and the open block of the fort interior. On the left side of the compound was the kitchen from which issued the delicious smell of roasting beef, with a privy and servants' quarters strung out beyond. The buildings were constructed of logs set in the upright fashion, chinked with mud thickened with deer hair and gray moss, and roofed with cypress shingles.

Elise and Little Quail followed the three men into the commandant's quarters. When they were seated, an African servant brought wine, bread and butter, and also a heavy cake spread with plum jam. Madame St. Denis, Doña Manuela, with a child hiding behind her skirts, came to see that they had everything they needed, then left them again. Then followed a rapid fire of questions and answers. St. Denis omitted no detail. He wanted to know the size of both forces, the weapons, the kinds of trenching done by the French, the behavior and manner of the Choctaws, the number of casualties. His grunt as he heard of the departure of the Natchez indicated surprise mixed with cynicism and he appeared to think that someone, perhaps the Choctaws if not the French, had been bribed to be deaf during the night, a charge Reynaud neither refuted nor admitted. He asked in particular after several women who were related to the people who lived near Fort Saint Jean Baptiste and appeared grateful for anything Elise was able to tell him about them.

They had been there perhaps an hour when the crowd began to gather outside. The news of their arrival had spread and people had come to see them with their own eyes. St. Denis ignored the growing rumble and mutter of voices for as long as he could. At last he looked toward the sound with a frown.

"I must ask you, my friend," he said finally to Reynaud, "what you intend here?"

Reynaud reached to take Elise's hand as she sat in the rough chair with its cowhide seat beside him. "I want one thing only: to secure your protection for this lady. She has suffered much and harmed no one. There is a woman here that she once knew who may offer to stand as her friend, to give her shelter. If you would see that she speaks to this one and that no one else is allowed to disturb her, you will earn my eternal gratitude."

"Done and easily," St. Denis said. "But what of you?"

The question went unanswered, for a shout, hoarse, imperative, came from outside. "Your pardon," St. Denis said and rose at once to go to the door, pulling it open.

Elise got to her feet, propelled forward by some unnamed fear. She was hardly aware of Reynaud beside her or of Pierre and Little Quail close behind. She stopped at the doorway, seeing beyond it a crowd of faces. In distraction, she recognized her old friend, Claudette, in the forefront, smiling, waving, as if she had been expected. There was also Pascal with his arms folded over his chest and grim satisfaction on his face. Beyond him was Henri, who moved forward with his eyes fastened on her face until he was stopped by the merchant.

The shout had come from none of these, however, but from a man who was clattering through the gate of the fort on the back of a horse he was guiding by plow lines, as if he had come from his fields. His hair had escaped from his queue and was whipping around his face and his eyes were hard and bright with excitement.

"Commandant St. Denis!" he yelled as he pulled his rearing mount to a halt. "Indians! The Natchez! Our Natchitoches brought the news. They saw them on the march. They're heading this way and are painted for war!"

18

IT WAS STRANGE, watching the French pour into Fort Saint Jean Baptiste: the distraught women carrying their crying children or bundled belongings; the men leading pack animals loaded with whatever they had been able to gather up in the way of food and supplies. It was as if some playful god had decided to switch the roles, turning the besieged into the attackers and the attackers into the besieged. The dust and confusion was the same, however, as well as the fear.

There were also not as many people. The number who had settled around the fort did not exceed three hundred, including Indian and African slaves. Of this count, perhaps eighty were men fit for fighting; a portion of them regular troops, a portion colonists.

Another difference was that Elise had nothing to do. Doña Manuela and two or three of the older women brought order from the chaos, assigning space in the barracks to families, directing older children to look after crying youngsters, setting women to making huge pots of soup and gruel with which to feed the gathering, seeing to the collection of bandaging materials and medicines. Elise, standing to one side, felt both useless and conspicuous. She was aware of the many sidelong glances sent her way, of the whispers behind hands, of the lifted brows. At one level of consciousness it troubled her, but at another, deeper level she cared not at all.

Claudette, with three children in tow, one on her hip and yet another under her apron, found her where she stood on the porch of the commandant's quarters. Her friend from her days as a correction girl was plump, her face rather blowzy and careworn from the strain of childbearing. She had always been a simple person. She smiled now, her brown eyes tired and rather anxious. "I have missed you, Elise."

If the truth were known, Elise had hardly thought of Claudette during all the years since they had last met. It made her ashamed. She forced a smile. "How have you been?"

"As you see," Claudette answered, indicating the children around her with a wry shrug. "You have no babies?"

Elise shook her head. "I am a widow now."

"So I heard."

There was a pause. Elise realized her friend must have heard much more. There were not so many French in Louisiana that news of those one knew could escape notice. "I am glad you are well and happy."

"Yes. I know you were not so lucky, for I spoke of you to St. Amant when he first came here and to young Henri who escaped the massacre with you. I would like to help you if you will allow me. I would like for you to come and stay with me."

"Claudette—" A hard lump formed in Elise's throat and she could say no more.

"I mean it, every word. I want you to live with me for as long as you like. Since the company sent out the so modest and pure convent girls with their dowries in caskets the year before last, you would think that we correction girls were mere women of pleasure, unfit as wives for the colonists, though *le bon Dieu* knows the men here are far from saints. But we who came first must stick together."

"Your husband, what would he say?"

"Jules won't mind," Claudette answered with a laugh. "There is very little that he minds."

"There will be talk." The words were blunt, but Elise could not help it.

Claudette shrugged. "When has there not been? I will feel privileged to hear the story of how you came to be the woman of the half-breed Chavalier. Now there is a man who could drop his pack outside my door any day."

"It appears that your husband does that often enough," Elise observed with dry humor.

"Yes," Claudette said, sighing, "a rutting beast of a man."

"Where is he?"

Claudette pointed and Elise, following her gesture, hastily

suppressed a smile. Claudette's rutting beast was short, balding, and potbellied, though the laugh lines around his eyes indicated a disposition that was tolerant and merry.

"Are you certain he won't mind?"

"He will be delighted when he sees you, though you must be careful to make it clear that you do not like your bottom pinched."

"I . . . may not be staying long."

"But of course you will! Where else would you go?"

Where else, indeed? Elise did not elaborate, however. There was no need, for Henri, impetuous, stammering slightly with excitement, came toward them.

"Madame L-Laffont, what a r-relief it is to see you among us, though who would have d-dreamed we would meet again like this?" He lifted a hand in which he held a musket to indicate the soldiers closing the gates and the men lining up to receive ammunition for their weapons.

"Not I," she said with a wan smile. "How have you been?"

"I am an a-assistant to M'sieu L-Lagross who has a trading post. I tend his horses and take care of customers, but also travel with him to New Orleans to buy goods. More, I am c-considered a man here and have been given this musket with which to defend the f-fort."

Elise admired the weapon he was brandishing. It was good to see that he was recovering from the effects of the massacre.

"M-may I say that you are looking well, m-madame?" he went on. "In truth, you grow more b-beautiful every time I see you."

"And you grow more of a flatterer," she replied, smiling a little at his gallantry, though she wanted also to cry as she thought of the battle that must come. The young and inexperienced were the most likely to fall, whether Natchez or French.

"No, no, m-madame, I assure you," he said, his eyes bright. "I must g-go now; I am needed."

"Yes. You will be careful?"

"But, of c-course, madame!"

He hurried away with a backward glance and a wave. Claudette, looking after him, said, "A nice young man. Now. Come and let me introduce you to the others."

There seemed no choice except to agree. In truth, it was not so bad; the women were suspicious, but their need to know about the welfare of the women who had been held by the

Natchez, to hear details of their captivity, to question Elise about the massacre, who had died and who survived, was greater than their moral outrage. Few among them could afford to set themselves on too high a form, in any case. It was not polite to inquire into a person's background in this backwater. There were more here who had been transported to the colony against their will than who had come by choice.

It was Claudette's oldest child, a girl, who brought Elise the greatest pain, though not from embarrassment but rather from a grief that seemed to squeeze her heart suddenly in an iron fist. She was playing with the girl, trying to keep from underfoot, when the child piped, "Look, Maman, the lady has on funny shoes."

From under the hem of her wrinkled and stained skirt could be seen the moccasins given to her by Tattooed Arm on the night she and Reynaud had been wed. The moccasins of white doeskin decorated with freshwater pearls and blue beads were the only reminder she had of her Indian marriage. But for them, it would be as if it had never taken place.

A sentry sang out. A Natchez warrior had been seen at the edge of the woods that had been cleared away from the fort. The Indians were gathering. Tension rose inside the stockade, but no one fired. There was always the possibility that the Natchez wanted only to talk or trade.

Elise saw Reynaud and St. Denis in close conversation. Beyond them was Pascal, a derisive expression on his face. He had not approached her and apparently did not intend to speak to her. It was just as well; she had nothing to say to him. Still, she did not like his attitude of condemnation or the vindictive glint in his eyes as he watched Reynaud. Most of all, she did not care for the knowing lasciviousness of his gaze as it rested upon her.

A delegation of Indians was seen approaching the fort. St. Denis, with Reynaud beside him, mounted to the parapet. A number of the other men also ran for the steps that led up to the walkway, joining the soldiers already in place at their stations. Elise hurried after them. She had grown used to knowing what was happening and did not intend to sit back and wait to be told simply because she was once more among Frenchwomen. It was unladylike to elbow for position, so she did it discreetly, with murmured apologies. So surprised were the men to see her there that they gave way. One or two tried to persuade her of the danger, but she only smiled and nodded and turned her attention to what was taking place below.

Path Bear, chief of the Flour Village who had been in command of the second Indian fort, marched at the head of the half-dozen Natchez that advanced alongside the river, coming from the direction of the woods. He swaggered forward with his men at his back and his hands on his hips. When he was within hearing distance, he lifted his voice in speech.

"St. Denis, commandant in this country of the Natchitoches. Is it you?"

"It is I," St. Denis called in the ritual greeting.

"I trust I see you well?"

"Well enough," the French commandant replied. "What do you want?"

"I come in peace to you who has ever had the interests of the Indian at heart. I wish to speak concerning the deeds done against us that you may intercede for us with your superior, the Governor Perier. Let us smoke a calumet together in a token of peace between this fort that you command and the fort of the Natchez on this side of the great river. Let us talk."

"We are talking now."

"But is this good, is this hospitality? Open your gates and permit me and my warriors to enter so that we may speak face to face as civilized men."

The words were smooth, but they sounded false to Elise's ear. Was it a trick like the one at Fort Rosalie when the warriors had come among the people asking for weapons and ammunition for a great hunt to supply winter food for the French as well as themselves? She could not tell. It might be her own prejudice against Path Bear that caused her to doubt him.

"Your people and mine are at war," St. Denis said. "I cannot permit you to enter the fort, but I rejoice in the opportunity to establish peace between us. You have only to say what it is you want me to tell Governor Perier."

An angry scowl darkened Path Bear's face. For long moments, he was silent, and when he spoke again, his tone had a harsh edge. "I see with you the war chief of the Natchez. It is strange that you harbor such a man if you so distrust my people."

"He came without an army of warriors at his back."

"Am I to blame that my brother warriors and I have been driven from our ancestral home and now must exist in the woods like animals? They joined me in the hope that I might lead them to safety and comfort. But, come, this shouting back and forth is without dignity. If we may not come in, then you and your officers must come out and hold council with us. Bring also our war chief, Tattooed Serpent, that he may join us in our entreaties.''

Did St. Denis hear the undertone of duplicity in Path Bear's voice? Elise wanted to turn and shout to the commandant to take care, but she did not quite dare to interfere, not yet.

"The fate of your people, who have been so helpful to the French in the past, is of deep concern to me," St. Denis said. "However, for the sake of the men and women of my own race who depend on me, I cannot leave the fort to treat with men painted for war. I repeat: If you wish me to send a message to the governor on your behalf, give it to me now as we talk.''

"You must come out!'' Path Bear shouted, waving a fist.

"Another time, when you come with the calumet of peace.''

"You come now!''

St. Denis shifted as if to turn away.

"You will come out to me or else I will give the order to burn the Frenchwoman!''

"You'll what?'' The voice of St. Denis cracked like a whip across the cleared ground and the river beyond as he swung back.

"I will burn the Frenchwoman whom I have with me, as your governor burned the women of the Natchez at New Orleans.'' Path Bear swung around, gesturing toward the woods. Two warriors appeared, supporting a woman between them. She could barely walk and stood with her head hanging, her white hair trailing around her face. Her clothing was no more than soiled rags.

The men on the parapet cursed softly and there was a buzz of voices punctuated by cries of shock as the news was relayed to those on the ground. Elise stood staring, trying to deny the evidence of her eyes. She wanted to think otherwise, but knew beyond doubting that the women with the Natchez was Madame Doucet.

"Burn that woman,'' St. Denis said, "and we will wreak a vengeance upon you more terrible than your worst imagining!''

Path Bear smiled, a ferocious lifting of full lips. "To do that, you must first come out of the fort.''

The Indian turned, striding away.

The people surged forward around St. Denis as he came down from the parapet. Some of the women were crying. Many of the children, seeing the tears and feeling the tense atmosphere around them, began to wail, too. The men were silent, but stared at each other with hard, sidelong glances. All except one. Pascal stepped from the crowd in front of the commandant and Reynaud, who walked beside St. Denis.

"Forgive me, Commandant," Pascal said, his voice laden with heavy irony, "but I think I speak for all of us when I ask what you mean to do with the traitor among us?"

"Traitor?" St. Denis frowned, his mind obviously on other matters.

"As that Indian out there said, we have given refuge to the war chief of the Natchez himself, the half-breed here that they call Tattooed Serpent. He has now betrayed us. What is to be done?"

"This man is Reynaud Chavalier," St. Denis said sharply, "no traitor."

"And yet the Natchez came on his heels. Can he prove he didn't lead them? That he didn't come on ahead to gain entry to the fort? What will happen to all of us if, when the Natchez launch their attack, he opens the gate?"

"Don't be ridiculous!"

"Ridiculous? When this half-breed is the man who directed the building of great forts for his Indian half brothers to fight from, who must have led their forces in the siege we've been hearing about? He has turned his coat any number of times in the last few years, living with one race or the other as it pleases him. Why should he not turn on us again?"

Elise pushed to the forefront of the crowd, stopping beside Pascal. "This man saved your life after the massacre at Fort Rosalie!" she cried. "Have you forgotten?"

"No," Pascal said with a sneer as he turned to look Elise up and down, "nor why."

Beyond the walls of the fort, screams, thin and shrill, began. A sentry, his voice none too steady, called down. "They have driven a stake into the ground and are tying the lady to it. Now they are bringing brush."

Elise looked at Reynaud and saw stark desolation in his face. His glance caught hers and the expression was wiped away, becoming hard and grim and stiff with something that might have been acceptance.

St. Denis was speaking. "What a man may do for one people out of loyalty has nothing to do with what he may do to another."

"Maybe not," Pascal said, swinging back to the commandant. "But I say we can't take the chance. I say we send him back to his half brothers. Let him prove himself by doing something for the French. If he is the war chief and brother of the Great Sun, it should be no problem to him to save Madame Doucet from burning. Let him do it."

There were growls of approval. Frail with distance and terror, the screaming continued from outside the gate. Elise, her eyes wide, whispered, "No." She said again, louder, "No! The man who leads these warriors is Reynaud's enemy. He has tried before to usurp his position. War chief or no, he may kill Reynaud the moment he is in his hands, without giving him a chance to free Madame Doucet."

St. Denis, his face hard, turned away. "This is wasting precious time. We will mount an offensive to save this woman."

"Wait," Reynaud said. His voice was not loud, but it carried authority. As St. Denis paused, turning his head, he went on. "I will go. There is no need for more."

"No," Elise said, but if Reynaud heard, he gave no sign.

"I cannot permit this, not if what Madame Laffont says is true." The words of the commandant were clipped, impatient, for time was growing short. Already the word had passed of the brush being piled high around the Frenchwoman beyond the walls. Her screams had turned to great, racking sobs mingled with prayers. Several of the Frenchwomen had closed their eyes and begun to pray while one elderly woman had her rosary in her hand, slipping the beads through fumbling fingers as her lips moved soundlessly.

"You cannot stop me," Reynaud said, "nor should you, for the sake of those here. Only prepare the offensive, in case I fail. And if that is not in time, give me leave to put an end to the torment of Madame Doucet."

Elise heard the gasps around her, felt her own indrawn breath as she realized what he meant. If he could not save Madame Doucet, if the offensive did not reach her in time, he would kill her. That offer, so brief, so humane, so cruelly kind, was an indication of his Natchez blood and of his unflinching courage. Elise felt her heart swell inside her, felt the burning press of tears behind her eyes.

St. Denis stared at him a long moment, then inclined his head in a deep bow. "It shall be as you say."

Then Reynaud turned toward Elise. She moved forward even as he took the long strides that brought her to him. That others watched mattered not at all. She reached for him and he caught her hands.

"Don't go," she whispered. "Don't go."

"I must, don't you see? It will be better this way."

She shook her head as tears blurred her vision.

He stared down at her, at the pale oval of her face, at the liquid amber-brown of her eyes, at her trembling lips. There was nothing he had ever wanted so much or ever dreamed of wanting as his desire to stay with her. But it could not be. He was an outcast, without a home, without safety or comfort to offer. If he had not known it before, he must accept it now. He could not ask her to share so precarious an existence as that which lay before him. It would be cruelty and he had hurt her enough. He had thought to teach her love and succeeded only in bringing her pain. It was better to end it now. A clean cut, as swift and sharp as a knife stroke.

"Forget, *untsaya àthlu*," he said, his eyes bleak. "Remember only that I loved you. Let happiness find you."

From the wall, the sentry called, his voice breaking, "The murdering savages are firing the brush."

Reynaud released her and stepped back. He ran with lithe strides toward the gate. It was opened a bare crack for him, then shut again when he was through.

Wife of my heart, he had called her. Elise raised shaking fingers to her mouth, staring after him, then, with a gasp, she lowered her hands to snatch up her skirts and run for the steps to the parapet. She clambered up them in haste, stumbling as she reached the top and was caught by a soldier. Then she was at the wall, holding on to the logs with their hewn points with fingers so tight the knuckles shone white under the skin. With burning eyes, she stared toward the edge of the woods where Reynaud stood talking with hard, abrupt gestures to the Natchez warriors.

Near where they stood, Madame Doucet writhed, coughing, screaming once more in the midst of a pall of smoke that boiled

up from her feet. Bright tongues of flames licked at the brush
and rotted logs piled high around her. The crackling of the fire,
growing louder, could be heard plainly. The smoke turned yel-
lowish at the bottom, thickening, making ready to explode into
a leaping conflagration. In a moment, it would be too late. The
smoke and heated air would sear Madame Doucet's lungs. Death
would be quick then, though the flames might first reach her
feet and her gown, racing up them with such flaring agony that
the end would be a release.

Reynaud made one last gesture. He swung away from the
warriors, turning his back on Path Bear to run to the woman
at the stake. He kicked the brush and burning brands apart,
sending them flying. Around Elise, a ragged cheer went up,
rising higher as Reynaud tore at the bonds that held Marie
Doucet.

The cheering was silenced abruptly as Reynaud, wreathed in
obscuring smoke, reached to take his knife from his belt. The
blade flashed in the sun.

Then he was running toward the fort with Madame Doucet
cradled in his arms. The figure of the elderly woman was limp.
Her arms dangled and her head hung back with her white hair
streaming, smoking slightly, as was the straggling hem of her
gown. The gate of the fort opened. Reynaud stepped inside. St.
Denis came forth, carefully taking the Frenchwoman into his
arms. Reynaud stepped back, bowed, then swung on his heel,
passing through the gate once more. Outside, he moved with
swift strides to join the Natchez.

"Murdering bastard!" came a strangled cry. A man raised
a gun, fired after Reynaud. Another musket crashed and another. From the direction of the forest, gunsmoke blossomed
as the Natchez returned fire, covering the retreat of their war
chief.

Reynaud ducked, increasing his stride to a loping run, dodging until seconds later he reached the protection of the trees. His
voice was raised in a shouted order.

Inside the fort, St. Denis, staring down at Madame Doucet,
lifted his head in sudden concern. "Cease firing," he bellowed.
"She's not dead! She's not dead!"

The ragged volley of shots died away. The Natchez warriors
faded into the woods, disappearing from sight. Within moments, the only thing left to mark the fact that they had been

there was the stake and the scattered brush, still smouldering, around it.

The French spent the night in the fort, being uncertain as to how far the Natchez had gone or whether they would return. There was a great deal that had to be done before order could be brought from the chaos. Bedding had to be arranged and an evening meal served to the multitude. With nerves on edge, the women fell to wrangling over who had contributed the most to the community supper, who had appropriated whose quilt for her children, and who should have the honor of sleeping in the church or barracks rather than in the servants' quarters or the guardhouse. For the most part, Elise was ignored.

Slipping away from the uproar that would have made the Natchez smile as everyone talked at once in the manner of gabbling geese, Elise went directly to Madame St. Denis and offered her help with Madame Doucet. She was there when the elderly woman, still unconscious, was undressed and bathed. It was she who put a soothing ointment and loose bandages on the few burns she had suffered. Elise also helped to place her in a clean linen nightgown and combed out the thin white hair with its singed ends. When the other women began to wonder who would sit with the poor thing while they tended to husbands and children, Elise quietly volunteered.

It was good to have something to do, to prevent herself from thinking. But she also felt that by her ministrations she might in some small way lessen her remorse for leaving Madame Doucet behind. As much as she had tried to tell herself that it had not been her fault, everything that had happened, she could not believe it. She had known the older woman was ill, that she was not herself; she should have watched after her more carefully.

Madame Doucet lay still and white in the bed, unmoving as the hours crept past. Outside were the sounds of revelry as if the French had decided to have a party to celebrate their relief at the passing of danger. Lanterns lighted the parade ground behind the commandant's house in front of the barracks. The music of fiddle and mouth organ, along with the shuffle of feet, lilted on the night. Voices became louder and laughter rose now and then, perhaps from the passing of several bottles of wine. Elise heard it, but she could not bring herself to look out or to think of joining. She sat on, staring at nothing in the dim room lit only by a single bedside candle.

The noise died away finally. The only sound to be heard was the pacing of the sentries on duty. The night moved toward the hours just before dawn when the world was darkest and the human spirit at its lowest ebb.

"Elise," Madame Doucet said, her voice cracked, husky. "Is it you?"

She had not been asleep; still, the sound from that figure, motionless and quiet for so long under the coverlet, startled her so that she jumped. She recovered instantly, leaning forward. "It's I. How are you?"

"I don't know. I feel so . . . odd."

"You have been through a great ordeal. You should not talk now. Would you like something to drink?"

At the older woman's slow nod, Elise brought water in a gourd dipper and raised Madame Doucet's head, holding the dipper to her lips. When she was done, Elise took it away again.

"You are good to me," Madame Doucet said.

Elise caught her breath. "I—no. I left you with the Natchez and I'm sorry, truly sorry."

Madame Doucet's lips moved in a faint smile. "It wasn't your fault. I was afraid."

"Afraid?"

"Of living, I think."

"Perhaps, but you are alive now and must have rest. Try to sleep." Elise reached out to take the thin, blue-veined hand that lay on the covers. The fingers curled around her own, though with little strength.

"I saw death today."

Was she wandering in her mind, as she had so often done at the Grand Village? Perhaps if there was no answer, Elise thought, the older woman would drift back to sleep.

Madame Doucet opened her eyes, staring up at Elise. "I was afraid of the Natchez, of the pain, but not of dying. I wanted to die. It seemed a good, glorious thing that was near, so near. When Reynaud came, I asked him to kill me, but he would not."

Tears. So many had been shed, yet Elise could not prevent the rise of more, could not stop them from spilling warm and wet down her cheeks.

"My dear, my very dear. Don't cry. It's not so bad. Reynaud said I must wait and so I am waiting."

It was perhaps an hour later, as the cocks began to crow and the dawn light ran pale into the sky, when Elise felt the fingers of Madame Doucet grow lax and saw that she breathed no longer.

19

E LISE WENT TO stay with Claudette in her two-room house within shouting distance of the fort. Claudette and her husband slept on a bed made of peeled saplings in one back corner of the front room. Their children slept in the other corner, tumbling over each other like puppies. Elise had a rough cot in the second, smaller room among the stacked furs, bundles of cloth and blankets, and boxes of pots and knives and beads, which represented the trading ventures of Claudette's husband. It appeared that most of the men of the community dabbled in trading during the winter season even if they were planters during the rest of the year.

The days were filled with cooking, cleaning, tending the children, helping Claudette as she grew larger with pregnancy. As the summer advanced, Elise sometimes worked in the indigo and tobacco fields that Jules cultivated, weeding and picking off insects and worms. She was busy and that suited her; the work helped to keep her from thinking and made it easier to sleep at night.

There were times, however, when she would watch Claudette waddling about at the center of her home and family, secure in her husband's affection, needed, swelling with new life, and her envy would be blighting. There would be no child born of her Indian idyll with Reynaud. She should have been relieved under the circumstances; instead, she was bitter. That much, at least, she could have had. Instead, she was left with thoughts and memories that haunted her waking moments and left her lying rigid, with clenched teeth and knotted fists, in the dark hours before dawn.

Reynaud had been forced to choose, for nothing, for nothing. His choice had not saved Madame Doucet, would not save the Natchez. And he had known, even as he made it, that it was useless. Gone. He was gone, swallowed up by the wilderness. He had renounced her for her own sake, forcing her to adhere to the choice he thought she had made when she walked out of the Natchez fort. And yet it had been against his will, she would swear it. He had not wanted to leave her, any more than she had wanted him to go.

She had so many regrets. She wished there had been more time for love, for laughter. She wished that she had made him know that she loved him with words and deeds. She wished that she could call back the night they had spent on the trail so that she could draw close to him once more, could take back the moments of scorn and anger. She wished—

Dear God, how she hated lying alone.

She felt so puny, caught in something beyond her control. They were all people, weren't they? What then did the differences matter? Why could they not all live together without greed and fear, pain and death, and the terrible wrenching of the soul caused by duty and honor? She was French, but she felt bound by invisible cords to this half-breed Reynaud–Hawk-of-the-Night–Tattooed Serpent. The cords were drawing tighter, strangling her as surely as if he had died and she must follow him into the afterlife. Her throat ached, and her heart, and mind, and body.

He was gone, and it was for nothing.

News came from the French expedition at the Grand Village. The French had been shocked, taken totally by surprise when they had approached the Natchez forts the morning after the capitulation and discovered that the tribe had fled during the night. There were charges leveled against Loubois and his men of incompetence at best and collusion with the Indians at worst. The Natchez had not only vanished; they had taken with them every pot and pail, every scrap of booty taken from the French during the massacre except for the useless cannons and a few rounds of shot. They must have made several trips during the night to remove such heavy pottery and ironware, such a storehouse of goods. That the soldiers and their Choctaw allies should have slept on, unknowing, seemed impossible. It was suggested in whispers that some of the gold taken from the colonists and the paymaster's stores at Fort Rosalie might have been slipped into the pockets of those guarding the Natchez to persuade them to turn a blind eye to the escape.

As for the captive French women and children, they had indeed become the hostages of the Choctaws. Loubois had naturally refused to pay the ransom demanded at first, but as the plight of the women became more pitiable, he had entered into negotiations. Having no gold or goods with him, he had given the Choctaws time to feel that their demands would be met so that they allowed the prisoners a little more freedom. Loubois had then moved in secret to load the women and children onto the small ship, a half galley, that had brought him and his men upriver, then he had given the order to set sail for New Orleans. The only prisoners left in the hands of the Choctaws had been one man and a number of Africans.

The situation had been dangerous for some moments after the departure of the prisoners was discovered, but finally the Choctaws had accepted promises of payment and left in a dignified dudgeon. The French soldiers under Loubois had set themselves to the task of burning the forts of the Natchez and rebuilding Fort Rosalie on the bluff above the river.

The same source that brought the news of what had taken place after Elise and the others had gone also gave a thorough report of the earlier events. From being something of a pariah, Elise found herself a heroine for her part in leading the French women and children into at least partial freedom. The women of the community dropped in to visit, to satisfy what was apparently a long-standing curiosity about her. They asked infinite questions concerning her own experience among the terrible Natchez and stared at her as if expecting that she would be different from them somehow because of what she had been through. None dared ask directly what it had been like to be the woman of a tattooed war chief, albeit one half French, but the question lingered unspoken in the air as they fanned themselves on the porch in the warmth of the evenings.

The spring advanced into summer. It was heard that the children from Fort Rosalie who had been left unclaimed by family or friends, some twenty-four of them, had been taken in by the Ursuline nuns, an order only two years old but already making its presence felt in the colony. The surviving men and women had been given other grants of land closer to New Orleans,

though a few had returned to their old lands near the Grand
Village despite occasional raids by small Natchez war parties.
Elise sometimes thought of going back herself, of starting over
on her own lands. They were so far from the fort, however, that
it would be dangerous, and, in any case, she could not seem to
find the heart for the enterprise.

In June an itinerant priest passed through the Natchitoches
country, going to minister to the Caddo. He paused long enough
to baptize Little Quail and then to perform a ceremony of marriage between the Indian woman and Pierre Broussard, trader.
The service was brief, the celebration not much longer. When
it was over, the couple loaded their horses and rode away along
the trail into the forest. Little Quail had ridden proudly on her
own mount. It was an honor not often accorded to the women
of the Adaes and Caddo with whom she and Pierre would trade
or to any but the Sun women of the Natchez, but one that she
now accepted as her right.

"Do not be sad," the Indian woman had said to Elise. "We
will return soon and often. And we will bring to you what word
of Tattooed Serpent we can."

They did, indeed, bring word, though other news seemed to
spread on the air, "to take the wind," as the Indians phrased it.
It was said that Reynaud had joined his brother, the Great Sun,
and his mother at their camp on the side of a lake somewhere
up the winding reaches of the Black River. They were engaged
in building a fort on a bluff above the lake and were planting
crops to feed the people. The new location was only fifteen
leagues, straight across the Mississippi and over a swamp, from
their old village; and not much more than twenty, south and east
through the forest, from the fort at Natchitoches. It might as
well have been a thousand for all the good the knowledge did
Elise.

The defeat of the tribe had caused a splintering so that while
most of the Natchez gave their allegiance to the Great Sun and
his war chief, some followed Path Bear, and others had sought
sanctuary among the allied tribes, the Yazoo and the Ouachita.
The men under Path Bear were the ones responsible for the
attacks on the new Fort Rosalie, as well as the ambushes of
French military patrols and traders on the rivers in which a number of men had been killed.

On a sweltering day in mid-July, Claudette's sixth child was
born, a girl. Elise was named the godmother. She spent the days

that followed tending the baby with anxious care while Claudette alternately laughed at her fascination with the small, red-faced infant and sighed that the baby had delayed her entrance into the world too long to be blessed by the priest.

A trader paddling up the Red River, which lay sluggish and thick with mud in the August drought, brought word that a ship named the *Somme* had come from France bringing Alexis, Sieur le Perier de Salvert, the brother of the governor, who had been appointed the king's general in charge of quelling the Indian uprising. This energetic gentleman took a few weeks of rest to recover from the long voyage, then began to gather and outfit an expedition to hunt down the Natchez.

There was a tale, brought perhaps by someone aboard the newly arrived ship, that the Company of the Indies, which had been the most successful of the many bodies established to colonize Louisiana, was ready to throw up its hands and admit defeat. Their stated reason was the depredations caused by the savages. In truth, the company had been looking for an excuse to be released from its charter for some time due to the lack of profit compared to the enormous expense of the project. It was supposed that the crown would be forced to take over the colony once more, should the rumor be verified.

The weeks and months slipped past. With little appetite, Elise grew thinner. She also became restless, a condition that progressed to an irritable boredom and finally to a desperate need to do something, attain something, to change things in some way. She spent her spare energy while not tending her goddaughter studying Jules' farming methods and trading methods and sometimes made small suggestions for improvement. In token of her good advice, he made her a gift of a bolt of material, thinking that she would like to stitch herself a dress. Instead, she gave it to Pierre to trade for Indian pottery and baskets of the kind she had found most useful while among the Natchez. These she sold to the women of her acquaintance and with the money bought more goods to be traded.

The activity helped to pass the hours, but did little to stop the restless turning of her mind in its cycle of worry. Moreover, it was so unlike the usual occupation of women that it caused a ripple of censure through the village around the fort. The community was small and insular, rife with petty jealousies, quarrels and feuds. There was nothing a person could do that everyone did not know about immediately; nothing they could say that

everyone did not repeat and someone resent. A single woman
was an object of close scrutiny, of much discussion and a fair
amount of manipulation. It was assumed that, rather than useful
work, her greatest need was a husband or at the least a man.

Pascal, swaggering, cap in hand, had come to call on Elise.
He had cornered her on the porch, suggesting that she should be
well pleased to be asked to walk with him along the river. They
would take a bottle of wine, some bread and cheese, and a
blanket. It was some time since she had had the attention she
needed; she must be ready and he was equally ready to supply
it.

He had reached to fondle her breast. Elise had struck him an
open-handed blow in the face and sent him away with heated
words. Claudette, who had been shamelessly listening from inside the house, had come out carrying her babe to watch his
departure and to call out spurious encouragement mixed with
laughter. With the knowledge that his dismissal would be common gossip by morning, Pascal had packed his belongings and
gone into the Tejas country to trade among the Spanish. He was
not heard from again.

He was not the only man who thought Elise must welcome
his advances, however. Every day they grew bolder, particularly those who could not understand why she did not leap
at their offers of marriage while shouting hosannas to the
Virgin. She tried to tell them that she was already married,
but they only hooted, accounting the Indian rite she had shared
with Reynaud as no more important than their own relation-
ships with their Indian and African slave women. If they were
willing to overlook so sordid an episode, why could she not
do the same?

It was to escape such badgering, such close watch over every
detail of her life, that Elise persuaded Pierre and Little Quail to
take her with them as far as Reynaud's home when next they
traveled to the lands of the Caddo. She would visit with Madeleine for a few weeks until Pierre and Little Quail returned; the
two of them, she and Reynaud's cousin, could exchange news
and perhaps comfort each other. And in the house where she
had discovered a precarious happiness, where Reynaud had
worked, eaten, and slept, she might feel closer to him. She
would lie for a few nights in the bed where they had lain together
and she would dream.

Madeleine had not changed. She was as thin and composed

as ever. She welcomed Elise, gave her chocolate and cakes while speaking of trivialities, and showed her to her room to rest. They did not talk of Reynaud until the second day after Pierre and Little Quail had gone.

They were sitting on the loggia, enjoying the cool of the evening as the sun settled slowly behind the dark line of trees behind the house. They waved palmetto fans and kept their feet under their skirts to prevent the mosquitoes that were beginning to gather from getting at their ankles. At their elbows were glasses of mint tea, an aid to digestion, or so Madeleine said, while on the air floated the aroma of baking bread and roasting pork. The smells of the food did not quite cover the strong, yet delicate scent of the small pale brown and white flowers with the look of fungi known as Indian pipes, which came from the surrounding woods.

The air was growing cool as September waned. They looked up at the sound of fluttering wings and saw a flight of passenger pigeons overhead. The sound grew louder and the sky darkened with the bodies of the birds for long moments before they finally passed and it was quiet again.

"Soon it will be fall," Madeleine remarked.

"Yes. Nearly a year." There was no need to elaborate; they both knew that Elise could mean nothing except nearly a year since the massacre.

"I haven't told you how much I felt for your hardships during the siege. It cannot have been an easy time."

Elise's lips curved in a wan smile. "It wasn't, of course, and yet I would change nothing."

Madeleine nodded. After a moment, she said, "You are a different woman from what you were when your first came here."

"If I am, it's because of Reynaud— Oh, Madeleine, I'm so afraid for him!"

"As am I. There is no point, for he is a law unto himself, and yet—"

"Yes." Elise was silent for long moments, waiting for the other women to go on. When she did not, she said, "I have been fearful about what might happen to you if he is caught. Will they not confiscate his property as a traitor?"

"If you mean this house and land, no, *chère*, though it is kind of you to be concerned. This property was placed in my name as a safeguard against such an eventuality some years ago since the laws are liable to change concerning the property rights of those of mixed French and Indian blood. As a spinster and a native-born Frenchwoman, there is not one who can challenge my ownership. Naturally I hold it only for Reynaud, as it is his birthright.''

''His birthright? I understood it was a gift from his father.''

''A legacy rather.''

''But as an illegitimate son, surely he had no birthright?''

''Who said he was illegitimate, pray?'' Madeleine demanded, coming stiffly upright.

''Why, I assumed, as he is the son of Tattooed Arm—''

''You assumed that his parents were not married except, perhaps, in the Indian manner? I assure you, Tattooed Arm was baptized as a Christian and the union between Reynaud's father and herself was solemnized with all possible pomp by a priest, who duly recorded it. This Natchez woman was my uncle's first, his only legal wife.''

''Then, the woman in France—''

''Regrettably, she was but a—a concubine to my uncle, though in France she is known as his widow.''

Elise stared at her for long moments. ''Forgive me, I didn't mean to pry.''

''Not at all, though I will admit that I am surprised Reynaud should not have told you.''

''We touched on it briefly once, but I think—it may be that he did not care to go into it just then and there was never another opportunity.''

He had deliberately allowed her to think the worst of him in those early days. Why? Did he think she would not believe him or had he feared she would use it against him in some way? There had been Madeleine to consider and his half brothers and sisters in France.

''You are thinking of the title, I expect,'' Madeleine said. ''Reynaud is, of course, the count, or perhaps the man they call the Great Sun should be so designated; I doubt that Tattooed Arm herself could say with accuracy which is the elder. But it was Reynaud who renounced that title. He had no use for it here, nor did his brother. Neither cared for the estates in France or the position at court that they might have gained. The Great Sun considered himself a king and had power over the life and death of his subjects greater, perhaps, than our own King Louis.

What use had he for property or titles? All he requested from the estate was a chased silver musket and a throne chair. Reynaud brought these things to him when he returned to take up these holdings that had been his bequest."

"And you came with him."

Madeleine took the comment as an inquiry into her motives. "I was tired of the strain of living as a poor relation, keeping a lie alive, being grateful to a false countess for her condescension knowing full well that she had no right to the title she bore. My disposition is not frivolous, but neither is it contemplative or as self-sacrificing as is necessary for a vocation as a nun. I discovered in myself, in fact, a positive longing for adventure, and here in this new world with Reynaud, I have not been disappointed."

"You are not lonely here?"

"Never. There are always people coming and going: the guards, the traders, sometimes others visiting between the settlements, both Saint Jean Baptiste, and the *Prairie des Canots* on the Ouachita River above us."

"And you have had no trouble here with all the unrest?"

"None to speak of. Oh, there have been a few stragglers, but they were soon sent packing. This house has always enjoyed the protection of Reynaud's Indian alliance, of course, but more than that it is solid, a fortress once the shutters are closed, and is well protected."

"I expect it is reassuring to Reynaud to know you are here watching over everything."

"What else should I do? This is my life."

"It would not be the same if you were to leave, but do you never think of marriage?"

A barking laugh left the Frenchwoman. "Who would have me at my age?"

"Many," Elise said firmly.

"But I don't want them. I fear I am too independent, too much addicted to having my own way to ever submit to the authority of a husband. More, I saw the countess betrayed by my uncle, Reynaud's father. I well remember the day she discovered that she was not a married woman as she had thought, the day that Reynaud was presented. My uncle had not told her of his half-breed son, you see. It was a great shock. When I was younger, I might have been able to bring myself to trust a man enough to give my life into his keeping; but no longer."

"You trust Reynaud, I think."

"He is half Natchez, and though far from a simple man, he has still their simple honor."

Elise waved her palmetto fan back and forth for a few strokes before she said, "It seems odd that a man who was trying to keep secret a previous marriage should make a son of that marriage free of his home."

"At the time of the second marriage, Reynaud was away on a protracted journey with his tutor to Italy and Byzantium. His position as heir had not been made public at his own request, nor was it later. Only the close family knew—and finally the countess. My uncle announced it to her for revenge, I think, a punishment for his wife because of an affair at court."

"He sounds a hard man."

"A disappointed one rather. He had come to Louisiana with d'Iberville in 1698 and spent three years exploring the woodlands of Louisiana, pretending to be a *coureur de bois*, living with the Natchez. He was happy, but his duty lay elsewhere and he had to leave. France and civilization seemed so far away then that he thought he could forget his marriage with a beautiful *sauvagesse*. A mistake."

A mistake, but one Reynaud had done his best to rectify. Just as he had tried to make things right for her. Elise considered it with care on the following evening as she walked along the path that led to the bayou. He was very good at the noble gesture despite his denials; it was one reason that she loved him. It would be tempting to think that on that day almost a year ago when he had made his proposal that she share his bed in return for the safety of the others and herself that his motive had been pure, a desire to help her discover sensual pleasure. But it was not so. He had wanted her and he had done what he had to do in order to have her. That certainty and directness was also a reason for her love.

Where was he now and what was he doing? Did he think of her? Did he yearn for her as she yearned for him? Did he ever think of this place here beneath the trees where she had invited his touch for the first time, where they had made love among the leaves? Did he wish that they could return to that moment, could live it again? Did he ever think of what might have happened if afterward he had stayed here at his home, refusing to become the war chief? Did he ever wonder if the result would have been any different?

He had not refused. He had saved his mother's people, for a time at least. In the end, he had been forced to choose the Natchez as his own, though he had decided, in cold blood, that she would be better among the French.

Oh, but what would happen if Perier found the Natchez stronghold when he marched against them? Would it be the *Fort de Valeur* all over again? Would Reynaud spend his life running, hiding in the woods from a French vengeance he did not deserve? Or would the new king's general hunt him down like an animal along with all the rest, putting them to the sword?

Elise dropped to her knees and, stretching out a hand that shook with faint tremors, picked up a maple leaf, dry and half-crushed, left from the year before. It had been here on this spot that she and Reynaud had lain naked together like pagans, lost in the wonder of the senses. She bowed her head and tears welled over her lashes, dropping onto the dry leaf. It shattered under the gentle impact. She twisted the stem in her fingers, then let it fall.

She had been back with Claudette for over a month when they heard that Alexis Perier and his force of five hundred and fifty men, divided into three battalions, along with another one hundred and fifty Indians of various tribes in a separate corps, had ascended to the mouth of the Black River. Christmas came and went without news, then in late January it was said that the French force had sighted the enemy and a siege was underway.

For long days nothing more could be discovered, though Elise questioned every trapper and trader who came near the vicinity of Fort Saint Jean Baptiste. Finally a man who had been at the battle itself came. The French had fired their cannons for two days to little purpose, he said, when by accident a shell had fallen into the center of the fort where the Natchez women and children were gathered. There had been terrible screams as many were killed or injured. Before the day was out, a warrior had emerged carrying a calumet.

Perier had refused to treat with this man, but had demanded that the Great Sun himself come out, saying that his failure to do so would mean that every man, woman, and child inside the fort would be killed at sword point when the French took it. Finally the Great Sun had emerged with St. Cosme and Path Bear, leaving his war chief in command. They had spoken with the French general in a drizzling rain. As the rain turned into a downpour, Perier had suggested that the Natchez leaders take refuge in a nearby cabin built for the protection of the French officers. Once the Indians were inside, guards had been posted, making the men prisoners.

With the Great Sun as a hostage, Perier then demanded the surrender of the fort. Night had fallen before an answer was received. During the hours of darkness, Path Bear had escaped confinement. With the dawn, the first wife of the Great Sun, with her family, had come out to be with the Great Sun. She had served as emissary to the others, relaying to them Perier's threat to burn at the stake all the Natchez he now held unless the war chief surrendered himself and the fort. In the end, Reynaud had emerged with many of the woman and children and the oldest warriors. On his instructions some seventy of the fiercest fighters had remained in the fort, a force that might have been intended, should the French not keep their word, to serve as a death squad to avenge those who were killed. Two days later, after the French had greeted the Natchez and fed them as brothers, the seventy warriors had escaped in the night along a ravine and were seen no more.

In all, more than four hundred Natchez had been taken. "I know not what the commandant-general means to do with them," said the soldier, "but he sends them to New Orleans. They do say, among the battalions, that the commandant-general, with his brother the governor, will sell them as slaves to St. Domingo for the profit of the company. In this way, they hope to remove the leaders forever so that those still in the woods and those among the other tribes have no purpose. Without a descendant of the sun to rally them, they will be no better, no different from the other tribes."

Because of the inclement weather, Pierre and Little Quail had not left on a trading trip, but were spending these worst weeks of the fairly short winter at Pierre's cabin some distance down the river. Within an hour after listening to the soldier's tale, Elise was pounding on their door.

It was Pierre who let her into the cabin. She wasted no time on greetings. "I must get to New Orleans," she said, reaching out to catch his arm. "Will you take me?"

They left the following morning. The Red and the Mississippi rivers were high from the recent rains, with a seven-knot current flowing, winding down to New Orleans. The skies were overcast and muddy gray with the promise of more rain and the wind across the water cut to the bone in its chill dampness. Pierre had hired a Natchitoches warrior to help with the paddling; still, Elise and Little Quail did their share during the journey, mainly in an attempt to stay warm.

In New Orleans there was little sign that the Indian trouble was finally over. Elise had braced herself unconsciously to endure the jubilation of the townspeople, to bear with fortitude the expected diatribes against the bloody savages and particularly against their renegade war chief who had caused the war to drag on for so many months. Instead, life seemed to be going on as usual. Flatboats were unloading along the low levee that had been built before the city. Indians were displaying their bead work and baskets near the Place d'Armes, joined by Germans and Swiss, who came from along the section of the river above New Orleans becoming known as *La Côte des Allemands*, with their milk, butter, cheese, and winter vegetables. Men and women picked their way through the muddy streets on clogs, their miens preoccupied, faintly bored, certainly without excitement or anger.

The town had changed since Elise last saw it. In preparation for trouble, Governor Perier had caused a stockade to be constructed between the four forts that marked the corners of the town—Forts St. Jean, St. Charles, St. Louis, and Bourgogne—and ordered a moatlike ditch dug along the exterior of this wall. A church of brick, stucco, and wood had been constructed opposite the Place d'Armes. A hospital had been donated to the city by a dying seaman and it stood just outside the wall. The streets, always straight and wide, had been edged with ditches for drainage so that each block had its own moat around it like a small island. Footpaths had been laid out in many places, with the wooden bridges of hewn planks, which spanned the ditches filled with muddy water in which slops floated, continuing for many feet to provide dry, clean walking areas. These unique walkways looked so much like benches that they were not called sidewalks but *banquettes*.

Beyond the outskirts of the town was the gleam of water where a canal was being dug to help carry away some of the overflow. Behind that was the thick, encroaching forest with its gray streamers of Capuchin's beard.

The town was comprised of perhaps two hundred houses built of upright logs and plaster in the usual style, though there were a few of more than one story, most notably that occupied by the governor. The house of St. Amant and Helene was also of two stories. It was plastered and wainscoted on the inside and furnished with a certain agreeable luxury.

St. Amant, deciding to remain in New Orleans instead of trying to return to his concession at Fort Rosalie, had used his influence to obtain a minor post in the government. He was quite willing to work and had a great facility for settling disputes and getting along with people. Helene confidently expected that he would advance with all haste in his chosen career and might even look with some confidence toward the post of governor.

Elise had gone directly to visit the couple. She had hoped that they might offer her the hospitality of their home since she had no other place to stay in New Orleans. Having heard of St. Amant's recent appointment she also thought to learn from him the truth concerning what was being done with the Natchez prisoners instead of depending on hearsay.

She was not mistaken on either count. Helene greeted her with all the joy and affection of a sister. Rooms were offered at once, not only to her but to Pierre and Little Quail. The baby, little Jeanne, now just over a year old, was brought out by a serving woman to be admired and to show off her latest accomplishment of toddling about.

Afterward, over cups of chocolate, they spoke of Reynaud. Elise had been right to come to New Orleans with all speed. In three days' time the women and children of the Natchez would be put up for auction. Thereafter as soon as a ship dropped anchor in the river, the warriors, including the Great Sun and his brother, would be put on board in chains and sent to St. Domingo where they would serve as slave laborers in the cane and indigo fields on that island. The rumors had not lied.

"But Reynaud isn't of Natchez blood alone; he's half French!" Elise cried. "Can't something be done?"

St. Amant shook his head. "He must be treated as one or the other, as French or Natchez. If he is not to suffer the same fate as the Indians, then he must be tried as a Frenchman. His crime is still indefensible, that of being a traitor. The punishment, if he is convicted, might be hanging or even drawing and quartering. It is better to leave it alone."

"I can't do that."

"You have no choice, I fear, Elise," St. Amant answered, his voice soft.

"Could I . . . Is there any way I could speak to him?"

"I think not. The Indians are being held without communication for fear of an attempt at escape. That's something they are very good at, you know.''

"Then could I write to him, let him know I am here?''

"It would not be wise.''

She sent him a defiant stare. "What do I care about being wise?''

"Oh, but, Elise,'' Helene said, "you will have to live here when he is gone.''

"Do you think that matters?''

"Reynaud would think so,'' St. Amant said. "Your best chance of seeing him, I expect, will be at the auction. The Natchez warriors will be there; it is required, as a part of their punishment, that they witness the selling of their wives, their mothers, their children. Perhaps Reynaud will also see you.''

Elise made sure of it. She stood on the edge of the crowd wearing the gown of yellow-striped silk that she had worn the day they had made love in the woods, part of the wardrobe of gowns Madeleine had sent home with her, all those chosen for her by Reynaud. With her head high, she watched him being led out, his wrists bound with chains that were connected to those on his ankles so that, like all the others, he had to shuffle into the line drawn up between ranks of soldiers. His brothers, the Great Sun and St. Cosme, stood with him, with all the others in ranks to the side and behind them.

He looked tired, she thought, and there were new lines in his face, about his eyes. There was a scar she had never seen before on his jaw and powder burns on his arms. His leather cloak, hanging from a cord about his throat, was waterstained and his leggings caked with mud. And yet his eyes were clear, his bearing straight and proud. No shadow of defeat or fear could be seen on the copper-bronze mask of his features.

In that moment, his gaze, moving with indifference over the crowd, came to rest on her. Brightness leaped into his gray eyes, warming them, reflecting a sudden and deep hunger. He looked at the gown she was wearing and a faint smile touched his mouth. He made a slight movement, as if he would step toward her, but was stopped by the weight of his chains. Down the line, a soldier carrying a musket spoke. The light in Reynaud's face was extinguished, swiftly, firmly, as if with an extreme effort of will.

Elise drew in her breath, her chest swelling even as she felt the dissolving of tightly held distress. She had been so afraid that she would find him changed, altered in some way by the hard choice he had made, by his life away from her and the tragedy of what had come upon his mother's people. It had not happened. She should have known it would not.

Now the Indian women and their children were being led out. The women walked with their heads high, though here and there a child cried in fright. Buyers crowded around near them. Elise found herself staring at Tattooed Arm. The face of Reynaud's mother was flushed with anger and outrage glittered in her eyes. One man stopped in front of her and lifted his hands to her face as if he would pry open her mouth to inspect her teeth. Tattooed Arm gave him such a virulent stare that he retreated. A laugh ran through the crowd. Some of the buyers stepped back, but others walked around the women, ostentatiously holding handkerchiefs dampened with perfume to their noses since the living quarters given to the Natchez had not included facilities for bathing. That miasma was probably one of the most difficult things for the Natchez to bear.

It was degrading, a deliberate attempt to lower the mind and spirit of an enemy, to make them feel their captivity. It was not the equal of the tortures inflicted by the Natchez on their male prisoners, but it was exactly the same as that shown to women captives. Regardless, for people who pretended to be so much more civilized, such a display should not be necessary. It was, in fact, Elise thought, unworthy.

Still, it went on. Bids were made and money changed hands. Some of the women were sent to labor on the king's plantations, among them Tattooed Arm; some went to other large concessions and some to individuals. One by one, with their children close around them, they were taken away. There were no outcries, no pleas, but there were tears streaming down, glistening on the copper faces, and many a backward look toward where the warriors of the Natchez stood in stoic grief, watching, fiercely watching.

So Elise watched. It came to her that the destruction of the Natchez as a people had not occurred in the swamp country of the Black River. It was happening here, in this place, at this moment, as men and women, fathers and children, were severed from each other, never to be seen again.

They had such pride, such dignity, so much kindness in them, these Natchez. Yes, they could kill; they had killed. But had they not also died? When they had first come in contact with the white man, they had been seven thousand strong. When years later the white man had come again, their numbers had been reduced to only five thousand through the diseases transmitted by the first explorers. More had succumbed, and still more, until there was hardly two thousand left to fight back. Now how many were there? A few hundred, no more? Soon the word Natchez would be nothing except a name. Who would ever know then how they had laughed and danced, how they had made love under the moon and sung their songs of the corn, the deer, and the turkey? Who would ever know of the sweetness of the passion that flowed in their veins, of the exultation they had felt in rendering service to the one they believed came from the sun, of the joy they had felt in being alive?

Such thoughts were an escape. They were a way to deny the fact that the auction was over, the crowd dispersing. Reynaud was being led away. She would never see him again in this life, never touch him, never feel the warmth of his body against her own. She wanted to cry out loud, to scream her anger and despair, to rail against the unfairness—anything to relieve the rending, tearing pain inside her. She could not speak, could not move; so great was the press of tears that she could not breath.

"Elise," Little Quail said, shaking her arm. "Elise, don't look so."

She caught her breath with a gasp, then the wet, salty tears began to slide down her cheeks, turning cold before they touched her lips and dripped onto the front of her dress.

Pierre stood in front of her, shielding her from curious glances. "Ah, don't, Elise. Reynaud would not wish it."

"I can't help it."

"If you think they will torture him," Little Quail said soothingly, "Pierre tells me it is not done, not with prisoners captured in war."

"No, no, but if there was only something I could do!"

"You are a widow. Could you not ask for him to serve you?"

Elise gave the other woman a wan smile as she wiped at her cheeks with the palms of her hands. "It doesn't work that way with the French."

"You could try."

Elise went still, struck by an idea so extraordinary that the shock of it stopped her tears at the source. She said nothing, for Helene and St. Amant, engaged until now in conversation with friends, turned and started toward where she stood with Pierre and Little Quail. But she could feel excitement burgeoning inside her. And hope.

20

ELISE FORCED HERSELF to wait until morning, until after she had had the long hours of the night to consider the plan evolving in her mind. She discovered many obstacles as she lay staring into the darkness, but none that would cause her to abandon the scheme. What she meant to do had to be better than doing nothing at all.

She discovered Helene on the back gallery of the house. The day was so warm that she was having breakfast on the open, airy porch. The table was set where the thick, thorny canes of a rose brought with care by some women from France climbed to the second floor. The rose was just putting out new growth, and other splashes of greenery were supplied by evergreen palmetto growing in round-bellied clay pots beside the door into the house.

Helene was feeding the baby sitting in her lap milk-soaked tidbits of bread that had been dipped in egg and then fried. More of the *pain perdu*, or lost bread, so called because it was made from day-old loaves, sat on a plate in the center of the table along with a pot of chocolate. Elise greeted her hostess, stopped a moment to play with the little Jeanne, then served herself. Only then did she speak of her plan.

"I realize that I have trespassed shamefully upon your hospitality, Helene, but if you would be kind enough to listen to me, I would like to beg your indulgence even further."

"How can you speak so, when but for you I might have died and my sweet Jeanne with me," Helene said, her eyes warm with her passionate sincerity. "More, you protected me from the killing drudgery of being the slave of Red Deer and allowed me to share your home and food. Only say how I may help you.''

''You are too good.''

''Nonsense. Tell me, now!''

''It's difficult to explain without sounding a monster of conceit. You see, I need to have it known in the town that I had some small part in the release of the women and children at *Fort de Valeur*.''

''Small!'' Helene exclaimed. She paused in spooning the bread into the baby's mouth and was recalled to her duty by a piercing shriek from Jeanne.

When she could be heard again, Elise said, ''It isn't for me, truly. I hardly dare put into words what I have in mind for fear it will fail.''

''You need not explain if that is your wish,'' Helene said in firm tones. ''As for spreading your repute as the woman who led the captives to safety, nothing could be easier. Indeed, it is already well known, along with many tales of your kindness while with the Natchez. All that is needed is to build upon what is already there.''

''I knew I might count on you. But there is another thing.''

''Yes?''

Elise stared at the other woman for a long moment, then in a rush she said, ''I wish it to be made common knowledge how I was coerced into becoming the slave in all matters of the half-breed, Reynaud Chavalier, son of the Comte de Combourg.''

Helene dropped the spoon into the dish in front of her so that milk splattered across the table. ''But, Elise, you were his wife!''

''They need not know that, or at least it should be understood that it was against my will.''

''He was kindness itself to you, unfailingly tender and—and considerate, at least so I thought while I was with you.''

''Yes,'' Elise agreed soberly.

''If it is that you think people will scorn you if they hear of your alliance with him, then you may be right, but I can only say that I would not have thought you would so blacken Reynaud's name.''

''No, no, and I would not, if there was any other way! But they think him a traitor now, remembering only that he led the Natchez during both sieges. They forget the years he spent in France, his noble blood, the good he has done in the past serving as liaison between French and Indian—forget also that if he had chosen to lead the Natchez truly in the path of war, the outcome of the conflict might have been far different.''

''Then why—''

''The officials here can hardly value him less, no matter what I say. They mean to make him a slave, with orders to his new master, I don't doubt, to see that he does not long survive. If I can save him from such a fate, what does it matter how I do it?''

''Save him?'' Helene echoed in amazement.

''At least make the attempt.''

Helene sent Elise a look of unexpected severity. ''You will never effect an escape; the men are too well guarded. And if you should find men enough and make a breach, it is all too likely that every Natchez warrior being held will pour through it. We would none of us be safe then, this you must see.''

''Yes. I promise you it's nothing like that.''

As Jeanne began to cry, reaching for her breakfast, Helene picked up the spoon and began once more to feed the baby. Slowly she said, ''Perhaps you had better tell me.''

Less than two days later, Helene held a small soirée. Elise, dressed in her brightest gown, was spritely and gay, though when the subject was turned most adroitly by her hostess to the subject of the Natchez, Elise burst out with a furious denunciation against them, declaring with exaggerated firmness that selling them into slavery was precisely the punishment she would have chosen for them herself, if not some more drastic vengeance, and ending on such a tearful note that she had to seek composure behind her handkerchief.

Helene, appearing very upset herself, led the conversation into calmer channels. Later she was able to confide to several of the ladies present that her friend was still affected by her recent experience, but was holding up in the best tradition of a true heroine. It took only a suggestion of the nature of the trials Elise had undergone to elicit breathless inquiries to be told every titillating detail. Helene obliged, adding such small asides as would remind her audience of Elise's part in the rescue of the women who were, in the main, the friends and relatives of the ladies gathered under her roof.

On the following afternoon, Elise and Helene went shopping. The whispers that marked their progress were evidence of the effectiveness of Helene's tactics. Several people came up to them, speaking of commonplaces at first, but finding some way of leading up to the expression of gratitude for what Elise had done for their cousin, their sister, or their niece. Most looked searchingly into Elise's face. At that point, Elise had only to think of Reynaud languishing in prison to summon the correct expression of suppressed anguish.

Using the money she had gained trading, Elise bought a new mantle of blue velvet with Watteau pleats in the back and a hood lined with peach silk that framed her face to devastating effect. She also invested in a set of blue-dyed egret plumes and a small vial of perfume with a seductive undertone of the Far East, and had her feet drawn for the making of a new pair of shoes of peach and blue brocade with the latest high, curved heels.

She had an opportunity to display her new finery at a reception given by the governor a few days later. It was a gala affair, a victory celebration. The long room of the official residence was lighted by crystal chandeliers holding candles of myrtle wax, which shed their spicelike fragrance on the night air. Mirrors in gold-leaf frames reflected the candlelight, hanging above a pair of rather rough brick fireplaces in which flames roared at each end of the room. The plastered walls were hung with tapestries above the wainscoting and lined with rows of mismatched but elegant chairs borrowed from a number of households. There was punch for the men, a fiery brew concocted with five different liquors, and ratafia or a rough wine distilled from wild grapes for the ladies.

The attitude of the guests was one of happy but cautious relief. There was still the remaining Natchez at large to contend with—and there was the fear that the dispersal of the women and children and the ignominy to be visited upon their leaders would rouse them to reckless fury. Still, the fighting was at an end for the moment and they were ready to honor the victors. The room was therefore crowded with uniforms as the officers of the expeditionary force mingled with the guests.

Elise wore her gown of blue satin over its petticoat of quilted cream satin and her new shoes. Her new plumes dipped and swayed above her hair, which was piled in curls on top of her head with one shining ringlet trailing over her shoulder. She stood with Helene and St. Amant, watching the sheen of silk and velvet, the glitter of gold lace and silver braiding, the bright accents of uniforms. There was a pair of violinists gathered about a harpsichord in one corner, but the music had not yet started. Elise was content to watch, in any case, and to wait for the arrival of the governor. She had been promised an introduction.

"Ah, here he is now," St. Amant said.

Elise had expected to dislike the man on sight. It was not possible. Nondescript in appearance, rather large in bulk, he carried himself with the uprightness instilled during a naval career in the War of Spanish Succession. He was richly dressed, but hardly more so than most of the other men in the room, nor was his full wig any larger. His smile was genial, calm. He was rumored to be somewhat vacillating, but nothing of it showed in his face. If anything, his mouth was of a width to denote generosity. It was said that he was prudent, which must certainly be true since he had managed to remain in the good graces of the company while at the same time serving the interests of the colonists. Whether he was as broad-minded as some asserted remained to be seen.

He was coming toward them. St. Amant offered his arm to Elise, leading her forward. She curtsied low as she was presented. She wanted to smile since it would be polite to do so for what she had in mind, but she could not make the muscles of her face obey her.

"I am charmed, Madame Laffont," Governor Perier said, taking her hand and carrying it to his lips. "One has heard so much about you that it becomes necessary to express the gratitude of the company and the king for your good offices on behalf of your fellow countrywomen."

"You are too kind." Elise heard his words with a sense of fearful triumph.

"Not at all. I will not speak of the sacrifices you have been called upon to make, in common with others of your fair sex who were at Fort Rosalie, but I will assure you of my most sincere sympathy."

She murmured she knew not what in response and the governor moved on. Turning to St. Amant with eyes feverishly bright, she whispered, "It will work; I know it will."

"I pray you are right. I waited to tell you, knowing how vital you felt it to be that you first meet the governor in a social setting, but I have news. A pirogue arrived this morning from Balize at the mouth of the Mississippi. There is a supply ship in, tacking upriver. It should be dropping anchor by tomorrow afternoon. When it departs again, the Natchez warriors will be on board, to be landed in St. Domingo.''

"It will have to be in the morning then." Her tone was flat.

"Yes. When the ship comes in, the governor will be too busy with official business to give you a full hearing."

Elise squared her shoulders, giving St. Amant a firm smile. "It's just as well. The waiting has been too long."

She dressed carefully for the meeting in the last of the gowns Reynaud had bought for her so long ago, a gown of rich gold and green stripes with deep sleeves finished with falls of lace and ruchings of lace filling the low décolletage. From Helene, who had never quite dared to wear it, she borrowed a rakish hat of green velvet in the style of a soldier's tricorne that was made more feminine by a gold brooch on one side and a cockade of lace. Checking her appearance before she left the house, she thought she looked well enough, if rather daring; a woman who knew what she wanted and intended to get it but who yet had a certain vulnerability about the eyes and the rose-flushed cheeks. It was excitement and fear that caused that look, she told herself, but turned from the mirror with a sharp swirl of skirts and let herself out of the room.

She was ushered with formality into the office of the governor. He was seated behind a large table of cherry wood driving a quill over a sheet of foolscap at a rapid rate. A fire smouldered at the end of the room, filling the air with the smell of smoke. The plank floor was bare and only the thinnest of velvet hangings draped the windows.

"One moment," Governor Perier muttered without looking up. He came to the end of his document and signed it with a flourish. He threw down his quill, seized a sand pot, shook it over the page, and poured off the excess. Only when he had laid it carefully aside did he look up to see who stood waiting to see him.

He jumped to his feet immediately and came around the desk. "Madame Laffont, forgive me, I did not catch your name. I am desolated to have kept you waiting."

"Do not think of it," she said, smiling. She had been taken aback by his rudeness and so great was her relief that it had been unintentional that she was perfectly willing to forget it.

He took her hand and led her to a chair, then turned to dismiss his aide as he resumed his own seat. "You are gracious, indeed.

I trust I see you well this morning after the dissipations of the night.''

This was her cue to compliment him on the success of his reception in its many details, which she did not fail to do. They spoke of general things for a few minutes, then, in her impatience, she could not prevent herself from coming to the point.

"I know you have much to do preparing for the supply ship that is due, your honor, and so I will not take up too much of your time. I have been persuaded that you might be able to grant a small request for me if it should meet with your approval."

"I will be happy to do what is in my power."

"That is most generous of you. The problem is with my lands near Fort Rosalie. Due to the unrest still in that area, I am convinced it would be foolhardy of me to attempt to begin cultivation of them any time soon. In the meantime, however, I have no place to go, nothing of my own."

"There are many in your same predicament, I fear."

"Yes, indeed. I understand that they are being given other lands, however, and this is the crux of the matter that I wish to put before you." She lowered her lashes with what she hoped was becoming modesty. "You may be aware of what I have suffered at the hands of the renegade, Reynaud Chavalier?"

The governor cleared his throat. "Indeed."

"It seems only fitting that I receive some recompense stemming directly from this man. I understand that he has a holding of some thousands of arpents near the bayou known as the Duc du Maine. This is some distance from the present scene of conflict and should be comparatively safe. If it is in your power . . . That is, is there any possible way that the ownership of this land could, perhaps, devolve upon me?"

He leaned back in his chair, putting the tips of his fingers together. "Your request seems reasonable enough, Madame Laffont. However, I am sorry to have to inform you that this matter has already been looked into by this office with the view of confiscation, of course. The property in question is not in the name of this Chavalier, but in that of his cousin."

Elise had known it well enough since Madeleine herself had told her. Still, she knew she had attained her purpose, that of gaining his sympathy, by the honest regret in his tone.

"I see." She made a helpless gesture, looking at him with weary anger in her amber-brown eyes. "Then is there no way that I can be revenged upon this man? If he were a savage, it would be different, but since he is half French I feel such rage against him for the way he has used me that I cannot tell you the half of it! How I would like to have him at my mercy, if only for an hour!''

''The fury of a woman,'' the governor said, smiling a little unctuously as he shook his head. ''It is truly said that hell cannot match it.''

''I believe the reference is to a woman who has been put from a man, not one taken unwilling.''

He shifted in his chair, adjusting his papers. ''Yes, well, I regret that I must refuse your request, but it is not in my power to grant it.''

''If only there was something I could take from this man as he has taken so much from me, my pride, my self-respect. You must understand that I was forced to do the bidding of this man for fear of my life and those of other people; I was his slave. How much pleasure it would give me to see him in the same position!''

''But, madame, he will in fact be a slave in St. Domingo. Can you not find comfort in this fact?''

''Oh, yes, but if I had my dearest wish, he would be my slave, mine!'' The essential truth rang in her words. She wondered that the man across from her did not hear it.

''You speak in the heat of the moment. It would be quite impossible.''

''But why?'' she asked, her tone reflective, faintly intrigued, as if she was only just now considering the problem seriously. ''Reynaud Chavalier is not a savage. He has a great deal of knowledge that could be helpful in the planting of my land. With the uprising all but crushed, with his brother the Great Sun out of the colony and his mother a slave on the king's plantations, I doubt that he would prove a danger.''

''He was the war chief and might rally the group of Natchez into a cohesive force once more.''

''After being shown the might of France? Knowing of the men and arms that can be sent against him and also the temper of the man who governs this colony? I doubt it. Besides, I will undertake to see to it that he has no time for such a useless task. He will be the most peaceable of men.''

The governor rubbed his chin with a rasping sound and the look in his eyes was harassed. ''I don't know.''

''It isn't as if he were a true Natchez. He is the legitimate son of the late Comte de Combourg, you know—though he renounced the title in favor of his half brother—so he must be allowed to have some feeling for his father's people.''

''Can this be true?''

''The marriage of his father and the Natchez woman Tattooed Arm is recorded at the church; I saw it myself. It would be wrong to embarrass the young man calling himself the count, his half brother, of course, and I would not attempt to do so; still, it cannot be denied.''

''I see.''

''It is my understanding that the ties between him and the family in France, both of affection and gratitude, are enduring if not close. The possibility exists, therefore, that the present count could take an interest in the welfare of his half brother. Should it happen that Reynaud Chavalier had died in the meantime in St. Domingo, it could, perhaps, give rise to embarrassing inquiries at court. This is especially true if the colony should revert, as is rumored, to the crown. It might be better, don't you think, if this man were still in Louisiana should that happen?''

Perier stared at her and his gaze was no longer as pleasant. ''You are a most persuasive woman, Madame Laffont.''

''Why, thank you, Governor Perier,'' she said and smiled, knowing she had won.

The governor's aide went with her to the long brick-and-plaster building that housed the prisoner. He carried with him an order signed by Perier with a slashing scrawl. This he presented to the captain of the guard. The captain read it, raised his eyebrows, then shouted out a name. A turnkey came to see what was wanted, then, with a pair of guards in tow, stomped away to bring the prisoner. Elise stared at the wall opposite her, ignoring the curious stares of the men and their idle conversation, willing herself to remain in control of her features and her voice.

There came the measured clank of chains. A guard appeared, his musket held at the ready. Behind him, Reynaud ducked into the room through the low doorway. He came to a halt at the sight of Elise and the guard behind him blundered into him, then cursed and gave him a shove that made him stumble forward.

Elise had to bite her lip to prevent herself from crying out to the guard not to touch him. At her side, the aide nodded at the captain. The officer unrolled the governor's order and, in a droning voice, read it to the end. Rolling it up, he handed it to Elise.

She took it in her hand as if it were precious. Swallowing hard, she lifted her chin. "I assume everything is in order?"

"Yes, Madame Laffont."

"I will take the prisoner."

"As you wish. The two men here will remain with you until you have the man under lock and key."

"Very well. I am ready." She turned to Reynaud. Keeping all expression from her face with an extreme effort, she said, "You understand you are now my slave?"

"I understand."

His voice was rough, with a husky note as if he had not used it in some time. The look in his gray eyes as they met her brown gaze was suspended, yet tinged with wry admiration.

"You will follow me at three paces." Elise swung around toward the captain and the governor's aide. "Good day, gentlemen."

She swept from the prison without a backward glance, though she knew from the clanking of the chains and the tramping of feet that Reynaud and the guards were behind her. The hour was nearly noon, due to the time it had taken to write the necessary orders and affix the proper seals, and she saw with relief that there were few people on the streets. A cold wind was blowing from Lake Pontchartrain and she drew her mantle around her. She did not increase her pace, however, because Reynaud's chains made it difficult for him to take a normal stride.

She wondered what he thought, what he made of what had taken place. Would he be glad or sorry to be parted from the Great Sun and the others? Would he be ready to do as she had promised and forget the war with the French? Or would he make a liar of her and take himself off to join the remnants of the tribe? She did not know, but she would find out soon enough.

At the house, St. Amant stood waiting in the salon with his back to the fireplace while Helene sat on a small settee. As Elise entered, the Frenchman started forward, his mouth opened as if he would ask what had occurred. Then, as she stepped aside, he saw Reynaud behind her. He moved past her with no more than a brief glance of congratulation and put out his hand to clasp Reynaud's shoulder.

"Welcome to my home," St. Amant said quietly, then turned to the guards. "You may remove the chains."

The guards looked at each other, then the older of the two

ducked his head in a bow. "As you please, m'sieu, but are you sure it's wise?"

"Quite sure." When the men did not move, St. Amant added, "You may unlock these shackles or I will strike them from him the instant you are gone. It's all one to me, but I thought you might prefer to take them with you."

"Yes, m'sieu," the guard said. Moving forward with care, he unlocked the wrist and ankle bands and stepped back quickly with the chains in his hands.

Elise watched Reynaud rub one wrist, which was rusty from the iron band and dark with the stains of old, dried blood. Her voice cold, she said to the guards, "You may go."

When they had taken themselves out the door with a final backward glance, Helene rose and paced forward. She stopped at St. Amant's side. "I add my welcome to that of my husband," she said to Reynaud. "Our home is at your disposal, as once you made me at home in yours. Now, which do you desire most, something strong to drink, hot food, or a hot bath?"

Reynaud smiled, a slow curving of his well-molded lips. "All three, if it pleases you."

Helene nodded as St. Amant moved to pour a glass of rum and put it in Reynaud's hand. "A bath shall be brought to you in Elise's chamber and afterward something to eat. We beg that you rest and will not expect to see you until tomorrow, if then."

When the door of the bedchamber had closed behind the maid bringing the last pot of hot water, silence descended. The fire that crackled in the hearth seemed noisy, intrusive. Beyond the window, the sky had darkened still more and a light rain was falling. So cool had it grown that steam rose from the water that sat ready in the round, wooden tub.

Elise realized that she still wore her mantle. Turning from Reynaud, she put back the hood and unfastened the clasp. She fumbled a little, nearly dropping the garment of heavy velvet as she drew it from her shoulders. It was not surprising that she was a trifle overwrought after her interview with the governor, she told herself, but knew all the while that that was not the cause. Moving to put the mantle away in the crude armoire built of native cypress that sat in one corner, she turned to face Reynaud with her hands clasped at her waist.

He stood watching her as if he had never seen her before or else could not believe that she was really there. She met his gray eyes for a long moment, and when she looked away again, there was a trembling inside her, though whether from fear or anticipation or some more elemental emotion she could not tell.

She made an abrupt gesture toward the tub. Her voice strained, she said, "It isn't St. Catherine Creek, but it's the best that we could do."

"It will be fine."

Without removing his gaze from her, he slipped off his cloak, striped away his leggings and moccasins, and discarded his breechclout. With a smooth movement, he stepped into the tub and knelt in the water. He took up the soap and clean cloth, both left with a length of toweling on a nearby chair, and with quick, economical movements began to soap himself from head to foot.

St. Amant had made Elise free of his wardrobe for Reynaud's outfitting. The garments she had chosen lay across the foot of the bed. She turned her back, moving to straighten a perfectly flat sleeve.

Reynaud, scrubbing at the iron stains on his wrists, spoke. "How did you do it?"

She sent him a small smile over her shoulder. "By sacrificing your good repute, I fear."

"As if I had any," he said with grim amusement, "but go on."

She turned back to lean against the bed, explaining as best she could. Though she tried to put the story in some logical order, it sounded disjointed and pointless even to her own ears. He seemed to have no difficulty in following it, however.

"Masterly," he said, his voice quiet, dulcet, when she had done. "So I am your slave, helpless to prevent your revenge?"

She had never seen a man look less helpless, she thought, sending him a resentful glance from under her lashes. The firelight caught his wet body with a glistening red-gold sheen, emphasizing its power and strength and also, she realized, its angular, masculine beauty.

She shied away from his question, however, asking instead, "Will you be content to forget the war of the Natchez? Can you?"

His expression turned somber. "There was a man who died not so long ago among the Natchez. He had been a guardian of the temple, responsible for keeping the fire kindled by the sun, the sacred fire that had been kept burning for generations beyond number. On his deathbed, he confessed that he had let the fire go out one day years ago. Greatly afraid, for it was an offense for which the punishment was death, he brought profane fire from his wife's cook fire to rekindle the blaze. When the Natchez heard this story, they knew that this was the reason their lands had been taken from them, the reason they had been defeated by the French, the reason they were being punished. Because they had lost the sacred flame. It was for this reason that my brother, the Great Sun, surrendered to the French. The day of the Natchez is ended. And so why should I not be content? What else is there to fight for?''

''You believe as your brother does?''

''It makes no difference so long as I am not required to lead the tribe any longer.''

He was too civilized to believe such legends, of course, and yet she could not be sure. There had always been depths to this man that she did not know, could not quite reach.

''What of the others who are still at large?''

''Some, feeling their lives forfeited, will try only to sell them dearly. Others will blend their blood with that of the Chickasaw, the Ouachita, perhaps even the Choctaw, and so will live.''

''We heard that Path Bear escaped.''

''Yes. He will be gathering men now to attack Fort Saint Jean Baptiste again, I expect; he talked of nothing else after our retreat from there. It will be a mistake to take on St. Denis for he fights not like a Frenchman, but like an Indian.''

''We must warn St. Denis!''

''I did that long ago.''

''I never knew you had communicated with anyone at the fort,'' she said slowly.

''It seemed best that you not know.''

He rinsed his hair, raking it back with his fingers, then rose in a sudden cataract of water and stepped out. Taking up the toweling, he began to dry himself with vigorous strokes.

Watching him, Elise asked in dangerous tones, ''Best for whom?''

He paused, then, flinging the toweling aside, stalked toward her. ''For you, because to hear from me could only keep open old wounds, because it was less difficult to stay away from you that way, as I knew I should. But now you have arranged it so that I am legally bound to you as your slave. Why?''

"Is that what's troubling you?" she demanded, resisting an impulse to step backward as he advanced. "Do you resent being bound as my servant?"

He reached out to touch her face, a gentle brush of his warm fingers. "No, why should I? I have been your slave from the moment I faced you across the dining table of Commandant Chepart. You have held my love and my life in your hands since you first touched me under a winter sky. You are my wife and in you resides the sun that warms me, that heals me, that renews the spring of joy. I am yours."

"Reynaud," she whispered, her throat aching.

"But, again, why?"

"You left me once; it seemed best to make certain you could not do it again."

"Only because—"

She reached to place her hand on his mouth. "I know, but the parting was a small death. I love you, Reynaud, as I have loved you, unknowing, since I was given to you in marriage by the Great Sun."

"My meddlesome brother who thought he knew what was best for us."

"And did."

They were silent, thinking of the leader of the Natchez, St. Cosme, and the others who would be soon sailing for St. Domingo.

Finally Elise said, "Your mother, perhaps we can find a way to take her from the king's plantation after a time. She can come to us at the house on the Bayou Duc du Maine."

"You would accept her?"

"Gladly, but do you think Madeleine—"

"Yes, I think so. But by Natchez custom it is your house," he reminded her, his voice deep.

"Ours," she corrected with a quick shake of her head. "But perhaps someday we may all be able to return to my—our land near St. Rosalie and the Grand Village to rebuild. We could divide our time between the two places."

"Ah, Elise, I love you beyond the telling. If I had not before, I would now." His strong arms encircled her, drawing her closer against his naked, tattoo-marked chest and the heated length of his body. "And because it is so, and since we are together when it seemed we might never be so again, have you any orders for me, my mistress?''

"Yes," she whispered, holding his dark gray gaze, "love me, love me hard and long and always."

His gaze was warm with promise, his answer firm and resonant in his chest. "Elise, *chérie, untsaya athlu,* I live to obey."

Author's Note

TRACING AN INCIDENT that happened over two hundred and fifty years ago through various written accounts can be a fascinating experience; it can also be frustrating. The massacre of the French by the Natchez Indians at Fort Rosalie on November 28, 1729, and the subsequent events, has been mentioned by most major historians of the Louisiana scene. The problem is that few of them agree on the details. The number of colonists killed has been calculated at as high as five hundred and as low as two hundred and thirty-five. Estimates of the strength of the Natchez as a tribe vary from seven thousand to two thousand. One account states flatly that the Choctaws were the only other tribe contacted by the Natchez in the conspiracy, while another mentions massacres by Indian allies at other French forts during the months of the uprising. One historian speaks of only four Natchez warriors being burned at the stake by Perier in New Orleans, though several others include two women among those burned. One says that these unfortunates were captured by French soldiers; another claims it was done by Indian allies of the French, while yet another identifies the allies as the Tunicas. Of the Natchez captured and sold into slavery in St. Domingo, modern Haiti, one source says there were over four hundred, another only forty. Among the different authorities, the spelling of the name of commandant at Fort Rosalie is given as De Chopart, De Chopard, De Chepart, De Chepard, De Chepar, and D'Etcheparre. Some accounts are so obviously prejudiced in favor of the French that the tales of atrocities given must be discounted, especially when they are not mentioned elsewhere.

Others are so pro-Indian/anti-French that they, too, must be taken with a grain of salt.

Another case in point is the attack by the Natchez on Fort Saint Jean Baptiste, the present site of Natchitoches, Louisiana. The time it occurred is set down variously as the winter of 1729, directly after the massacre at Fort Rosalie; the spring of 1730, after the defeat of the Natchez at their fort near the Grand Village; and in the fall of 1731 after the scattering of the remnants of the Natchez following the capture of the Great Sun. It seems possible that the fort may have faced Indian attack more than once, which would account for the apparent contradictions. The attack mounted in October 1731, which resulted in the defeat by St. Denis and his Natchitoches allies of the Natchez, and the death of the chief of the Flour Village who supposedly instigated the Fort Rosalie massacre, are best documented. However, the spring of 1730 was the time of the most daring raids by the Natchez against the French, with several parties of soldiers ambushed and killed. There is enough evidence of a war party sent against the fort at this time to give reason to place the characters of my story there for a few pivotal chapters of the book.

I chose as my primary source of information for the writing of *Fierce Eden* the volume by M. Antoine Simon Le Page Du Pratz entitled *The History of Louisiana.* Du Pratz was a Dutchman who came to Louisiana in 1718. He lived for eight years at Fort Rosalie, working among the Natchez and eventually fighting them in the uprising of 1723. A year before the massacre of 1729, he left the Natchez country to take up a position as supervisor of the king's plantations near New Orleans. His history, published originally in Paris in 1758 and later reprinted in English, contains the most detailed account of the life-style and customs of the Natchez, along with a wealth of material concerning the natural resources of early Louisiana. The events leading up to the massacre, and following it, are given with impartiality. This book is also the basis for much of the background information available at the museum of the Natchez Indians, the Grand Village of the Natchez, at Natchez, Mississippi.

Other sources consulted include Alcee Fortier's *A History of Louisiana*; Garnie W. McGinty's *A History of Louisiana*; François X. Martin's *The History of Louisiana*; *Charlevoix's Louisiana: Selections from the History and Journal*, written by the Jesuit priest Pierre F. X. de Charlevoix; *Louisiana, The Pelican State* and *Louisiana, A Narrative History*, both by Edwin

Adams Davis; *Louisiana, A Pictorial History* by Leonard V. Huber; *The Natchez* by Charles D. Van Tuyl, including a short English-Natchez dictionary; *History of the Choctaw, Chickasaw & Natchez Indians* by H. B. Cushman; *The Grand Village of the Natchez Revisited*, Archaelogical Report No. 12, by Robert S. Neitzel; Lyle Saxon's *Fabulous New Orleans*; Harnett Kane's *Queen New Orleans*; Grace King's *New Orleans, The Place and the People*; with brief excursions into many others.

The depiction of the Natchez Indians, their matrilineal society, their practices, beliefs, and living conditions closely follows Du Pratz, though with an assist now and then from other sources. Where some important point that needed to be illustrated was obscure, I chose to use the known practices and traditions of other mound-building Indians of the Mississippi River valley or other matrilineal Indian societies, such as the Algonquin, Sioux, Seneca, Pawnee, Seminole, Kiowa, and Cree. The social customs of the Natchez were of great interest to the French and several sources seek to explain the structure of their society, including the practice of matrilineal descent, female ownership, marriage ceremonies, rights of divorce, female control of abortion, the lasciviousness of the women compared to the habitual virtue of the men, and, in contrast to the general impression of Indian women working alone in the fields, the practice of the Natchez men aiding them in the heavy labor of preparing the ground for planting. The Natchez men, in fact, had complete control of planting and harvesting corn, including their own feast and dancing at harvest time.

A number of Natchez depicted in *Fierce Eden* actually lived, including the Great Sun, who was indeed half Natchez, half French; his mother who was called by the French *Bras Pique*, which has been translated as Tattooed Arm; his brother, St. Cosme; and the chief of the Flour Village whose given name is not known. Historical personages among the French who played their appointed parts were Governor Perier; his brother, Alexis, Sieur le Perier de Salvert; the king's lieutenant, the Chevalier de Loubois; Louis Antoine Juchereau de St. Denis and his wife, Doña Manuela. All other characters are purely imaginary.

Those who are puzzled by the mention of the Bayou Duc du Maine, a name that does not appear on any modern map of Louisiana, should refer instead to the Dugdemona Bayou, the modern, Anglicized version of the same. This stream, called variously a river, a creek, and finally a bayou, meanders through the middle of the north and central sections of the state.

The Natchez as a tribe were destroyed after the events described in this book. The survivors were adopted into many other tribes, among them the Ouachita, Tunica, Tensas, Cherokee, Creek, and Chicksaw. Descendants of these survivors accompanied the Creeks and Cherokees over the Trail of Tears in the 1830s to the Oklahoma Indian Territory. Today there is a Natchez community at Gore, Oklahoma, where many live who can claim Cherokee-Natchez or Creek-Natchez ancestry. There are no full-blood Natchez living today.

For readers interested in further study of the Natchez Indians, I recommend a visit to the Grand Village of the Natchez, near Natchez, Mississippi. In the museum, there is an excellent diorama of the Grand Village, plus displays of pottery, bones, tools, trade goods, and other items found in excavations of the mounds from 1931–1972. There can also be seen the remnants of the mounds that once held the Temple of the Sun of the Natchez and the house of the Great Sun. The ancient plaza has been carefully reconstructed, rescued from beneath the silt of two centuries and more, and a replica of a Natchez hut, complete with cane thatch, has been built to one side. Beyond the edge of the bluff that holds the village site runs St. Catherine Creek where once the Natchez bathed and played. It flows quietly over its gravel bed and sandbars, beneath the tall trees hung with vines, beside the willows and rustling cane, clear and pure and timeless.

Jennifer Blake
Sweet Brier
Quitman, Louisiana

ABOUT THE AUTHOR

Jennifer Blake was born near Goldanna, Louisiana, in her grand-parents' 120-year-old hand-built cottage. She grew up on an eighty-acre farm in the rolling hills of north Louisiana. While married and raising her children, she became a voracious reader. At last, she set out to write a book of her own. That first book was followed by thirty-one more and today they have reached more than nine million copies in print, making her one of the bestselling romance authors of our time. Her most recent book is the hardcover LOVE AND SMOKE.

Jennifer and her husband live in their house near Quitman, Louisi-ana—styled after old Southern planters' cottages.

Capture The Romance
With

Jennifer Blake